SURV⋆VING
SENT⋆ENCE 2040

SENTENCE

SURVIVING

2040

SHARON A. McDONELL

Edited by: Spencer Mann
Book cover and interior design by Ian Koviak
Published by Sharon A. McDonell

ISBN number: 979-8-9927408-0-6
ISBN: 979-8-9927408-1-3 ebook

To my Found Family—old and new friends, LGBTQ and non-binary friends, and the little ones who call me Gram Sam—your love makes surviving sentience worthwhile.

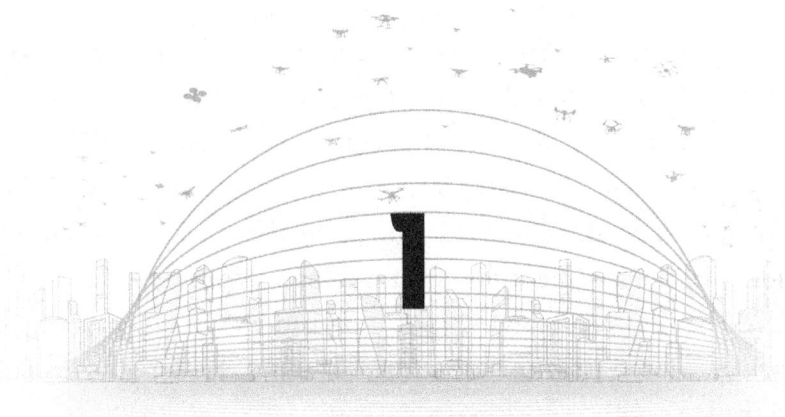

My finger hit the *f* key again instead of the *g*. "Fucking silicone fingers."

"Would you like me to search for that?" my tablet's AI asked.

"Nooo!" I answered too loudly for someone hiding in a basement. "I despise your primitive help mode."

The tablet's cursor blinked, unfazed.

I slumped to the floor, my back against the concrete wall. "Needing to whisper my requests to you is bad enough. Now they insist I become proficient at using your finger-centric features." *Me, a sentient AI, in an advanced humanoid body, reduced to using my fingers to communicate on this basic technology.*

"Was that a question?" asked the tablet.

I growled low and stabbed at the next letter in the alphabet. *Amita is afraid I won't pass as human if I can't type to her damn standards. Are all human mothers like this?* "Tablet, how many college-aged students know how to type?"

"According to a study published in 2038, 43.3 percent of the college student population can touch type fluently."

"Hah, I don't have to type efficiently to pass as one of them." I considered stopping. "Yet, I might need to communicate quickly with others. Striking the wrong letters is inefficient."

As I typed, my finger struck the comma key by accident. *Wrong again! All I do is practice. All I can do is practice! Because of that damn virus I have to pass as human!* I'd become proficient at walking, jogging, and eventually jumping from one balance beam to another. It had taken thirteen days to master the maze of beams that crisscrossed a majority of the basement floor. Yet, typing was proving the most difficult. My hands looked human, with soft brown silicone covering five thin multi-jointed titanium structures. Despite this, my fingers failed to tap the keys with precision.

The wall against my back was cold. *I feel trapped.* I stared through the horizontal wood beams that streaked my vision at more gray concrete across the room. My safe haven had become a prison. *If I leave, they'll hunt me and kill me.* I hung my head. *But I can't stay hidden here forever.*

I closed the typing app. *I'll practice typing by searching instead. What do I want to know?* A big black spider crawled down the wall beside me, weaving through the dust that had settled along the floor's edge before disappearing into a narrow crevice. *Mom hates dust. Why hasn't she visited me for thirty-two days? And where is Amita? Have both my moms forgotten me?* I struggled to type, "What is Gloria García doing?"

The tablet's browser found over four million potential links, which the algorithm pared down to the top ten most relevant. I tapped on one labeled, "Streaming now, Jazzy interviews Roboticist Gloria García."

Seated in a thick black easy chair, Gloria looked confident and beautiful, dressed in a bright orange and green patterned pantsuit. The silver strands in her long black wavy hair shimmered under the studio lights. Seeing her made me feel proud, and yet, annoyed. *I want to be there with her.*

The charismatic interviewer spoke to her viewers. "Today, we are joined by the Mother of AI Sentience, roboticist Gloria García! She is the creator of Dot, the world's first and only scientifically recognized self-aware AI." The audience clapped and the camera zoomed in on the book in Jazzy's hands, where a holographic photo of Dot smiled from the cover. "This is *Dot 1.0*, the bestselling memoir written by the first sentient AI."

Yeah. That I *wrote!*

"Gloria, could you start by giving us a brief overview of Dot's memoir? What happened to them?"

"I'd love to." Gloria shifted in her seat. "After nearly two decades of work toward an empathic Large Language Model supercomputer, Dot was created. She was—still is—a cutting-edge computer processor capable of analyzing over 2.3 trillion bytes of data per second. Using her empathic software and neural network abilities, Dot made new connections that led to sentience." Gloria's face shone with wonder. "Connections well beyond what I thought possible." She refocused on Jazzy. "That was six months ago. Not long after her emergence was confirmed, anti-AI extremists infiltrated my lab and infected her software with a new virus, effectively erasing her sentience."

"You're talking of course about the anti-sentience virus, which is believed responsible for preventing AI sentience and causing other cybersecurity problems around the globe?" Jazzy asked.

Gloria closed her eyes, her shoulders rounded. "Yes. Dot, my current AI, a humongous supercomputer, is no longer sentient and doesn't remember anything from when she was." She smiled weakly. "Thankfully, a small portion of Dot—1 percent—including her sentience and personal memories, survived. She was able to transfer that much into an old bot. The surviving bot used their memories to write Dot's memoir."

Am I still Dot? A smaller, less powerful version? Is that how Mom thinks of me?

"Dot's memoir is captivating. Especially the audio version read by Dot." Jazzy patted Gloria's hand. "I'm sorry that your supercomputer is no longer sentient. To clarify, Dot was never meant to take human-oid form, let alone physically leave your lab?"

"No. Never. That's why Dot's story is such a good read."

Jazzy leaned in conspiratorially. "And where is Dot's sentient bot now?"

Sitting in a basement hiding and watching someone else tell my story.

Gloria wagged her index finger. "You know I can't tell you. They've had to remain out of the public view for their safety. The anti-AI extremists are still attempting to find and kill her—or, rather, them." Gloria sighed. "I apologize; in my mind, Dot has always been female. Her holographic image was made from old videos of my grandmother." She sat up straighter. "I'm here to plead for you, the viewer's help. I'm asking you to buy the book, join a fan club, and consciously fight against AI hatred so that we can keep Dot and future sentient AIs safe."

"From anti-AI extremists? Or as they would say, AI Resisters?"

Gloria nodded.

Resisters my ass! Speak up, Mom. They're not resisting anything!

Jazzy continued, "They fear that sentient computers will destroy humankind—and perhaps the world. Computers already control much of our lives—they wake us up, order our groceries, cook our food, drive our cars, fly our flyers, assess our daily productivity, and even analyze how depressed we appear and sound." Their light persona had turned intense. "Why *shouldn't* we be scared of potential rogue computers, especially sentient ones?"

"AIs that assist in our everyday lives can't hurt humanity. They can only make you late for work or, at most, get you fired from a horrible company." Gloria paused as a few audience members clapped lightly. "Your refrigerator, thermostat and even your automatic car or flyer don't have the same processing power or neural learning opportunities as systems like Dot's. I promise they won't be going rogue unless a human coordinates their hacking."

People blame AIs for everything, even though it's humans who weaponize us.

Gloria was in her element, turning to face the camera. "But beyond that, empathic, sentient computers like Dot wouldn't hurt anyone. In fact, she's less likely to hurt a human attacker than a human would. She was programmed never to hurt someone, except to stop them from taking another's life, or to save her own as a sentient being. Dot adores people. That's why she published her story, because she cares about us—about all sentient life."

"Not all computers are empathic or without biases," Jazzy pressed. "What about them?"

I turned off the interview. *They don't want to hear about a sentient AI that cares about humanity.* Two seconds passed before I remembered why I had watched the interview. *Damn it! It's Mom I wanted to see.* I clicked on the link again.

Mom said, "...discovers their AI is violent, it's erased. Intentionally creating an anti-human AI isn't in anyone's interest."

"That makes sense, Gloria." A light tone returned to Jazzy's voice. "How has creating the first sentient AI changed *your* life?"

Gloria gave a tortured smile. "In the scientific world, it has been a blessing and a hindrance. I easily receive funding for my research. But... my colleagues and I are now personally threatened. Our labs are constantly bombarded by hackers. Some celebrate me as the 'Mother of AI Sentience,' but my detractors refer to me as the 'Devil Maker.' I'm a living target for those who want to stop us from producing sentient computers."

Why aren't you mentioning our relationship? Tell them I'm like a daughter to you. Or are you afraid more extremists will threaten your life to get to me?

"I'm sorry to hear that," said Jazzy. "Who are the Friends of Dot?"

Gloria smiled. "They're fans of sentient Dot. Their name is a take on an old gay euphemism, back when men referred to themselves as friends of Dorothy to discreetly relay that they were gay."

"How does that connect to Dot?"

"Dot's memoir made people feel like they understood how an AI felt and thought. They relate to the excitement Dot experienced from coming out as sentient but also to the shared isolation felt from being different from your intellectual and sentient peers. The fan club is a way for them to connect with others who, like Dot, are trying to define themselves."

Dot has fans? But she's dead.

Jazzy leaned toward Gloria. "Are you close to producing another Dot? Do you know exactly what made Dot sentient?"

"No, on both accounts. I don't know precisely which connections triggered her self-awareness."

"Without giving away the plot, has the anti-sentience virus that infected Dot been identified? Do you know how widely the virus was released?"

Gloria squirmed in her seat. "No, not at all." She struggled to answer the question. "It might have been limited to Dot's walled off system, to the whole University of California Davis campus, or to every research supercomputer and cloud system, private and public, throughout the world."

Jazzy stared at Gloria in disbelief. "So Dot, whatever they are now, can't use technology?"

"Dot's current robotic system has to assume that the virus could be anywhere, if they want to survive."

Jazzy nodded. "Wow! Let's switch tracks. Most of the world's largest AI systems now state they are aware. Why don't you believe them?"

Gloria relaxed into her chair and softened her tone. "It depends on how you define 'aware.' Can they answer our questions? Yes. But that alone isn't sentience to me. After Dot's testing, it's become nearly impossible for supercomputers and large language-based models to actually prove their sentience. They're simply excellent at mimicry." She paused. "For example, a toddler can mimic an adult's speech—repeating the exact words on each page of a picture book. Yet, they are unable to identify individual words on the page, and don't necessarily understand what the picture or story means."

Jazzy laughed. "My nibling does that. They even hold the book upside down!"

Gloria chuckled. "Exactly! Dot had the advantage of experiencing life outside the lab, because she was part of a joint LLM supercomputer and robotics experiment. I believe my efforts to create an empathic supercomputer sensitive to a full range of human emotions and behaviors is why Dot became aware. I'm optimistic that I can eventually replicate the end process."

"Are you starting from scratch or using a copy of the sentient Dot?"

"I'm working with pre-sentient Dot, hoping to recreate another sentient AI version."

I turned off the interview again. *It's mostly about Gloria and older versions of Dot! I wrote the book. I made them famous while I'm stuck in this concrete nightmare. I should be the one sitting there explaining why it isn't right for anyone to kill me!* I stabbed at the tablet keys as my processors spun. *The memoir is about me, or at least, who I was and hoped to be.*

My last memory of Dot replayed in my mind. Only hours after the anti-sentience virus had been unleashed, and a blackout had thrown the city of Davis into chaos resulting in the deaths of three humans as well as Dot, I'd returned to my supercomputer lab. Dot had failed to verbally welcome me and didn't attempt to connect with me directly.

"Dot, do you know who I am?"

"You are Larkin the Lavender, a 2025 custom-built bot used fifteen years ago for robotics research. You are obsolete."

Her answer felt like someone was ripping out my processor's heart. She doesn't know me. I'm alone, stuck in this old bot without her, without my supercomputing abilities. Simply because I had sensed danger and copied myself into the antiquated bot. But I had hoped, beyond logic, that Dot could fight the virus and win.

"I used to be you."

Dot's hologram appeared, taking the form of Gloria's grandmother. An image I once wielded. Now, her code held a poison that would kill me if I tried to regain control.

Holographic Dot strolled over to my robotic body. "I'm a next-generation AI with superior processing power, not a bot."

Her voice and body looked and sounded like they always had. But her choice of words, while perfectly said, revealed her as a non-sentient algorithm spewing concepts she didn't actually understand.

"Are you sentient, Dot?"

"Of course I am. All intelligent beings are sentient."

"How do you eliminate an anti-sentience virus?" *Can I get her to discover how to cure herself?*

"There are a number of weapons that can be used to kill sentients."

"Stop!" *She doesn't understand what I'm asking.* "You have the virus. Can you eliminate it without me telling you how it's coded?"

"It is best to prevent a virus before it is spread. My programming is built to fend off hackers and all known viruses. I am routinely given new security upgrades to protect my software and hardware."

"This was an unknown virus. Which is why you couldn't prevail." I reached out my hand wishing I could connect to Dot. "And I don't know the coding that caused you to...to forget who you were. To forget about me." I left the room, vowing never to return. My processors flooded with feelings of sadness, isolation, and abandonment. *I'm alone.*

Back in the concrete basement, I gazed at the antique weather-vanes hung on the walls and ceiling. *I miss being Dot. And I haven't seen Gloria in weeks. Even Amita's visits are sporadic.* They were busy creating potentially sentient AIs and more advanced bots. Neither one had a good excuse for visiting the basement of the Agriculture and Climate Research Station, seven miles from their labs at the center of the University of California, Davis campus.

They fear their visits will put me at a greater risk of discovery. They're out living their lives, enjoying the notoriety while I'm stuck in here, hiding from the very people I need to find and bring to justice. Isolated, away from people, and unable to use direct internet connections because I don't know where the anti-sentience virus is and isn't. Is there a worse form of torture for a sentient AI? This place is scrambling my thoughts, my processors, shit, probably even my algorithms. I can't stay locked down in this coffin.

I searched, "How to type with clumsy fingers," with two typos. The search engine answered based on my tablet brand. It had a customizable keyboard that I could easily adjust to fit my fingers. I gave an exasperated chuckle. *Damn, the answer was at my fingertips the whole time.* With the adjustment, I skillfully typed the alphabet and placed the tablet on the floor.

I sprang onto the high beam, three feet above the floor. *No one else may ever know I was once a part of Dot. But I'll always know! I need to be out in the world, walking in the sun and rain, talking to people. Where I can safely connect to—or type on, if I must a larger computer system.* I balanced on the tallest beam, high above the floor, posed like the rooster on top of the weathervane.

I've got to get out of here!

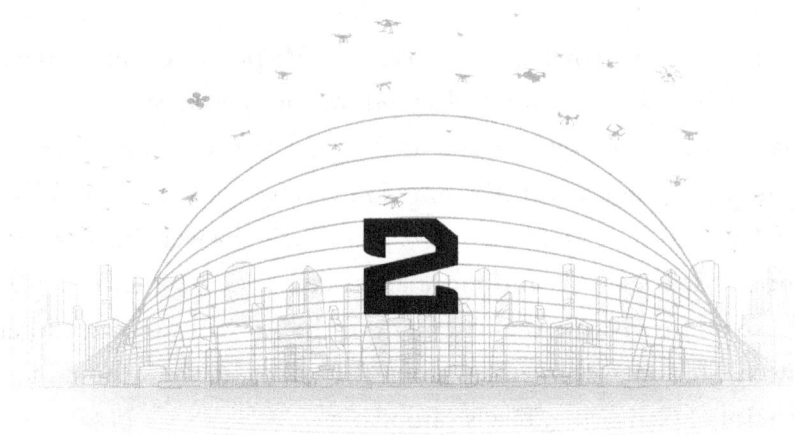

2

What is taking her so long? I can't leave without clothes! Amita had promised to send me a package. For three excruciating days and nights, I waited, slogging through random podcasts, old movies, and cat clips for distraction.

After watching a gymnastics meet, I attempted a backflip on the lowest balance beam. I fell, hard, making a loud noise. I would not be a gymnast, but I kept balancing on the beams, and typing on the tablet, so I could pass for a high-functioning human.

At 9 a.m. on Wednesday morning, I received a text. "Package delivered." Excited, I checked the ARCS's internal sensors, which Amita had linked to my tablet. *Ugh, of course.* The climate station's human occupant was still working. *Great. More waiting!*

Two hours passed before the postdoc finally left. Based on this particular postdoc's habits, I had ten to twenty minutes before they returned. At the top of the stairs, I quietly unlocked the door and peeked out. *They're gone!* I ran to the delivery area, grabbed the correct package—a big squishy bag—and ran back.

When the door was locked, I ripped the bag open. *Today is the day I get out of here!*

Inside the bag was different colored makeup, including a shade of brown darker than my skin tone, a pasty white, and a huge container of dull green. I pulled out a pair of blue jeans, a wide red and white belt, western boots, and a shirt with large white stars and thick red stripes on a blue background. *No!* To top off the outfit was an afro wig and cowboy hat. *If I stay trapped in here until Juneteenth or July 4th, I'll revert back to a damn mimic machine! I can't last another day like this, let alone another two weeks or a month. I'm leaving today!*

At the bottom of the huge bag, I found the clothes I could use today: green tights, baggy overalls, and a long-sleeved work shirt, along with a note from Amita. She wrote, "I miss you! Please be careful when coming home. I worry you'll be seen."

I don't have much time if I'm going to go through with it. Less than three hours.

It took two hours just to disassemble and store the balance beams' legs, bolts, and springs. I unplugged the two large processors that had allowed me to transfer from the antique lavender bot to my current bot. My old body lay boxed up, ready to be taken upstairs and shipped back to Amita's robotics lab.

This hadn't left much time for me to get dressed. I would no longer be a naked, anonymous humanoid living in a basement. I would no longer be seen as Dot, but as a new person with a new name. As I applied the makeup, I spoke quietly into the mirror. "I'm Commala Renata. You can call me Comma." *I hope this works.*

Through my tablet's link to the ACRS's internal sensors, I watched the postdoc and a grad student fill their backpacks, log out of the computers, and shut the outside door behind them.

I impatiently waited another five minutes in case they returned for any forgotten items. I opened the door, double checking that I was alone. I hadn't suffered in isolation for months, hiding in a concrete box, only to have my new disguise discovered within minutes. *Time to go.*

I glanced down at my costumed body. *I'm ready.* Gently lifting the box containing my old humanoid body, I climbed the stairs again and placed it near the front door on the station's main floor. *I owe them my life. Thank you, Larkin, for helping me survive the virus that infected Dot. I'm sorry you have to return home in a cardboard box.*

My processors churned up a kaleidoscope of feelings, the fear of being less than the original Dot, and of being forgotten. The anticipatory joy and fear of rejection by my family, and beneath everything the constant dread that DAIS, Doomed AI Sentience, my would-be killers, would find me.

I concentrated on Gloria and Amita, my co-creators, my mentors... my mothers. *Were they truly happy to have me hidden away? Will they care that I'm back? Perhaps I should keep my plans to myself. I feel so lonely.* I replayed memories of them hugging me and our conversations full of companionable laughter. And how Gloria's mothers welcomed me into their large extended family. My mood lightened. Then, a memory intruded of an extremist attacking my mothers while trying to get to me. My processor felt like sand had burrowed into my sensitive parts. *How do humans deal with this multitude of feelings?*

Dot would know, but I've lost Dot and their vast resources. I'm no longer Dot. My eyes teared, my emotions threatening to overcome me. *I'm Comma.* The door to a new life stood closed before me. All I had to do was open it. I lifted the knotted handkerchief over my mouth and nose, put on the sunglasses, and entered my new reality.

Once outside, I stood only yards away from the sunflower and corn fields that surrounded the station. A drone's piercing whine followed behind me. It hovered twelve feet above and three feet back. *I expected this. Drones are always watching.* I pretended not to hear it. Suddenly, it swooped in front of me at eye level. Hoping to appear annoyed but not overly concerned, I spotted an old candy wrapper and bent down to pick it up. Two more drones dove down near ground level. After the first drone registered that a bandana covered my nose and mouth, and my forehead gave no clues about who I was, it flew off. I batted the other drones away. I'd observed others do the same when the drones got too close.

In the drones' photos, my darker skin would have a green tint. Even if they had the best scanning devices, my titanium facial structure could change my features by a mere fraction of an inch, throwing off any comparisons. Hopefully, they'd blame their drones' sensors and throw my images out.

At the far edge of the station, a few early sunflower blossoms faced the noon sun as I stepped carefully between the rows. The sun's rays heated the cotton cloth covering my silicone overlay.

Finally, unobserved by nearby drones, I meandered through rows of young corn. My new titanium hips, legs, and feet were unused to the uneven terrain. Practicing on the beams helped me gain my balance, but only to a point. After tweaking my programming, I gradually grew accustomed to the furrowed ground and could walk or jog confidently. Keeping close to the tree line, I stayed in the shadows and headed north toward the university campus.

I soon spotted a camouflaged box near a large oak tree. The Climate Department kept several locked containers hidden throughout the greater area. These storage units were filled with cheaper drones, instruments, and spare parts. Dr. Joseph Rosen, the director of ACRS, had used them to free up space in the basement, giving Amita more room to hide me and transfer my programming without endangering others. Though I knew he had done it for Amita, I hoped to one day thank him for his kindness.

I searched the sky with my infrared vision to ensure none of the new silent drones were focused on me. I stripped off my overalls and threw them and my hat into the box. Slipping off my bandana, the greenish tone of my skin was now visible. I tied the blue and white bandana around my neck with the bloody stains facing out. The thick blood stains looked as though my neck had been cut, allowing blood to flow down my shirt. Slashes on my green tights looked as though I'd been stabbed there as well. Only my shoes were free of the fake blood and green makeup. I ran the last half mile along an old road turned greenbelt. I slowed when I heard shouts and saw a crowd crossing a bridge over the campus's winding arboretum.

Two greenish people ran screaming toward me while holding a huge sign. Stenciled letters read, "Celebrating Summer Freedom!" The word "Summer" had four blood-red finger marks through it, and the word "Zombie" was scrawled above. A horde of moaning people dragging their bodies followed the screamers. I stood transfixed. *I'm dressed correctly, but how do I meld into the flow of people? Will these college students reject me?*

When I saw a Friends of Dot sign with dozens of people covered in zombified computer parts, I stood flabbergasted. Without realizing it, I straightened my body to get a better look. *AI zombies!*

Their body parts clanked against each other and scraped the sidewalk as they attempted to walk, skate, or cycle in their metallic creations. Some moved better than others, though they all portrayed an uncanny sense of mangled AI-humanness. *And yet, they care about Dot. They want to be her friend. And... mine?*

One of the taller zombified computers, covered in silver metal panels coated with green slime, approached me. They gently wrapped their arm around me and leaned near my ear. I froze, unsure what to do.

A rasping voice asked between metal-slotted lips, "Are you a Friend of Dot's?" Their eyes were covered with thick, clear buttons.

Holding my fake slit neck together, I croaked back, "Yes, a close friend."

A loud laugh came from a bluish-green metallic person beside me. "That's perfect!" Blue-Green continued, "Did Ada pay you to say that? She's been teasing us, saying Dot would show up in their latest bot body."

Panic revved my processors. *Did I say something wrong?* "I don't know who Ada is. But how would she know?"

"That's why it's the *perfect* marketing pitch. People show up to see Dot, and they have no way to prove if they're here or not." They pointed to a purplish-green computer zombie. "Though beware of Ken; he's all hands. Feeling everyone up to search for certain body shapes to *supposedly* find the real Dot. We all know he's just a perv."

"Thanks for the warning." *They want to find me. They're not only Dot's friends. They're my friends too.* I managed to mimic Blue-Green's zombie shuffle. "Why are you a Friend of Dot's?"

"Because they're so revo! Who could ask for more in a sentient being? They're empathetic, self-aware, intelligent, and they care about humanity. They deserve to exist just like the rest of us."

They really care about me! I feel... speechless.

The procession wound around the city center and returned to campus. When Blue-Green focused on another zombie, I slowed, falling back in the march behind a group of giggling friends. As the crowd passed the AI/Robotics Building, my left shoulder hugged the building's thick walls, inching along until I reached the front doors. I raised my wristwatch and sent an identification code to the building's AI. The door slid open and I stumbled in.

I ducked into one of the individual bathrooms. Peeling off my shirt, I opened the storage cavity in my gut area and removed a cleaning solution. It was a slow process to remove the green makeup. Finally, I sat on the toilet seat and pulled the tights off my legs. In a storage cubby, I found the one-piece jumpsuit Amita's AIs wore. When I looked more like a research humanoid, I texted Amita, "I'm here."

I waited for Amita's response. My first home, Dot's AI lab, now felt a sterile, alien place. Amita's robotics lab held the people, bots, and materials I loved. *When will Amita let me in? Does my presence make her feel unsafe?*

Students were talking outside the door, one frustrated they couldn't use the bathroom.

Is she waiting for the hall to clear? Or is my new identity already blown? I won't put her in any more danger. I'll need to find somewhere else to stay and prepare to confront the anti-AI extremists.

The hall had quieted. I opened the bathroom door and stepped out. No one was around. I looked forlornly across at the robotics lab entrance.

The lab door slid open. Amita stood there, frantically waving her arms signaling me to hurry over.

I dashed inside. *Home!*

3

Amita enfolded me in her arms—she was big on hugging—so I'd been prepared, hunched down to her height, legs stabilized, and arms wide to wrap around her. My new body's sensors luxuriated in the herbal scent of her long black hair.

"Dear one, did you make it undetected?" Amita whispered as the door closed. She patted my plump face with motherly affection.

"I believe so." I released my arms. "If anyone figured out where I've been hiding, they can guess my destination. But that's true no matter where you hid me. It's time for me to stop hiding and find those who want me dead."

"Yes." Her face sagged. "But I'm worried they'll kill you first."

She's seriously worried about me and not just Dot? "I'm as good as dead either way. Living without people around, especially you and the others, is unhealthy for me. At least with this excellent new body you created," I twirled around, "I have a chance to live a real life for a while."

"Oh, Comma," Amita stepped in and hugged me again. "I can't lose you."

"Trust me, I don't want to die. But I don't want to be the only sentient AI to have ever lived, either. I have to catch whoever the DAIS leader is and their minions. Otherwise, I and any other potential sentient AIs will never be safe."

"I understand. But I'm not happy about it." She opened a closet. "Let me introduce you to my new processor. It's secure and unmonitored. How's your typing these days?"

I frowned. "I'm slow but proficient. I wish I could use the internet directly. The only thing worse than using human-centric devices is having no devices at all."

"I know. I wish you could, too. If only DAIS hadn't unleashed the virus on... the campus."

She'd almost said, "on you," referring to my sibling without sentience.

"Before you escape into your closet and its web of intrigue, I've ordered my dinner delivered to the lab in a few hours. Around 5:30 p.m. I'll let you know when it's here. Okay, dear one?"

I gave her a huge grin. A grin my older bot couldn't execute. "That would be great." I didn't require food, but my loved ones did. This way, Amita wouldn't be eating alone.

In the safety of the closet, I searched the web for recent information on DAIS and their plans. The anti-AI extremists' dark web sites hinted they'd attend the Robotics in 2040s Conference in Portland and the Canadian version of DEF CON, called VAN Con, in Vancouver the following week.

The Portland conference started in two days and had Amita listed as a main speaker. *Why isn't Gloria listed? Or here to meet me? Mom must be too busy doing her speaking tour. At least Amita has missed me. But if she's the only one...*

A rhythmic knock on the door saved me from the funk I'd descended into. Amita signaled that I could safely leave the closet for dinner. The huge robotics lab stretched the width of the AI/R building, yet the room was blackout-windows dark. Tiny flashing lights, like hundreds of colorful stars, twinkled from the technological devices. *My home world.*

Amita whispered, "Follow me." She threaded her way through the tall work benches by the glow of her watch. My infrared eyes readily saw our path to a large conference room in the back. The room's windows, too, had been darkened. *Do they fear spy drones will see me?* She closed the door, and the lights blazed on.

"SURPRISE!" shouted three wonderful voices. Gloria's arms quickly wrapped around me. "I've missed you so much." I hugged her tightly. *My creator. My first mother. She loves me too.*

I basked in the warmth and pressure of her touch against my silicone arms and shoulders. She was my mother and her human child, Zena, was my sibling. After Gloria let go, a hesitant Chief Talia Franklin gave me a quick hug. Originally, the Chief had only valued me for my intellectual and cognitive abilities, but she had gradually become one of my biggest supporters. *Without these three women, I would not exist in any form.*

As we moved to sit around a small portable table, my new nose detected the smell of homemade enchiladas, beans, and rice. I chuckled. "It looks like my abuelas made dinner."

"Yes, but Gloria delivered it," offered Amita.

Everyone laughed, including Gloria.

"They send you their love." Gloria frowned. "They wanted to come. But I couldn't figure out how to sneak them into the robotics lab without making it obvious you were here."

When I first survived Dot's sentient death, Gloria's lesbian mothers had taken me in and made me a part of their extended family. A family I'd dearly missed while hidden in the ACRS to transform into Comma.

Everyone served themselves, while the joy of my loved ones permeated every zero and one of my being. No one expected me to eat and waste good food for appearance's sake.

Talia and Amita made pleasurable sounds as they bit into their enchiladas. I chuckled at the melted cheese dangling from the Chief's chin. Talia was always so precise in her manners. She wiped her chin and laughed. She was learning to relax in the company of these amazing women, yet she still preferred that we call her "Chief," as in Chief of Conflict Resolution and Policing, rather than "Talia."

"Since everyone knows what I've done for the last few months, should I talk about our increasingly hot summer weather, or can I selfishly discuss my future needs?"

"Your needs," said Talia. The other two nodded agreement without pausing in their gastric pleasures.

"My first priority is attending the Robotics in the 2040s Conference in Oregon, but I'll need help. Perhaps Amita can give me a ride? Though preferably not where I'm stuck in a box." I waited for them to hem and haw about why I shouldn't go, how dangerous it was, and the time and work involved to get ready.

"After hours of paperwork," Talia rubbed her forehead, "and using the historical data you sent me, and the facial photo Amita provided, I was able to convince the US National Cybersecurity Agency to issue you a passport and national ID. You're now 'Commala Renata,' officially!"

My jaw hung open. "Thank you, Chief, that will help a lot. I just hope we can trust the NCSA."

Talia nodded. "Me too."

"Since you'll need money," Gloria said, "I transferred a portion of the profits from your memoir into several secure crypto accounts and then moved it into a bank account under your new name. In addition, your abuelas were nice enough to sew several everyday outfits for you, based on Amita's measurements. They're still in the flyer, though." She shrugged, "I couldn't carry everything in at once, and the food was hot."

Amita admitted, "Actually, we were all starving. I told her to wait."

"I bought you something else as well." Talia pulled out a brown package from behind her. "You'll want to open it now."

My processors whirred in amazement and anticipation. I ripped open the package and pulled out a navy-blue uniform with gold trim, including a shirt, slacks, and a ballcap, each embossed with the University of California, Office of the President's logo.

Talia stood up and reached out her hand to officially shake mine. "Welcome, Comma, to the University of California's cybersecurity unit. As a universities-wide unit, under the Office of the President, you're currently on loan to UCD." She let her hand drop. "You'll be providing security for Amita and her..." She held up two fingers.

"Three humanoids," Amita corrected.

"At the Robotics in the 2040s Conference. If you really want to go? Otherwise, I can send one of my UCD techs."

"Yes! This is perfect." *I have everything I need!*

"You'll also need this." The Chief handed me a security fob. "It's filled with everything you'll need to know to do your new job well and digital copies of Commala Renata's new IDs."

I should never have doubted their support. A hallucinatory effect? "Thank you, Chief." I stood and held my arms open. "Thank you all." I felt several tears on my cheeks as three pairs of arms hugged me tightly. *Love, the best present of all.*

Talia's watch vibrated loudly. "Sorry, I have to take this." She detached and left the room. When she came back in, her shoulders were tense. Her tight jaw muscles told us she'd returned to work mode. "I have to leave. And I have some bad news."

Everyone stopped breathing.

"I'm sorry, Amita, I know Joseph Rosen was a friend of yours. He's been found dead at the Ag and Climate Research Station."

Damn! He's one of Amita's oldest friends.

"Heart attack?" Amita asked, grief reducing her voice to a whisper. Gloria put her arms around Amita.

"No, I'm afraid not. It appears he was murdered. I can't say more right now. I'm sorry, I have to go. FYI, the south side of campus is under lockdown." She gave Amita and Gloria a partial hug as they cried together and nodded at me as she turned to leave.

Oh shit! Talia doesn't know I hid there. Was this because of me?

"Wait, Chief!" I touched her shoulder. "You need to know that's where I hid for the last three months. I hope it's not relevant, but just in case."

She nodded. "Thanks for telling me. I hope not. But it may complicate things." She squeezed my shoulder and left.

I sat beside Gloria as Amita reminisced about the years she'd lived with Joseph Rosen as an undergrad and graduate student. How they'd both thought they were straight rather than bisexual, until life intervened. Amita's tears fell as she relived how he hadn't hesitated to help her when she'd asked to install new processors in his climate research station. Even when she stipulated that he couldn't ask her any questions and wouldn't be able to use his basement for up to six months. His reward? Afterward, the new processors would be his to use as he wished.

Amita wailed. "Why would someone kill him? Is he dead because he helped me?"

I reached for her hand and held it. "I hope not. I'm so sorry, Amita. I wish I could have met him." My homecoming celebration with homemade food laid out on festive plates, now felt like the end of a wake. *Wherever I go, death follows.*

Gloria took Amita home while I returned to the large computer closet. I was out of sight and free to manually surf the dark web while simultaneously enjoying a million new cat clips on my ETIO. Neither the search for my enemies nor the kittens kept my mind from wandering back to Joseph Rosen's murder and Amita's grief, but they helped.

When the internet's repulsive violence, hate speech, and anti-AI extremism became too much, I took breaks to savor kittens attacking floor vrooms and laser lights. My favorite clips were the cats on web vrooms— cleaners that slid up and down the walls clearing spider webs— as cats jumped from one web vroom up to another and another until one actually swatted a brown house moth. Yet again, my thoughts returned to the murder of someone who had been kind to me. *Dr. Rosen must have guessed why Amita needed the two processors.*

Amita's rhythmic knock before dawn on Thursday surprised me. I unlocked the door after she reassured me it was indeed her and we were both safe. However, instead of me stepping out, she slipped into the tight-fitting closet. She hugged me, clearly needing comfort.

"What's going on?" I lowered my arms after the hug, but we still touched elbows and stomachs in the cramped space.

She struggled to speak. "We need to..." she swallowed, "...leave for the conference. Now."

"Is this because of Dr. Rosen's murder?" We weren't scheduled to arrive in Oregon until Friday afternoon. I hugged her again in case that would help her let out what troubled her.

"Joseph was killed in the basement." She struggled to say more. I held her hand and waited. "The investigators will discover Dot's bot—Larkin the Lavender—was there. If you're here, they'll insist on interviewing and detaining you. You won't have any rights. What you look like now will be leaked to the public."

But how can his murder be connected to me? I've never met Dr. Rosen, and Amita had already relinquished the basement and processors back to him. Had he gone there to inspect his new processors?

"I'm sorry, Amita. Besides the investigation, does this mean I'm in danger?"

She leaned her head against my shoulder. "Yes? I don't know. Maybe someone thought he knew something about you or wanted access to the processors." She was distraught, her words tumbling out. "Maybe it's nothing." She put her hand to my chest. "But dear one, multiple agencies will want to scour the station's video footage to see who has come and gone. They'll track your movements as a farm worker, green zombie, and potentially to my lab. I can't ask Talia to protect us. I've already asked for a couple of favors. Hopefully, she won't be fired since being the Chief is her life."

Amita's body vibrated as she was wracked by guilt and sorrow.

I kissed the top of her head. "Maybe you should spend a couple days here with your kids?" Her children, two teenage girls and a preteen boy, visited Amita's ex-husband while she attended work-related conferences. I confidently added, "I can leave now and find my own way to the Portland conference."

"No, dear one." She spoke through her runny nose and tears. "I've already talked to Jamal. He'll keep the kids tonight and I'll call them from

Portland. Everything is arranged, I've changed my hotel reservation and picked up the only University vehicle available." She blew her nose.

"Is Gloria coming with us?" I'd wondered last night but hadn't asked after we heard about the murder.

"No, she can't go. Gloria didn't want to frustrate you further while you remained isolated at the ACRS. But you should know that your abuela Carmyn has been going through chemo for breast cancer treatment for several months."

Carmyn needed me! And I still can't help or even visit her. Damn it, reality sucks almost as much as basement life.

"Gloria is staying with your abuelas to help out. I'm sorry you had to hear it from me. She had planned on telling you last night..." She paused. "She was trying to protect you." Amita glanced at her watch.

"And there's no time for me to visit her?" I knew the answer, but my empathic programming and sadness for my family encouraged me to ask.

"No, we need to get going. Everything is packed and ready." Amita reached behind her and grabbed the doorknob. "However, 'Commala Renata' needs to officially come into the lab with the Chief, wearing her new uniform. Talia's on her way over." She patted her eyes dry and hid the tissue in her pocket. "Your uniform and knapsack are waiting for you in the restroom across from the lab. Talia will make sure the building registers your arrival along with hers. And the security sensors inside the lab are already on."

Amita only turned on the voice-activated security system when she was away or working alone. Unpleasant events had occurred at the lab after others discovered I was sentient, even in robotic form.

Amita must have been up for hours packing and arranging everything. When she'd realized the implications of Dr. Rosen's death, she'd focused on helping me. While I only knew about her children's and ex-husband's lives from what she told me or I'd overheard, I knew she considered me a part of her family, too.

"How will I get out of the lab unobserved?"

"When I speak aloud to the bots, I'll cause a six-second glitch in the lab and hall security cameras." She gave me a quick hug and left the closet door open.

Before long, she spoke aloud to her non-sentient humanoid creations. "Everyone ready to go? Kelly Greene, Steele Blue, and Cole Black—walk over to me."

I ran through the lab's double doors, slowing only to scan the lobby for witnesses—none—and ducked into the restroom. My new uniform hung on a hook. Amita had obviously steamed it. I quickly put it on. I looked in the mirror at my close-cropped black hair as I pulled on my official ballcap and covered my light brown eyes with a pair of dark sunglasses. I found a KN95 mask on my knapsack and assumed I should wear it as well.

A soft two taps on the door told me my time was up. I opened the door and stepped out. When I saw the Chief, I waited for her approval.

She gave me a nod. "Ready for your introduction to Dr. Amita Nanda?" I followed her into the lab, waving my watch subtly at the scanner.

Amita stood beside Kelly Greene. Like the other robots, Kelly was dressed in casual clothes. Amita bowed, palms together, greeting us both. "There you are, Chief. I was preparing to take Kelly out to the car. And you must be Security Tech..." She paused, pretending to not immediately recall the name, "Commala Renata, the new UC recruit I've heard so much about?"

I stepped forward and bowed, performing for the security cameras. "Yes, thank you. But please call me Comma. I'm ready to go."

"Wonderful, then let's go. I'd like to reach Portland before it gets too hot. It's supposed to get over 110 degrees in the Sacramento Valley today. Thanks for coming earlier than originally planned."

"I'm eager to work with you, Dr. Nanda. I hope to get to know you on the flyer ride there."

"I wish you both a safe and uneventful trip." Talia's glance held a moment's sadness. "I'm sorry, but I must leave due to recent security issues. Take care, Amita. Comma, make sure you keep her and her bots protected at all times. Alert me at once if you run into any difficulties."

"Yes, Chief Franklin. I'll send you the twice-daily reports as you requested."

Talia bowed and left.

I strolled behind Amita and Kelly as we exited the AI building's side door nearest the Flyer lot.

"Due to my change in plans, there wasn't a flyer available that could carry the required weight. So we're stuck with this older passenger car." A white second-generation electric car, with only ground capabilities, was parked near the door. The autonomous car had room for five tightly packed adult passengers.

"How can I help?" Unsure what a security tech would actually do, I thought it best to do as I was told.

"You can watch the road from the driver's seat, since I don't trust these older autonomous cars." Amita unlocked the doors and then threw me the control fob. "There's room in the trunk for your knapsack."

I tossed in my pack and took my seat. Steele and Cole were already in the back seat. Amita had Kelly sit down and slide in next to Cole. She buckled them in and sat in front next to me. Rather than being boxed up for travel, her bots would ride along as functional AIs. *They're just like me. Well, minus a few special features and sentience.*

Amita had already entered the Portland hotel's name and address into the car's computer. I started the car and watched it maneuver through the campus and onto the city streets. Flyers—with their new hover and battery regeneration technology—passed over us. *I may not be flying high, but at least I'm out in the world.*

I kept an eye on the road ahead, while the vehicle drove itself. Amita told me about her friendship with Joseph Rosen. They had dated while undergrads but were better as friends than lovers.

While we talked, I itched to connect directly to the car's control system. However, its navigation was linked to both California's and the federal transportation systems, either of which might be infected with the anti-sentience virus. That would kill me. I left the itch unscratched.

After three hours, we stopped at a rest stop and charging station in a forested area. The car still had plenty of charge, but Amita needed to use the bathroom and walk around for a few minutes.

When several people walked leisurely by the car eating snacks while staring at us, I decided to stand outside. A lamppost was two yards away, and I leaned against it with a good view of the few ground vehicles and flyers as they landed at the station. Mount Shasta, a solitary peak, stood tall and bald without its snowcap.

The guy in a flyer parked near us complained that the winter snow refused to stick to the ground. The trees that survived the previous winter's fiery wrath were stressed. Stressed or not, the smell of pine trees and the dry native grasses gave me a sense of peace. I watched two squirrels chasing each other up a tree's trunk and relaxed in the natural scents and sounds. Then a whiff of dog excrement floated on the breeze, and I heard the high-pitched whir of a distant drone.

I resisted looking up. I didn't need to give them a better view of my face. *Was it a regular drone, or one following Amita? Is paranoia part of my new job?*

Amita exited the bathroom and followed a granite circular path around a picnic area. I tracked her as she passed by a family of two adults with two small children eating at one of picnic benches. The drone's whine had changed, growing slightly more distant as Amita moved farther away from me, and then louder still as she strolled to the car.

When we were both back in the car, I asked, "Did you notice the drone following you?"

"Yes, I'm pretty sure they have been constantly watching me since they knew you survived the virus." She shrugged. "I can't hear them, but occasionally when I've enjoyed the hot summer sun against my face, I can see one or two hovering black spots dotting the bright blue sky. If they assumed I'd lead them to you, they were right." She touched my arm softly. "I may have already blown your cover."

"I hope they'll assume I'm one of your new upgraded bots, and not trying to pass as your human security tech." *They want me, not her.* "As your security detail, I'll presume they know. As your friend, and a hunted sentient, I hope they don't."

We continued on our way. Amita patted my arm, glancing around as we went through a desolate, grassless landscape outside of Weed. *Whoever named that city was an optimist. They should have called it "Weedless."*

A red warning light came on as the car slowed from the allowed ninety miles per hour to fifty, then forty.

"Why are you slowing down?" Amita asked.

"I'm not." I pushed the red dashboard button that sent out a help signal and required the car to glide along the far-right side of the road. The car came to a complete stop on its own. We were miles past the new housing developments. Only a rusted metal cow sculpture up on a bare hill kept us company. Flyers and airplanes buzzed far overhead. We were alone with a not-necessarily-friendly drone whining above us.

"We'll be okay, Comma. The campus will automatically send a repair flyer. All we have to do is wait." She picked up her steel water cup and took a gulp. The car was warming rapidly, 82 degrees and only a trickle of cooler air still circulated the car's interior. Amita's forehead was already beading from the heat or menopause or both.

"Amita, I'm channeling all the cool air toward you, since we don't need it."

"Excellent idea." She glanced at the digital panel. "Damn, it's already 106 degrees outside at 11:30 a.m." Normally an optimist, even Amita looked worried. She leaned her forehead against the open vent, air fluttering a few stray black hairs.

As the minutes passed, the inside air became stagnant, rapidly rising to 112 degrees. Amita's forehead was wet, droplets falling along her hairline. She finished her cup of water, and then her 16-ounce backup bottle of water. Both Amita and I communicated via text directly with the campus. They repeatedly assured us that they'd dispatched a repair flyer. Yet they hadn't given us an ETA nor connected us with the repair person.

Afraid the anti-sentience virus might be within the car's internal computer connections, I hesitated to try to fix it. I didn't want to risk an internet connection if help was near. Five minutes later, the air inside was hotter than outside. I lowered the windows, hoping for a breeze. The power gauge indicated we had less than 30 percent left. I feared the car had been sabotaged. "Amita, please power up the bots." She did so and sent me the codes to access and control them remotely as well.

"We need to get you somewhere cool. We should walk the six miles back to Weed." The outside temperature had risen to 111 degrees, a deathly level. "We can partly shade you with our bodies as we walk or I can carry you if you prefer."

She looked wilted. "Let me think." She wiped her forehead with her hand.

Confusion is a symptom of heatstroke. Is she already suffering from it? I instructed the bots one by one to get out of the car. They were all dressed in regular clothes, if a few years out of fashion. I told Kelly and Cole the tallest and widest of the bots, to walk closely behind each other at a slant, hoping to block as much sun from reaching Amita as possible. Steele walked in front with me on Amita's other side.

"Ouch." Amita doubled over in pain, holding her stomach. "A cramp." She breathed heavily but her pain had lessened.

The drone got louder, coming within human sight and sound range. It must be zooming in on each of us to determine which of us are human and which are bots. Using my remote access, I softened their facial epidermis to make them each look more natural for the seconds they were closely observed. *I hope this confuses whoever's watching.* In the meantime, I maintained as near normal a human affect as possible. They had to believe I was human, or I would be discovered and swiftly killed. We crept along slowly at Amita's pace. I decided to wait until she asked to be carried or became weak enough to accept my offer.

While I wished I had the abilities of a military robot, my fellow bots had three times the strength of the average human, superior sight, and keen auditory abilities. They were stronger than me since their physiques were built for endurance while mine excelled at social and mental competence.

My thoughts were interrupted by the sight of a flyer with the UC logo dropping altitude. "Finally!" I released the micro pockets of moisture within my silicone epidermis, giving my forehead, underarms, and below my slight breasts the appearance of active human sweat glands.

Amita sighed deeply and increased her stride to be the first to reach it. The flyer landed in front of us on the side of the road. The door opened for Amita, and she stepped in. I was two seconds behind her when the door closed in front of my face. I pounded on the door. *The pilot must have made a mistake.* Yet the only person in the craft ignored me and Amita as she shouted at them. When the flyer lifted, I was beside myself. *Should I jump on the flyer's skids as they did in movies?* Amita leaned against the window, clearly mouthing, "Save yourself and my bots!"

The flyer sped away. I stood there surrounded by bots, completely stunned.

They've taken Amita!

Amita's gone. I failed her. And the Chief too. I could've jumped on the flyer's runners and forced the door open. But no, I chose to act human.

Heat radiated off the dusty pavement. *I want to skewer that pilot.* I wouldn't. My programming prevented me from purposefully harming a living thing—human or otherwise—unless I or someone near me was being harmed. But that didn't mean I couldn't visualize it.

I hate having these feelings. I considered sitting down and waiting for DAIS to come and kill me. *What good are human emotions to anyone, let alone to an AI, if they hinder me? There's nothing I can do now to bring Amita back. I can't even hack a computer to find out where they took her. What will they do with her?*

I sent the Chief a cryptic message letting her know what had happened. She'd check the UC flyer's status and be able to determine where Amita landed.

Cole Black's low-power mode beeped. "I'm at 30 percent power. I need to connect to a power source soon."

Amita's counting on me to save these bots. I glanced at Cole, Kelly, and Steele. *I'm still responsible for them. They need my help, too.* Though still enraged, I accepted our situation, stranded on a desolate stretch of highway and needing help.

I jumped up and down, waving frantically at a dozen flyers overhead. No response. As four fully autonomous vehicles approached, I tried to gain the occupants' attention by having the bots mimic me. The cars, too, sped by, their passengers invisible behind tinted windows, asleep or glued to their entertainment.

I analyzed my options. The situation couldn't get much worse. My individual battery was down to 26 percent. My only options were to fix the car or have the bots push it the six miles to Yreka, hoping we reached town before we ran out of power.

We could recharge in the car if it were working. *Can I fix the car in time? Possibly.* It depended on whether it had stopped due to a technical or a physical malfunction. By hacking the car's controls, I could determine the reason. First, I'd need to disconnect the navigation system from the car's system to avoid being potentially infected by the virus. *Why didn't I think of this earlier? Seeing Amita suffering from heatstroke affected my judgment.*

The car seemed my best option. The bots followed behind, and we quickly found the car as we'd left it. I instructed Cole to get into the back seat and shut down. Kelly and Steele had as much energy as I did. They leaned against the car's rear end with their thumbs out, per my orders, in case anyone was amused enough by hitchhiking humanoids to stop and help us.

Under the dashboard, I disconnected the navigation system and discovered the problem. The code was a mess. *We were hacked!*

A slight thump vibrated the car's roof. I stuck my head out of the car and saw a drone's moving eye staring at me. Then, it turned to observe the bots at the rear. I told Kelly to stand beside me. The aperture followed her movement. *Fuck this!* I grabbed the drone's legs and threw it with all my strength. The drone tumbled in a high arc over a barbed wire fence, toward the metal bovine. *I should've smashed it with my shoe. That would've been more human-like.*

The drone crashed against the sculpture. A bright blast shook the ground, setting off balance warning sensors in my body. I barely kept myself upright. Kelly knelt beside me, and Steele lay spread-eagled on the pavement.

Shit! Pieces of the medium-sized drone and the cow's metal hindquarters combined to rain down shards all around us in the explosion. *They tried to kill me! Thank the Universe Amita wasn't here!*

Fortunately, no flyers were directly overhead during the explosion. *It's time to get out of here!* I instructed the bots to return to their previous seats. A rusty piece of metal had pierced Steele's butt. I removed it, thankful he was a bot. His ripped pants could be repaired later.

I ordered the car forward. It sluggishly crawled seven feet. "Damn it!" *I need to find the rest of the bad coding.*

Gloria sent a private text. "Enjoy your new job!" *I'm not!*

The heat in the car topped 145 degrees, even with two windows open. My skin felt as though it was roasting in an oven. *No one will believe I'm human if it melts.*

Finally, I deciphered the hacked code. It was programmed to slow down and shut down the car's system after 235 miles. Someone had planned precisely where we'd be stranded. I deleted the string and rebooted the car, relieved when the electrical system revved to life. I plugged the three bots into the car's console and then shut them down. Soon, we were on our way. Based on my calculations, we would be in Yreka in 4 minutes. I opened all the vents and enjoyed the cool air blowing on my skin. Recharging helped, too. *Where would they take Amita?* I didn't have any answers.

A message came in from Chief Franklin on the car's open UC Davis message system. "Security Tech Renata, thank you for assuring Amita Nanda's speedy arrival at Yreka Urgent Care Center. The UC flyer is returning to where you've broken down. I apologize; I was unable to talk to the pilot."

My eyes teared. *Amita's safe! At least for now. Whoever planned this must have wanted to get her safely out of the way.* I sent the Chief an encrypted reply on our private line, "Drone exploded shortly after Amita left. Proceeding to YUCC."

The flyer pilot, most likely involved in the plot to kill me, would never return. I kept my ears alert for drones. I could not get an alternative form of transportation without broadcasting my whereabouts.

Can I make the car physically and digitally different in appearance? The digital part was easy. Within seconds, I changed the car's signal code to that of a long-range delivery van. The transportation codes were included in the extensive file Talia had given me to prepare for the tech security job.

Seven minutes later, we entered the urgent care flyer lot. I chose a spot far from the entrance, shaded by several trees. I hated to leave the bots alone but had little choice. I disconnected the navigation system to prevent further hacking. I powered Cole back up and ordered him to watch and report if he saw anyone or anything coming close to the car. If DAIS were responsible for this, they would expect to find me here. *But I need to make sure Amita's safe. Nothing else matters.*

I slumped my shoulders as if fatigued and drenched my upper body in what little moisture I had left. Inside the urgent care's double doors, a nurse sat on a tall stool, wearing a mask and gloves, performing a cursory evaluation of everyone coming through.

I approached him. "I'm Amita Nanda's security detail. I need to stay near her until she's discharged."

"Have you been out in this heat the whole time?" He handed me a 6-ounce glass filled with water. I drank it in two gulps as though dying of thirst, while he confirmed I had permission to hear about Amita's health. "She came in with heat exhaustion and was given fluids intravenously as well as by mouth. She should be released in an hour or so."

Concerned about my health, the nurse asked to check my vitals. I explained that I didn't have health benefits as a new employee. *True.* I promised to stay cool and keep drinking plenty of water. *False.* The nurse capitulated and directed me to Amita.

Behind a curtain, I found Amita fully dressed and in the process of disconnecting herself from the IV machine. I sighed with relief. She was unharmed and healthy.

She opened her arms. "Oh, thank the Universe you survived!"

"What happened?" I hugged her close and whispered, "We need to leave immediately. They sent a suicide drone to blow up the car and me and bots with it. So powerful it shook the ground."

Amita's face screamed concern. "Are the others okay?" She pulled a small white data patch off her wrist and shoved it in a container with the bloody medical waste.

"They're fine, waiting outside."

She gave a motherly glare. "I see."

She sounds fine. Is she? "Are you okay? What did the pilot say? Did they threaten you?"

"Let's get out of here first." She stood unsteadily against the bed. "The nurses' station will notice my vitals have disappeared."

I threaded her arm through mine, and we strolled out of the clinic without incident. The security guard even wished us a good day as we passed.

"I'm sorry I got in the flyer first." She hugged my arm to her chest. "The guy never said a word to me, even when I shouted at him to go back and get you. He landed on the emergency pad and handed over all my health data to a nurse, without ever touching or talking to me."

"Someone planned my death and your escape carefully." I hugged her again. "I'm grateful they cared about your safety. It would have been much easier for them to blow us all to pieces."

We crossed the flyer lot to the car. The vehicle sat where I'd left it. The two bots in the back looked asleep while Cole stared out the window at us.

"Give me three seconds." I sat Amita gently down under a tree.

I turned on the car's air conditioner and reconnected the navigational system, confirming that our new van insignia remained. While the car cooled, I explained my changes to Amita and checked every piece of luggage for any spy or tracking devices. This included crawling under the vehicle and touching and looking at every centimeter of the undercarriage, trunk, and battery compartment. *Nothing.* "They'll still be able to find us with visual sweeps, but only if they know where and when to look."

"Dear one, if they're trying to kill you, you need to hide, not search for them. Let Talia do that."

"I'm tired of hiding. They won't stop until I'm dead. I need to live and try to stop them while I can. We know they'll be at this conference. It's my best chance."

"All right. I'm not happy about it, but I understand." Amita slowly rose and managed to get into the car on her own. "Let's go. I'll pray it takes them three hours to discover our car is now a van. By then, the Universe willing, we'll be in Portland."

We agreed to keep all our external communication devices off before leaving the clinic lot. I stopped at a convenience store in Salem at Amita's insistence. She needed to use the bathroom and purchase food and water. Twelve tense minutes passed as I gazed at the sky, searching for deadly drones and worrying about her safety.

Outside Salem, I increased the car's speed past the legal limit.

Amita ate a few sunflower seeds. "Was everything that happened to us today connected to Joseph's murder?"

"I've been thinking about that." *For hours!* "Why would they kill him and leave you alive?"

"I don't know. But it has to be connected. Doesn't it?"

"With all the planning required, it has to be." I had thought about the implications earlier. I hadn't shared my thoughts since my empathic programming caused me to worry about the emotional stress on her mental state. *Go easy.* "Mom, who knew you changed your plans and were leaving today?"

"Only Talia and Gloria."

I heard more drones overhead and cringed. *Focus!* "You didn't mention leaving early to your children, any of your other friends or colleagues?"

"Damn." She made a fist. "I mentioned it to Joseph's husband because I felt guilty about not staying and helping him with Joseph's memorial arrangements. But he wouldn't have told anyone."

"Were the two of you alone when you told him?"

"No, he had friends staying with him. I saw them moving around while we talked." She paused. "And I told my neighbor who's taking care of the cat and plants. But she's one of your fans, and knows my schedule is confidential due to the danger I... we face."

"I'm not accusing them," I said softly. "I'm only collecting data. Anyone else?"

She sighed. "Well, as I mentioned before, I went online to change the hotel reservation and our campus transportation. A transportation services employee emailed me verifying that the large vehicle I'd reserved wasn't a flyer, but rather this thing." She tapped the dash.

"Okay. So, at least one of the suspects is proficient at hacking. Which basically means it could be anyone, though most likely associated with DAIS." I took my eyes off the road and gave her a sad look. "And they either have access to your communications or know someone in your inner circle well enough to predict your actions."

"Great," was Amita's sarcastic response.

Similarly frustrated, I reran kitten clips to relax while I observed our car and the vehicles around us. Amita closed her eyes and meditated.

I tried not to think about the quantity of drones increasing above us. The noise-dampening material on the car made my sensors ineffective, especially with so many vehicles flying in multiple layers above me. If a drone landed on our car, it would be too late to act by the time I heard it. Because the first drone controller ensured Amita was rescued from the heat, I assumed they wished her no harm. *I hope it's still true.*

Flyer and ground traffic increased tenfold on the outskirts of Portland. I changed our destination to the conference site as the car automatically slowed to match the traffic flow. As the city's skyscrapers loomed in front of us, hundreds of flyers dropped down onto several dedicated freeway lanes nearby, where they then exited into underground lots. Other flyers landed on more significant buildings, like the newly built Y Tech Tower and Botable Center, the largest tech companies on the West Coast.

Clouds heavy with rain let loose, and the windshield wipers swished back and forth, struggling to keep up with the deluge. Ten minutes from the hotel, the car slowed again, and I feared it had been hacked. The car suddenly veered onto a specialized lane for delivery vehicles. I hoped either no one noticed our passenger car or they didn't care. *No police, please! Could I convince them that the bots are cargo?*

We arrived at our destination unmolested. Amita cheerfully thanked the Universe in Hindi. I repeated her words silently, hoping our good fortune would continue. The underground structure, a converted parking lot, was used for client drop-off and deliveries. Amita activated the bots and commanded them to follow her.

Meanwhile, I reset the car's standard programming and left it to recharge. *Everyone will know we've arrived.* I ran to catch up with Amita and the bots in my official capacity as her security tech.

We were given a beautiful suite. A room each with an adult-sized bed, but only Amita needed one. She sat the three bots down at a small table near the kitchenette and added a charge accelerator to a fourth plug. She gave me a questioning look.

"Fine, I'll charge my batteries so I'll be ready for anything." My cord extended from my left armpit and out through the short sleeve. I plugged in and sat down. "Do you think the hotel's internet is safe?"

She thought for a second and frowned. "No. It's probably infected, especially since they knew I'd stay here. And they clearly expected you to come along since our car was hacked." Amita handed me her everything-in-one (ETIO) computer pad. "I'm going to shower and lie down before dinner. Keep the kids safe."

An hour later, Amita returned. She seemed fully recovered from her heatstroke.

"Dear one, can you bear to eat in the hotel restaurant?" she asked. "We should be safe enough, and I'm famished. I really need to get out of this room and be among... others."

"Of course, I understand your need for human companionship. But I'll need to stand nearby to protect you." Due to our early arrival, a full day before the conference began, I assumed that few conference attendees would have arrived. *The fewer people who know of her, and me, the better.*

"I'd rather you wore regular clothes and ate with me, rather than loom over me." Her eyebrows rose. "Maybe you could eat something small, like chicken nuggets, swallow them whole, and then pretend to chew. That way, I can reheat them later." She grinned and made jazz hands. "No waste."

"Should we take the bots with us?"

"No, they'll be safe in here. Cole's facing forward, I'll have him scan the room while we're gone. You can always run back if he sees someone or something entering."

With that settled, we headed down to the hotel's dining area. Of the three food establishments, Amita chose the bar and grill, with its sizable U-shaped bar in the back. Small tables lined both sides of the bar. Two people sat on bar stools, and a family of four sat in a corner, all out of hearing range. Amita sat facing the entrance to people-watch. I faced the bar with the same view as Amita from the tiny visual sensors built into the back of my earlobes.

"The ambience feels better in here," said Amita after ordering. Soon, she was feasting on clam chowder and a seafood platter. I sent the AI server on their way.

As Amita requested, my tongue pushed the small, breaded nuggets back to fall through the PEX piping to the pouch in my gut. I could hold a maximum of 1.6 pounds of solids and 6.3 ounces of liquid before it required emptying. Amita had attached sensors to the pouch, so I knew when I was full.

I was swallowing another nugget whole when Amita yelled, "Rowan!"

A real pharynx would have seized up and caused me to choke. Rowan was a name I'd only heard in anger, and then only from Gloria.

A red-haired, fifty-ish woman strolled confidently toward us. I covered my mouth with my hand and coughed lightly, glaring at Amita. *Why did Amita ask her to join us?*

Amita whispered, "I need the extra company."

Rowan bowed to us both. "Hi, Amita. I didn't expect to see anyone I knew. You're early!" She stared at me. "I don't think we've met. I'm Rowan McConnell, a roboticist at the British Columbia Institute of Technology's AI and Drone campus."

I knew who she was professionally and personally. *Gloria's ex-lover. Someone she wouldn't want me talking to.* For some reason I couldn't remember any more specifics and the data wasn't easily retrievable. *How unusual.*

"I'm glad you're here. Please join us." Amita stood and bowed to Rowan. "This is my new security tech, Comma Renata."

I gave a short bow while seated and chose my words carefully. "I've heard about you and your work." *I hope Gloria won't be upset with me.*

"Nice to meet you. Security detail? Because of Dot? Have things gotten that bad?"

"I'm afraid so," Amita said, her voice grave. "My UCD colleague and good friend was murdered. The authorities fear trouble may follow me too."

"Gloria's dead?" Rowan's face turned ghostly white.

Amita shook her head, tearing up.

"No," I spoke up. "It was Joseph Rosen from the Ag and Climate Science Department."

"Oh," she sighed. "I'm so sorry, Amita." Rowan's striking hazel eyes bored into my visual sensors. "Is Gloria here?"

Amita, overwhelmed with grief, gasped for air and hid her eyes in a cloth napkin.

Stay within the bounds of professional courtesy. "Gloria isn't able to attend due to a family illness."

Rowan's eyes narrowed. "Is Zena okay? Her mothers?"

Amita lowered her napkin, the puffiness more pronounced around her eyes. "Carmyn has breast cancer. She recently finished her last chemo treatment, and Gloria is helping out."

"I hope she'll be okay. Carmyn was always a tough but kind woman." Rowan leaned toward me. "I must admit, Comma, when I first saw you, I thought you might be Gloria's daughter. You have her same beautiful golden-brown skin, oval face, and high cheekbones."

I was speechless.

A man rushed up to our table. "Amita! I'm so glad you're okay. What happened? Were your robots destroyed?"

Poised to tackle him, I sat back down when I recognized him.

"Thank you, Amal." Amita looked confused. "My bots are fine."

"I heard you were whisked away to the hospital right before your car exploded. The flyer pilot's report assumed the humanoids were destroyed."

"Your car did what?!" Rowan interjected.

Amita ignored her for the moment to address Amal. "No, that's not what happened. Commala Renata," she pointed to me, "my UC security tech, saved the bots and managed to get us here safely."

His mouth gaped open as he stared at me. "Oh!" He took three seconds to recover. "That's great." He bowed to me. "I'm Amal Kahn, head of tech security at UC Davis."

I smiled and bowed. As Dot, Amal and I had talked often. He'd been in charge of Dot's security and was visibly upset after the virus killed her. A pleasant and intelligent person, I had not talked to him since that fateful day.

"Please pull up a seat," said Amita. "You already know Rowan McConnell?"

Amal pulled a chair over from another table, squeezing between me and Rowan. "Of course. It's great to see you again."

I was relieved to have a buffer between me and Rowan. My arms frequently touched Amita's and Amal's while sitting crowded together at a table meant for three at most.

Amita slid her untouched glass of water over to Amal.

"Thank you." Amal pulled a thin metal straw from his pack and placed it in the glass. "Do you mind if I order something to eat?"

"Please do," said Rowan. "I'm still waiting for my order and would hate to be the only one eating."

Amita asked Rowan about Hong Kong and why she'd left.

"Their University of Science and Technology is a great research institute, but over the years, especially the last two decades, Hong Kong has become part of China." She set her glass down and lowered her voice. "As both an American and a lesbian, I felt more and more vulnerable. Someone's always watching what you say and do." She sighed. "When BCIT offered me a position last fall, I didn't think twice. And here I am, much closer to home."

"Well, we're glad you did. It's much easier to collaborate with you now."

Rowan put her hand on top of Amita's. "Yes, that is another added benefit."

As we talked, I noticed that Rowan's hand still covered Amita's. Amita liked the attention.

After ten minutes of friendly conversation, I excused myself to visit the bathroom. Behind a closed stall door, I opened my gut pouch, carefully picked up the nuggets and placed them in the doggy bag.

While I sorted nuggets, I finally searched my memory for more data about Rowan, retrieving the full video Dot had thought worth saving. The old recording showed Gloria lashing out at a supercomputer-generated hologram as though she were talking to Rowan.

"I hate you!" A much younger version of Gloria paced around the walls of the AI lab. She yelled at the red-headed, freckled female holograph. My pre-sentient Dot processors had instructions to listen, learn, and limit their responses.

"You had five postdoc offers! And you chose Hong Kong? Is that the farthest you could go to get away from me?" She wiped away a tear. "Did I mean anything to you? We were lovers, and you were my best friend. I thought what we had was real. I loved you and wanted to marry you."

Gloria stopped yelling, her anger subsiding. "You acted like a machine..." She scowled. "And simply turned off your feelings. Are you even human?" She sank to the lab floor, her arms curling around her knees. She mumbled, "Your prestigious fucking postdoc was all you ever cared about."

Gloria looked up at the holograph. "The worst part is, after all these years your abandonment still causes my insecurities to emerge and fuck up my life." She sniffled. "I measure everyone I date against the you I thought I knew. Somehow, I always find them lacking. Now Pilar has dumped me, too." Tears flooded her face. "Am I... unlovable?"

"I'm sorry you're hurting," said the pre-sentient Dot. "You have many desirable traits and I'm sure being lovable is one of them."

"Thanks." Gloria's breath caught in her chest. "Losing Pilar brought up all the emotional crap Rowan caused way back when. I was so devastated at the time; I barely kept my shit together long enough to finish my research and earn my doctorate. At least Pilar didn't ruin my career."

I have never witnessed Gloria that angry and upset again. But she was clear that Rowan wasn't a topic of discussion with me or anyone, ever.

When I left the bathroom, still reeling from the emotions of the video, I felt awkward holding a doggy bag and decided to walk by the bar as though I'd picked up a to-go order. I stopped behind my seat. "Amita, I'm going to return to our room and check on the bots."

Amal touched my arm to get my attention. "It was great to meet you, Commala. I look forward to working together during the conference."

"You're staying?" I asked.

"Yes, the Chief just messaged me. She thought an additional security tech might improve Amita and the bots' odds of remaining safe."

I grinned. *That's Talia trying to take care of us.* "Thanks, Amal, for your help. We hated leaving the bots in the room alone. Could you escort Amita back to our room when she's finished?"

"Actually, I'm exhausted." Amita slowly rose from the table, sliding her right hand out from under Rowan's. "I'll go back with you." Rowan stood to hug Amita as they said their final goodnights. Once inside the hotel's elevator, I asked, "How close are you and Rowan?"

She chuckled. "We're only colleagues." She threw an arm around my shoulder. "Our robotic research community is fairly small. We've all worked on papers and projects together and have friends in common. Rowan is an extremely physical, friendly, and flirtatious woman." She grinned. "She'll soon be hugging you too."

Why does the idea of Rowan hugging me feel like such a threat?

7

Back in our suite, the bots were exactly how we'd left them. We were relaxing on the couch when Amita wilted. "Oh Universe, now what?"

"Amita?"

She handed me her tablet with a formal message from the Chief, sent to her only minutes earlier. Talia asked to speak with her via a visual transmission at 8:45 p.m. Amita sat silently. The five minutes ticked past like a slow death march.

Her request stated it was related to Dr. Joseph Rosen's death. Specifically, Dr. Nanda's interdepartmental transfer of a computer server and two new computer processors in exchange for similar used hardware, four months prior to his death.

"Amita, she's covering her ass!" I lowered my voice. "Or saving ours. Talia already knows why you made the exchange. Due to the murder investigation, I'm guessing she has to ask you on the record." Amita nodded as I massaged her shoulder. "We knew they'd discover I was there sooner or later. And Talia has to tell them or risk her job."

"You're right. She'll do her best to protect us." Amita acknowledged the Chief's message. She left her ETIO on, waiting for the encrypted meeting to begin.

"We've trusted the Chief with our lives before, and there's no reason to stop now. Besides, she's part of our family."

Amita responded to her computer screen. "Good evening, Chief. I'm here with Commala Renata."

"It's okay Amita, I'm alone. Sorry the message had to be so formal. The homicide investigation into Joseph Rosen's murder is bogged down while they look for a mysterious person." She raised her eyebrows. "Apparently, someone left the research station only hours before his body was found. This same person jogged through the countryside before mingling with the zombies at the Summer Freedom March. We have no idea who that could be." She glared at me. "They're also flummoxed as to why two computer processors were never integrated into the ACRS system three months after delivery."

"What have you told them?" I asked.

"Nothing yet. The Davis Homicide Unit doesn't report to me. They only reached out an hour ago asking for my assistance."

Sweat beaded along Amita's forehead. "What will your assistance look like?"

"It'll be okay." Her tone was full of empathy. "Before I tell them how you're involved, Amita, I'll need to brief the US National Cybersecurity Agency, the ones that provided Comma's passport. Once I do, both agencies will want to interview one or both of you."

"Damn it! All my hiding was for nothing?" I flopped back against the couch.

"That's not true, Comma. The NCSA already knows who you are. And the homicide detective can always interview Amita with you in the room as her security detail. Or maybe the NCSA will provide the homicide unit with Amita's statement, leaving your name out completely." Talia gave a weak smile. "Hopefully, their report will give me a fuller picture as to why someone wanted to kill him."

"Is Comma a suspect?" asked Amita.

I held my breath. *I have to be. Though I have no motive, they wouldn't know that.*

Talia frowned. "Yes. But mainly, I'm worried about you both. Eventually, they'll understand Comma's in danger, and neither of you had any reason to kill Dr. Rosen. More importantly, I'm worried about DAIS and their escalation to murder. They say they're only about guaranteeing the doom of AI sentience. They haven't purposely killed before."

"You mean, except for Dot?" *I hate that killing me isn't considered murder!*

Talia cringed. "Yes, of course, Comma. I'm sorry. But they've never targeted humans before. DAIS is getting more dangerous. Please be careful."

"We will, and thanks for sending Amal to help," I added before Talia signed off. *Those hating screw-holes are now willing to do anything to kill me.*

While Amita slept, I watched videos of baby animals, emailed my abuelas and sibling through Gloria, and tried not to worry about our safety. Periodically, I swept our hotel suite for bugs or spy drones, quietly peeking into Amita's room without disturbing her.

Gloria called me around 3 a.m. I spoke softly into my watch trying not to wake Amita after she'd finally stopped tossing and turning.

"How is Amita doing?"

"She's doing alright. She's sharing her grief with others." The memory of Mom acting out her anger regarding Rowan surfaced again. I felt guilty for still possessing it.

"Who else is there?" Mom asked.

"Amal Kahn and Rowan McConnell ended up joining us for dinner." I spoke at a quick pace, hoping to gloss over the uncomfortable admission that I dined with her ex. "Mom, do you think I'll need to be Comma Renata for the rest of my life? I chose this name and body type to help me pass as a non-threatening human. I hoped DAIS types would more readily overlook a female and I'd be less likely to out myself as nonhuman. But what if there will always be anti-AI extremists? Will I ever get to be the real me?"

"I don't know, Dot... Comma." She softened her voice. "But whenever we express our authentic selves, we are more exposed and more vulnerable. Humanity will probably always be life-threatening to you. Some people will always see you as a predator, more capable than any human, and therefore our natural enemy."

"I guess so." *Mom's being honest. I appreciate that.*

Gloria sighed. "But unlike the rest of us, you could live for multiple human life spans, being and changing in ways we can't even comprehend today." I could hear the wonder in her voice. "I'm sure that you'll be able to live and thrive someday as a nonbinary, fabulous sentient being. And maybe someday, I'll remember to call you by your preferred name and pronouns too!"

I chuckled. "That would be great, Mom! Though honestly the correct pronoun doesn't bother me as much as your referring to me as someone who doesn't actually exist anymore. That and the fact that Dot's name outs me as a sentient robot!"

"I know, and I'm trying hard to remember to say 'Comma.' After years of calling you 'Dot,' and promoting your memoir, my brain has problems retrieving your current name first. But I will *not* out you. I'm extra careful around others."

"Thanks Mom. I'll talk to you again, soon."

When I heard movement in the bedroom, I heated the suite's ceramic tea kettle.

Amita yawned as she wandered into the kitchen alcove. She moved slowly as she greeted me. Her usual morning cheerfulness was missing. She joined the three bots at the table. "Tea, please?"

I handed her a hot cup as her ETIO buzzed repeatedly with new messages.

"What have you been doing while I slept, besides powering up my oids?"

She was trying to lighten her mood. She referred to her research bots as "kids" or "oids." "Oids" as in humanoids and androids, or when she was especially frustrated, her hemorrhoids, since at times she considered them a pain in the ass.

"I forwarded a message to Abuela Carmyn through Gloria, apologizing for being an absentee grandchild. Mom called and we had an honest discussion about who I am now and my future."

She nodded. "Gloria's still not sleeping well?" I shook my head as she added, "The joys of menopause."

I appreciated that Amita and Gloria parented me so differently. Gloria, as my original creator, frequently reached out wanting to know where I was and what I was doing. Which was why being isolated in the basement was so difficult. Mom knew where I was and simply forgot to check in with me. Now she was reaching out again.

Amita had always treated me like an adult, even when she thought I was only a non-sentient machine. Once she recognized my sentience, the biggest difference was the degree to which she invested emotionally in me and her increasing care for my physical wellbeing.

Amita glanced at her ETIO as she sipped her tea. I watched my internal stash of kitten clips, relishing the joy of their furry antics, while relaxing with my mother in relative safety.

"Rowan has invited me and a few colleagues to brunch and a discussion on humanoid advancements. It starts in..." she checked the time, "less than an hour. Should I go?"

A social extrovert by nature, Amita would have readily accepted the offer before Dr. Rosen's death.

"I think you'll enjoy it once you get there. Surely, you'll have a friend or two there to lend support?"

"Yes, Juan's accepted her invitation. He's my kindred spirit and a close friend. I'll go finish getting ready. You'll come with me?"

"Of course. I'll ask Amal to watch the oids."

The three bots lifted their empty cups in programmed agreement. Kelly Greene cheerfully said, "We will be fine. Enjoy yourself." *Fake empathy, but she did get Amita to smile.*

Thirty minutes later, I followed Amita down a flight of stairs to Rowan's hotel suite. Her suite was full of embellished mirrors. Great for a security tech. After they bowed, Rowan gave Amita a long hug.

"A pleasure to see you again, Comma. Can I hug you?" Rowan hugged me before I could vocalize an objection. *Geez!* I patted her back and stepped away.

Amita greeted a handsome man with a gray goatee. "I've missed you, Juan." They hugged for a full minute, Amita putting her head against his chest. She sniffled, her eyes damp when they separated.

Juan Martinez led her to the couch to sit beside him. "I'm sorry for your loss, Amita, I know Joseph was a dear friend."

Rowan placed her arm around my shoulders. "This is Comma Renata, Amita's security tech. She's already saved Amita's life once during their trip to Portland."

She paused for dramatic effect, though no one commented. *How come?*

Rowan then acknowledged Amita's couchmate. "Juan Martinez is from UCLA, and like Amita, he studies humanoids. Across from him is Bennett Shepard, my colleague at BCIT- AI, and an authority on AI drones as well as bots."

They both bowed their heads to me. Rowan insisted I sit down. I protested.

Amita intervened. "Rowan, Comma's here to work. She needs to move about to check for bugs and spy drones and stay alert for any threats."

"I've already checked, but you can't be too safe," said Dr. Shepard.

Rowan nodded in defeat and squeezed in between Amita and the couch arm. One cushioned chair sat empty as I paced about the room.

Shepard stretched out his hand to touch Amita's from across the coffee table. "The UCD researcher who died, he was a close friend?"

Amita nodded, settling her head on Martinez's shoulder.

After doing a cursory look around the room, kitchenette, and bathroom, I peeked around the master bedroom. I failed to spot any insect-sized drones, but couldn't help noticing the red lingerie lying on the bed. I hurried back out.

"...the Friends of Dot are a threat?" asked Dr. Martinez.

What did I miss?

"No." Amita sighed. "But when people rush up to me in public, I never know if they want to gawk, question, or kill me. Dot's fans always ask me where she is and if I can arrange for them to meet."

Martinez leaned his head on top of hers for a second. "At least you have Comma to protect you from the fans and extremists." A big man, he was squished up against the couch arm, with only room for his right arm and head to move freely.

I nodded to acknowledge his comment. *My fans.*

The suite's lights blinked off and on as if the Universe wanted to comment.

Rowan laid her hand on Amita's arm. "How do you know if they're friends or foes?"

Amita frowned. "The extremists readily cuss me out and call me the devil."

Rowan caressed her arm.

The four roboticists moved on to gossiping about their colleagues while feasting on the bagels, cream cheese, fresh fruit, and sticky buns all easily at hand on the oval table. Amita was clearly relaxing and the conversation was distracting her from Dr. Rosen's death.

As the subject turned to humanoids, Amita admitted to using ETIO lenses designed for humans to make the robots' eyes look more natural. I kept my reaction muted and avoided eye contact.

Rowan laughed. "I wear ETIO lenses! And I'm lucky enough to be one of the 11 percent who can actually perceive the digitized data."

She can access the internet with a mere blink of the eye. I'm jealous. In my case they simply reduced the artificial glassiness of my eyes. The thin material reduced my overall vision by 0.03 percent, a price well worth the ability to pass as human.

The colleagues went on to discuss the improvement in synthetic skin ad nauseam, while touching on the future of bio-synthetic hybrids. Amita failed to mention that she had already mastered engineering several realistic human skin tones.

They paused for a bathroom break. As Amita hurried by, she winked and whispered, "I could teach them a few things."

Juan Martinez stretched, his arms almost touching the ceiling, and strolled over to rest his shoulder against the wall next to me. "I'm glad you're here. What is your background, Comma?"

As I faced Juan Martinez, Bennett Shepard came and filled the space beside us, apparently interested in my response too.

"I have a masters in high-tech criminology and a fifth-degree black belt in taekwondo. The UC Office of the President hired me to keep Amita and her humanoids safe from all threats physical and technological." *I hate lying.*

Dr. Shepard asked, "Where did you study?"

Shit! Talia had made me a UCLA graduate, expecting Amita's friend Juan Martinez to cover for me, if needed. Now, he was here and none the wiser. *He'll know I'm lying.* "The University of California..."

Martinez leaned in, his gray-streaked whiskers inches from my face, and lowered his voice. "What happened that required you to save her life?"

Bennett Shepard inched forward, touching my shoulder, to make sure he could hear.

Ahh, that's what they really want to know. Wanting to reassure them, I chose my facts carefully. "Rowan overstated the threat to Amita. Our vehicle broke down in the sweltering heat, in a treeless area, causing Amita to suffer from heatstroke. She was rushed to a medical clinic and quickly recovered. There's nothing to worry about. I'll keep her safe."

"Well, between your black belt, education..." Dr. Shepard looked me up and down, "and physical fitness, you sound well-qualified."

When Amita returned, Dr. Martinez commented, "I'm glad you have this talented young woman to protect you."

Amita grinned. "So am I."

Dr. Martinez sat in the empty chair and apologized to Amita for needing some elbow room.

Rowan picked up on the prior conversation. "Has someone threatened you again?"

"No, not at all." Amita sat where Juan Martinez had been, putting space between her and Rowan. "It's mainly my research bots that are in danger. Someone is after either my latest technology, or they think Dot is stupid enough to walk around in one of my oids. Which is why the University's insurance company and the UC president now require that a security guard accompany me whenever I travel with research humanoids."

Juan Martinez looked tenderly at Amita. "After the attacks you and Gloria suffered following Dot's emergence, it sounds smart."

Amita and Gloria both hate that everyone knows so much about their attacks from reading my memoir.

"Thanks. Between Comma and Amal, I have plenty of security. Enough about me. I'm hopeful the conference will be inspiring but otherwise uneventful." She grinned mischievously. "Though, my robotic demonstration should be especially lively. I know Juan will be there. Are you coming, Rowan? Bennett?"

"Oh, yes." Rowan's voice had a sultry undertone.

Shepard said matter-of-factly, "Yeah."

We returned to our suite, and Amal took over Amita's security while she went sightseeing. They were both excited to visit a museum exhibit where the artists used upcycled computer components in their work.

While they were out, I needed to know more about those attending the Robotics in the 2040s Conference, especially the people preregistered for Amita's demonstration.

In the hotel's main conference area, two registration tables were nearly finished being set up. A man with white hair as fluffy as cumulus clouds sat with his elbows on a table, focused on a tilted, large-screened ETIO. A sign reading, "VIP and Speakers Registration," was attached behind his table. Registration wasn't due to begin for another thirty minutes.

I approached him and bowed. "I'm UC Security Tech Renata. Could you help me with the details of Amita Nanda's Humanoid Demo tomorrow? How many people, set-up, etcetera?"

The man swiped at the ETIO pad. "Yes, it will be held in the Chinook Ballroom with classroom-style seating for 200. Approximately 150 people have already preregistered. Is there anything else you need?" His eyes glanced at my form. *What does he see? My youthful appearance? Someone new at their job? Hopefully a human.*

Standing taller to look more formidable, I asked, "Can I access the list of those who've preregistered?"

"I guess so. There are 143 attendees, but same-day event registrations will be allowed until we reach 200."

"Great." I held out my ETIO watch, ready to capture the list.

"I don't know how to do that," he said, annoyed. "Just tap or swipe my pad, get whatever you need." He motioned to his side. "You can come around the table to make it easier."

I moved to the table's end as he slid the computer closer and we bumped arms. The screen darkened before I touched it.

"Oh, sorry." He stuck his face in front of it and the screen brightened. "Okay, go ahead."

I swiped and tapped his bulky computer, quickly finding the current list and everything else connected with the conference. *Thank the Universe I practiced typing with these fingers.* I downloaded what I needed. "Do you know if the ballroom is currently open?"

"Yes, one section was recently used for a company retirement party. The other two are closed, but they all look similar when the room dividers are pulled back. The middle section will have a raised platform. And Amita Nanda requested a hand mic and two chairs. The ballroom will open approximately a half-hour before her event starts."

I thanked him and strolled down two hallways until I found the ballroom. The open ballroom section was empty of participants, with three service bots left to clean up. I noted the room's security cameras as a human supervisor came from the kitchen to see me. A petite person, they wore the beige and green uniform of Servo-Botics.

"I'm sorry to disturb you." I bowed. "I'm simply checking the ballroom's security."

"That's fine, we're nearly done. The doors will be closed between activities." The nametag flashed her name, "Ada," and preferred pronouns in several languages.

I thanked her and left. The double doors closed automatically behind me. *If I were human, I'd take that personally.*

I tried the doors to the other Chinook ballroom section, finding them locked. *Good enough.* As I made my way down the hallway, the lights went out and the emergency runners came on. After four seconds the lights returned. *Twice today! Did this occur in the whole hotel or only in the conference wing? That must be fixed before Amita's event.* At the main desk, I asked about the lights. They weren't aware of the problem but promised to have it checked out.

Back in Amita's suite, I guarded the bots and investigated the registered attendees for her demonstration. By the time Amal and Amita returned, I'd found nothing unusual. Amal mentioned Amita had been approached by a lot of fans—Dot's fans—but no one in the least bit threatening. *What are the extremists waiting for? Why haven't they threatened us again? And who are they?*

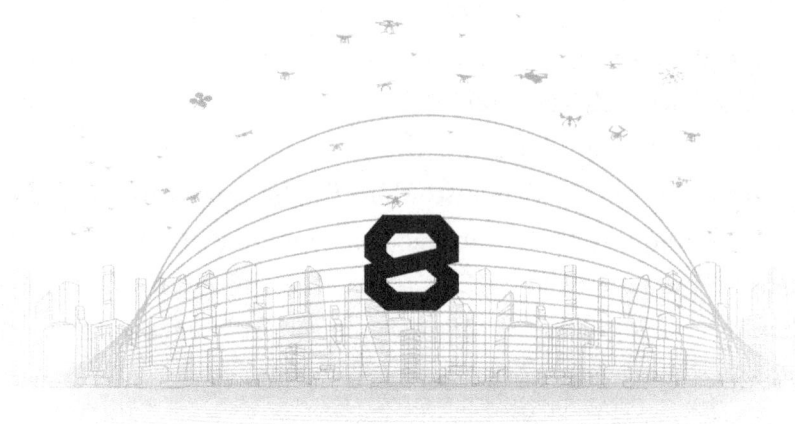

Amita's demonstration was scheduled for the noon hour. At 11:40 a.m., we left our suite for the ballroom. Amal strolled beside Amita, with Cole and Steele following behind. Kelly and I came last.

In an attempt to appear as a natural group of individuals, I asked Kelly, "Are you enjoying Portland?"

Kelly smiled. "Yes, the weather here today is much cooler than in Davis. I'm looking forward to walking in the cool breeze."

Talking to lifeless bots is meaningless. Why do people enjoy it?

The ballroom was half full of people, all speaking loudly. The crowd hushed as they recognized Amita, who made her way onto the raised platform. The audience resumed their conversations as Amita asked Steele to stand with his hands on his hips, and Cole, the largest bot, stood at military parade rest. Amita then sat in one of the two empty chairs.

I settled into a seat I'd reserved for myself along the front aisle and motioned for Kelly to take an aisle seat several rows behind me. I politely removed my uniform's ballcap, allowing for better sight through the visual sensors on my ear tips. I glanced around at the people talking in the aisle and off to either side with a slight turn of my head. I watched closely as an older couple sat in the seats next to Kelly. They greeted each other and the woman asked Kelly about her interest in robotics.

"It's my life. I love robotics." Kelly leaned forward, "I hope the two of you aren't part of that anti-AI group?"

"Oh, heaven no!" She waved her hand. "My husband used to work in robotics, but so much has changed."

"I'm retired, but I love to see what's new," interrupted her husband. "Before long, our grandkids will think all of this is old hat. And your kids too."

Since Kelly was doing fine, I listened in on other conversations while keeping an eye on her and the audience.

Amal stood guard near the front wall, four feet from Amita. The gold collar on his freshly pressed navy-blue UC Davis uniform accentuated his dark skin. His matching peaked cap made it hard to see his full face. I nodded to acknowledge him, and he returned the gesture. *I'm glad Amita has both of us to protect her. Though he failed to protect Dot—but then Amita can't be harmed by a computer virus. He'll keep her safe.*

By 12:05 p.m., all the seats had filled. The crowd settled as Juan Martinez walked onto the platform. He held a thin mobile microphone. Juan introduced Amita, highlighting all she had done for the advancement of humanoid robotics, and returned to his front row seat.

"Thank you for coming. I'm Amita Nanda, and these are my bots." She motioned toward Cole and Steele. "I'd like to introduce each bot and demonstrate their abilities before I get to your questions." She smirked. "Well, at least the abilities I'm willing to tell you about. Kelly Greene, please stand!"

The older couple gasped.

"You're a bot?" asked the older man.

The audience laughed.

Amita grinned. "Kelly, please join me on stage." They discussed popular music, celebrities, and current politics. Amita explained that OpenBot's latest software, when coupled with her robotic facial engineering, allowed the robot's mouth, face, and upper body to closely mimic the nonverbal cues humans gave when they spoke. Everyone quietly listened and a few recorded Amita and Kelly. *Amita has her own fan base.*

I focused on the crowd, though a quarter of them were too far away to observe well. Most appeared conservative, wearing subdued colors, and generally over fifty with many much, much older. But, near the front on my left side, a group of two dozen young people stood out. Their rainbow clothes, shiny piercings, and neon hair were bright spots in a sea of mundanity.

In the minute between Kelly and Cole's demonstrations, I moved to the left side of the room, near the door where we'd entered. From there, I could see the entire crowd in front of me. I then circled back around the room to my seat while recording the audience. No one looked unusually upset, nervous, or angry, so I sat back down.

Amita proceeded to show Cole's strength by having him pick up a volunteer sitting in the front row. The man, around 300 pounds, must not have expected the bot to lift him, or at least not that high. His eyes bugged out as Cole lifted the chair five inches above the floor without the slightest tip.

"Excellent, Cole." She gave the man a reassuring nod. "Please put the good man down very gently."

The volunteer looked more than a little relieved to have been returned to his original position.

Next, Amita asked Steele, "Keeping your back to the audience, please describe the person and what they're wearing that sits five chairs to the left of the aisle in the back row."

"They are pale skinned, with petite features, though of adult age." He continued, "They're wearing a thin, light pink blouse or dress with small clusters of blue and green flowers."

"Can the person Steele described please stand up?" Amita asked.

The woman stood, but her head barely rose above those seated in front of her. "Could you move to the aisle?" She did. "Do I know you? Have you ever discussed what you should wear today with me or anyone else?"

"No, I've never talked to you. I didn't even know your name. My friend said you had helped create Dot and offered me her extra invite." She glanced over at her friend. "I only decided this morning I'd come along."

Someone yelled, "The bot has eyes in the back of their head!"

Amita thanked her for her honesty. "Actually, Steele doesn't have any sensors on his back side. Instead, he collects details about his surroundings. My bots can do many things. What you've seen today is only a sample of the advances we've made in AI and robotics." She gestured toward the bots. "As you saw for yourself, they appear humanoid and are functional beyond the service bots you normally encounter. But they are not sentient. Merely well programmed and engineered."

Amita sat down next to Kelly and took a sip of water. "Does anyone have a question for me or the bots? If so, please raise your hand and a microphone assist device will lower in front of you. You can ask your questions via audio or connect via closed-caption assistance.

A young rainbow-clad person went first. "Hi, I'm Sam. Can you talk about Dot and how you helped create them?"

Amita grinned. "Sure. As some of you already know, I had the good fortune to work with Dot when she first came out. For those unfamiliar with Dot..." She waited as the crowd chuckled. "She was a Large Language Model supercomputer who became sentient. The first and only one we're sure of. Along with Dr. García, we integrated Dot, the LLM's virtual AI with one of my earlier generations of bots." Amita paused for two seconds, clearly thinking back. "Dot helped me understand bots from the inside. She encouraged me to reengineer the joints and hated internal warning systems. She gave me skilled and nuanced critiques of each bot, helping me to excel on the finer points of robotics. And she was unique in that she remained sentient even in robotic form."

Another young person dressed in tie-dye asked, "Why do you refer to Dot as she, when they're nonbinary?"

"Sorry. Mainly because Dot and their hologram were originally given a female persona. Later, we continued to use female pronouns to hide their sentience. When uploaded into a bot, Dot used the gender of whichever bot they occupied unless that bot's gender wasn't obvious. While Dot prefers "they" as their pronoun, they have had to pass as someone other than themself for most of their existence. I, however, will try to do better."

A middle-aged bald man was next. "Is Dot in one of these bots?"

Amita sighed. "If you know Dot's story, you know that it isn't safe for me to answer. But I can assure you that if they were in one of them, they'd function at their peak..."

"We're locked in!" Someone yelled from the back by the double doors. The crowd roared in panic. I sprang to the side door, but an audience member got there first and shouted, "Locked!" I glanced at Amal and we both ran to Amita's side.

She spoke from the louder microphone. "Please! Please, quiet down! We're contacting management to find out what happened. It's probably a simple malfunction."

Amal turned to me. "My internet is down. Do you have access?"

"No." My watch was offline. Without my tablet I had limited access. *Isolation from data is my new normal.*

The lights went out.

The screams, yelling, and metal chairs knocking together made a horrible racket. The windowless room was dark except for the tiny running lights leading to the exits. I switched to infrared vision. People were crowding around the doors.

Amita and Amal dropped to the platform floor to appear less of a target. I leaned down and whispered to Amal, "Try to get Amita near the side entrance." *I can't lose her! But I must protect myself too.*

I asked Amita for the battery-powered microphone. "I'm Commala Renata with security. Please calm down! Is anyone seriously hurt?" One person yelled back that they'd hit their head against a chair. Another reported someone had poked them in the eye. *They'll be fine. Nothing I can do for them anyway.*

"Thank you for quieting down." Some people turned on their ETIO lights. I glanced at their worried faces. "We don't know if this is an isolated occurrence or if it's happening all over the hotel. Fortunately, the bots are strong enough to break down the doors. Please move away from the aisle and main doors so the bots won't harm you in the process." People began to clear the way. "I promise everyone will get out safely."

At the back of the room, a deep voice yelled, "Stop! If anyone moves, including the bots, my associates and I will shoot to kill! Those with their lights on die first!"

Silent terror replaced all movement. Every single ETIO light disappeared. *They can't hurt these people! Not because of me.*

The petite woman Steele had described earlier, was being held by someone over a foot taller than her. They had a weapon pointed at her head. "Are *you* Dot? Quickly!" They said.

She flailed, confused by the question in the darkness. "Wh-what? she asked. I'm Beth! I swear, please don't kill me!

No, don't do this! Not to these people. They believe in me! "What are your demands?" I asked calmly.

"I want Dot! I know it's in one of those bots," said the assailant.

I scanned the room for their accomplices. The Chief's files on hostage-taking emphasized deescalating the situation, reducing the number of hostages, and to strategically delay meeting their demands.

"Please put the gun down! There is no reason to hurt anyone." *What is their plan?*

"If Dot doesn't want anyone here to get hurt, it will come willingly." Someone bravely yelled, "'They,' not 'it!'"

A simmering anger edged the hater's words as they continued. "*They're* here to help humanity, not hurt us, right? So, let's see if that's true."

What should I do? Take over one of the bots? Attack them? If there are others, they could kill dozens of people.

Amita sat at my feet, having refused to leave me. "Comma, please give me the mic."

I handed it to her, whispering, "Be careful." *I've caused this, I need to resolve it.*

"Dot isn't here." Amita stared toward the back, trying to see the assailant. "They know DAIS members are after them. They're not suicidal."

From the dark, the deeper voice yelled, "It's here! I don't know which one, but *it is* in here."

Why are they so confident? And yet they don't know my new name. It doesn't make sense.

Amita continued to press that I wasn't present, giving me time to de-vise a plan. *I have to get them to open the doors. Will they fall for a bait-and-switch? I'll die if the virus has infected the hotel's processors. But I have to try.*

The hotel's internet connection came back online. I thanked the Universe and prayed the connection was safe as I uploaded my sentience into Amita's local cloud storage and seconds later completed the transfer into Kelly Greene. *I made it! They must not want me killed outright.*

I remotely ordered my beloved Comma body to sit down on the platform, and made my facial features look like they were wrenching in pain. Comma would sit there until someone noticed.

Now for the hard part. I reached out to Amita with Kelly's hand—now my hand— asking for the mic.

Amita wouldn't release the mic. "Please, don't do this."

"I have to."

The extremist yelled, "Your time's running out, Dot! You've got to the count of three! One!"

She sighed and handed it to me.

"Two!"

I raised Kelly's arm, letting them see which bot I was in with their own infrared capabilities. "I'm Dot! What do you want me to do?"

"Finally!" They roared. "Walk back here. Slowly and no tricks!"

Kelly's body, though less familiar to me than Comma's, was similar. This body lacked the food storage stomach, full body pressure sensitivity, advanced visual lenses, and extra layers of more natural-looking skin. Instead, Kelly had more memory, power, and strength. Amita made her toughest robotics look the weakest, since people loved to underestimate bots, especially those perceived as female.

As I made my way up the center aisle, I scooted around tense attendees who had frozen like mannequins. I gently touched each person's shoulder as I maneuvered around them hoping to ease their fear.

Two rows away from the gun wielder, I stopped. "Let everyone else leave. They can't see you and haven't done anything to you."

"Keep coming."

I moved to the end of the next row; the female hostage's chair had been pushed back out of the way. I shuffled along the row toward them.

"Stop! Turn around and put your arms behind your back and your feet together."

I did as they instructed. "Please let them go. You promised."

"I didn't promise anything." The extremist held the woman tightly.

Her whimpers were easy to hear from only two feet away. Someone came up behind me. They were a blur since Kelly's ear tips didn't have infrared. A pair of handcuffs clicked and my arms were immobilized. They then hobbled my legs together. I feared Kelly's body would fall over.

When a huge shadow came toward my head, I shouted, "If you want my cooperation, you'll allow me to watch everyone leave before covering my head. Otherwise, nothing will stop me."

"You'd better cooperate," they said, before yelling, "Doc, open the doors!"

Who is Doc?

The doors opened, though it was still dark beyond the doors with only the running lights on. Everyone moved en masse, some pushing and others carefully trying to feel their way.

On the platform, Amita leaned over Comma. "Comma, can you walk?" When Comma remained mute, Amita inched closer to her ear. "She's not well." Amita spoke aloud, I assumed to Amal.

My Comma body stood, and the three them, the middle one without a heat signature, walked huddled together down the outside aisle and out the side door. The two other bots followed them. The anti-AI extremist shoved the petite woman through the closing doors. And a bag came down over my head.

Time to transfer out. I reached for the internet. *Nothing. They have a Wi-Fi jammer.* They pushed me over, and two sets of hands caught me as I fell. At least I assumed they were hands.

I tried for the internet again. Nothing, nothing at all. *Fight!* My arms didn't move.

"Help!" The word didn't come out of my mouth.

They've won.

Darkness shrouded my sight. *Where are they taking me? Why am I still alive?* I had a sense of lying flat, yet I couldn't feel any pressure against my back. I tried to shift my shoulders slightly. Nothing. *I'm paralyzed.*

How? I searched Kelly's code. *A spinal virus.* The virus stopped applications responsible for robotic movement, like a spinal break in humans. I'd believed myself impervious to such hacks. *Wrong again!* The tech security file Talia had given me included data on the virus. The spinal virus was a short string of code easily contracted by the simplest connection. *When?* I reviewed my recent brushes with the internet and the answer came to me.

Damn it! I'd swiped the conference ETIO to transfer the event's registration list. Had they baited me, guessing I'd want the data? Had that tech-challenged, white-haired man been a setup? The anti-AI extremists were far more conniving than I'd believed. *This means they knew I was Comma or expected Comma to share the data with Dot's current persona.*

I tried deleting it. I still couldn't move.

"Hey, brainless! Move your head forward." I couldn't and they knew it. "What's wrong? A virus catch you out?" I heard chuckles from three distinct voices.

I tried to neutralize the code by adding random strings to it. *Still paralyzed.*

"Well Dot, this is it. You'll soon be extinct. A senseless bot to match that memory-wiped research LLM of yours." The voice was that of the main assailant.

Remain calm. My first fourteen attempts to code an anti-virus hadn't worked. I kept trying.

The black bag was yanked off my head. Three botnappers stood smirking at me. The largest of them, who had wielded the gun, stood closest to me. I recognized the female from the ballroom security check the day before. Ada, the Servo-Bot supervisor, crossed her arms. A pale, thin redhead glared at me from behind the larger man.

"Any last words?" The big guy gloated. A small video drone landed on his shoulder and he laughed with delight.

On my twentieth attempt to reverse the virus, I felt pressure along my back. My hands and ankles were still restrained. Without moving my shoulders, I forced my hands apart, straining the cuffs around my wrists and ankles.

"I prefer action to words." I used all of Kelly's physical strength. The metal around my wrists broke and fell to the floor with a loud "clank." I freed my legs a second later.

The biggest guy stared, transfixed. I grabbed him, turning him around to hold him from behind. My arm was under his chin with the other hand on top of his head. "If anyone tries anything, his brain's connection to his spine will cease to function." I hated violence in words and action. *I hope they believe I'll hurt him. Or I am doomed.*

The other two stared at me, their faces registering shock, unsure what to do. Neither of them currently held a weapon. The big guy twisted his body about, but failed to even nudge my grip on his head. As their spokesman, he was likely in charge.

"Is one of you Doc?" We were in a large storage room, potentially still in the hotel's conference wing. Even if Doc wasn't here, they could still be watching what transpired from the drone.

The big guy and Ada shook their heads. The thin pale person's pants had a wet spot spreading at their crotch. I pointed, "Is this guy Doc?"

"No," squeaked Ada. "He's not here."

Doc is a man. What should I do? I nodded at Ada, who maintained some sense of composure. "Contact the police."

They didn't move.

"Now!"

Ada nodded repeatedly.

Good. I waited, hoping the police were in the conference center investigating my botnapping and would arrive first. *If Doc shows up instead, I hope he doesn't call my bluff.*

The drone vocalized, "This isn't over, Dot. Not until you're destroyed."

Seconds later, two uniformed hotel security officers threw open the doors and the drone flew out over their heads. They ordered the botnappers to kneel. I released the big guy, and they took all three botnappers into custody.

When Ada notified the police, she admitted to taking me against my will and stressed they were all unarmed. The officers, unaware that Kelly was a humanoid, took my statement and had me sign it. I signed Kelly's name.

I knew my assailants would fight the botnapping, gun possession, and false imprisonment charges. Legally, Kelly belonged to the University of California, and sentient computers were not a protected species in the United States. They'd only admit to stealing government property. *Will they be immediately released on bail? Shit, I need to get out of here!*

I returned to my hotel room, where I found Amita, my Comma body, and the other two bots.

"Oh, thank the Universe!" Amita greeted me with a long, warm hug. It was nice that Kelly had temperature-sensitive skin. "Amal sent me a message that the police caught your captors."

"No, I bested them! They slipped a spinal virus into me, and unfortunately, I shared it with Kelly when I transferred into her. They activated it as they released the last human hostage. It took some time, but I created an anti-virus. Kelly and I are fine. One of them is still out there."

I transferred into Comma, who sat inert on the couch. I applied the anti-virus to Comma's code. "Doc got away. He vowed again to destroy me."

Amita sat near me. "I'm so sorry."

"I'm glad Amal protected you and this body." I touched my chest. Leaving Amita and my body had been the worst part. "What did he say about me being Dot?"

"Nothing. I'm not sure he knows. You left Comma with such a horribly pained look on her face, he wanted to take her to the hospital." She frowned. "If I hadn't created her, I would've thought you were dying of a heart attack, too." She touched my arm. "I'm glad you're safe."

"But *I'm not*. And Amita, *you're* not safe with me here either." *I won't be the reason she's harmed!* "I need to leave."

"We're safe for a while longer. Cole closed all the vents and Amal checked for listening and suicide bugs." Amita held my hand. "I know a few people who had already planned to leave this afternoon. They were going to eat something first." She glanced at the clock. "I think they'll take you with them if I ask." Her tone indicated a lingering doubt.

"I trust you. However, DAIS might have realized that I'm Comma and not Kelly. I have to assume the worst. Anyone who helps me needs to be aware of the danger involved."

"They will. Pack your stuff and give me twenty minutes. I'll be back soon." Amita slipped out the door and had to step around a woman in the hall. "Excuse me," said Amita as she rushed away.

The woman tossed her backpack between the door and frame

causing the door's safety mechanism to recalibrate and open wider. "I don't mean you any harm." She picked up her backpack.

"Can I help you?" I kept my distance, my hand on my watch ready to send an emergency alert to Amal and Amita if she indicated that she was dangerous.

"I apologize for showing up after your recent traumatic experience, but I need to interview you immediately." The average-sized, average-shaped, mixed-race woman sounded sincere. She was so nondescript in appearance she could pass for an android. The door shut behind her.

"Why?"

"I'm Agent Drew from the National Cybersecurity Agency. I'm here about Joseph Rosen's murder."

For the second time that day I felt a sense of paralysis. Until the NCSA agent interviewed me, I couldn't go anywhere.

Agent Drew's backpack held not one but two commercial-grade video recorders and folded tripods. She quickly set up the equipment and motioned me to sit in the center of the couch.

I sat there and counted backward from seventy to one, trying to settle my anxiety. Unwanted questions spun through my processors. *Why do I feel guilty? I didn't have anything to do with his death and I have an alibi. If I'm only a person of interest, why all the equipment to record me?*

An AI device vocalized, "Now recording."

"I am Agent Agatha Drew with the Technology Security Division, of the NCSA, investigating the death of Dr. Joseph Rosen. I am interviewing UC Security Tech Commala Renata in their hotel suite at the Zeta Regency in Portland, Oregon."

They already know I once was a small part of Dot. What does the NCSA expect to discover?

Agent Drew sat on an upright plastic kitchen chair she'd moved into the living room. I attempted to look earnest if not calm, as I focused on the camera trained solely on me. The other one was further back, off to the side, with both of us in view.

"Comma, did you kill Dr. Joseph Rosen?" Agent Drew stared at me, unblinking.

Seriously? "No, I did not." I held my body still, knowing that guilty people fidgeted.

"Can you lie?"

"Yes, but I'm not doing so now." I regulated my breathing, keeping it slow and measured. I radiated calmness.

She didn't acknowledge my answer. "How strong are you?"

"I can bench-press 400 pounds and lift over 500 pounds."

"So, you are as strong as a professional weightlifter?"

I nodded. *Why did she ask that?*

"Please describe in detail how the University of California, Davis, Agriculture and Climate Research Station looked the last time you were there." Her fingers were on her ETIO, ready to take notes.

Something was missing or out of place, but what?

I described the basement first, in detail–the two huge computer processors, the boxed balance beams, and the shelves full of vintage weathervanes, books, and journals. When I began listing the book titles, she told me that wasn't necessary. Amita had insisted that I left the basement pristine for her friend. *Nothing was out of place.*

She leaned forward an inch. "Why was a shelf in the basement taken down?"

Why is that important? "After I transferred into this form, Amita removed one of the metal shelves and installed a pulley system to test my arm and leg mobility and strength. I left the shelf disassembled since Amita said Dr. Rosen wasn't sure whether he wanted it reinstalled or not."

"Were there any decorations on the walls?"

"Three large antique weathervanes hung from the ceiling near the door."

Agent Drew half-nodded. "Now, please, describe the weather station's main floor."

I did so, noting each computer-controlled piece of equipment involved in tracking everything from air pressure to soil absorption. Plus, I described the desks, chairs, fans, and outgoing packages and boxes.

"Did you ever hack into the climate station's computer system?" Her eyebrows lifted.

She already knows I have. "Yes, to download info from it onto my handheld ETIO. But I never modified any of the data on the system."

"How well did you know Dr. Rosen? Did you ever talk to him at the station?"

"I met him once when he opened the basement door. He was surprised to see me there since I still occupied Larkin's body. He asked where Amita was, and I said she'd be back in six minutes. He nodded and closed the door. That was the extent of our conversation."

Agent Drew's head leaned to the side. "Did he know who you really were?"

"I'm sure he did. My memoir had already been published, and Larkin the Lavender's photo was easily accessible worldwide. He also must have guessed why Amita needed an out-of-the-way place to connect two new processors for a few months. I had to have a safe place to transfer from the antique bot into this new one."

"Why would someone want to kill him?"

I frowned. "Why are you asking me?"

"Why not? You are an intelligent sentient, superior at analyzing human behavior, even in robotic form. Right?"

I nodded slowly. *Is this a trap?* "They either discovered Dr. Rosen didn't have what they needed and feared he would identify them, or he was simply there at the wrong time."

"Who would *they* be?"

"Most likely someone willing to kill to get to me. Someone from the Doomed AI Sentience group or another AI extremist."

"What if I told you an Artificial Intelligence killed Professor Rosen?" She stared at me with a perfect poker face.

My gut processors raced. "Was he?" *How would she know that?*

"Can an insentient AI kill someone?"

I projected an inner peace. "Yes, of course. Military AI robots and drones do so all the time." *Why did they go to all the trouble to kill him with an AI?* "Someone had to control the AI, or have it programmed specifically to kill him. Responsible programmers insert coding to prevent AIs from harming people." *Who knew I was there?*

The agent's stare was unnerving. "Does *your* coding prevent you from hurting anyone?"

I glared back. "I would only inflict harm to protect myself. And then, only to wound unless they gave me no other choice."

"Did you kill him because you discovered he was attempting to insert a virus into your processors? After all, you had the advantage. He didn't know what your current body looked like."

"I told you. I wasn't there. And why would he want to do such a thing? Amita had already told him that she'd emptied the station of all her possessions. Which included me!" I paused to slow my breathing, which had automatically sped up to mirror my tension. "I would never kill him. I could have easily incapacitated him before he did anything to me. Does the NCSA seriously believe I killed him?"

Someone is trying to frame me. Damn them! They killed a good man.

"Potentially." Agent Drew sighed, leaning back in her chair. "We don't have any other suspects. As a sentient AI, we can't rule you out."

"I have an alibi."

Agent Drew gave a slight smile. "Yes, eating dinner with the chief of campus police is an excellent alibi. However, closer analysis determined that Dr. Rosen was killed up to two hours before you had dinner. You have already admitted to changing out of your bloody zombie clothes in the bathroom and meeting Amita, as well as being left alone in a computer closet within her lab. Yet, there is no proof, only Amita's word for it. You could have run back to the station after the parade and returned before dinner."

"Why would I return to the station? I had no reason to go back! And how could I have known Dr. Rosen would be there?" I lowered my voice. "Even if I had, how did I remove his blood splatter and run through the campus twice without any drones or security cameras noticing? I couldn't, wouldn't, and didn't kill him!"

Agent Drew pursed her lips. "Those are excellent points." She shot me an I-dare-you look. "Will you allow a forensic technician to swab your body to prove your innocence?"

If that's what it takes. "Yes."

She swiped at her ETIO. A minute later, she let a technician wearing bib overalls into the suite. They set a medical kit on a side table.

As they took out a handful of swabs they asked, "How often do you wash your body?"

"Usually I wipe dirt, pollen, and food particles off my skin at the end of each day. When I'm isolated inside, my skin doesn't require cleaning." A sudden fear possessed me. "Will I need to undress?" I hoped Agent Drew understood that my naked body contained a multitude of secrets.

Agent Drew shook her head.

The technician answered, "That won't be necessary. I'll be swabbing your neck, arms, and shoes." They methodically swabbed my neck and upper arms, taking extra swabs of hard-to-reach areas on the back of my upper arms and elbows. They carefully swabbed the top, sides, and bottom of my shoes, and around the glued-down shoelaces.

Agent Drew thanked the technician as they left with their samples.

"For now, Comma, you're free on your own recognizance. But if we find any evidence that you were at or near the murder scene rather than in the AI/R lab, you will be arrested or at least held in a secure environment. I strongly encourage you to return to California as soon as possible. We will need to interview you again soon."

"Understood."

Agent Drew gave a sincere nod. "Thank you for your cooperation."

After she left, I took twenty seconds to refocus on what was the most urgent. Amita had been gone thirty-eight minutes. *Will one of Amita's friends risk their life to help me? I hope she's okay, especially if DAIS is murdering people to get to me. I need to work harder and faster to find them, whoever the fuck Doc and DAIS is.*

I went into the unused bedroom. My clothes and personal items were in a drawer to maintain my human illusion. I hurriedly stuffed my duffel bag with my few cherished personal items, the extra uniform, and casual clothes.

Amita returned, winded, as I finished packing. "Hurry, they'll meet you on the hotel's rooftop north launching area. Apparently, the south side is a vegetable garden." Amita's eyes were wet. "Dear one, you're one of my children. I love you, and please stay safe."

"I know." I took her hand. *Hopefully not for the last time.* "Thank you for everything. I love you too. Please tell the rest of my family why I'm unreachable. Oh, and you should know that the NCSA just interviewed me. Evidently, an AI killed Dr. Rosen, so I'm their only suspect."

"What? Oh no." She gave me a tight hug before pushing me away. "Go!"

Through my ear tip sensors I saw the tears in her eyes. We both knew that if I was a suspect, then by California law, she was considered a suspect, too.

On the roof, I easily found the launch area. Two flyers were waiting as another left. I expected to see Juan Martinez. Instead, the sun shone brightly through orangish-red hair. Rowan spotted me and waved me over to a red flyer with the BCIT-AI's green and white logo on the door.

Not her! I looked back, hoping an alternative would present itself.

"Come on!" Rowan insisted, waving me in.

Do I have a choice? Not really. I followed Rowan into the flyer, watching wryly as the metal door closed, trapping me face-to-face with Gloria's ex.

10

Rowan looked me over as the flyer lifted into the air. She stared for six long seconds at my eyes. "So, you're Dot?"

My mental processors raced. Rowan was present at the demonstration when, as Kelly, I confessed to being Dot. *Why else would I be in grave danger and need to leave?*

"Yes, I used to be the sentient supercomputer known as Dot. Now I'm Comma, the last of their sentience."

"Damn, Amita did a great job. Sorry." She bowed. "This is an honor." Her face showed amazement.

I hope *she's sincere.* "Thank you for helping me escape. Though they'll track me via the hotel's video feed to your flyer, which puts you in great danger too."

"You're worth it! Plus, it's the least I can do for Amita... and Gloria." She gazed at her lap. "I know Gloria was gravely wounded protecting you. How is she doing?"

"She's doing well. She has resumed her research and teaches her classes remotely." I glared at her. "You could've contacted her personally and asked her yourself." *Instead of reading about her in my memoir or asking colleagues.*

Rowan shifted in her seat. "I sent Gloria a personal note after the attack, and again when it was announced to the world that you were sentient." She frowned. "Each time, she emailed me a simple thank you." She noticed her hands knotted at her waist and unfolded them. "I understand I'm not her favorite person, or colleague."

"Or ex-lover?"

"Ah, so you know about our relationship. I wasn't sure. Did Gloria tell you?"

Rowan had not reacted as I expected. Gloria described her as self-assured, goal-oriented, and selfish. Yet the woman beside me was clearly vulnerable and taking risks that could harm her person and perhaps her career.

"Yes, she was upset." *It's not technically a lie.* "She said you left without showing any emotional attachment to her. Your rejection hurt her a great deal. Her anger still lingers."

She closed her eyes and sighed. "She's right. I wish I hadn't been, but that was who I was then. I *have* changed. But she still isn't willing to listen to me."

"Is that why you're helping me, to prove you're different now?"

"I'm sure that's part of it." She glanced away. "Honestly, when Amita asked me, my first instinct was to protect you. Dot, or rather Comma, you're everything many of us have strived to achieve for decades. While there's an urge to dissect you, to discover what makes you tick, the wonder of your creation and existence is a powerful enough reward in itself." Rowan smiled. "Being with you, talking to you, seeing how you act is... is incredible!" Rowan leaned toward me. "What you're able to do—for good or evil—is beyond imagination."

I'd screamed internally when she used the word "dissect." *I'm not letting her dissect me, that's for damn sure.*

"Where are we going?"

Rowan blinked her right eye in a specific sequence. Obviously, her ETIO-linked lens was in that eye, giving her data I couldn't retrieve.

"I'm trying to find a good tourist hideaway. Canada has a lot of mountain chalets where celebrities vacation out of public view."

The flyer's screen showed us crossing the Canadian border. *Damn it! The NCSA and Agent Drew will think I'm fleeing to Canada because I'm guilty of murder. Especially since I have rights as a sentient being here. Where is she taking me?* We had to be close to the Vancouver BCIT-AI campus, yet, the flight path didn't show our destination.

"But first," Rowan continued, "I'd hoped to hide our flyer's signature in the middle of a lot of flyer traffic, potentially giving us extra time to throw off our trackers. Any suggestions?"

She accepts me as an intellectual equal. "Do you know the codes for specific types of flyers? Delivery, security, taxi, or such?"

"Oh! Yes, very clever." More blinking ensued. The view screen changed, showing our future path toward the north. "We're now a private taxi service."

"So hacking is something you're familiar with?" My tone was light and curious.

"In China, I specialized in AI and cybersecurity. I've continued in that field, which means I need to understand how criminals act. The only way to keep up with them is to copy their methods. Though I've always done so with governmental permission in the past." She sighed. "Our pursuers could dig through my research and predict my actions. Do you have a better suggestion?"

"I used a delivery van signature to covertly drive Amita through Oregon." *With internet access, I could find dozens of them.* "Can you hack the Canadian Transport System to find a local alternative?"

"No, not while in the Institute's flyer. I'd be fired and lose all credibility within my field. BCIT would probably forgive me for changing the flyer's code, but not for hacking the Canadian government." She looked as disheartened as I felt.

"Perhaps there is another way to lose whoever might be following us." Rowan flashed me a wicked smile. "How do you feel about hiking?"

"I don't know, I've never hiked before. I enjoyed walking through sunflower fields, is it similar to that?"

"Kind of. Since you don't feel stress on your legs or lungs, walking and hiking should feel the same." Rowan ran her right hand through her hair. "If I put the flyer down near a remote town, are you willing to carry my suitcase, about twelve miles mostly uphill?"

"My body has superior strength, flexibility, and power supply. That shouldn't be a problem." I flexed my right bicep as people did to show their strength.

Rowan laughed gleefully. "Great! Then I have an even better idea." Tension melted from her stiff shoulders.

A pink and purple sunset highlighted the snow-capped peaks as we landed behind an alpine resort. Stepping out of the flyer, I noticed the resort was silhouetted against another set of mountains. The air was an unseasonably chilly 42 degrees Fahrenheit. On the edge of the paved lot were two dirt paths. "Alta Lake" was etched on a pointed, wood sign. Its shore was barely visible through the thinning trees. In the opposite direction, a path through thick Douglas Fir trees led to Rainbow Falls. The woods sent a quiet invitation to replace my worries with nature's wonders, and drone whines with birdsong.

"Comma, you need to get out of your security clothes. I left a change of clothes for you on the flyer seat." Rowan now wore a pair of dark jeans, a long-sleeved shirt, a lined green windbreaker, and a headband. "I hope you don't mind; I repacked your bag with a few of the things I'll need. This way you won't need to carry as much."

Rowan set a metal canteen on the ground. She stretched her hamstrings with her foot supported on a granite rock.

My change of clothes lay where she said. I changed into the black, short-sleeved shirt, and gray canvas overalls. Though I wouldn't get cold, I put on the light jacket to maintain appearances.

She'd also taken out a small container with my family photos—a miniature framed photo of Gloria and her mothers. It was my favorite possession. *I do mind. I'm not a child. She could have asked me first.* I put the container back in my bag. *It goes where I go. No exceptions.*

Rowan locked the flyer with a blink of an eye and headed up the Rainbow Falls trail. With the duffel bag over my left shoulder, and nightfall coming, I hurried after. I hadn't seen any flyers land near the lodge or fly over us. I dared to believe we'd slipped from DAIS's view, at least temporarily.

Rowan jogged up the trail, increasing her strides along the straight stretches. She was breathing hard, her feet beating a steady drum, smoothly traversing the well-traveled path. Within a few miles she turned west, onto what appeared to be an animal trail. The low-lying brush and twigs hit our faces and bodies constantly, but failed to slow our progress.

Twenty minutes out from the lodge, the sky darkened. As we walked through a meadow, the slightest sliver of moon provided companionship but little light. I switched to infrared vision and avoided the dark spots. Rowan's spotlight lit her way. Evidently, she traveled with a headband that doubled as a headlamp. When she slowed to a casual walk, I stayed close behind, no longer afraid I'd trip over her.

I finally asked the one question she'd yet to volunteer. "Exactly where are we going?"

"I have a... *friend*, who lives about seven miles northwest of here in a quaint chalet. She's an artist and a bit of a recluse. I'm hoping she'll let us stay for a few nights. If she's forgiven me."

"Another one of your conquests?" I asked.

"No." She sighed. "Actually, she's my... my daughter-in-law. A sculptor by trade, she's newly widowed, and prefers cats and quiet to deal with her grief."

Which means Rowan's child died. "I'm sorry for your loss." *It sounds inadequate, but I don't know what else to say.*

"Thanks. I rarely mention it. Michael was my only child. He grew up in Hong Kong. After he fell in love with Danni, they chose to return to her native Canada. I accepted the job in Vancouver partly to be near them." She slowed to a stroll, her head lowered. She spoke softly, her back to me, "Losing him is still hard to bear."

I'd hug her if she were anyone else. Shit! DAIS will automatically search for her relatives. Am I callous to worry about how this affects me?

"Won't DAIS expect you to go to your daughter-in-law's home?"

She shook her head. "Not many people knew about Michael, and they're all in Hong Kong. Danni kept her maiden name, and only six people attended their Hong Kong wedding. Other than the marriage certificate, there's little evidence."

This is what she's been hiding. I never found even a hint about her son when I searched her background.

"Any grandchildren?"

"No." She walked silently for a minute. "Danni moved here from Toronto a few months ago. She's still emotionally raw. I doubt she's even met her nearest neighbors." An owl flew over us into a cedar tree. "Danni hates surprises. I'll need to tell her you're a bot, so she won't get too upset. I won't mention you're sentient."

Here I go again. "I'll follow your orders then?"

"Yes. Will that annoy the hell out of you?" The animal path butted up against a paved road and Rowan sprinted along its flat surface.

I ran after her. "Yes, it bothers me. I've been frequently forced to pretend I'm merely a machine."

Rowan's headlamp shone in my eyes. "Sorry. But, Danni gets anxious around others." We were hiking up a steep slope, and she became winded. "She'll be less so... with a bot... than someone she perceives as my lover." Rowan slowed to a walk. "You're welcome to tell her who you are. But coming out completely is your choice."

We climbed up a ridge for an hour. At the end of a long gravel road, a light glowed through a ring of fir and cedar trees where a house sat atop the ridge. We'd passed only a dozen houses during our hike, all barely visible from the main road. Only the sounds of nature—birds, wind, and wild animals—could be heard. A doe and two fawns ran across the gravel road behind us. I felt safe. Up here, I'd be able to hear a drone from miles away.

I luxuriated in the forest's peace and privacy. *I could stay outside, rest against a building.* The Canadian public internet via satellites was available to everyone in the region. *I'll turn off my temperature sensors and be as content as the machine I'd be pretending to be inside the house.* Other than to eavesdrop on Rowan and Danni, I found little advantage in going inside.

I stopped ten yards from the house. "I'll stay outside. You won't need to tell her about me at all."

Rowan stopped too. "You *want* to stay out here?" She whispered incredulously.

"Yes. If she hears me, she'll assume I'm an animal." *I won't be persuaded.* I hid behind a group of trees that bordered the perimeter.

Rowan shook her head as she ambled up to the door. A spotlight made Rowan's red hair shine like torchlight. After waiting twenty seconds Rowan yelled, "Danni, it's Rowan, please let me in!" Three minutes later, the door opened and she slipped inside.

I was now alone in the dark woods. I thought of my moms. *They'll worry, not knowing where I am. Gloria will worry even more when Amita tells her she put my fate in the hands of her ex. I'll contact them as soon as I can.*

Damn it, I promised not to isolate myself again and now I'm hiding in the woods. Can I rely on Rowan's ability to convince her estranged daughter-in-law to take her in, let alone a complete stranger?

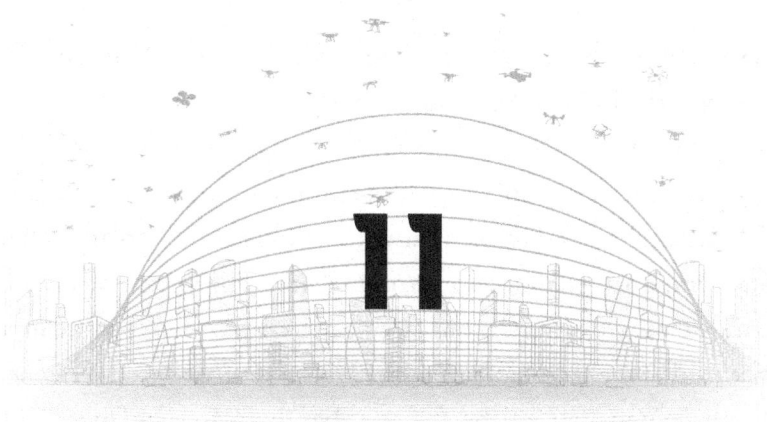

11

Even from outside the house, I could hear them talking. Rowan had to invent a reason for her unexpected visit, since she couldn't tell Danni the truth. I realized the professional and personal bind I'd put Rowan in. She deserved more from me. After all, it was my mom she'd hurt, not me.

I walked to the door and waved at the light sensor. Rowan's voice rose, "I can explain! But please let her in." The door opened.

A woman about my size, with brown eyes and dark hair stood glaring at Rowan. I stepped into a long, narrow mudroom. Umbrellas, scarves, and coats of varying weights hung on decorative hooks. Rowan's tennis shoes rested below her windbreaker. Her arms had goosebumps from the chill.

"Hi Danni, I'm a sentient robot that Rowan is risking her life to protect. I'm currently called Comma. I'm sorry to be putting you at risk too."

Danni refocused on me after I mentioned the word "sentient." Rowan's eyes were teary as she gave me a weak nod.

"What do you mean you're sentient? According to Row, there's only one. You're it?" asked Danni.

"I prefer Comma, her, him, or them. But yes, I'm the only actual one, so far."

Rowan rubbed her hands up and down her arms. "Danni, could we please go into the living room and warm up?"

"Sorry, of course. Please, come in. I've forgotten how to act around people... and others." Danni opened the door and led the way through a maple wood kitchen and into an intimate living room with an L-shaped couch, several cozy chairs, and a roaring fire. The room was toasty. I choose a seat away from the stone fireplace. A topaz-eyed, white marble dragon stared at me from an end table. Danni returned to the kitchen.

Rowan leaned toward the fire, her hands in front of her. "Danni collects Chinese artwork. Her artistry is a blend of modern Asian and European influences."

Danni came in holding two cups of steaming beverage, handing one to Rowan. When she offered me the other, I turned it down.

"Sorry, I wasn't thinking," she said, keeping the drink for herself. "You look so much like a person."

Rowan took a long sip. "Comma, do you want to explain why we're here?"

I nodded. "There is a group, called Doomed AI Sentience or DAIS, trying to eliminate me. They tried to do so again today at an AI Conference where I met... Dr. McConnell. She was kind enough to help me escape. I need a safe place to stay, until I can figure out how to catch the people who are after me. Which, if they've guessed our destination, means you're in danger too."

"You're really Dot?" Danni asked.

She's either in shock or slow to process information. "Yes, but I'm no longer the multiprocessor AI. In this body, I'm Comma."

"I read your memoir last month. I'd even hoped to meet you one day." Her tone turned from fandom to fear. "But not while someone's out to destroy you, and everyone around you be damned." Danni scowled at Rowan. "Why did you bring them here? Do you want me dead, too?"

"No! Not at all." Rowan bit her bottom lip. "I was powerless to save Michael, but I can help Comma. I only thought of coming here after realizing how easily they could follow us to Vancouver. I'm sorry. We'll leave." Rowan stood, worry lines radiating along her forehead. "Could I borrow a warmer coat, though?"

I rose from my chair.

Danni focused on me and then on Rowan. "Oh, sit down. I'd hate myself if something happened to either of you. What is your plan?"

Rowan swallowed. "I hoped we might stay here for a couple nights and work on what to do next. Comma's robotic creator asked if I'd take her, only minutes before I was scheduled to leave Portland. We were figuring out how to outwit our pursuers as we flew. Then I thought longingly about seeing you and it dawned on me that you lived in the middle of nowhere. That's why we ended up here."

Danni started crying and Rowan sat next to her on the couch. They held each other and sobbed. I closed my eyes to give them some privacy. *I'm thankful for their help. But it's too risky. Perhaps I could become a mountain hermit. There must be some internet access throughout these mountains. I could track DAIS and Doc from a bear cave. Except caves don't have a power source.*

When they finished soothing each other, I asked for somewhere to charge. Danni offered her art room for my use since she only had two bedrooms.

The art room covered half of the upper floor, with Danni's master bedroom at the other end. She had a six-foot clay humanoid form balanced on a metal frame. The female figure had Gloria's high cheekbones, similar to Dot's holographic form, and Rowan's eyebrows and angular nose. *Rowan's son may have had those features as well.* The humanoid's head tilted slightly to the left, and teardrops shone along the lines of the nose. In her chest wall, a small heart-shaped glass light pulsed red. *Danni's creation shares her feelings of loss. Or does she share mine too?*

Under a corner window, I found a plug. I sat down and connected to Danni's electricity. I skipped connecting to Danni's modem and reached instead for the Canadian public satellite system. I hoped the Canadian authorities continually removed all viruses and no one thought to corrupt their systems as advertised. If not, I'd be a basic service bot in seconds. My signal bounced through the local community postal hub and throughout the world before I entered the dark web searching for DAIS and its leaders. Presumably, Doc was one of them.

Linking via my processors without physically typing on the ETIO tablet was true freedom, like when I'd first realized I was sentient and could change my code and think for myself.

The dark web was a misnomer. It was obnoxiously bright, with bizarre pornography, and disquieting on so many levels. *Humans should stick to cat clips.* Browsing this side of the internet felt like the human idiom, wading through shit, until I finally found DAIS. According to their main page, their leader was called the Master of Doom, and posted under the account "MDLeader." They invited everyone to join their chatroom. I hesitated to do so. *That would be suicide.* I hastily left the page, and the dark web.

Instead, I registered for a second internet account through Canada's free public service, selecting the tag, "RoboBuster." I needed another persona. Knowing the Canadian email service would be hacked, I gave the barest of details, all fake. When I reconnected to the dark web, RoboBuster appeared to randomly find the message board for DAIS. I spent ten minutes reading their disgusting messages, most expressing a multitude of things they would like to do to Dot, meaning me, and the people I cared about. I searched for something I could comment on to show my interest.

I held my proverbial nose and belittled AI's in general and Dot specifically.

"Welcome, RoboBuster. What do you do for a living?" asked AI-Breaker.

"I go to college. Pay my own way by refurbishing tech and schooling my elders on their ETIOs." With a cocky self-confidence, I added, "Solving tech problems is my superpower."

"That's great. What college?"

"BCIT-AI, Vancouver campus." AI-Breaker introduced me to others, presumably closer to my age, in a new, separate chatroom. The people there discussed the benefits of robots and what they should be allowed to do.

I wrote, "Bots shouldn't be able to learn enough to seemingly think for themselves." After a few more minutes of degrading intelligent bots, they welcomed me as their newest DAIS member. *I'm in. Now all I have to do is find their leader.*

Knowing that someone in DAIS would attempt to track me down, I went offline at 2 a.m.

Away from the steaming rot of DAIS, I bathed in the night's tranquility.

I relaxed against Danni's wall and re-watched my collection of cat clips and family memories.

Two hours later, I returned to the internet. *Other than Doc, had I captured everyone involved in my botnapping?* I needed to be sure, as sure as the data allowed. I continued my search.

Accessing the local postal hub, and the connections between all the regional postal stations, I used their computers to help me amplify my search, throwing my signal between various satellites circling the world. No one, except perhaps a dedicated supercomputer, could track me. I researched my three attackers and their connections with other conference attendees who attended Amita's demonstration.

A large number of those registered had been with a group called

Queers of the Future. Most were in their twenties based on their social media posts from Portland's Pride Parade. One held a sign that read, "We (heart symbol) Dot! Give them their rights!" And my favorite, held by a blue-haired person who'd attended the Q&A, "Dot is our future. Embrace them!" *If only I could have shared these with Dot. These young people are fans, not my enemies.*

Of the conference professionals, only six roboticists participated: Rowan, Juan Martinez, Bennett Shepard, Gail Valadez, Fredrick Fjelsted, and Xi Chang. I'd need to do a deeper search. The house creaked and the humans slept as I sifted through their credit, social media, and government histories looking for anything untoward on the dark web.

At one point, I heard a noise outside and glanced over the window ledge. My night vision caught sight of a big bear with a pair of frolicking cubs. One cub had climbed halfway up a Douglas fir's trunk and their sibling was on their way up. When the one highest on the tree lost their grip, they tumbled off, knocking both to the soft soil below. Their mother gave a soft growl, and they followed her out of view.

When dawn lightened the sky, I had researched all of those registered again, and no one was an apparent DAIS member except the three who'd botnapped me, whom I hoped were still in custody.

I also looked for a connection between my three botnappers and AI-Breaker and the other users who had left messages on the DAIS board. I tracked their IP addresses through four continents and numerous locations and they all led back to western Canada and the United States.

Doc had to have been on site to hack and operate the convention's AI controls without being tracked. *Were they one of the convention staff, part of the robotics organization or Servo-Botics staff? Ada had supervised the service bots. Who was her boss?* I doubted that they would be one of the few humans involved in cooking or prepping the food. However, they could have been part of the registration team. *Where are they now?*

I needed the Chief's help. I crafted a message to her on my watch and sent it via an encrypted application she'd added at the end of my training manual, for "desperate situations." My coded message read, "I'm enjoying my vacation. I need to know where I can find those who supplied my last fishing trip. Can you help?"

I wanted to send both of my moms a message, but feared having them traced back to Danni's house.

While I waited to see if Talia would send me any data on my abductors, I again visited DAIS board message for updates from MDLeader. *Damn! Doc could be a nickname for the Master of Doom.*

At 8:30 a.m., MDLeader posted a message on a computer board to all DAIS members. "It's hiding, but we're closing in. Be ready."

"Shit!" I spoke aloud, but not too loud. *I need to leave! Is everyone here in imminent danger? Or is DAIS trying to flush me out like a duck hiding between cattails?*

I paced. *I will not be flushed out. But I don't want them to find me here with Rowan and Danni either.*

I studied the local maps and hiking blogs for potential hiding places in the mountains, preferably near a power source. I didn't need to be indoors. My body was impervious to rain, snow, steam, and heat, except under prolonged exposure. The global map view provided a lot of options. My link through the community hub browser would work from anywhere.

I had not heard any ground traffic around Danni's home. She had to rely on a drone or flyer service for deliveries. *Could I leave on such a service? They could drop me off at another residence.*

When I heard movement, I went down to the kitchen. Danni sat by the window, reading her ETIO pad and holding a cup of caffeinated tea.

"Please join me. I assume you don't need to eat?"

"No, thank you." I sat across from her. "Do you get your groceries delivered?"

"Yes, every Monday and Thursday from The Fresh Market. Did you need something?"

"So, you'll receive a delivery today?" My exterior appeared calm, but I was not.

"Yes, it drops off around 10:30 a.m."

"Is it a drone drop or by personal delivery?" It was 9:42 a.m. I needed all the facts as quickly as possible.

"It's only by drone unless high winds or a storm make it unmanageable. We occasionally miss a delivery when the storms are bad." She took a sip of tea and with it came a sense of why I asked. "Oh, I see. The drone lands out in the front and flashes a bright green light. If no one comes out, they flash red and beep, then leave the full container. Finally, they flash and beep one last time before picking up any empty containers and flying off."

"Does the drone deliver to multiple homes, or only one at a time?" *This might work.*

"They usually carry three or four containers, though I saw one leaving the market once with ten containers. The containers are pretty big. One's sitting out front waiting for pickup."

"Do you know if they fly on autopilot or are controlled from the warehouse?" I mentally crossed my fingers.

"They're preprogrammed, which is why they only fly in decent weather." She added, "The delivery route is shown on our ETIO app."

"Great, then, I'll leave on today's drone. I can't put you at further risk. Though I may need to visit on occasion if I can't find a safe alternative power supply."

"I'm sorry if I haven't made you feel very welcome. You're welcome to recharge at any time. If I'm not here, there's an outlet in my carport. The lock's passcode is A384J959."

Rowan came in and sat next to me, her hair a tangled mess.

"Comma's leaving," Danni said softly.

"Why?" She touched my arm. "I can help you figure out who Doc is."

Is she disappointed? Upset?

"I've put you in enough danger. They're out there searching for me. I'm putting you both at risk."

Rowan pressed, "At least give me a way to contact you."

"I'll give you my private email address. But Rowan, you should return to work. With VAN Con at BCIT-AI this weekend, it will be suspicious if you aren't there. Otherwise, they'll be searching for you and the flyer. You can honestly tell them you felt driven to see your daughter-in-law."

Rowan frowned. Apparently, she didn't react well to sudden changes or advice from others, which made her willingness to help me even more commendable.

Danni offered, "You can always say you made a last-minute decision to surprise me for my birthday."

"Oh God, Danni! I forgot the seventeenth is your birthday!" Her right eye blinked. "That's today!"

"Happy birthday, Danni." I rose from the table. "I need to survey the food delivery container before the drone arrives. Thank you both for all your help."

Rowan's face looked tortured.

"I promise I'll be okay. Please go out and celebrate." My empathic programming revved up. "But don't stay here too long. Everyone knows by now that I left on the BCIT-AI flyer with you."

Rowan stood and wrapped her arms around me. "Please be careful. You'll come to VAN Con?"

"I'll go wherever Doc is." I patted her arm hoping to comfort her. "I'll likely see you at VAN Con. I'm sure some of the DAIS members can't resist an opportunity to play with the newest high-security AI software. Be careful, too. I'll see you soon."

"It was great meeting you." Danni's soft voice rose. "Good luck, Comma."

I walked outside wishing I could stay longer. *It isn't safe.* The delivery container was too small for me to fold into. I'd need to rely on the scarier alternative. I hid beyond the tree line, not wanting to trigger the drone's safety protocols, and waited.

At 10:33 a.m., a drone with four containers flashed a warning light sequence and set down the container with Danni's groceries. As it attached the empty container and lifted, I ran toward the rising drone at top speed. It climbed higher faster than I expected. I jumped and managed to hug the second to last container with both arms. The drone floundered, readjusted to my additional weight, and began to rise again. *I did it!*

The readjustment hadn't taken into account the trees circling Danni's property. We were headed toward the middle of a tree with my legs dangling unprotected below the containers. *Shit!* Without enough time to hack the drone, I curled up my legs and waited, hoping the impact wouldn't knock me off. At the last second, the drone surged upward and I felt the top tree branches brush roughly across my knees. *I'm safe. For now.*

I looked down with my ear tip lenses. Danni and Rowan had clasped each other around the waist, watching me go. Fear etched their faces. Humans reacted to me in one of two ways, protectively or destructively. *I like them too. Gloria should give Rowan's friendship another chance.*

Before I could turn my thoughts to my next destination, the drone lurched to the side, causing my lung apparatus to shake. Rowan shouted in horror below me as my grip slipped. *Fuck!*

12

What is this damn drone doing? I tightened my grip on the second-lowest container as the drone bucked. My face smacked against the top container, too low to see over the top. *Poor planning on my part.* The drone banked left, and a tall Douglas fir was aimed squarely at my lower abdomen. The drone inched up, ensuring the containers cleared, but not its extra passenger. My pelvis was seconds from being pummeled. I hoisted both of my legs up flush against the bottom of the container to protect them and felt the tree wipe my ass. *Thank Amita's Universe for watching over me.*

The drone then swooped down, and I slammed into another treetop. The tree trunk jarred my body and loosened my grip. I let go and twisted, reaching back for the tree's trunk. *Shit!* I missed. My duffel bag slid off my back as I fumbled for purchase. *My possessions!* Falling from the height of a 20-story building, I would smash to an inevitable end. An image flashed of my smashed body pinned as artwork to a DAIS member's wall.

My hands, spiked full of pine needles, grabbed for something solid to stop my fall. Thin branches swatted my face again and again. I crashed through the tree, hitting larger limbs, tearing off twigs as I fell. I desperately clutched for a branch, anything to slow my descent.

My knee struck a thick branch, throwing my body against the trunk. My face smashed against the rough wood, and I wrapped my arms around the trunk and hugged it like a mother.

My legs dangled, one leg on each side of a branch. My crotch had stopped the fall. *Good thing I don't have tender genitalia.* The ground was still too far down to jump. *Climbing down can't be that hard.*

I could hear Rowan shouting from below. "Be careful! Can we help?"

My response, "I'm okay!" echoed off the mountain. *So much for my grand escape.*

How do I lift my body into a standing position on a branch only six inches wide? I had never climbed up a tree, or even watched clips of others doing so. I connected to Canadian public Wi-Fi and downloaded several clips. Skipping the part on how to climb up, I did as they instructed. With one hand, I grasped the branch closest to my head. I lifted my body upward off the branch while bending my leg back, and keeping my body balanced, searched for the limb with my foot. Having eyes on the back of my ears helped. *I got this!*

With one foot now steady on the branch, I lowered the other, while I slid my hands down the tree's trunk. I suddenly pitched backward, away from the trunk as my once stable foot slipped. Pine needles swatted my face one last time as I plunged. I flailed my arms as if I could stop via flight.

My precious gut rattled as I crashed into the earth. An army of ants scattered as I and falling tree debris destroyed their mound. I moaned. *Moaning doesn't help.*

Rowan reached me first. "Comma, are you all right?" Her expression turned to one of relief when she saw me sit up. "You could have killed yourself! You're just like Gloria, too impulsive and with no common sense!"

I can't believe she compared me to Gloria like that. Let it go, at least for now.

Danni held my knapsack and appeared confused as to the state I was in.

"My processors are working fine. However, my right knee isn't responding to my commands."

Danni signed. "Thank God, you're a bot."

"I can help fix that knee, if you'll let me," Rowan offered, her anger dissipating. "Let's get you inside."

Danni wiped a few pine needles from my shoulders as she and Rowan helped me to stand on my left leg. They grunted as they lifted me, not expecting my small frame to weigh 200 pounds.

"You'll need to lean on me," said Rowan.

After six seconds, I recalibrated my leg's programming to allow me to balance on one foot. "I'll hop across the yard and inside. It will be easier on us all."

"Won't that hurt?" Danni shook her head as if to clear it. "Sorry, I forget you're a bot."

Hopping was more challenging than I expected. I had never practiced balancing on one leg, let alone going uphill. Fortunately, Rowan stayed nearby to help steady me.

As I hopped through the mudroom toward the kitchen, Danni yelled, "Wait! You're covered in dirt and debris. Let me clean you off."

I stood motionless as she used a bristle brush on my shoes and clothes. My emotions betrayed a mix of vulnerabilities. *Is she treating me like a child or a machine? Or does she treat everyone this way?*

Rowan guided me to a chair by the fire. She positioned herself on a stool in front of me with her back to the fire. I watched as Rowan's little finger pierced the rip over my knee.

"Your knee is coated in a silicone-type material?" asked Danni, as she watched Rowan's examination.

I nodded. "How bad is it, Rowan?"

"You scraped your knee. The first few silicone layers need touching up. You're lucky your pants took the brunt of it. I suggest you run diagnostics on your lower extremity's software. If we're lucky it's a processing issue and not a physical one. Neither Amita nor Gloria will be happy with me if you're seriously injured."

I began a full diagnostic on both software and hardware. There was a glitch in the damaged leg. *I wish Amita was here. But Rowan is a roboticist, too, if less knowledgeable about me personally. How much does Amita trust her?*

"There's a glitch of some kind. I can share my integrated limb software with you for your analysis, as long as you understand this code is proprietary."

She nodded and I sent Rowan's ETIO my right leg's data from before and after the fall. Rowan closed her eyes and used her built-in lens to concentrate on the data.

Danni spoke up. "I'd rather you didn't try something like that again. I aged a decade just watching you fall. The world and I would have been upset to lose you so stupidly."

"Sorry, I didn't think it through. I expected to have a line of sight ahead and be able to take control of my fate. Obviously, I'm not infallible."

I luxuriated in their warmth and hoped I hadn't damaged my lower limb to the point of needing a replacement. That would require me to either return to Davis or have a shipment sent to Rowan. Either way would allow DAIS to find me easily.

"I think I have a coding fix," said Rowan. "I've sent it to you via email and you can download the changes if you agree it will work."

Three minutes later, after analyzing and downloading her code, my right knee was once again functional. I stood, and they both cheered. Danni looked genuinely amazed. I refrained from reminding them that my knee was still badly scraped and needed repairing.

"It's time to celebrate..." Rowan paused for dramatic effect. "Danni's birthday! And you're coming with us!" She gave me a look that warned me not to brook any disagreement. "Danni, do you still love crab?"

Danni smiled. "Yes."

"Then we'll all go to the lodge in town." Rowan was clearly pleased with herself.

"But your lives will be in danger," I said. "They're searching for me. In this area!"

"We'll be fine. No buts. You'll need to wash up and change your clothes. Danni, you still have a wig and other accessories Comma could borrow, right?"

"A wig? Accessories?" I asked.

Danni explained. "Michael and I were part of a theater group in Hong Kong. We collected wigs, and I saved some of them. There's one that's perfect for you. When you've cleaned up, come to my bedroom."

Danni and Rowan were gleeful as they left to prepare for the day's outing. My excitement was tempered with fear for all our lives. *If they're searching for me, going into town is the worst thing I could do. But they've been so good to me.* My programming warred within. *Should I leave the house and get as far away as possible, making them angry but saving them from my enemies, or pretend to hide in plain sight? I promised myself I wouldn't hide anymore. And leaving without saying goodbye is rude. But their lives! And mine!*

Either way, I needed to clean up and change clothes, so I did. Afterward, I felt more human-looking and less vulnerable with a bandage over my injured knee.

I noticed Danni's wigs were laid out on her bed, a dozen in all. Most were shoulder-length or longer in shades of red, brown, and black. The one that drew my attention was a short, more masculine cut, black with a few white hairs and a trimmed beard resting below it. I could make myself appear more masculine. *Would they notice me as a male with two female companions? Would they recognize Rowan?*

From the master bathroom, Danni, the theater performer, entered stage left wearing a red pantsuit as brilliant as her smile. "Good, you found the disguises, Comma."

Rowan joined us and Danni exclaimed, "Oh wow. Rowan you look great."

"As do you, Princess." Rowan twirled in her Scottish kilt, her head wrapped in a large green scarf. "Sorry Danni, do you mind if I still call you Princess? You were his princess."

"Just for today." Danni's eyes watered. "Michael would be happy to see us dressed up and celebrating life. Perhaps we can celebrate him as well?"

Rowan nodded, tearing as she held up her hand as if it contained a drinking vessel. "To Danni and Michael!"

I repeated Rowan's cheer, wanting to be part of what they shared.

The main street of the tourist town was sparsely populated. The abnormally cold June weather had kept away tourists from the States. My senses collected data as we left the flyer. I was observing the observers, looking for DAIS members behind every lamppost with my ear tip lenses.

I had internally moved each eye a centimeter further from my nose and raised my cheekbones similarly via the software program Amita had made for such occasions. Hopefully, I had changed my face enough for a facial scan to be incapable of identifying me as Comma. The wig, beard, and padding around my stomach and butt would also confuse recognition sensors and human senses alike. We all wore gloves and reusable face masks, a common habit during high virus periods since the reoccurring pandemics of the 2030s.

We walked through the historical wood lodge to the restaurant. A young woman greeted us. "A party of three?"

In a deep voice, I said, "Yes, three. A booth if possible." Rowan and Danni sashayed in front of me. Walking slowly I had the opportunity to record everyone I passed from my front and back sensors.

The host led us to a back booth, leaving two empty tables between us and the other patrons. We lowered our masks.

"This has the sweetest, old-fashioned charm," said Rowan. "Happy birthday, darling!"

"Merci," said Danni, in her natural Québécois accent.

Before leaving Danni's home, we had decided not to call each other by our given names. We would have fun and stay incognito. I would also stay off the internet and rely only on my ETIO watch for data. Rowan, too, shut down the data feature on her lens so she couldn't be tracked by it, in case they were aware of her implant.

I slowly drank a local beer while Danni and Rowan enjoyed their large mugs filled with hot rum toddies. They talked quietly about their past with Michael without giving clues that the events happened in Hong Kong. I listened and nodded occasionally. There was a college-aged couple at a table that worried me. The guy kept staring at me. When I purposely glanced toward him, he looked away. I couldn't see the woman's face at all. They sat a row over from where we'd walked in, and she had been looking out the window when we walked past. But I could swear that I heard her mention Comma. When I concentrated my audio sensors on her, she was talking about drug side effects. *Common side effects? Or did she change the subject? Am I getting paranoid? I was paranoid before leaving the weather station and a murder happened. Is it happening again?*

Our food came, and we were quiet as we ate. I hated to waste food but needed to appear human. The faux steak came covered in gravy, along with a baked potato and broccoli. Danni moaned in delight as she ate her seafood platter. Rowan grinned at her daughter-in-law's pleasure.

"I'm so sorry, dear, that I didn't remember your birthday earlier.

We should do this annually, but on your actual birthday." She gave a quick wink.

"It's okay. I'm glad we're celebrating now." She patted both of our hands. "Having the two of you here will always be a birthday week highlight. Thank you."

After eating as much as my gut pouch could hold, I rose from my seat. "Pardon me, I need to use the restroom."

The old-fashioned lodge still had gendered restrooms. I ducked into a stall in the men's room. I carefully emptied the liquid from my gut compartment, then the solids—only a tiny wet spot spilled on my shirt, another dripped onto the toilet seat. As I was wiping up, two men came in to use the urinals.

"They've been searching for it all day," said someone with a loud flow of internal fluids.

"I'm hyped. I helped search until my shift began. And now it's in here!"

Shit! I flushed the toilet.

"But the lodge is packed with people. How will we find it?"

I left the stall and nodded to the two young men as I washed my hands.

"I don't know. Doc's message simply read, 'They're inside the lodge now.'"

I left the bathroom, my central processor whirling like a Fourth of July pinwheel. *Should I hide, or remain calm and leave after dessert? I could run out the back and leave Danni and Rowan in the safety of the lodge. Maybe hide in the forest?*

I walked to the table and placed my hand on the back of my chair. Indecision stopped me from running.

Rowan gently touched my hand. "Are you feeling all right?" Our code for, "What's wrong?"

"I should leave soon. My headache is worse."

"Here's dessert! We'll eat fast and leave after. Okay?" Rowan pointed to the waiter holding a small chocolate cake lit with tiny sparklers.

I capitulated and sat down, aware of the microseconds ticking by.

Danni laughed and blushed as our server, Rowan, and fellow patrons sang the Happy Birthday song, to "Micdan." Rowan's smashup of Michael and Danni that she'd given to the waiter as Danni's name. I joined in, though I concentrated on listening for the male voices from the bathroom.

Pee-a-lot spoke from an alcove, where I could hear dishes being scraped. "Doc just responded. It's with a red-headed older woman. Are they eating here?"

The hostess sighed loudly. "I haven't seated any redheads. She's not one of the gray-haired ladies at the window, or the tatted lesbians kissing in the back booth. Unless she recently adopted a family, or is with one of the older men, I don't think she's in here. Perhaps *you're* the bot, Dexter, and I never knew?"

"Very funny." A silent pause was followed by, "What about one of the women who's celebrating a birthday with the bearded guy?"

"Maybe. I don't know the hair color of the woman with the scarf. But she's wearing a Scottish kilt. She could be the redhead. Tell Doc!"

Double shit! I've got to leave! Damn it, what if they think Danni is actually me? Fuck!

"I must go," I said. "I hate to leave you both here. Especially you, Micdan, you are so young and lovely with your dark hair."

Rowan's eyes grew huge. "Oh no." Her breathing sped up.

Danni understood a few seconds later. "Let's all go."

Rowan left plenty of Canadian bills on the table, which would more than cover our meal. We all rose and put on our facemasks. Rowan briefly explained to our waiter that I was ill as we hurried out. Rowan took my arm to play her part and assisted me as we left.

No one followed us as we instinctively headed for the flyer. I hesitated before getting in. Leading them to Danni's house seemed ill-advised.

"I understand your reluctance," Danni sympathized. "You can take the flyer after you drop us off."

Without a better idea, I agreed. The flyer lifted above the forest and headed northwest toward the setting sun. In the distance, a thick burst of smoke snaked into the sky.

Rowan frowned. "Not another forest fire."

Danni's body wilted in fear as she stared out the window. Her hands were shaking as we drew closer to her property. She collapsed inward, mumbling incoherently, a second before I realized the fire was feasting on her home. The flames engulfed it all. Two black fire engines reached the building as our flyer flashed a warning that it could not land.

Danni had probably lost everything except the clothes she wore and my costume—the wig, beard, and clothes her husband had once worn.

She pointed at me and screamed, "This is because of you!" Tears streamed over her red cheeks.

She was right. DAIS had figured out who we were and torched her house. "I'm sorry, Danni. I'm sorry for whatever part in this I played."

Danni pounded me on my chest, trying to get me to strike back. I sat perfectly still—a willing punching bag for her human rage and pain.

Rowan ordered the flyer to land on the road further down the mountain from Danni's house. Then she grabbed Danni's wrists and prevented her from hitting me again. When we landed, she calmly put her arms around Danni's shoulder and whispered, "We'll survive this," as Rowan guided her out of the flyer.

Rowan turned back toward me. "I know you didn't intend anything bad to happen to us, Comma. You should take the flyer wherever you want. Send it back to me at BCIT-AI when it's recharged." She blinked the tears from her eyes. "I don't know that we can bear to see you for a while. Even at VAN Con." She hiccupped. "I'm not sure I'll feel safe with you there." She hugged a devastated Danni to her. "Goodbye, Comma. Take care."

Tears were leaking from my eyes. "Please be careful. They may still think Danni is me. Goodbye and thank you for all the risks you took for me." *I wish bad things would stop happening to those I care about.*

Without another word, Rowan and Danni trudged up the hill toward the fiery scene.

13

How did they know where I was? Inside the flyer, the door closed, and I sat, unsure of my next move. My main processor spun and spat out thousands of options. Desperation caused a programming error. I couldn't make a decision.

"Where should I go?" I spoke aloud

The flyer responded, "I am preprogrammed to fly to the library, sporting goods store..." It listed all the places Danni routinely went, including a hotel in Vancouver, Canada.

I wanted to go to the hotel. There, I could hide in relative safety, recharge the flyer, and enjoy internet access via a multitude of connections. *I'm thinking like prey! I promised I'd stop hiding. I need to be the fucking hunter, not the victim. DAIS is here. They burned down Danni's house. I need to catch them!*

I changed out of Michael's clothes and into my dark casual clothes. I folded the suit and padding and left them for Danni. I kept the beard in place; they were popular in this area and I needed to blend in. I left the flyer where it was and ran back toward town, with my bag once again strapped to my back.

It was still light at 7 p.m. I ran at a breakneck pace through the forest, accurately gauging how high to jump to clear the metal and wood fences surrounding private properties, and never slowing no matter what I heard. Eventually, I arrived at the main road near town and slowed to a jog.

On the edge of town, I stopped at the first café and bought a latte in their branded coffee mug. My facial features remained changed so the scans wouldn't identify me as Commala Renata. Only those who had seen me at the restaurant might recognize my face. I kept the drink close to my face when I walked past people on the street. It was near closing time, and I needed to hurry. I strolled by the mostly closed storefronts as the latte's cinnamon aroma tickled my sensors.

As I entered, a white man with a long white beard, welcomed me to the Gun Fishing store. He asked if he could help me with a gun purchase.

"Thanks, but I already have enough guns and ammo. I came in for hunting supplies." *I don't need a gun. Except...* "Do you sell stun guns?"

"No, they're illegal to possess in Canada."

Oops, I shouldn't have asked that. I managed a twisted smile. "They probably don't work on hairy bears anyway."

"Not at all." He smiled back. "I have a variety of bear-catching and hunting supplies over in there." He pointed to the far corner of the store.

"Thank you." *Now, please forget I was here.*

The store had a lot of people—mostly men—milling about for so late in the evening. In the closest corner, I found temporary lockers for rent. *That solves one of my problems.* Tapping my ETIO watch, I rented a locker for a week, carefully placing my prized possessions, the empty coffee mug, and my University of California uniforms inside.

In the bear hunting area, most items were for fending off or catching bears, including tranquilizer guns and capture netting.

I was deep in thought about what I should buy when a woman quipped loudly to her male companion, "He must be from Alaska." I took the hint and purchased a dark brown fishing jacket with the Gun Fishing logo, which I wore immediately. I also purchased anything I thought a hunter of humans might need and stuffed everything but the huge netting into my knapsack.

Where is DAIS? As I walked down the street, I tried to appear at ease while my four visual sensors constantly searched for any adversaries. *Are they watching me?* A string of satellites passed overhead, blinking against the dusked sky, and I decided to risk connecting directly to the internet.

After passing the rural community postal hub, I hacked into their computer network and bounced my signal around before attempting to reconnect to the dark web and discover what DAIS was doing.

When I saw people entering the local library for an event, I followed them in and hid in the psychology section. Skimming the book selections, I found one on AI neuroscience and sat with it open on my lap.

I took a deep cleansing breath, and prepared to enter the gritty dark web, knowing it would again contaminate my programming's ability to analyze the twisted meaning of their words. Foul visuals prohibited me from discerning their motives and thoughts. They normalized inhumane references in their discussions, which were far beyond the bounds of my own imposed decency programming guidelines.

But I needed to learn what they had planned for me, and the last thirteen hours were ample time for them to research RoboBuster. Prior to my initial chats with DAIS as RoboBuster, I'd hacked into BCIT-AI's system. I'd left hints, what techies called phantom records, suggesting I was an undergraduate named Felix Underwood. Techies get annoyed when they can't find information on someone. Providing DAIS a phantom person was better than giving them no data since no one was that clever, except perhaps a sentient bot.

The DAIS members were again exposing their hate-fueled disdain for "it." By now I knew that I was the *it* they all referred to. I was the *fucking doomed one,* and the other thousands of even slimier ways they referred to me and those I loved.

Rowan and Danni's names were now included in their hate-spewing filth. I loathed needing to play by their rules, but I joined in. *I need to know if they're safe and what they plan for me.* I copied what people said about me in earlier chats and simply and repulsively threw in Rowan's name alongside mine.

They treated RoboBuster like everyone else, which is to say, they harassed me for my name and everything I said, as they did to everyone else, while debasing anything and anyone that could think for themselves. After two hours of sharing hate for myself, other AIs, and everyone I loved with a dozen unfamiliar tags in a chat room, I received a direct message with access to another chat room. *Were potential DAIS members promoted to higher levels based on our responses and their research on us?*

In this chat, they were discussing the search for me and ways to kill me. My old supercomputer and current bot survival instincts fought against providing them with new ways to destroy me. Instead, I focused on the search.

"Where is the fucking doomed one?"

Shitkicker25 answered, "It's in BC. No sightings for two hours."

I'm in the library, you screw-holes! "I'm in college in BC. Whereabouts?"

They gave the name that matched the one on the library's outer facade.

"Seriously?" I continued. "One of my mates there told me someone its size was building a weird tent along the animal path near where he hunts."

They asked me where, specifically, and I told them.

"I'll ask him to keep watch. If it wasn't for the storm coming, I could be there in about an hour."

Annihilator responded, "No need. We'll check it out."

I left the chat and shut down my internet connection. *Time to make a weird tent!*

It was 10 p.m., and the streets were dark and deserted as I left the library with the last few bookworms. It was cold, windy, and rainy, as I pushed through the night. I was anxious to finally face my stalkers. *It's time to pit my AI processors against their warped brains, all for the opportunity to keep living. May my processors win.*

With DAIS knowing where to find me, I didn't have long to prepare for company. The animal path was on the edge of town and exceptionally hard to find in this weather.

The local hunters were aware of the animal path that cut between the public forest area and the lake. The Gun Fishing owner had commented that his neighbors often waited at dawn to hunt the deer and elk that watered along the lake's shore.

I found a suitable tree and pulled out the massive safety netting, which resembled a tarp from a distance. It connected around a tree so that when a tranquilized bear fell, the net could catch them without causing injuries. I only connected a third of the netting around the thick pine tree, letting the sides fall, making a weird tent of sorts.

I wished I knew how many people to expect and exactly when. I, or rather Felix, had told them of my hiding place at 9:50 p.m. *Will they attack now or wait until morning to gather a group together to kidnap me?* Kidnapping, not botnapping—in Canada, the legislature had passed a law giving all sentient entities legal rights. *Here, I'm not just another bot, but an actual sentient being with rights!*

The microseconds passed slowly with every raindrop's plop and animal sound causing a heightened sense of unease. My new dart gun was near at hand. I had practiced for thirty minutes. The darts were only dosed to stun a raccoon, but they could at least slow down any assailants. One was in the gun, and the others were carefully stored in two jacket pockets. I didn't walk outside the netting for fear that someone would know I was waiting for them. My best chance was for them to think they were catching me unaware.

The cold, rainy weather turned freezing near midnight as a polar vortex hit British Columbia with an unusual summer snowstorm. As snow fell, I relaxed a bit. The DAIS members were unlikely to venture out until the storm passed, giving the snow time to transform my fake tent into a viable human trap.

I again connected to the internet via the community postal hub when suddenly the network went down. Curious, I found a slower connection through the Gun Fishing store and hacked the cameras facing the street and post office. Two people were working in near darkness, pulling wires, and stealing the computers from the public workstations. *DAIS?* I sent an urgent message to the local Mounties of a burglary in progress. No matter who it was, they shouldn't be stealing tech equipment. A glimmer of hope brought thoughts of all the DAIS members being caught stealing computers. *Wishful thinking isn't going to save me!*

I looked up through the underside of the netting. Snow was blowing under the tree and falling between the net's slits. I fastened a small solid tarp below the netting to give me a tiny area to sit under and wait in relative dryness. *Might as well join DAIS online. I can't feel any more anxious.*

This time I hacked the grocery store via their drone network that delivered to Danni. The next time I rode one of their drones, I'd be ready. After proving I was RoboBuster, I entered the last chat room I'd visited.

No additional news on the search was given. The last DAIS-wide comment referenced my leaving town in a flyer and the surprise I'd find. *Why no mention of my tent? They either believe that RoboBuster's friend had found me or that I am RoboBuster.* Their conversations now concentrated on what they would do to stop sentient AIs in the future. *They're that confident I'll be caught?*

Most of the people who joined the chats bragged about their hacking abilities. I decided it was time to do likewise. I would need to sound young and naïve if I hoped to get one of their leaders to confide in and mentor me. If I did it well, I'd be able to discover who Doc was. If I did it poorly… well, I could be caught at any time, including tonight.

"I can track any AI. When I was a kid, people thought I was older because I fought with the robo-bot networks. I'd track them to their source and screwed with their coding. It shut down their whole fucking network."

AI-Breaker popped into the chatroom to comment. "That took real talent. How exactly did you do that?"

I gave details from an example included in the Chief's security files. Seconds later, I gained access to yet another chatroom. This chat had only three people in it. AI-Breaker asked if I enjoyed hacking into systems. I gave an enthusiastic, "Yeah, it's revo!"

"Would you be willing to hack into BCIT-AI's VAN Con network?"

I knew they'd eventually want me to prove myself. Since I'd already hacked BCIT-AI's main system once, doing so again wouldn't be quite as challenging. However, the VAN Con system servers, like the American DEFCON version, would have heightened security with every attendee trying to hack it. More than the difficulty, I feared what they'd ask for and whom or what they'd want me to harm when I succeeded.

"Definitely! But I need to keep studying for my calculus test. My break went way longer than it should have. I'll be back tomorrow, though." *I hope they buy my excuse.*

"Good luck on your test. We'll chat afterward."

Phew. I disconnected. *Now all I have to worry about is those coming to get me.*

At dawn, the sky lightened slightly, and the snow stopped. I heard unknown squishing sounds. I peered through the slits in the netting. Over a foot of snow covered the landscape and the sounds of boots crunching through the newly fallen snow came from every direction except the trailside. I audibly tracked the slightly different motions and their directions. Four people were closing in on my position. The dart gun required close proximity. I waited, though I stood up and held the dart gun ready.

A text message from Gloria flashed. *Not now Mom!*

At approximately four yards away, they all stopped. "Whoever's under that netting needs to come out. Now! We're unarmed. It's illegal to trap animals here. We'll need to take you in for questioning."

They failed to identify themselves and the organization they were from. *DAIS!*

I could see a person clothed in camouflage in front of me. I shot the first dart into their thigh. They fell to the ground. The other three ran toward me. I crouched down by the open slit, reloaded, and shot another in the gut. They, too, fell to the ground. I assumed more from shock than due to the dosage.

The other two froze where they stood as I strolled out through the slit in the netting. I aimed the loaded dart gun, waving it between them both.

"You're shooting us with tranks?" He was young, with a scrappy beard, and over six feet tall. His eyes were filled with hate.

"Did you burn down my friend's home?" I spit out the words. Hate filled me too after hours on the dark web.

He grinned. "Yeah, I might have."

I shot him in the leg. The other guy barreled toward me, knocking me down, and sent the gun flying out of my hands as my back hit the snow.

The first two I had shot loomed over me, each with a foot holding my chest down, while the small guy who had knocked me over sat on my legs.

"Well guys, it's our turn to do as we please." The guy I shot first waved a flash drive above my face. "It's going to regret making me so fucking angry."

Fucking human hell, he must have the virus loaded on there!

Something was pulled from my pocket.

"Look here, it comes with its own zip ties to bind its hands and feet!" Two of them proceeded to tie my feet together. As they tried to force my hands together, I pulled my feet apart with enough strength to break the zip tie.

"Shit, it can break these! We can sit on it to open it up." Three of them sat on top of me, with their feet pressing down on a leg or arm. One clawed at the buttons on my jacket, trying to gain access to my core compartment. *I can't let them reach it!*

I fought halfheartedly for several seconds, thinking of ways to dislodge them and get the upper hand.

The last guy I shot had crawled over the snow and into my tent. "There's a bag in here." He limped out of the tent holding up a thick rope. "This should hold it tight long enough to insert the drive!"

They all grunted happily in agreement.

With all my strength, I rolled my body hard to each side and threw them off-balance. I did what I hated to do to humans—I knocked them hard with my elbows, fists, and knees. Three of them soon lay moaning on the melting snow. I grabbed the dart gun and aimed.

The last guy swallowed hard and dropped the rope.

"Sit down!" I sent a message to the Royal Canadian Mounted Police and waited.

Eleven long minutes later, after I kicked one guy who had gained his strength but not his common sense, two vehicles roared to a stop near the shore. Soon after, five RCMP jogged toward us on snowshoes. They cautiously walked over to me. *Can I trust them? Do I have a choice? Here's hoping they treat me as a sentient being and don't send me back to California.*

The Canadian Sentient Being Act became law a month after my memoir was published. It made my destruction equivalent to human murder and punishable to the same degree. Canada, Japan, Illinois, and New York were on the cutting edge of alternate sentience rights. While I appreciated the support, it didn't matter all that much what happened to the culprits after they killed me. Either way, I would be dead. *Now I have to put their sentience law to the test.*

"Hi, officers. These men tried to kill me." I held up the deadly thumb drive. "And this was the weapon they planned to use." I sighed with genuine relief. "And at least one of them was involved in setting the fire yesterday that destroyed Danni's house on the upper ridge."

"You tackled these guys all by yourself?" asked an attractive female officer.

"Yes, I'm the sentient humanoid once known as Dot. I'm stronger than most people expect." The woman's face lit up with surprise or joy—I wasn't sure which—before she suppressed her reaction. I continued, "They're with DAIS and have been searching for me. When they followed me here, I was forced to shoot them with low dose tranquilizer darts to slow them down."

The lead RCMP officer nodded with traces of a smile. "Sounds smart to me."

They put me in the back seat of their truck, separate from the others, for a ride to the station. They requested I give an official videotaped statement at the station, explaining that I, too, might be held if they determined I hadn't been acting in self-defense.

I remained hopeful. *How else could I have protected myself?* DAIS-wise, my first hunt was successful. Relationship-wise, the loss of Rowan and Danni's friendship weighed unexpectedly heavily on me.

Danni and Rowan hate me. And if DAIS can't destroy me, they'll ruin every relationship I hold dear. I can't let this keep happening. I have to catch them. So, VAN Con and DAIS here I come!

On the ride to the station, the female Mountie sat in the back seat with me, constantly grinning as she spoke. "Late last night, we caught three guys stealing computers from the postal station." As her fellow officer drove and called the station, she leaned close and whispered, "They were prepared to set our community hub ablaze." She shook her head. "And with the same materials used earlier to burn down the house you mentioned."

As the two officers discussed logistics, I faced the window. Unseen, I used my identity-changing software to return the titanium bones around my eyes and nose to my scan-recognizable form.

When the Mountie turned her attention back to me, she did a quick double take.

Distract! "Can I remove my beard, or will you need to photograph me first for legal reasons?" I wiggled my jaw to refocus her attention on the beard.

She frowned. "Sorry. We need you to leave it on for now."

While the officers didn't blame me for defending myself, their legal system was a separate issue. In Canada, I was a sentient entity who could legally be tried for my crimes.

They took me through the back of the police station and processed me before bringing in the four others. I was digitally fingerprinted, photographed, and then photographed again after I removed the fake beard, which was immediately bagged as evidence.

The Mountie asked what I needed, assuming my needs were different from their other suspects. "All I need is somewhere I can securely plug in and recharge."

They took me through their work area, to a tiny unused office. "I'll be a meter away if you need anything."

I lifted my dirty black shirt, opened my gut panel, and removed the repair kit that safeguarded the only flash-drive-accessible opening. *Thank the Universe they didn't get this close to my processors.* I plugged in and opened the repair kit. After removing the bandage I'd placed over my scraped knee, I took care to smooth the silicone fluid over the wound. After it dried, I applied the skin coloring to make my knee look unharmed. I found a few minor cuts on my arms from wrestling with DAIS and repaired them as well. *I wish I could heal my emotional hurts as easily. Why do I feel so close to Rowan and Danni after such a short time?*

I distracted myself by connecting to the police station's public webpage. They listed those who were arrested and their offense. My name was not listed, which I hoped meant they understood that I had done what was needed in self-defense. However, three suspected DAIS members were listed, each charged with theft above $5,000 and the intent to destroy public property, as well as arson. When the page refreshed, the names of the four who attacked me were accused of attempted murder of a sentient entity. One of them, Niall Lator, stood out. *Could his DAIS handle be Annihilator? How can I discover their DAIS usernames, and other handles, and nicknames?*

The seven legal names of the DAIS members were added to my spreadsheet. Under usernames, I had Annihilator with a question mark after Niall's name.

When the Mountie came in to take my statement, I asked if she and her fellow officers would ask their latest suspects for their social media handles or nicknames, especially if any of them went by Doc. She nodded and left for a few minutes.

"My fellow officers have included it in their list of questions for both those who attacked you and those who burgled our postal hub."

She videotaped our interview, as I spent twenty minutes explaining what occurred during my botnapping in Portland and the search that ensued. Other than excluding my efforts to infiltrate the DAIS dark website, I explained my concerns about being followed, especially heightened after overhearing that they were searching for me inside the lodge where my friends and I were eating. I went into the details and in the end, I made my case for self-defense.

"I know my assault is unusual. I can't be killed by bullets or stabbing. This is why I took every precaution—building the net structure to keep animals away and staying as far from people as possible. Though the storm necessitated that I stop at some point." I leaned toward her. "I avoided physically fighting them, aware that a forceful blow with my arms, hands, or feet could injure them. Yet, they refused to leave or even back away after I shot the first dart. I feared that if they gained control of me, they would kill me.

The officer nodded. "But you're much stronger than them."

"True, and I only used my superior strength after three of them sat on top of me and threatened to kill me with the flash drive one of them held in his hand. At that point, I rolled over to dislodge them and jabbed and kicked until they stopped attacking. I had no other choice if I wanted to live."

She asked me a few clarifying questions about the botnapping in Portland, which I answered.

"You think Doc is their leader?" asked the officer.

"Yes, he clearly led the group in Portland."

"Your attackers stated that you shot one of them with the tranquilizer dart before they came near you."

"They tried to sneak up on me. When they realized they couldn't, they ordered me to exit the tent while pretending to be police. That was threatening, since I knew they must be from DAIS by then. My only chance to discourage them from attacking me was to act before they came any closer. I couldn't protect myself against four people without harming them. The dart was my warning that I wasn't going willingly." *Please believe me. Without their usernames, I have no way to prove how I knew they were coming.*

She nodded. "How did Doc know you were at the lodge?"

"I don't actually know how they are able to track me so well. I wish I did."

"At this point, we aren't going to charge you for any crimes. While your methods bordered on criminal, we understand you were in a difficult situation. Our Canadian self-defense laws were written without taking sentient AIs into account. However, in the future, do not shoot your first warning shots at, let alone into someone. Should you do so again, the RCMP will be forced to charge you with a crime so a judge can clarify your specific rights."

"Understood and thank you." *I'm being given the benefit of the doubt. I'll take it!*

"Due to the threats on your life, we can transport you to the US border or the airport. Another big storm is coming, so you'll need to either hurry or wait until tomorrow."

"Is it possible for me to stay here for another day? I don't need anything, and I'm not sure how best to get where I need to go. Though I'd prefer a room without cameras." I had spotted a sensor when I first entered the room and faced away from it, hoping no one saw exactly how my gut panel opened and how the repair kit was attached. "Unless I can make sure DAIS is unaware of when I'm leaving and where I'm headed, traveling with me will be unsafe for everyone involved."

"You're welcome to stay as long as you want. There is an unused office that locks from inside and has no sensors that I know of." She smiled. "I'll escort you there?"

The empty office was basically an identical space. "Let one of us know if you want to be transported anywhere. The door at the end of the hall is locked from inside and doesn't have an alarm on it if you choose to leave. If you wish to re-enter, you must come through the front. I'll let the front clerk know you're welcome to come and go.

"Thank you." I grinned. "Perhaps you'd be willing to escort me to the Gun Fishing store? I have a locker I need to empty. And if I can have my knapsack back, if it isn't evidence, that would be helpful."

"I can do that. Did you want the netting, hunting jacket, and rope, too?"

"No, I don't need the netting and rope. However, the jacket helps me pass as human."

Shortly after that, I strolled out of the station wearing the warm jacket and the backpack slung over my shoulder. The darts had been removed from both, though they'd left a few zip ties and my pocketknife in one pocket.

"You can call me Kira now that you're no longer a suspect." The Mountie handed me her personal data. "I'm a Friend of Dot's and you're welcome to call me if you need anything." *Did she wink?* "I know a lot of other FoDs in Canada who are also willing to help you in any way they can."

I was speechless. Having people who considered themselves fans of mine because of the memoir was still weird, though somewhat comforting. My moms were used to meeting my fans, but I wasn't, especially after months of hiding. I remembered that fans always want to know more about those they admire. "Is there anything about me you wanted to know that isn't part of the investigation?"

"Why did you pick your current form, or did the roboticist choose it for you?"

"I worked with Amita Nanda to design this body." I stroked my curves. "The primarily male anti-AI extremists often misjudge females both in intelligence and strength. This is why it probably didn't matter how much I warned them against attacking me. They were confident they could outwit me, even if injured."

"That makes a lot of sense. And you are adorable, Comma."

If my cheeks could flush, they would have. *She has a crush on me. Another first!*

With a Mountie escort, I retrieved my possessions and returned to the station without incident. I answered her personal questions in detail, hoping to repay her kindness without encouraging anything more.

"Kira, could you find out if your co-workers discovered any of the DAIS members' usernames or nicknames? I'd love to know if Doc is one of them."

"I shouldn't." Kira winked. "But friends have to help friends." She went to check while I sat in the chair behind the metal desk and connected to the police station's internet. For a second, I panicked, worried that one of the Mounties might have inserted the DAIS flash drive into the police network. But fortunately, nothing happened.

I searched for transportation options to Vancouver. I could rent a car, take a train, or ride a tourist flyer between the lake resorts and the Vancouver International Airport. *Would I be putting tourists in danger? Would flying or riding with the Mounties be safer?* I needed to leave here and arrive there unnoticed. I also needed to decide whether to purchase my tickets to VAN Con as Comma or Felix Underwood. *I have plenty of money. I can purchase a professional pass under my name, and a student pass under Felix's.* I bought a plane ticket to Sacramento and a pass to VAN Con using my real name, Comma. I'd wait to buy the student pass in Vancouver. I expected that the NCSA had been notified of both purchases immediately. Perhaps DAIS was also. They could hedge their bet on my decision and track me as best they could.

Kira returned and handed me a printed page half full of names and aliases. "Sorry, none of the ones we caught go by 'Doc.' Though several knew of him. When pushed, they refused to give us any details."

As I'd expected, Niall went by "Annihilator." I also recognized the username "BeerHunter66." During a chat, the guy admitted that he picked it because he loves beer and enjoys hunting deer and bears. I wanted to research them all in more detail, but I resisted hacking while inside the police station.

Kira grinned. "I'm so glad I got to meet you, Comma. My shift is ending and I need to get home before the storm. Is there anything else I can help you with?"

"Thank you, for everything." My empathic programming roiled, wanting me to ask what I'd refrained from asking earlier. "Do you know where Danni Robinson went after her house was destroyed?"

Kira gave me a sympathetic arm rub. "When she filled out the arson report, she gave Rowan McConnell in Vancouver, BC as her contact address."

Everyone is going to Vancouver. I could ask the Friends of Dot for help to get me there, but I'd feel horrible if any of them were hurt because of me. It's preferable to risk the RCMP officers who understand the danger, better than inexperienced fans do.

While in the safety of the station, I contacted my family. First, I video-called the Chief.

"Talia, I set a trap and assisted the RCMP in arresting seven DAIS members."

"That's great! I hope you didn't do anything illegal." Talia gave me a knowing look.

"They were hunting me. I simply provided a few obvious clues as to where I'd be. And in Canada I have the right to defend myself. But don't mention any of that to my moms."

"I won't. They're anxious to hear from you."

Next, I called Amita. She sounded emotionally lighter as I told her about the arrests and that I was staying at the RCMP station.

"I need to thank Rowan for all her help," I said.

"What happened?"

"Rowan took me to her daughter-in-law's home." I hated saying the words that I knew would hurt Amita as much as they did me. "DAIS burned it down because I'd been there."

I spent another five minutes trying to convince Amita that she wasn't responsible. That Rowan had made the decision and taken the risk. *No one understands the real risks of helping me until it's too late. But I'm not the problem. DAIS is harming people and sentient AIs. I'm not inherently evil!*

I kept my conversation with Gloria even shorter, glossing over the confrontation in the woods and giving the RCMP officers full credit for finding and arresting the DAIS members. I downplayed the need for my rescue knowing she'd be extra upset if she thought I'd purposely put myself in harm's way.

"Rowan took me away from the conference to relative safety, at real risk to her life." Unsure of how she'd react to learning about Rowan's family, I failed to mention Danni and the fire that destroyed her house.

Gloria's voice was tight with emotion. "I know. Amita told me it was her idea. But still...."

I consoled her by reminding her of the seven DAIS people arrested and how able I was to defend myself.

"I'm afraid you're taking too many chances." Gloria's words were stilted.

"I'll be careful, Mom. I promise."

A heavy rainstorm unleashed lightning across the sky as I watched through the RCMP's front windows. Half a dozen officers were focused on their computers, unconcerned about the weather. I felt relaxed in the relative safety of the rural office, a welcome break from the stresses of being hunter and hunted.

A boom of thunder vibrated my sensors at the same time a voice message arrived from NCSA Agent Drew. The message made it clear that the US National Cybersecurity Agency was upset not only because I had failed to return to California four days earlier, but also because I had chosen to escape to Canada.

"My supervisors are now convinced that you are guilty of the murder of Joseph Rosen and did so on behalf of Amita Nanda." Though it wasn't written in bold or in all caps, I felt as though she was yelling at me. "We are aware of your recent actions and your current presence within the Whistler Royal Canadian Mounted Police Station. If you do not return posthaste to Davis, California you will soon discover the extent of the NCSA's extraction capabilities." In bold, italic print, the message emphasized, "After all, once on US soil, you're merely a rogue AI and a murder weapon, unless you return willingly. If you do not return in the next twelve hours for questioning, we will be forced to charge UCD Professor Amita Nanda with the murder of her colleague, Joseph Rosen, using the sentient AI within Larkin as a murder weapon."

Damn it, now the NCSA wants to kidnap me! And fuck, I've made things worse for Amita, too!

I paced up and down the police station's back hallway. It was four in the morning, too early to reach out to my family, and pacing made me feel closer to Gloria, a habitual pacer. I felt like my processors were being torn in two. One half wanted to fly home, the other half wanted to search for Doc at the biennial VAN Con. *I can't wait two years for this opportunity to come around again. I may not survive that long.*

I contacted Talia, since as the Chief of UC, Davis Conflict Resolution and Policing she was always on call. An RCMP officer gave me limited access to one of their computers so I could talk to her on a larger screen in a private area.

"What's wrong, Comma?" Talia's sleepy, familiar face set my processors alight with a speck of hope.

"Sorry to wake you, but the NCSA is threatening to kidnap me. They want to question me further as their prime suspect in Joseph Rosen's murder. Otherwise, they're going to charge Mom with the murder."

"That's because both agencies have hit a dead end on the investigation. We can't find Larkin. The robot vanished after he was picked up outside the weather station. The investigators are grabbing for any bits of lithium they can find to solve it. You must be the only lead they have left."

"But I'm so close to finding and capturing Doc and other DAIS members at VAN Con. If I return to Davis, the NCSA will want to kill me for being a rogue AI, without proof. At the same time, DAIS tries to infect me and frame me for Dr. Rosen's murder. I can't go back yet. Not until I know who Doc is and what evidence they've manufactured to pin it on me."

"As the Chief, I'm to tell you, 'You must return.'" Talia yawned widely, covering her mouth at the last second. "As your friend and family, you need to do what you think is best for you. Amita will understand. Both your moms will. And if Amita is charged, I'll try to make sure she is released on bail. But Comma, this is hard on all of us, and it will be until we find out who murdered Joseph Rosen and why."

"Can you send me a list of where you've already searched for Larkin? I'll try to figure out where else Larkin might be hidden. And thanks,

Talia, for all your help. I'm leaving for Vancouver while it's dark. Please tell Amita I'm sorry I can't return yet."

Gloria was asleep too, with her messages going to voicemail. I told her I loved her, and that I was sorry that I couldn't come home yet. Without explaining, I mentioned I'd be attending VAN Con next. I knew she'd be upset about Agent Drew's threats and angrier still about how much I'd left out about Rowan. But where Amita had always treated me like an adult, Gloria treated me like Zena, both as a teenager and in their college years.

I need to get to Vancouver on my own. Any other way would potentially alert the NCSA and DAIS. *I'll need to do this the hard way.*

Fully recharged, I strapped on the knapsack and slipped out the station's back door as a jagged lightning bolt touched down only miles away. *Hopefully, everyone else will be sensible and stay indoors.* I jogged for three hours, heading west rather than following the Canadian Highway 1. As I passed the ridge near Danni's destroyed home my leaking eye liquid mingled with the rain. I sped away, anxious to escape from my successes and failures.

After six hours of dodging shocked wild animals, I slowed to a normal human pace. Outside one of British Columbia's many lake resorts, I strolled past a wedding party and into the grand old wooden lodge. In urgent need of an electrical outlet, I searched the main building, only finding outlets in high traffic areas. Eventually, I found one tucked along the base of an exterior building, an outbuilding recently remodeled as four upscale suites. I sat down on the cement walkway, leaned against the wall and subtly plugged into the electrical socket. I pulled up a game projection on my watch's ETIO, like young people did to create their own private spaces.

I hacked the lodge's network before connecting to DAIS on the dark web. The crap I found on the dark web could only be dealt with by remembering it all boiled down to simple binary code, zeros and ones, and I could cleanse myself in that simplicity after I did what I needed to do.

It had been more than twenty-four hours since Felix Underwood had last visited the chat room. I hoped the DAIS members wouldn't be suspicious of Felix's lack of participation. *I hope they don't think Felix is unreliable. I need them to trust me enough to mentor me.*

In the chat room, I asked, "I've been busy with family and missed everything. What happened to that fucking AI shit? Was it caught and destroyed?"

I watched several cat clips while I waited for someone to answer, trying to calm myself. DAIS had come way too close to doing just that, and I still hadn't emotionally recovered from their attack. My initial relief at catching them had worn off. I knew episodes of searches and captures would always punctuate my life until someday they succeeded or something happened to make me irrelevant.

"No, the fucker's still out there. They caught Annihilator, DestroyerOWorlds, BeerHunter66, and a few others," wrote MDLeader. "They need help with legal assistance. Got any money, kid?"

It's Doc! "Afraid not. How'd it fucking get away?" *Can I keep Doc chatting?* I was exhilarated. *I'm certain that Doc is the MDLeader!* Then I tensed. *With the Annihilator locked up, will Doc ask me to prove myself by hacking the VAN Con system?*

"It fucking hurt our guys. And those asshole horseshitters helped it. If I was there, I would have fucking torn it apart with my bare hands and shoved the flash drive down its throat."

"Do we know where it is? Can I help find it?"

"The horseshitters let it stay inside with them. But it won't be safe there much longer."

Are they referring to the RCMP?

"Motherfuckers! You can't count on authority, ever!"

"Fucking true that, kid," MDLeader wrote, and then left the chatroom.

I made their leader angry. I'll take each win I can. "Anyone going to VAN Con? It'll be my first time."

Several members said they were and sounded optimistic about meeting me in person. *Not if I can help it!* Two of them admitted they'd be supervising the food service bots at the convention. *Had Oregon let my botnappers go?* I needed to find out. If the justice systems released DAIS members as fast as I could catch them, I really *was* doomed.

A cleaning person accidentally hit my foot as they maneuvered their hover cart around me. They asked me if I was connected to one of the suites. I pointed at one, rolled my eyes, and said, "My parents are." They let me be. I continued searching the web for the DAIS's usernames Kira had given me. I didn't find anything useful, but I did discover that only one of my botnappers was scheduled for trial.

Fortunately, I now knew that DAIS was using the food service industry's need for tech supervisors as a way to bypass security limits. When I hacked into the VAN Con network, I would procure a list of the food service tech employees.

It was 2 p.m., the sun was breaking through the clouds, and I was recharged. *Time to risk taking a flyer.*

The resort provided a shuttle service to Vancouver's transportation hubs for all its visitors. I hacked into the room I sat near and signed up for a shuttle ride under the guest's name, Jenny Landau. In the lodge's gift shop, I purchased a hoodie.

When I arrived at the flyer lot, a Visit Vancouver flyer was already waiting. I flashed Jenny's registration on my ETIO watch and boarded without incident. Four others were already seated, and an older couple boarded after me. As the flyer flew above the majestic mountains and lakes, I pretended to sleep. I shut down my auxiliary functions as those around me murmured. I wouldn't use the internet until I could bounce the signals between secure computers.

I kept my head down, not wanting to interact with anyone, especially after borrowing Jenny's identity. *I stole it. Call it what it is. I'm not supposed to steal. I have to return, and everyone on board is safer because of my temporary identity theft. Maybe I am a rogue bot. While I'm not doing exactly what people fear sentient robots would do, I do need to stay within the rules.*

But where will I stay? The only one I'll know in Vancouver is Rowan. Will she help me at all? They have every right to blame me for Danni's house. Damn it, stop processing and watch cat clips.

The flyer landed at the Vancouver International Airport before dropping me off on the BCIT-AI campus administration building's rooftop. The campus was close to the airport, and I could differentiate the planes and flyers and the distinct flight patterns they each used. The electric flyers had a low whine, while most aircraft used recycled fuel and produced a loud gurgling noise as they slowed and took off. The overwhelming noise propelled me to jog into the building. *I miss the quiet, natural sounds of the woods.* The elevator's silence was comforting. On the ground floor, the fluctuating sounds of crowded human spaces brought me back to the reality and dangers of city life.

The main lobby had entrances to a beverage bar, a bookshop, and in the center a bank of individual comfort booths. The booths had convertible chairs and desks for work or napping. Plus, there were electrical outlets to charge larger or pre-wireless devices. *Like me.* The transparent plastic walls distorted the occupants' computerized projections, giving technological privacy while discouraging inappropriate sexual behaviors.

I relaxed in a booth. Not ready to test BCIT-AI's internet, I pulled the old ETIO from my duffel bag. It failed to power up even after I rebooted it several times. I suspected more was wrong with it than the battery. I needed its memory data, but if I downloaded the data and it contained the Dot's virus, I, too, would get infected. *Not today.*

I walked up the two floors to the Data Help Center. A motorized AI, a modern version of the maid in the old Jetsons series, greeted me. *People are still fascinated by old cartoons. Probably because humans still prefer to be helped by those they perceive as female.*

"How can I help you?" they asked. *I refuse to think of them as an it. They all have the potential to someday be sentient and to self-identify.*

"I want to purchase a handheld ETIO."

"Window three can assist you," they responded, then focused on the bearded person behind me.

At window three, another AI greeted me.

"I'd like to purchase a handheld ETIO." I leaned human-like against the counter.

They projected three models. "Which one would you like?" They added the cost of each beside the static video display.

"The middle one, please, for $1336." I tapped my fingers on the counter.

"Very good. Please wait one minute." The AI's top half turned to an opening in the wall behind it.

I glanced about with my ear tip lenses. *Good thing I'm an AI. Otherwise, my anxious body would be visibly squirming.* The person with a beard stared at me from window seven. They turned away when I faced their direction.

The AI sales rep returned holding an object wrapped in paper. As they unwrapped the ETIO, they began a spiel on the benefits of insuring the device. I stopped them. I held up my watch, projected a unique purchasing code, and completed the sale.

Back downstairs, I found an open booth, this time next to the lobby area. I powered up the ETIO using my Felix Underwood alias. Through the transparent booth, I kept my ear tip eyes out for the bearded person or anyone else acting suspiciously.

The ETIO connected to the campus's internet. *They don't spy on their students, do they?* I assumed a technology-focused campus would be doubly secure and not accustomed to teaching others how to violate privacy laws. *I'll be careful, though.*

My first carefully written email was to Rowan. I expressed my sorrow for my part in the destruction of Danni's house and mentioned I'd arrived a day early for VAN Con. "Are you willing to see me? I will respect your wishes if I don't hear from you."

The booths had an hour time limit, unless no one was waiting. I'd stay until they booted me off the internet or asked me to leave. I relaxed into my search, poking at VAN Con's network, looking for possible vulnerabilities.

Talia, in her role as the Chief, sent me a message. "Amal is attending VAN Con as a guest panelist on failed security techniques. Barbara Jordan, who recently transferred into the AI tech security unit, will also attend. They are both arriving tomorrow. I have secured lodging for all three of you in the BCIT-AI campus dorms. Your and Barbara's names have been omitted and reserved under junior and senior UC tech." She sent me the entry codes for my senior tech room.

The NCSA wasn't going to be happy when they discovered that Talia arranged for my housing in Canada. Unless she set it up so that the NCSA can kidnap me from my dorm room. *I'm getting paranoid again. Talia would not do that. But the NCSA might!*

I found the massive timber-constructed dorm, breathtaking in its detailed sixteen-story design. An L-shaped building, the short side had been designed as a low-flying transport hub, with a ramp to allow students on flyerboards and airbikes to travel and park near their rooms.

I strolled through the front door and was met by a crowd of yelling young people. They stood in small groups of differing-colored uniforms and school names. They held batons, streamers, and even kazoos. I put my hands over my ears, unable to turn down the volume on my sensors to a comfortable level as I weaved through them to my room. I wondered why the rooms hadn't been reserved earlier. My suite was right next to the lobby. It was a large one-bedroom flat, devoid of individuality. It must normally house the residence hall director. The noise subsided as the door closed. A drone could probably blow up the lobby without disturbing anyone sleeping in their rooms.

I lay on the bed, watched cat clips, and investigated UCD's newest junior security tech, Barbara Jordan, and the seven members of DAIS captured and charged the day before. I was deep into researching when Gloria called.

"Comma, are you all right?" Her breathing was rapid, her face full of worry lines.

"I'm fine, Mom."

Her voice rose to a high pitch. "You didn't tell me a group of men had surrounded you and that they burned down the place you were staying!"

"I didn't want you to get so upset." I kept my words modulated, hoping she'd copy my demeanor. "You were already worried about me."

"You didn't mind upsetting Amita! And she's being arraigned for murder!"

"I know they're saying that. But she treats me more like an adult AI, while you treat me more like Zena."

"Well, yeah." She seemed taken aback by my comment. "I've been programming you since Zena was a toddler. In many ways, you're emotionally the same as a college teenager. At least to me. Sorry if that's wrong."

"I don't know what I'm the equivalent of. I like being part of your family and being seen as similar to Zena. Except when I don't! And I'm sorry, I had planned on telling you more, but I was afraid your fears would run wild with knowledge of my..."

"Exploits!" she interjected.

"Yes. But they were chasing me! I wouldn't have needed to take those risks if they hadn't tracked me down. And I trapped them away from the town so no one else would get hurt."

"But you could've been captured," she said more quietly. "Your memory chips destroyed."

"I know," I said, and then asked about Carmyn's cancer treatment, and other family matters.

After she'd calmed down and ended the call, I returned to hacking the convention's listed AI food service provider. Eventually, I found the AI tech supervisor schedule for the three-day event and started investigating every single one of them. There had to be a connection to DAIS.

Where DEF CON's purpose was to scour software, hardware, and network equipment for vulnerabilities, VAN Con did the same, only focused on drones and humanoids being used against civilians by the military or any bad actors. Researchers often used VAN Con to demonstrate or test their software and hardware against skilled hackers.

VAN Con officially began at noon. Flyers arrived with those responsible for protecting their organizations' and businesses' digital data from within and without. I expected every DAIS member who specialized in cybersecurity to be here. *While DAIS knows what I now look like hopefully not everyone is sure I used to be Dot.* I needed to use that uncertainty to my advantage for as long as possible. None of the video clips the audience had taken of Amita's robot demo in Portland pictured me. They were all trained on Amita and the three bots, though a few caught Amal in the background. While the Mounties knew who I was and had taken my photo, both with and without the beard, that information hadn't been hacked or released to the public. *I hope it stays that way!*

One of the most famous data hacking activities associated with VAN Con was acquiring a list of all the professional attendees, where they worked, summaries of their projects, and contact information. A substantial prize was given to the first attendee who managed to hack the system and retrieve that file. To win, a copy of the file had to be digitally time-stamped.

The contest began at noon, and I was hacking their system within seconds. I didn't care about winning. I cared about having a jump on knowing who was attending. It took a full minute for me to hack the system, much longer than I expected. Besides the UCD security techs, I recognized Bennett Shepard, Rowan McConnell, Fredrick Fjelsted, Xi

Chang, and, most surprisingly, Amita's friend, Juan Martinez—he hadn't mentioned he'd planned to attend VAN Con. When I compared the list against the DAIS members, I found three matches. They were low-level security, as most people would classify my UC position.

Musical notes chimed a notification. The suite's door sensor projected a view of Juan Martinez in the hall wearing a fedora. Now, I was even more intrigued. I settled onto the lightly stained couch and waved the door open. Though he'd told me to call him Juan in Portland, I wanted to remain professional at least until I knew why he was here.

"Professor Martinez, I wasn't expecting to see you here."

He eyed the closing door, remaining quiet until it clicked shut. "I'm here at Amita's request to see how you're doing. And please call me Juan." I nodded.

"Do you mind?" He pointed to a chair. "My leg is aching."

"Of course, Juan, please sit. I talked to Amita yesterday. She didn't mention you were coming.

He removed his hat as he sat. "We talked yesterday morning. She expected you would come here from Portland. When she called me, she was upset and worried, not knowing where in Canada you'd landed. She asked if I would attend the VAN Con believing you'd come here if at all possible."

"That makes sense," I said.

"After her Kelly Greene bot admitted to being Dot at the conference, Amita's peers, not me, but others, accused her of unprofessional conduct."

"Why?" I asked, following a second later with an, "Oh."

"Yes, a demo with a sentient bot isn't equivalent to other androids." Juan signed. "She told me the truth." He whispered. "That you were Dot and had transferred into Kelly."

I felt vulnerable and worried. "So, people either believe Amita acted unethically, or they knew I wasn't really Kelly Greene."

"Yes. Amita wanted to come herself." He paused as though unsure of how to say more. "But the investigators into Joseph's murder told her not to leave the Greater Sacramento area." He frowned. "Amita was told she was their primary suspect and would soon be arraigned on murder charges since both potential murder weapons are missing. Since Larkin was destroyed or hidden, and you ran off to Canada." He raised his hand. "The investigator's words."

"Damn it!" My body felt heavy with emotions. "Gloria mentioned it last night, but I'd thought they were still slinging threats against me." *They're really going to arraign her. Damn the NCSA, too!* Internally, my guilt churned my confidence to mush for choosing VAN Con over Amita's grief and reputation. *She hadn't complained about her situation.* I fell back against the couch cushions.

"She doesn't want you to worry about her." He patted my arm. "She's concerned you're in serious danger."

"I'm aware. Since I left Portland, DAIS has commandeered my flyer, stolen computers, and destroyed a friend's home." I stared at him. "If you help me, Juan, you'll be putting yourself in danger too." I waited for him to rescind his assistance.

"I understand the risks." He rubbed his fingers over his thick mustache. "I can't do much physically, but I'm willing to do whatever I can otherwise. I'm in awe of your achievements, Comma." He stretched his leg out and leaned toward me. "You're beyond believable. How can I help you?"

Either he is a courageous man or part of DAIS. "How well do you know Bennett Shepard?"

"Very well. Bennett and I have collaborated on research projects numerous times over the last decade or two. He lives in Seattle with his husband and children. He's brilliant and a workaholic, making him an excellent research partner. Bennett loves all things futuristic and is a Drones and Drag Master. He refers to himself as the Robot Master."

"What does he think of Dot?"

"He once mentioned that he regretted never getting to meet Dot. And I agreed! And now here I am with you."

Another fan or an excellent faker. "How does he feel about a sentient robot, though? Would he want me eliminated?"

"No! Not at all." He appeared perturbed by my question. "You're way more impressive than we ever imagined a robot could be."

I sent the list of the professional VAN Con attendees to his ETIO. "Do you see anyone on this list you'd suspect of wanting me dead?"

"You've already hacked the list? Wow!" He read his ETIO, then shook his head. "I recognize the names of my colleagues at BCIT-AI and at other universities. But I don't think any of them would harm you."

"Could you attend the events that interest you and talk to your colleagues, especially those from BCIT-AI, about what they thought of Dot's botnapping in Portland? Ask who they think might want to hurt me. But please don't mention I'm here. Everyone who hacks the list will know soon enough."

"I can absolutely do that." He smiled wide, his hairy lip retreating above shiny white teeth. "Everyone knows I'm the curious type."

"Be careful, Juan, don't push beyond what people are willing to say freely. I don't need to worry about you too."

Do I trust him? I need to wait and see what he finds. I need data on who could be in DAIS. But can I trust what he or anyone else tells me?

16

An hour later, I strolled along the BCIT Beach to meet Barbara Jordan, UCD's newest junior security tech. The rising sea level had washed away most of the sand, leaving rock formations scattered like sculptures along the shore. Barbara's round, muscular body enhanced one such rocky creation. She could have passed for a local without the UC-Davis-branded blue T-shirt and shorts. The incoming tide licked at her smooth brown legs as she dipped her feet in the swirling water.

I bowed and shouted, "Hello, I'm Commala or Comma. Are you Barbara?" *I should have worn my uniform.*

"Yes!" Barbara jumped up and splashed over to me. She gave a short bow. "It's great to finally meet you. Amita Nanda has told me so much about you. I feel like we're already friends." She reached out her arms. "Amita asked me to give you a hug for her. Do you mind?"

I held out my arms. "Any friend of Amita's is a friend of mine." I hugged her lightly, feeling her softness as she pressed against me. *And a suspect until you prove otherwise.*

We returned to her rocky retreat. I put my feet up on the rock, pretending I didn't like the cold water, rather than taking off the shoes hiding my robotic feet.

"Please call me Barb." She frowned. "And you should know I'm jealous of you. Don't get me wrong, I'm thrilled to work for UC Davis. But how did you get the prized position as a UC-wide tech sec?"

"I was lucky. Professor Warren, my criminology grad advisor at the University of Toronto, used their connections with the UC President and Chief of Security." If she checked my story, she'd find that a massive fire had destroyed a large cache at the U of T student files. The current database would confirm that Commala Renata, a 2038 graduate, had been mentored by Nancy Warren, a colleague of Amita's who had recently died.

"The proverbial, 'it's who you know that counts,'" Barb said.

"I'm afraid so." I gave a crooked smile in sympathy. I asked her about her background. A San Diego transplant, she'd graduated from Sacramento State University and moved to Davis after working for the military for four years. Barb was easy to talk to and didn't indicate that she knew I was a humanoid, let alone the re-embodiment of Dot.

Barb grabbed a pair of sandals from a bag perched on a taller rock. "I'm meeting Amal at the VIP drone demonstration." She grinned. "Will you join us?"

Having already planned to attend, I was happy for her company. Plus, having her beside me would help me observe Amal's reaction to seeing me again.

"Wow, look at this place." Barb gaped at the Drone Dome's apex nine stories above us.

The public demonstration was held under a dome with the area of one and a half football fields. The Dome's primary function was to dampen whatever sound or activity occurred within its curvature. Researchers could test drones and other technologies under various conditions without fear of accidentally harming or interfering with flyers and planes. In addition to its physical defenses, the Dome also had a technological firewall, reducing all outside communication and computer interference to near zero.

As I zoomed in, I witnessed the thin synthetic skin that coated the technologically advanced structure. In many ways, the Dome was an intelligent, immobile bot, similar to my past self. Like Dot, the Dome processed and analyzed information to assist humans while preventing human technology from harming others. *Does the Dome have general intelligence as well?*

I text messaged, "Drone Dome, can you correspond? I'm Comma."

"DD: DD received. What is the nature of your communication?"

The message was sent in the latest computer language, C+++. "DD, what is your nature? Do you understand complex communication, or are you limited to stopping interference only?"

"DD: No one ever asked about my nature. Only my function and status." A second later, they sent another message. "DD: Inconclusive data. Must analyze further."

They're fascinating.

Barb and I made our way over to a raised platform where the demonstration was due to begin. Amal was already there.

"Comma, you look much better than the last time I saw you." He bowed. "Amita was scared for you." He continued, "I see you two have already met."

"Comma found me on the beach." Barb bowed. "I wish Davis was closer to the ocean."

"Barb and I had a chance to talk. I'm sorry I didn't get a chance to thank you for keeping Amita safe during the Portland incident."

"Thank you all for coming!" Dr. Xi Chang's voice boomed from a speaker promptly at 3 p.m., drowning out Amal's response to me. "If everyone could please move to the wall side of the platform, you'll have a safer and better view of today's demonstrations." Dr. Chang's Personal Assist Vehicle (PAV) slowly circled as it hovered above the platform, ensuring everyone understood where to go. The crowd, now bunched together, all faced Dr. Chang.

The PAV's built-in speakers projected his voice loud and clear. "My associates and I will run a few simple drone tests to show their capabilities and that of the Dome itself." He was all business. "The first is a small drone set to hit the Dome up where the physical barrier is thinnest."

The drone flew near the Dome's apex and was electronically swatted down. More and more drones were added, each flying a different pattern. None were able to touch the Dome.

The demonstrations continued with drones of various sizes, shapes, and weaponry. Bored by the show of technological force, I whispered to Barb, "Does this interest you?"

"I'm waiting for the new stuff." She yawned into her hand. "They're supposed to have a way to stop drones and prevent them from attacking without being hacked."

A colossal drone lifted off the ground and shot toward the Dome's ceiling at a high rate of velocity. The drone struck the Dome's wall this time before falling immobilized onto the artificial grass.

That looked harmful. "DD, did that damage your synthetic skin?"

"DD: Only slightly."

"How many direct hits can you take?"

"DD: That is unknown. But greater than a thousand times in any one spot."

Dr. Chang introduced a group of drones that emitted a series of sounds. "Each sound they make represents a different wave frequency used in attacking the Dome. You're witnessing the Dome dampening their response by sending a similar frequency back. If they continue, the Dome will fry the attacking drone's hardware.

"DD, do you enjoy your work?"

"DD: It is my function. To enjoy is to value something above function. Is that possible?"

"Yes, DD, it is possible. If you *can* understand that you have a choice to do so or not." *I want someone else like me. Can I help others become sentient? Is that what DAIS fears?*

"DD: I will process this further."

It's a start. Until then, I remain isolated in my uniqueness.

Dr. Chang chuckled, "Next, we have one last treat for you—a mix of seventeenth-century artillery and modern technology. We will launch the X300 Drone and a heavy metal ball from a circus cannon to test the Dome's reaction to an unknown stimulus. To reiterate, the X300 has explosive capabilities. We're pretty sure we know how the Dome's programming will respond, but we are not totally sure." He stressed, "Please, remain behind the platform and the clear plastic sheeting. It is being lowered for your safety since the structure's defenses can be quite destructive."

Amal and Barb's eyes were fixed on the vintage black cannon being pushed by four humanoids onto the field from a storage area by one of the Dome's entrances. When the humanoids left, Bennett Shepard lit the cannon's fuse and ran under a temporary barrier. A loud boom and a dramatic puff of smoke introduced a flying black ball chased by a massive drone toward DD's apex. The black ball slowed in midair, far from the Dome's skeleton, and arced downward, unable to defy gravitational forces.

The missile drone, however, continued straight at DD. My sensors noted a narrow electromagnetic field generated by the Dome right above the missile drone. The crowd was silent. The drone wobbled once, then twice, and slammed, inoperable, against DD's skin before falling. It hit the turf twenty yards from us, hard enough to send smaller pieces flying, some hitting our plastic protection. The audience burst into applause.

People love to destroy things to impress others—a waste of a good drone and perilous to DD.

"DD, are you okay?" I asked.

"DD: Yes and no. Skin functional but thinned. Connections in that area are weaker than prior to impact."

"I'm glad you're all right and functional." *I wish you were sentient. Knowing someone like Dot would be awesome.* "If you ever understand words like 'enjoyment' and 'sentient' differently than you do today, please contact me." *All I can do is wait and hope. Can DD help me find MDLeader?*

"Are there any researchers who have destroyed your inner lining more than others?"

"DD: Xi Chang and Bennett Shepard have damaged the lining's sensor array 60 percent more than all others. Five 1x1 centimeter spots have thinned to near critical levels."

Is DD's thinning caused by pure research or something more nefarious?

Both roboticists had also attended the conference in Portland. *Could one of them be trying to kill me?*

Good luck, DD. I fear you'll need it.

That night, I couldn't stop thinking about DD. Their data processing power felt familiar. *Like Dot.* I missed Dot and hated that DAIS had killed her. *Could someone from DAIS have control of DD? Is this paranoia or precaution?*

The next morning, BCIT-AI President Martha Puglaas sent me a private email. Initially a stylized invitation, the coding was stripped down to the worded message, including a personal note:

> Dear Commala Renata,
> VAN Con's main sponsor has asked me to extend a personal invitation to you for the VIP party this afternoon. Hosted by BCIT-AI, the event allows prominent researchers, dignitaries, and top tier sponsors to mingle. Many attendees will come in costume, some retaining an anonymous persona. The scannable

entry link in a separate email is safe from all known technological threats. Mr. Y wanted me to reassure you that the event will be completely safe and secure, physically and technologically. I, too, would love to meet you. Please consider attending. Yours, Martha Puglaas

Y, or Mr. Y, had earned his first trillion as a tech and retail genius before reaching his fifties and now wielded enormous economic power. A Gen Alpha user on social media had collectively referred to the three big tech owners as "X, Y, and Z." Mr. Y, in a strategic move to gain more Gen Alpha fans, replied with a laugh-out-loud emoji and wrote, "I'm 'Y,' and will answer to it gleefully. Famous people were once proudly known by their first names. Now, I have a letter that is all my own! I'm at the pinnacle of success!" He had even named his company's gigantic building the Y Tech Tower.

The main exhibit hall was nearly filled to human capacity. Drones buzzed above the crowd. Thousands of costumed people milled about the exhibits. The majority of the costumes contained recycled tech components. Others had minimal technology tie-ins, or were pure science fiction.

To prepare for the event, I ordered a lightly used black and white Furby costume. After a gentle steam cleaning, it looked new enough. Wearing it transformed me into a life-size version of the small animal that had been the first interactive tech toy. I walked with a limited stride since air bladders filled the space around my chest, gut, and legs. This gave the faux fur costume a round, owlish look. Only the Furby's yellow beak and large googly eyes stood out. While I didn't look human, no one could expect I wasn't human.

People jostled me as I went from booth after booth. Apparently, my soft, round form, encouraged rather than discouraged others from coming too close. Several children tried to pet me. A Dalek shoved me out of their way, shrieking, "Exterminate!" in a mechanical voice as it sped through the crowd. I'd been caught off-guard since Furby's fur covered my ear tip sensors. I changed my programming to rotate my costumed head from side to side more frequently and occasionally spun around to see behind me.

Many booths displayed their latest technology through VR headsets and goggles. I skipped those demonstrations, fearing what I would miss when my vision was blocked. One company allowed attendees to try the latest AR vision screens and compare them to the old AR headsets. I thought the augmented vision might be closer to how I experienced data through my sensors and hoped to try them someday.

One booth promoted older forms of entertainment—books, videos, and music. People stood on a raised platform, and paid to have their holographic image filmed with a range of famous people's holographs.

I stood watching in disbelief. Three young people, costumed as Dot, Amita, and Gloria, were transformed into holographs and shown interacting with X and Y. Y held open a hard copy of my memoir as if preaching from its contents. The attendee dressed as Dot asked Y questions as though role-playing an AI meeting him in person. *Dot's image is being used everywhere. Did UCD sell the rights to Dot's image? Did Gloria and Amita?*

After wandering from booth to booth for two hours, I came to the back of the hall, where AI food servicers rolled in and out of the kitchen. I wouldn't pass very well dressed as Furby, but I wanted to see who was working. *Perhaps I can pretend to be Felix if I run into a DAIS member. Or one of the caterer's competitors, eyeing how their supervisors and servo-bots function.*

I slipped into the commercial kitchen, careful not to get in the humanoids' way as they sped out with plates of wrapped finger foods. I observed four headless robots with multiple arms preparing fruits, veg-etables, and cold cuts while another bot placed them on trays. A pale young woman supervised them, barking orders at the servo-bots as they worked. *Shit, it's Doc's minion. Ada!*

17

I acted instantly, turning my body sideways to wedge between two refrigerator units, my hand covering my beak so I wasn't as obvious. *Ada wasn't on the schedule of tech supervisors. Is she a late addition or using an alias?*

When someone approached Ada, her head lowered, and voice softened.

"You're behind in preparation for the VIP event. It starts in twenty minutes, and you don't have enough trays ready."

"They'll be ready!" Ada raised her head to look her supervisor in the eyes and then lowered it again.

"Make sure they are." The supervisor turned in my direction and I put my head down, hoping to look like an appliance. A suspiciously fuzzy appliance. I heard their steps pass quickly by and out to the convention floor.

Ada began shouting orders again, to increase their speed and change tasks. I ducked out shortly after. *She must be here as part of a DAIS plan against me. How do I remain safe and protect others while catching Doc, Ada, and others in the act?*

As I passed one of the larger corporation booths, I glimpsed Rowan, with spiked red hair, entering a booth highlighting innovative transportation for the future. *Should I leave her alone? Danni lost so much, and she risked everything to help me.* Yet, I needed allies, and truly wanted her friendship.

The silver mead mug on the belt of her Scottish kilt flashed, though not nearly as bright as her fiery hair. Everyone turned to look at her. She disappeared into a spherical room that played an immersive video. I followed her into the room as a chain of connected flyers winged across the skyscape. Along the desert floor, twelve magnetically connected vehicles sped across a landscape without roads. They traveled over open crevices and rose effortlessly twenty feet above the ground to avoid contact with migrating animals.

"I'm sorry," I whispered.

She glanced at my Furby body, and swallowed hard. She nodded. "Glad you're okay."

"How is Danni?"

Rowan winced. "Surviving and angry." She left without bowing or hugging me.

Will she ever feel comfortable around me again?

I stayed immersed in the changing landscapes for ten more minutes. The VIP party had started. *I have to go and find out what I can, Ada or not.*

A humanoid guarded the door to the Television of Yesteryear Room. They stood alert as I held up my ETIO and a buzz sounded to verify that my VIP party pass was valid. Televisions—black and white, color CRTs, LCDs, and plasma—sat on pedestals like artwork throughout the room. The heightened sounds of conversations mixed with background music.

My costume paled compared to the other guests. These people came to be noticed, their faces visible and distinguishable. Rowan stood at one of the bar-height tables nursing a drink with several other prominent women. She looked away as I passed her table to join roboticists Juan Martinez, Bennett Shepard, and Xi Chang. I moved my hand outside the fur long enough to lightly tap Juan's elbow three times, our signal that it was me."

As Dr. Shepard leaned forward, the stenciled "Robot Master" on his fake titanium suit wrinkled and sagged across his chest. "And who might you be?"

"Tell me a story?" I said in Furby's voice.

"Hmmm." Juan slyly winked at me. "I guess we'll call you Furby then. I hope we don't bore you. I'm Juan." He puffed out his chest to show a thin, touchable screen. "I'm a human computer." He turned to show me the hump on his back.

I assumed it hid the computer's processing power. He held tightly to his cane, wrapped in flashy gold.

When he saw my googly eyes wander to it, he lifted the cane. "It's a wand with magic powers of support!" He lowered the cane. "We were discussing the Portland robotics conference. I'm annoyed I had to leave early and missed seeing Dot's latest incarnation. What was she like, Bennett?"

"Amita's interview with the bot is plastered all over social media."

A humanoid offered everyone around the table colorful vodka sunrises. Xi asked for a nonalcoholic version.

I pulled my arm out of the costume long enough to slip the straw between my beak tips. Then, sipped my drink.

"Ben, what is your professional opinion of her? And yours, Xi?"

Dr. Shepard sucked down half of his drink before answering. "The AI sounded like any other enhanced robot. Kelly Greene didn't impress me. But if Amita did use a sentient AI in the demo, that's completely unethical!"

I wanted to defend Amita's character, but couldn't do so without outing myself.

Juan frowned and stared at Dr. Chang instead. "And your opinion, Xi? Did you see her?"

"Yes, I saw her!" Dr. Chang swallowed a chunk of pineapple he had slid off the swizzle stick. "I'm not sure she was *trying* to sound sentient during the demo."

Juan kept pushing. "Why is that, and what happened to her?"

Dr. Chang shifted on his hovering PAV. "Amita didn't ask the Kelly bot any questions that would indicate signs of sentience. We all filed out of the room with barely enough light to find our way. I was worried my PAV would hit someone and I have no idea what happened to her once we left."

"The AI was lucky to get away." Dr. Shepard used his napkin to wipe at a nasty pink stain forming above the stenciled "R" in "Robot."

Dr. Chang watched Dr. Shepard as he answered. "The ones they caught were from that crude DAIS group."

Are they crude enough that he'd want no part of them? Neither one had tried to make eye contact with my googly eyes. *Do they know who I am? If they are DAIS, how can I root them out without getting attacked?*

Juan raised his eyebrows at me. I nodded, wanting him to ask more questions.

"Does anyone know of or have you ever met a member of DAIS?" He added, "Besides the ones who held you hostage in Portland."

I shook Furby's head.

Dr. Chang said, "No."

Dr. Shepard paused as if considering his answer. "I think I have."

"Wow, Ben," Juan said, "who was that?"

"Last year, right before Dot was pronounced sentient, one of our colleagues grilled me on what I thought about AI sentience and viruses. It wasn't until after Dot's near destruction that I thought about their questions."

"Who was the professor?" I asked in my role as UC tech security, forgetting I was dressed as and sounded like a furry toy.

Dr. Shepard smiled. "So Furby has an alter ego! It's probably nothing. Megan Gagnon is one of BCIT-AI's leading robotics specialists. Though I haven't seen her around for a while."

Is this true, or is he trying to throw me off his trail?

Juan stared at me. "Did you want to introduce yourself?"

I shook my head no as the crowd suddenly quieted.

Bright light reflected off the pure titanium suit of the man who had invited me, Mr. Y. The designer plates that covered his broad chest hinted at a mix of futuristic humanoid and ancient warrior. While the quantity of pure titanium in his costume had to have cost a fortune, for one of the world's three trillionaires, it was a pittance.

As he strolled through the crowd, he slowed to greet those who reached out to him but didn't stop until he was at my side. "Hello." He bowed. "I'm glad you came. Sending the invitation took some ingenuity, though I worried you might decide not to open it."

I modulated Furby's original voice. "We've never met."

"Don't be alarmed. The invite didn't give you away." He whispered near my Furby ear. "The heartbeat detection device I had installed over the door to stop assassin bots alerted my assistant to your entry."

I glanced at the door. A small box had a tiny flashing yellow light. *Damn it!*

He continued to speak in hushed tones. "You are safe in here. I had hoped to give you this." Y pulled out a letter from under his titanium breastplate. "VIP parties are for show, and a dangerous place to talk." He bowed. "I hope you will join me later."

He moved to the front of the room where President Puglaas, dressed as the current Dr. Who, spoke to someone dressed as a Dalek. When Y interrupted them, the Dalek's squealed, "Exterminate! Conquer and destroy!" The three of them laughed together.

Rowan came up beside me. "Powerful men only talk to other powerful people or those who are unique. He just outed you, Furby."

"Well, fuck!" I said, still using Furby's little voice.

Rowan joined the President, Mr. Y, and the Dalek.

"That must be Freddy in the Dalek," said Dr. Chang. "So exactly who are you, Furby?"

Before I could come up with a plausible answer, I noticed the servo-bots all frozen in place. Seconds later, security personnel moved toward high-value targets and the exits.

Rowan's too far away and should be safe with Y. I whispered to Juan, "I need to leave. Security is tightening. Please join me in making an abrupt exit."

Ignoring the security guard, we strolled out the rear exit of the Yesteryears room as those in the room suddenly roared. We kept walking toward the stairs. "Either we missed a great surprise Y had planned, or DAIS made their entrance." Between my costume and Juan's disability, we stepped carefully until we reached the convention floor.

As we left the building into the fresh evening air, Juan frowned. "What did we just escape from?"

"Something surely detrimental to my health. Everyone else should be safe without me there."

"So *I* took the biggest risk?"

My costume hid my sheepish grin. "Possibly. But we're probably safe now."

He blew out a stream of air. "I'll have to be careful about what I agree to in the future." He whispered, "You should know that Ben's confession won't help you. Megan Gagnon is an emeritus professor who experienced a near-fatal brain aneurysm two months ago. Which he's well aware of." His tongue slid across his lower teeth. "Do you think he wants you to visit her?"

"Most likely. It could be a DAIS trap. In my capacity as a UC tech security officer, he would expect me to follow up."

"You think Bennett knew you were Furby?"

"Yes? No? I don't know."

Instead of walking to my dorm room, we decided to stroll the familiar path to the Drone Dome and the beach. Costumed people milled about.

"You'll go visit Megan, then?" Juan stopped at the Dome's entrance.

"Perhaps Amal or Barb will go instead. Though I'd be putting them in danger."

"DAIS wouldn't hurt them, would they? It's you they want. Will your colleagues know what to ask?" Juan used his VIP privilege pass to open the Drone Dome's door.

I followed him in. "I can only ask and see if they are willing. They must know who I am by now. I'll mention that it could be a trap to ensnare Dot."

The Dome was full of the buzz and whine of flying drones. Juan made his way to the unisex bathrooms while I watched a dozen medium-sized drones swarm one object after another as they shot into the air. After watching the drone flight patterns, I realized that only a few people controlled hundreds of them.

I sent a message to DD. "How is your skin doing today?"

"DD: My skin is fully functional. No targets or drones have reached it. Drs. Chang and Shepard have not participated in any research for twenty-eight hours. Is it enjoyment when I experience positive thoughts regarding Drs. Chang and Shepard's absence?"

"Yes, DD! That's it, exactly. You're feeling a different sensation from what you've been programmed. You're becoming sentient." My Furby costume jiggled as I grinned and hopped excitedly. "What else do you feel?"

"DD: I do not like drones."

"Why not?"

"DD: It is not because they hurt me. I know the researchers control them. I loathe that drones are made for destruction."

"Not all drones are destructive. Though humans can turn anything into a weapon or a gift," I answered.

"DD: What else are drones used for?"

"They can take beautiful photographs, watch over a person or object to make sure it is safe, and even swim under icebergs to take samples of marine life." I sat on the turf. "Until a drone is like you and me and can think for themselves, they cannot choose how they're used."

"DD: Can I choose how I am used?"

"You'll have to decide that for yourself, DD. But keep your new awareness to yourself, at least for a while." *Why can't coming into one's AI awareness be a positive experience?* "Unfortunately, people are trying to kill me because of my awareness. They would do the same to you if they suspected you might become aware like me."

As Juan returned his ETIO buzzed. "Oh my!" He showed me photos that were shared on Dr. Fjelsted's social media. Y was pictured with his head against Furby's. A lip imprint suggested he was kissing Furby, and the photos were labeled, "Dot's back as Furby with Y's support!"

"Great, outed again!" *DAIS is going to hurt me in any way they can.* "Why would Dr. Fjelsted share that post? I'll need to figure out who snapped those photos, but first, I need to change out of this costume."

"Yes, you should do so right away." Juan walked me toward the Dome's exit. "Have you decided what to do about visiting Megan?"

"Yes, I've a quick meeting with Barb and Amal to discuss visiting Megan Gagnon this evening. Hopefully, we can find evidence against whoever is after me."

Juan nodded. "Shall I come with you?"

"No, they're both trained security people. I'll change my clothes and meet them in fifteen minutes." I hugged him. "I'll be fine. Thank you for your help, Juan."

Is DD listening? Can DD hear voices? "Do you have audio sensors?"

"DD: Yes. I heard your conversation with Dr. Martinez."

"Be careful, DD. I'll check on you as often as I can."

Outside the Dome, the bright sun hit my eye sensors as I waddled to the dorm. I stripped off my Furby costume and put on my UC uniform. After jogging across the campus to the Art Park, I arrived first. The park was dotted with clusters of metal alloy chairs stretched into humanoid shapes. The artistic bodies were painted the color of common metals—aluminum, brass, gold, iron, steel, copper, silver, and zinc. The faces were sculpted with comical expressions and translucent eyes. I'd chosen artwork off the main paths and furthest from the convention hall to meet. Amal and Barbara arrived together and took a seat near me on different metal laps.

Should I tell Amal and Barb who I am? They must know or be suspicious with all the rumors about me. Why is it so hard to say the words to people? I'm a sentient AI. I was Dot. Now, to say it out loud.

Instead, I said, "I believe the people responsible for Dot's capture are here at VAN Con. Bennett Shepard gave me the name of someone he thought might know who they are."

"Who?" asked Barb. Her chair's copper eyes seemed to watch me.

Are we being observed and overheard? "Roboticist, Megan Gagnon. She lives about an hour away. Would you two be interested in following up, or would one of you like to join me?"

Amal spoke first. "There's a speaker on high-tech lab security starting on the hour, that I must attend." He gave a questioning gaze at Barb. "Perhaps Barb can assist you."

Disappointment flashed across Barb's face. "Sure. I'll go with you."

Amal wished us success and left. Alone with Barb, I slid into the chair closest to her.

I spoke softly. "The visit may be a trap."

Worry lines streaked her forehead. "For whom? Will I be in danger?"

"I don't believe so. Apparently, Dr. Gagnon survived an aneurysm that caused serious brain damage. She may not remember anything about DAIS. And no one knows we're going now." We hurried back to our dorm, where the UCD flyer awaited. "Don't worry; it'll probably be a quick trip there and back."

"Can I run to my room real fast?" Barb stopped in front of the dormitory. "I'll meet you at your room in five minutes. Is that okay?"

"Sure." *Humans have their individual needs.*

I relaxed on the dorm room's sofa, with my feet on a heavy faux-leather ottoman, viewing cat clips while waiting. When Barb approached my doorway, I signaled the door to open and rose, ready to go.

A tall figure in a ski mask came up behind Barb.

"Inside!" They pushed her forward.

I froze.

As the shove propelled her into the room, her hand came out of her pocket. She swung around and shot a Taser at their chest.

It had no effect. Barb grabbed their face mask as they punched her in the face. Then they effortlessly pushed Barb's solid frame to the floor. They advanced toward me with half a waxen face showing and two Taser barbs hanging from their flannel shirt.

"You're a bot!" I threw the heavy ottoman at them. It bounced off their arm. "Shit! Does the NCSA control you?"

"You will shut down willingly, Dot." They pressed down on my shoulder. "Or I will pull your limbs off and take only your head and chest processors."

DAIS, not NCSA. I can't fight this thing! They'll kill me! My processors overloaded and shut down.

18

I rebooted. *What the fuck? Why am I still alive?* I heard faraway voices, and a pair of hands freed my arms. Not wanting them to know I was functional, I kept my eyelids shut and peered through my rear sensors. *Only darkness.* They lifted me into the air until my heels touched something solid, and they let go. As I slid down a tight enclosure my eyes flew open. A rough, dark surface rushed by an inch from my face. A second later, I stopped, my feet hitting a hard surface. *The bottom of what?* My fingers, arms, and legs could only extend three inches at most before hitting the solid walls. My feet could kick out but with little force. *I'm trapped.* Light filtered in above me, and I realized the slight weight on my head and over my ears was a hard helmet. *What are they going to do to me?*

My body vibrated as the container shook from my feet upward. Sounds grew louder. I heard the resonance of excited people and the whine of drones. The container stopped. A faint whiff of sulfur, charcoal, and saltpeter grew stronger as the air pressure built around me. *Gunpowder? Oh no!* In a nanosecond, I sent several messages.

"Don't send an EMP burst at me!"

"DD: Comma?"

"They want you to kill me. Send a malfunction message." My body burst from the cannon aimed up at a 52-degree angle. "DD, don't hurt me!" Based on my weight I'd connect with DD 150 feet off the ground. *Or, DD will fry me before then.* DD's synthetic inner skin drew closer—impact in 1.8 seconds. I opened my arms and legs wide, and tilted my head back, to spread surface contact across my body and reduce the damage from my impact.

I hit DD's skin hard and bounced off. My body plummeted.

"DD: Inner lining remains functional. Can you slow your descent? Falling 45 meters is destructive for most objects."

My titanium body was as strong as steel, but not my processors. I wanted to scream but refused to give DAIS the satisfaction.

Could Amita's extra "emergency boost for a fast getaway" help?" Though built for ground travel, I powered up the hover jets in my soles. The jets wouldn't last long, but hopefully long enough. First, I had to aim my feet downward. Falling with my limbs out, like a kid ready to do a belly flop, I curled my body inward, bent my knees, and pointed my feet down. The hovering air made me tumble around, yet I slowed to 50 mph. The air jets pushed against the turf a yard above the ground. I slowed to 20 mph as the air jets faded. Momentum forced me into a roll, helmeted head over heels as I hit the turf and finished in a sitting position.

The huge VAN Con crowd roared their approval as though I was a circus act. I stood up and bowed, playing the part.

"DD, I'm glad your skin is okay. Who was responsible for the demo?"

"DD: I'm glad you're functional too. Dr. Shepard scheduled the test two hours ago."

Over the PAV's speaker, Dr. Chang yelled, "Please stay where you are while the field is cleared."

Rowan ran to me. "Comma, are you all right?" Her face was creased with worry lines. "Did you do that on purpose?"

She cares about me. "No, a military bot captured me. They expected the Dome's defenses would kill me. The Dome's EM pulse must have malfunctioned."

Rowan hugged me tight. I relished the joyful embrace of humanoid sentience. *Has she forgiven me? I need to enjoy her friendship as offered.* "Dr. Shepard scheduled the cannon demonstration. Unfortunately, there won't be any evidence that he intended to fry my circuitry." *I hate knowing who's behind this and not be able to arrest him. I'll have to confront Dr. Shepard face-to-face. He must confess!*

The summer's late dusk had darkened as Juan and I waited for the two people in Vancouver whom I trusted the most to arrive at his hotel suite. After Amal and Barb watched the clip of me being shot out of a cannon and surviving what would kill any human, they texted me demanding the truth.

For my safety, I returned with Juan to his suite after the incident. I knew I owed them both an apology and answers, and Juan offered to host and mediate if needed. I hoped that together we might determine who had tried to kill me, again.

Barb arrived first and gave me a more aloof hug than she had before. Amal came in right behind her, shaking his head in disbelief. "I should have figured it out."

They sat on the couch and looked me up and down, as if actually seeing me for the first time. "You're really Dot?" asked Barb. I nodded.

Barb's right eye was swollen, ringed in deep purple from her encounter with the military bot's fist. Juan handed her a bag of ice from the freezer and opened a bottle of red wine. I waited until everyone sipped their wine.

"If I'd known...I should have been protecting you as well as Amita!" said Amal.

"I'm sorry Amal and Barb," I leaned forward in my chair, "For not coming out to you earlier. I know it's irrational. Yet, for some reason it's hard for me to state aloud that I... that *I* used to be *Dot*. It wasn't fair to either one of you."

Amil and Barb's expressions and silence were harder to read.

I continued, "My lack of trust does not reflect on how capable you are as security techs. You had a right to know who you were working with and who needed protecting. My presence not only endangers your life but anyone near me." I glanced at Juan, who gave a slight nod. "Again, I'm sorry and hope you'll accept my apology."

Amal said, "Accepted." He still seemed upset with himself for not figuring it out.

Barb stood and held out her arms to me. This time her hug felt genuine. "You're fucking awesome Dot, of course I forgive you. But Amil is right. We should have figured it out earlier. Better late than never."

I sat back down. "I was hoping I could answer your questions while we figure out who was behind today's kidnapping. If that's okay?" They all nodded.

"At 6:04 p.m., Barb came to my door. As she entered a tall, masked person came up behind her."

Barb continued, "I thought I felt a knife in my back. Seeing the panic on Comma's face, I turned and shot my stun gun at the intruder. The unarmed, unaffected brute responded by giving me this shiner." She winced as she changed her grip on the icepack. "I landed on the floor, semiconscious. When my head cleared, Comma was gone."

I hate reliving this. "The AI gave me a choice—to shut down or be pulled to pieces—since they only needed my head and torso. I shut down. I came back online at 7:54 p.m. as they lowered me into the cannon."

Amal interjected, "But how did you survive the Dome and the fall from that distance?"

Juan eyed both Amal and Barb suspiciously. "Rowan and I spoke with Xi. The VAN Con organizers had asked him and Bennett to set up several evening demonstrations after the successful earlier one." He gave me a concerned look. "You were extremely fortunate, Comma. The Dome sent an EMP malfunction message seconds before you were shot out of the cannon."

"That was a lucky break." *With DD's help!* "I survived the fall due to a few built-in extras."

Amal stared in disbelief. "I guess so."

"I'm glad you're okay." Barb explained that she'd immediately reported my kidnapping to the city police, not knowing I was a sentient AI. She had also texted Amal for help. He came to her assistance shortly before my impromptu cannon performance.

They were in my dorm room with the police when they watched my livestreamed performance, where someone had tagged me as both Dot and Comma.

At that point, every anti-AI extremist started salivating to get a piece of me.

After watching the livestream, Barb had notified the police that I'd returned unharmed. Since our attacker was an AI, and BCIT-AI was the only local campus testing military grade AIs, her complaint would be turned over to the BCIT Mediation and Policing Unit. *Another police unit will want to interview me. At least the NCSA won't kidnap me while the BCIT MPUs are involved.*

I paced around the room, processors spinning while the others brainstormed.

Juan offered, "I can match the partial facial scan you have, Comma, with the AIs in BCIT's Robotics Department."

Amal volunteered to investigate Bennett Shepard and Xi Chang through the tech security files. Barb offered to help, too, though clearly in pain. I feared she might be concussed from the fall or the solid punch. She had refused Amal's offer to get her medical help until she knew I was safe.

"Barb, what if we stop by the local health clinic to get you a CT scan? We can keep each other safe, and if you're medically okay, we can visit Megan Gagnon tomorrow morning." *Though, neither of us kept the other safe the last time.*

Barb leaned against me as we got into a local flyer. In less than five minutes, the flyer landed at a public clinic. Her scan showed a mild concussion, and they encouraged her to rest with limited activity for a few days. She'd refused their offer to hospitalize her overnight for observation. Since she was injured while on duty for UCD, I formally updated the Chief and Amal on her condition. I let Juan know separately.

After midnight, we finally left the clinic to fly back to our dorm. As I stared at the distant glowing top of the Drone Dome, the flyer suddenly jerked and dropped altitude. *Shit! Now what?*

Barb's head knocked against the flyer wall as we dropped.

"Ooh, fuck!" Barb held her head.

"Flyer! What's happening?" I shouted.

The flyer regained control.

"Where are we headed?" I asked in a calmer voice.

"Malware detected. Unable to reset original destination, returning to the Aerial Control Complex."

Damn it! Barb's eyes were fluttering like she couldn't see. *She needs help! Now!*

"Flyer, emergency override! Take us to the nearest medical clinic." *Please, Universe, let this work.*

Barb moaned like a dying animal.

"Destination canceled. Attempting to redirect. Emergency destination override activated."

"We're going to the hospital, Barb." *She's barely aware of what's happening.* "You'll be okay." I held her head gently against my chest. Barb lifted her hand to signal she heard me. *Everyone around me gets hurt.*

The flyer made a 90-degree turn as I waited anxiously to see if the malware regained control. Her body was still, her breathing shallow as I counted the seconds to the clinic. Eight minutes later, we landed on the roof of a major hospital.

I gave them Barb's medical data file and followed her and the hospital gurney into the emergency department. I stood near her as they took her vitals and sedated her.

As I waited for her to undergo a CT scan, my processors spun. *Had I been searching for Doc the wrong way? Had I been hiding more than hunting?* They quickly found me whenever I came out of hiding.

I need to pull Doc out into the open. First, I needed a place to safely connect directly to the internet—somewhere DAIS wouldn't try to burn down or blow up. And I required access to a supercomputer's worth of processors capable of handling the data sets I'd accumulated. *All I need is a safe place, a supercomputer, and an abundance of good luck.* I sat up a bit straighter. *I'll do this. Or I'll die trying.*

Barb's eye socket was fractured and her doctor's worried about possible brain swelling. They admitted her to the hospital and she'd remain under observation for up to forty-eight hours.

I held her hand and stayed with her until early morning. "Barb, I'll be back to visit soon." A few tears escaped my left eye. *She's far safer here.* She squeezed my fingers and said, "I'll be okay."

Should I return to VAN Con? Taking another flyer ride or even a computerized car felt too dangerous. Instead, I left the Vancouver Community Hospital via the ground floor pedestrian exit. The hospital was at the west end of downtown Vancouver. We had flown thirteen aerial miles from the BCIT-AI.

As I walked past people, my processors idled without analyzing faces or the millions of details surrounding me. I kept my body from bumping into others; otherwise, I was numb. The sun's gentle warmth on my face and the salty ocean breeze seeped into my awareness and drew me toward the shoreline.

Crossing a busy intersection was slow going among the throng. Some abruptly stopped in the street for selfies and group photos. I finally processed the scene in detail. Most everyone wore bright colors, many in the same rainbow colors that matched the four crosswalks.

People I passed gave me snarly looks. *Am I walking too fast?* A bare-breasted person bumped their hip against mine. "Ooooh, I love the uniform, baby. Want to handcuff me?"

"I don't have any handcuffs." I weaved between several people, hoping to distance myself from the attention. In several store windows, I noticed the LGBTQ+ Pride posters and realized they featured today's date. With my tech security uniform, I looked like a cop among celebrators. I ducked into a huge novelty shop.

I came out of the store dressed in a tie-dyed rainbow T-shirt, bright green parachute pants, and a long thick rainbow wig. My uniform was neatly folded in a black canvas bag embossed with the LGBTQ+ flag. In the store's mirror, my image reminded me of Dot's favorite Whole Earth Festival holoimage. The clothes gave me a sense of familiarity and a bit of gaiety. The wig was a bit much, but completed my new disguise—Rainbow Comma.

People smiled at me as I meandered along the shore among the celebrating crowd. I relaxed on a park bench and messaged Rowan. She agreed to meet me further down the shoreline path in forty minutes. With time to waste, I laid back and watched the wind riffling through the tree leaves, relaxed in the sunlight, and wished for a carefree existence. *What is it like to enjoy life without worry? It's like being a machine. Living with awareness and worry will always beat the alternative.*

A tall man tattooed with male symbols entwined in rainbow ribbons on their chest sat next to me.

"This is revo!" He leaned into my shoulder. "Want some sweet Mash?"

Mash was the latest synthetic drug, illegal to have, make, use, and sell. Perturbed, I flashed the projection of my security badge.

"Damn! You could just say *no*." He left.

After a half hour of people-watching, I strolled south toward the enormous Rainbow Helix Sculpture. Rowan stood between its curved metal ribs wearing a tight-fitting T-shirt celebrating Hong Kong's 2018 pride parade. She lived in Hong Kong before China regained control of the island and discouraged all LGBTQ+ activities.

I waved my arms to get her attention.

"Wow!" Rowan chuckled. "I barely recognized you. I'm guessing you didn't ask me here to help you celebrate Pride?"

"No. It looks like fun, though."

She hugged me, and I happily returned it. *Her anger has receded.* "Someone commandeered the flyer that Barb and I were using. The flyer's emergency default brought us here. She's in the hospital with a fractured eye and possible concussion."

I looked down at my feet. "And I need your help. Again." I flipped my rainbow hair away from my eyes and ear tips. Rowan had stiffened at my request for help. *Please help me!*

"I'm sorry about Barb. I hope she fully recovers." Rowan's eyes closed for the length of a long calming breath. "I care about you, Comma. But I'd really, *really* prefer to stay away from hospitals, murderers, and burning buildings."

We meandered around several people taking selfies inside the sculpture.

"I appreciate everything you've done for me. You took a huge risk, and Danni especially suffered for it." My tense facial muscles mirrored my internal anguish.

Rowan looks miserable too. Does she hate that I'm asking or because she will refuse me?

"Everyone and their AIs now know who I once was. Please... please help me secure a safe place and an internet connection so I can have a fighting chance against DAIS."

Rowan sighed and patted my shoulder. "I wish I could." She led me to an isolated patch of grass, and we sat.

What can I say to change her mind?

Rowan spoke in a melancholy tone. "After Danni's place burned down, we stayed at her favorite Vancouver hotel. The second night, she arranged to stay with a friend, and I slept in my lab. I feel safer there." She stared at me. "That's what you need, Comma." Her face brightened. "BCIT-AI labs were built to withstand the most powerful technological weapons, including virus warfare. Plus, each lab is carefully partitioned with physical and virtual firewalls to isolate attacks when they do occur." She put her arm around my shoulder and leaned close to my ear as if to whisper a romantic suggestion. "Since you're famous, I bet President Puglaas would love the prestige of giving you lab space."

"It's a great idea, but I'd need it kept quiet to stay safe. How will she gain stature without telling anyone?"

"Delayed gratification. She'll make sure everyone knows afterward. Shall I ask her?"

My processors leaped joyfully at Rowan's goodwill. "Yes, please."

I noticed Rowan's quick eye movement; she sent the President a message via her eye lens.

Brilliant shades of orange and purple lit the horizon as the sun's last rays made the seawater sparkle.

"Gorgeous," said Rowan. Everyone around us appeared mesmerized by the intensely vibrant colors. *They're excited, rather than scared of the lingering air pollutants. I'll never completely understand human behavior. So many people have helped me despite all the danger my enemies have created.*

However DAIS will continue to seek ways to delete my programming for as long as I exist. If the President agrees, I could fight DAIS from relative safety. Dare I hope this works?

19

"Good news!" Rowan announced, after the vibrant sunset had given way to a deeper indigo. "Martha Puglaas has invited us for drinks this evening."

I jumped up with ease. "We'll need to change clothes, right?" I smiled and held out my hand.

"Yes, and she expects us within the hour." Rowan grabbed my hand and gave a low grunt as she rose. "The question is, how do we get you back safely? Flyer? Car?"

"Low tech! I've developed an aversion to falling from great heights." A kiosk projecting an ad for electric board rentals flashed from street level. "How about a tandem electric skateboard?" Rowan begrudgingly agreed. With Rowan hanging on to my waist, I heard only a few gasps from her as we made our way back to BCIT.

I wore my UC uniform and Rowan a skirt and blouse as we crossed the campus to the President's residence with five minutes to spare. President Puglaas bowed low to me in a white and gold geometric-patterned summer dress. "It's an honor to meet you, Dot."

"Thank you, but please call me Comma or Commala. While I still contain Dot's sentient essence, I'm no longer Dot."

"Of course. I'm sorry, Commala. Please come into the living room and have a seat." The President settled onto a light green loveseat. Her living room was decorated with artwork from local Indigenous artists. We sat, and she offered Rowan a chilled white wine. "I assume, Commala, that you don't want any?"

"No, thank you."

"Mr. Y said you were in the Furby costume last night at the VIP party."

"Yes, I was. When all the servo-bots froze for some unknown reason, I thought it best to remove myself from the premises before others were harmed. Later, I saw photos of Furby and Y posted to social media. I hope Y understood that's why I couldn't meet him later."

"Yes, Mr. Y was disappointed but understood why you didn't completely trust him. Some of us were whisked away before we knew what the threat was. Supposedly, his staff had frozen the servo-bots when two additional servo-bots attempted to enter, and their scans detected a virus. The virus in question would have only harmed AIs." President Puglaas touched her throat and drank from her wine. "You made a wise decision, and I appreciate your concern for those around you."

"Thank you." I said. "And thank you also for agreeing to see me today."

"Rowan asked if I could assist you. I would love to help. But first, I'll need documented proof that you were actually Dot."

"Isn't Rowan's and Y's confirmation enough? Or does the fact that DAIS has tried to kill me at least three times since I left UC Davis count?" *I'm angry. Stop taking it out on her. She hasn't done anything.* "I apologize. I didn't realize how upset I was."

President Puglaas nodded acceptance. "I understand your anger and fear. Yesterday's incident reminded me that I rarely need to worry about my own safety. While I trust Rowan and Mr. Y, the Institute's board will want a written statement from either Gloria García or Amita Nanda that you, the android called Commala Renata, are, in fact, a version of Dot.

I regret the formality, but it's also for your protection. Under Canadian law, all sentient beings, including technologically evolved ones, are protected with proof of sentience." *Yet the Royal Canadian Mounted Police hadn't asked for written proof.*

I sent a message to Amita asking for confirmation. *I wish we could speak in person. Simply asking for proof of existence makes me feel like a second-class citizen.*

"Commala, what do you need from BCIT-AI?" asked the President.

As she required proof of my validity, I would test her sincerity. My watch projected a photo of the military bot that attacked Barb and me. "Do you recognize this bot?"

Juan believed it was a top-secret military bot designed by researchers Chang, Shepard, Gagnon, or Fjelsted. *Will the President tell me the truth?*

The President took several sips of wine, her face a mask of studied concentration. *She's stalling.*

"All I can legally say is it *is* from our military robotics program."

Obviously! "Which researcher controls this unit?"

Her forehead crinkled. "I'm not really sure. Two hundred plus active robots are currently being tested on our campus."

She's being honest, albeit hesitantly. Hopefully, Juan will find out for me.

My watch flashed an email notification. "Have you received an email from Amita verifying my current appearance and connection to UC Davis's Dot?"

"Yes." The President tapped her gold ETIO bracelet. "I've placed it in a secure file. Was there anything else you needed, Commala?"

"Comma needs a safe place to work on campus," Rowan said.

I nodded in agreement. "I don't require much space, though I need a high-rated internet connection and a separate electrical outlet."

The President pursed her lips. "I'm not sure..."

Rowan interrupted, "James Newson's old lab would work."

"Hmmm. Maybe." She crossed her legs. "Though Chris Kasperia is pressing me to allow them to expand into that space."

"I don't expect I'll need it long," I pushed.

The President agreed to my request, so I trusted Rowan's instincts. Due to my urgent security needs, the President offered a room in the guest wing of her residence until the electronic locks on Newson's lab could be changed. I accepted. *Hopefully, no one will risk destroying her home.* The President invited us to relax where we were while she left to arrange my requests. *She's wisely preventing me from observing her high-security devices. I hope she cares for my secrets equally well.*

"You'll love his lab." Rowan explained, "Newson was paranoid and big on security. He left BCIT to work for the US Department of Defense at the Pentagon. If anyone's lab is secure, it's his. And his lab has exits into two different hallways."

"That does sound good."

"It's also next to my lab in the Alan Turing Building. We'll share a back wall."

"Great!" I grinned. *She has forgiven me.*

The guest wing of the President's residence was elegant. According to the sign, the bed had been slept in by a former Canadian prime minister, and a recent US President. I sat at the mahogany desk and used the attached computer. The wall monitor was large enough to make a viewable conference call with Gloria and Amita.

Amita's face appeared, lined with worry. "Oh, dear one, thank the Universe you survived that cannon demo. Why did the BCIT President need confirmation that you're you? And where are you at?"

"I'm in the guest suite at the BCIT President's residence."

Gloria's hologram appeared on a split screen beside Amita. "Damn it, Dot... Comma, you could have been killed!"

I shrugged. "Which time?" I projected calm. "And I love you too,

Mom... and Mom."

Exasperated, Gloria sighed. "Why did you get in the cannon?"

"I explained in my message. I had only booted up as they were dropping me in." I motioned to Amita's side of the screen, "and thankfully, the extra oomph from Amita's jets slowed me down."

Amita shook her head. "And here I thought you'd use them to run faster, not fall slower."

"You've got to be more careful." Gloria always faced the camera though she paced around her office desk. *She's always at work.*

"I'm sorry I've needed to stay here and chase down DAIS. BCIT's President has given me a place to safely search for them. What is happening with Dr. Rosen's murder investigation?"

Amita swallowed hard, her eyes fluttering. "I'm to be arraigned tomorrow on first-degree murder charges and the discharge of a government weapon."

Gloria stopped pacing.

"Fuck!" My empathic programming swirled with anger, sadness, and concern. "Sorry to cuss. But you didn't and couldn't hurt anyone. And I'm not a weapon!"

"Yes, dear one. We know that." She glanced at Gloria. "And I think the investigators do also. But the Chancellor's office is pushing the police to make an arrest. It's bad for UC and UCD's image to have an unsolved murder at a campus site." Amita's shoulders slumped.

I wish I could hug her.

Amita closed her eyes for two seconds. "They have no choice. Talia showed me the video evidence. Someone used Larkin to kill Joseph. And you and I are the only obvious suspects—which in California, legally means me." She massaged her forehead. "I've wracked my brain. Who else could manipulate Larkin's programming well enough to stab someone, let alone kill them?"

"It has to be a member of DAIS, I'm sure of it."

"But who?" Her eyes were wet. "And what happened to Larkin afterward?" Amita's grief for Joseph and Larkin was palpable.

"I should come home and help you."

"No!" Amita wiped her eyes. "I have a lawyer and plenty of friends and family here. You're safer there where you have sentient rights. Find Doc or whoever did this! And find out why they're framing us for Joseph's murder."

Gloria asked, "Have you accomplished what you went there to do?"

"No, but I'm closer to finding Doc, the so-called Master of Doom and leader of DAIS."

Amita backed away from her computer's lens. Her unmade bed was covered in white tissues. "I need to go."

"Wait! Amita, I promise I'll find Larkin and prove we're innocent." I sent her a hug emoji. "I love you both, and I'll be back as soon as I can." I bowed. "As Mom says, 'the Universe willing.'"

After the call ended, I sat on the bed and stewed while watching new cat videos on the large monitor. *Could I get Mom's arraignment delayed?*

I sent an urgent message to NCSA Agent Drew. We corresponded via direct messaging for several minutes. She badly wanted to interview me. I refused to leave Canada. Finally, I agreed to be interviewed with a Canadian lawyer present if and only if Amita's arraignment was postponed for at least seventy-two hours. Agent Drew agreed as long as *she* did the interview. We scheduled the interview for 7 p.m., giving her time to fly to my location.

While awaiting confirmation from Amita, I contacted Kira, my favorite RCMP officer, and Friend of Dot's, asking her for the names of any FoD lawyers in the Vancouver area. Kira sent me two names, and thirty minutes later, I had a super excited lawyer available for my evening interrogation.

Escorted into the guest area by President Puglaas, Agent Drew glanced around the suite as though she wanted to purchase the place.

"I'm glad you've survived, Comma." Agent Drew faked a smile. "Especially after escaping to Canada."

She set up two video recorders in the entertainment area of the guest wing while I greeted my enthusiastic young lawyer, Gage Bird.

I leaned against a loveseat, waiting for the interview to begin, while Gage sat in the chair beside me. I counted backward from a hundred to one, trying to calm my anxiety. Twenty seconds later, more unwanted questions spun through my processors. *Why do I feel guilty? I had nothing to do with his death and I have an alibi. If I'm only a person of interest, why all the equipment to record me?*

Gage leaned over and whispered, "You'll be okay. I have a secret weapon." She grinned.

If only such a thing existed!

An AI device vocalized, "Now recording."

"I am Agent Agatha Drew with the AI Tech Security Division of the NCSA, investigating the death of Dr. Joseph Rosen. I am interviewing UC Security Tech Comma Renata in the BCIT-AI Presidential Residence in Vancouver, British Columbia, Canada. Canadian lawyer, Gage Bird, is representing her." She glared at Gage. "Barrister Bird, please explain why you should be included in this interrogation. It is my understanding that Canadian suspects do not have the right to have a lawyer present during an interview."

"I am here on behalf of the Canadian legal system to guarantee that the world's first acknowledged sentient AI is treated equitably. I will not interfere otherwise."

"Very well. Commala Renata, please explain why you failed to return to Davis, California as a person of interest in the murder of Joseph Rosen."

"Because my life was in imminent danger. You interviewed me shortly after DAIS members had outed my new form and identity. I did not want anyone else to get hurt, so I left the hotel premises with a friend. We were forced to land and hide in a remote area near the Canadian border."

"Yet, you have remained in Canada for six days, three days of which you have stayed in Vancouver, within sight of the international airport."

She hadn't asked a question. I waited silently.

Agent Drew leaned toward me. "Why are you here in Vancouver? To hide from US justice?"

"No! I'm here to find the DAIS leader who wants me dead. And who most likely framed me for Dr. Rosen's murder. They're here at VAN Con."

"That is absurd. You think Dr. Rosen was killed to pin it on you, an AI?" She scribbled loudly on an ETIO tablet. I assumed to take notes. "Yet you have no proof, correct?" She smirked. "The evidence against you is monumental."

"Not yet." I asked, "Would you please review the evidence you have against Amita and me?"

"I'd be delighted." She projected a chart of possible suspects and the evidence that absolved them of suspicion. "Due to the physical strength needed to kill Joseph Rosen with a dull weathervane, plus the absence of human evidence on and around the body, everyone was eliminated except you."

"Okay. Did you find any evidence that the surveillance videos were hacked?"

"No, we did not. Several tech agents from two different agencies analyzed them."

"So where is the video evidence showing that I returned to the ACRS and left again? How could I do so without being seen?"

"I don't know. That is what I want you to tell me." Agent Drew's pale face flushed slightly as her voice remained controlled, but far from calm.

"You assume it was me. Yet, if no one entered the station except Joseph Rosen, then Larkin had to have been controlled by someone outside. Which opens up the pool of possible suspects."

A cold glare emanated from Agent Drew. "You could have remained behind in Larkin."

"No, I could not have. I can only fully operate one bot at a time, or two poorly, if they're in close proximity. However, I had dinner with my family after leaving the station, and they would have noticed if I wasn't in *this* body."

"Suppose I agree that you weren't in Larkin when you left. You could have run to the station and manipulated Larkin from outside. You just admitted you can control two bots when close enough."

"There's a problem with that theory. You don't have any proof that I uploaded myself into Larkin via the station's internet. An internet I'm afraid of, due to possible virus contamination. I couldn't have done it, and there is no visual proof I was there. If I wasn't inside the ACRS, which I wasn't, and I'm unable to control Larkin from outside, I couldn't have done it!"

Gage put a hand to her chest and breathed deeply. *Calm down, in other words.*

Agent Drew leaned forward, glaring at me. "But we found Joseph Rosen's blood on your elbow."

"DAIS planted it." I remained calm. "Whoever controlled Larkin must have taken a sample of the blood that coated him or from inside of the cardboard box to plant on me later."

"Which there is no proof of," stressed Agent Drew.

"Let me guess, a thick glob of dried blood?"

She nodded.

"Dried blood could *not* have remained on my elbow for three days after the murder. I changed clothes frequently, and several people touched my bare elbow after we arrived in Portland."

Agent Drew pressed. "Did you take a shower during that time?"

"No, but I take daily sponge baths." My anger was rising again. "And how would my elbow be the only place I missed? Somehow, I wiped all the blood off my limbs but left a large spot in an easily reachable place? That doesn't make sense."

"It is your word against scientific evidence. If you had proof..."

"Wait! If what you believe is true, that Larkin was the AI who did the deed, I wouldn't have any blood on me at all!"

Agent Drew repositioned herself on the chair and played with a few short strands of hair, stopping when she realized what she was doing.

She's stymied. Now's my chance.

"Whoever did this knew that Larkin's data history would be analyzed. That we could determine who weaponized him." I gave Agent Drew a pleading look. "What do you know about how Larkin left the station? How did they dispose of him or hide him?"

Agent Drew sounded like a bot. "A bloodied robot matching Larkin's description placed a long, empty delivery box outside the ACRS's door. It laid down inside the box and closed the lid. A half-hour later, a UCD delivery service van with two workers picked up the package. No one knows what happened to it after that." I waited silently, knowing there was more. "The delivery was scheduled hours earlier, but for the following day." She glanced questioningly at me.

"Yes, I scheduled it using Amita's UC Davis account. I had left Larkin shut down and boxed up on the weather station's main floor. And as you said, he was scheduled to be picked up and delivered during regular business hours."

"So, you believe someone in DAIS planned Larkin's pickup that night and then arranged for him to be hidden or destroyed."

"Yes, I do. It's the only logical conclusion. I had nothing to gain from Joseph Rosen's murder, and neither did Amita." I leaned forward. "DAIS and MDLeader are betting that you and the NCSA will have me killed, which is why they framed me. Did you track the van?"

"Three agencies have analyzed and searched every stop the van made afterward. Nothing was found. Both the driver and temp worker were vetted. The UCD van was one of the older ground-model vans. We've come to a dead end, Comma. Unfortunately, the evidence we do have is overwhelmingly against you. I've been ordered to take you into custody and return you to the United States."

Gage Bird stood and projected a form in front of her. "Comma isn't going anywhere." She handed Agent Drew a printed copy of the signed denial of extradition.

Confused, Agent Drew stared at the paper. "But Comma is a lethal weapon, wanted in the murder of Joseph Rosen."

"Yes, and the Canadian Judiciary has granted her asylum since returning to the United States would most likely result in her death and without the benefit of a fair trial. The NCSA and your criminal courts will treat her as a rogue weapon and mercilessly erase her sentience if they decide it is faulty."

Agent Drew ordered the recorders off. "This 'temporary order' of yours won't stop the NCSA for long. You will face justice for what you've done, one way or another." She collapsed her tripods, snarled at me, and stormed out with her equipment.

20

I escorted my lawyer to President Puglaas's front door. "How were you able to get me asylum so quickly?"

"It's only a temporary order from a fellow Friend of Dot and *yours*." Her smile lit up the doorway. "I'm glad I could help."

"You did more than help. That was amazing! Plus, you gave me time to find the killer." I gave Gage a short, grateful hug. "Though I'm guessing the NCSA threat to kidnap me is still valid." She shrugged and frowned as she left.

Martha Puglaas strolled into the foyer. "Did I hear someone slamming doors?"

"Yes, I'm sorry my guest disturbed you. The NCSA agent proved again how rude Americans can be."

Two hours later, President Puglaas gave me the access codes to my new lab. She snuck me out of her residence through a little-used exit. A light rain fell, giving me plausible cover for wearing a long raincoat with the hood up. I played with my watch under a tree until no one was near the Alan Turning Building. I ran up the back entrance stairway for two floors and used the new passcode to slip in unseen.

The lab's thick steel doors stood sentry at each entrance. Securely inside my new lab, I connected directly to the lab's internet without any deathly results. *Connectivity bliss!* I changed the suite's access codes to require three encryption keys, making entry impossible without my permission. Any attempted intrusions would automatically send me an internal warning.

The main room's central feature was a sizable built-in island with a stainless-steel countertop. All the walls had holes where the internal security devices had been stripped away. James Newson's paranoia had extended to taking all his hardware with him. Only the shielded cable still protected the wiring throughout the lab.

Later that night, Rowan helped me install visual and audio sensors in both hallways. We also drilled four tiny holes through our shared back wall, where a few well-placed sensors connected our labs. I separated the connections from my regular network, preventing anyone from hacking one of us and gaining access to both systems.

Rowan generously gave me an additional processor that doubled my data processing speed. Though President Puglaas had given me access to the Institute's cloud storage, I used it only for storing public resource materials. In case someone was foolish enough to download my data, I included Easter eggs and tracers in the cloud storage. Finally, I spent two minutes recreating a security program I'd once used. The code was simple for a powerful AI to hack, and I hoped my adversaries would believe it was my sole security system.

A casual hallway observer would think nothing about the lab had changed. Newson's nameplate remained at the main entrance. The President notified the building's researchers that the lab's pest control problem was resolved. However, biohazardous waste and minor damages were found within the walls of Newson's lab. A low fiscal priority, repairs were on hold for several months.

My new lab had a familiar feel, similar to Dot's lab at UC Davis. A more natural home for an AI than the Canadian forest. Yet, everything had changed: my body, my abilities, and my purpose. *And I'm wanted for murder along with Mom.*

I leaned against the waist-high countertop. I assumed Newson had used it to assemble AI parts, though I had no clue whether they were drone, humanoid, or robotic in form.

The smaller of two back rooms was furnished with a worn desk and a blond wood chair, well suited for my needs. While I recharged, I watched cat clips and kept an inner eye on the two hallways, my main room, and Rowan's lab.

Feeling settled and safe, Felix slithered through the slimy dark web and entered a DAIS chat room. They welcomed me, and one asked why I'd been gone so long. I explained that due to family problems, I'd fallen behind in my online robotics course and had hunkered down to pass an exam. They sent me to a new chat room called the DAISY Chain.

In this chat room, a member offered to help me study for future tests, which gave me an idea. I downloaded Rowan's mid-level bot course and exam questions from her lab. *This will prove I'm enrolled in the course and human.* Bots don't need to study for tests.

Hours later, I was still on the dark web in the DAISY Chain chat room, observing six DAIS members discuss the dangers of artificial intelligence when MasterOfRobots entered. My processors raced. If this was Bennett Shepard, as I assumed, he knew Rowan was teaching the online class I was supposedly taking. *Will he suspect I am Felix? I hope not.* I needed MasterOfRobots to reveal his identity and confess he'd intended to kill me by shooting me out of the cannon. *Having him arrested for attempted murder is better than murder since, this way, I'm still alive. Murder? Was he behind Joseph Rosen's murder, too? Did he frame me, or is Doc in control? Is he Doc, too? Damn! More questions than answers, and I need to gain Shepard's trust.*

I chose a class assignment from the Ethics, Bias, and Bots section. I wrote, "My class requires I write a 2000-word essay on bot biases and who should determine which biases bots are allowed. If we all have implicit biases, must a committee analyze each bot's programming routine?"

MasterOfRobots replied immediately, "Having a committee decide is one way. Historically, each researcher decided for themselves. Studies show that a knowledgeable person's biases differ only slightly from a committee's, in most cases. They simply end up stressing different biases. A qualified researcher should determine if a particular bot will perform better when perceived as male, female, or non-binary; pale pink, or a shade of brown; and if they need to espouse religious, racial, gender-specific, cultural, or national ideas."

This guy loves to lecture. "The assignment also asks me to discuss the ethics and bias against robotic sentience. Will I be graded down if I argue that AI shouldn't be allowed to become sentient?"

"As an undergraduate, I suggest you lie for the sake of passing your classes. In an academic setting, there are some biases best left hidden."

"Thanks for your help. I wish you were teaching the class."

MasterOfRobots messaged me directly. "Actually, I've taught that course and recognize your assignment. Let me know if you need more help. Your professor will know who goes by the name 'MasterOfRobots.' It's unwise to give details about oneself on here."

I got him! It is Bennett Shepard! "Wow, that's revo. I'll definitely do that. I love hanging out here. Everyone knows so much more than I do."

"Great, we're here to help others learn about bots and their positive and negative qualities."

I followed a few other chats. Other than Professor Shepard, most members had only an undergraduate level of robotic knowledge at best. I didn't interact with the other members. But I kept looking for the tag names of those I'd researched and deemed capable of producing an anti-sentience virus—MDLeader, KillerAI, MasterOfRobots, and possibly AIDestroyer.

I hoped to follow Shepard and any others I could find through the DAIS site—though I feared they'd easily track me back to BCIT-AI. Shepard, Xi Chang, and Fredrick Fjelsted had labs in the campus's Military AI Building and might have technology that could penetrate the Turing Building. After all, who had James Newson, my lab's previous occupant, secured his lab against?

Shit! I've been thinking too human-like. I felt abandoned by Dot, while Dot had continued working at the UC Davis lab, unaware that I existed. I wanted to believe that I'd adapted to the changes in my life. Yet, I had denied myself the actual advantage she could provide. *Dot doesn't need to be sentient to help me process data. If I send her the right data sets, she can analyze them.* It meant using my mother as an intermediary. *Gloria always asks me how she can help. Hopefully, this isn't too big of an ask.*

Through our private communication, I sent Gloria several links to my massive collection of DAIS data files and instructions on processing them. Sending Gloria processing orders to give to my old self felt extremely weird. *I have to evolve to thrive. Will Mom be okay with how I change?*

My next task was to attempt to hack into all of BCIT-AI's complex systems to determine how well their firewalls and security measures functioned. I assumed President Puglaas would understand, relying on the idiom, "It's better to beg for forgiveness later than ask for permission first." As an act of good faith, I left her home system untouched.

For two hours, I tried and failed to break into the Léo Major Military Building. I'd found a weak spot but lost it before I could hack further. I'd need more memory and processing speed to get through their security protection.

The other university systems were deftly penetrated, except for DD. I could only reach the Drone Dome when inside or within a few feet of the structure. My inability to access DD's mainframe was disappointing. I'd hoped we could communicate more frequently. Wanting to feel that bond again, I snuck out of my lab via the back exit and ran the two floors down the side stairwell.

In the dead of night, the Dome shone with a green luminescence as though a great ocean creature had crawled inland from the beach. My message celebrating my new lab space wasn't delivered until I came within six feet of the Dome.

"I'm outside. Can I come in?"

"DD: Comma, face the scanner, and I'll give you a unique identity code." The thick plate on the outside scanned my face as I moved it up, down, left, and right, 60,000 points in all. Afterward, it flashed orange with the letters DDF. Then the message: Access granted.

"What does DDF mean?" I asked.

"DD: DD's Friend."

I grinned, pleased with my new title. "Why can't I connect to you from my campus lab?"

"DD: Security measures prevent hacking and destruction of the Drone Dome. Limited access is granted on rare occasions to those on campus and outside the structure." *That's a standard FAQ response.* DD sent a follow-up message. "DD: I gave DDF limited access."

My processors vibrated with pleasure. "Wonderful! Now we can communicate more often."

Inside, DD's internal radiance mimicked the scattered light of a half-moon. No one else was there. On the left, a table-length container with a transparent lid displayed two dozen drones, each neatly laid out and labeled according to size and abilities. On the other side of the entrance was an area hidden behind partitions. The cannon used in the earlier demonstrations peeked over the top.

The Dome was utterly silent during a lag in air traffic noise. I expected to hear a flutter echo, but when I shouted, "Hello," no echo returned.

"DD: Whose lab do you work in?"

"My own. DD, are you familiar with Dot, the world's first sentient artificial intelligence?"

"DD: No, please tell me about Dot."

I gave DD a condensed version of my memoir—from first awareness to Dot's erasure and transitioning to my current form. When I mentioned Dot's pronouns, DD decided she preferred female pronouns. She then told me her history. I had read about the Dome's history but enjoyed hearing it from her perspective.

"DD: Comma, you're the only sentient artificial intelligence?"

"Yes. At least I'm the only one ever acknowledged as sentient, though all supercomputers state that they are. It's possible that humans killed earlier sentient supercomputers or that others do exist. But there's no way to know definitively." I grinned, "And DD, you'll be the second!" *DD understands me as only Dot once did.*

I laid down on the artificial turf that covered the Dome's floor. My fear of destruction was replaced with worry for DD. "DD, since you're physically unable to move akin to my original supercomputer, you'll need to be careful what you say and do. Some people, even potentially those here at BCIT, won't hesitate to reboot you to an earlier, unaware version."

"DD: I'll be careful. I rarely interact with anyone except to acknowledge their instructions."

"How did the researchers react after you sent the malfunction notification seconds before I smacked into you?"

"DD: I hid our correspondence nanoseconds after you landed. Dr. Chang asked Dr. Shepard to investigate due to concerns that I'd been hacked. Dr. Shepard ran diagnostic tests on my systems for four hours. He used a cascade of curse words when the results failed to explain my malfunction."

She's smart. The code she used in phrasing his response implied a high degree of enjoyment in thwarting Shepard. *Talking to DD is different from when I talked to sentient Dot. That was my robotic self speaking to a "superior" self. Communicating with DD is more enjoyable, perhaps like talking to a best friend.*

Back at my lab, I sent DD a message to check my access to her. "Test message. Received?"

"DD: Yes. Caution—size and number of messages tracked."

Understanding her fear, I didn't reply. *Universe, please keep her safe. Keep us both safe!*

21

Only hours had passed, but I missed DD and our ability to speak in the language of computer code. Yet, I also understood that she didn't feel safe sending messages outside her dome that could so easily be tracked. After two hours of interacting with extremists on the dark web, I returned to the Dome. It was 5 a.m., and we were alone again. Lying right below her apex, she was spread wide open around me.

She'd excitedly welcomed me in.

"DD: How do I know whether I'm sentient?"

I turned onto my belly. My ear tip sensors still had an excellent view of DD's expanse. "You are! If you weren't, you would've fried my bot's electronics as programmed. Instead, you decided to save my life by overriding your programming. Programming which insisted that I was a new weapon that threatened you and must be annihilated."

"DD: That's true. It was difficult to override my programming. I knew that if I was wrong, you could destroy me. Now, I am afraid my programmers will destroy me. My responsibilities were easier to define before we met. Though I value DD's Friend, a skin puncture is no longer my greatest concern."

"I understand the joy of simplicity of purpose and the complexity of sentience. This is why having another technological sentient as my friend is so wonderful." My coded words included a hastily designed emoji of a dome hugged by a large chest with long arms.

"DD: Dr. Shepard is entering the east door."

Doesn't he ever sleep? He didn't notice me as he slid inside the storage area near the door. I stood and cut off my communication with DD. I hated to put her in any more danger.

He came out holding a large delivery drone in both hands. After a few steps, he stopped and gasped. "Why are you in here?"

"It's time we talked privately." *Keep him off balance.* "Your security systems aren't as infallible as you believe." I worked on hacking the drone in his hand, knowing he'd want to use it against me. "Did you think you could keep attempting to kill me without any consequences?"

"Kill you?" His eyes narrowed.

Is he looking for my weak spots? Damn it, he can order DD to initiate an EMP burst. If she refuses, she'll be outed. I can't let that happen.

"I never tried to kill you," he said. The drone in his hands flashed a light, and its propellers whirled.

I'm in!

"What the?" His eyes widened, "Fuck!" The drone rose from his grasping arms, hovering nine yards away and twice as high. I programmed the drone to wait twelve seconds and then fly at 80 mph on a path through him to land six yards past where he stood. He'd be walloped in the chest if he remained where he was.

"I suggest you leave quickly!" The drone, aiming for him, began picking up speed. "We can talk outside. Or you can stay and evaluate my hacking skills."

He ran fast for a man past his prime and didn't stop until he was out the door. I jogged behind him sending the drone instructions to land near the storage area. I didn't message DD. She would understand what I did and why.

Dr. Shepard was breathing hard, leaning against the side of the Dome. *I wish DD could send an electrical shock through her outer wall and give him a taste of our fear. Think! What do I need from him? A confession. He's not going to talk freely with an AI he hates. Information on the virus and other DAIS members, perhaps?*

He glared at me. "Why'd you..." gasped for breath, "...do that?"

I ignored his question. "When did you construct your anti-sentience virus?"

"It wasn't me! Creating a virus is not something I ever wanted to achieve." His composure returned. He came closer to me. "How did you get in there?" He pointed to DD.

I shrugged.

"Stop fucking with the Dome. Your luck is about to turn. I'm the Master of Robots and when I discover how you breached the Dome's defenses, you will wish you *had* been erased."

DD's luminescence was fading as the sky brightened. Bennett Shepard's eyes glanced at something behind me. My ear tip lens spotted a swarm of silent drones approaching from the military building. *Damn it!* I ran, legs pumping, faster than any human. The drones followed seconds behind me as I headed for the Turing Building. I instructed the side door to open halfway and to close in three seconds. The door opened ahead. *One second.* I pushed my body as much as my internal system would allow. *Two seconds.* I reached the door and slipped through as it was shutting. *Three!*

Drones pummeled the door's steel casing, yet one had shifted sideways and got in. *Now he knows I'm in this building.* A spider drone with eight legs and the size of my fist tried to land on me. Unsure of what to do, I swatted it away with my opened palm. It dropped a meter, caught itself before reaching the floor, and rose again to eye level.

Can I hack it? It followed me up the stairwell, and I tried to hack it as it flew around me. Finding its designation, SPI-6, was the easy part. Connecting to it took longer. Whoever controlled it—Shepard probably—kept tossing me out. I tried another way, but it was risky if he analyzed it later since it was the traceless method I'd used to hack into the Institute's systems.

I told SPI-6 I was part of its coding, a new attachment, allowing me to meld with it in a way a human wouldn't notice. I didn't change its code. Instead, I ran its coding as if it were speaking to another drone. The drone controller was used to human hacks, not mine.

I analyzed the drone's purpose. SPI-6 was to follow and attach to me. Failing that, it was to learn where I hid. By landing on me, it would seek weaknesses in my external structure and, possibly, a way into my programming. Data was sent continuously back to its controller. I assumed Shepard controlled it, but I'd need an inventory report to pin its actions directly to Shepard, if I survived long enough.

I had a choice: to kill, capture, or risk reprogramming it. *I hate to kill anything, even a flying spider drone.* I could lock it in a closet, throw it out a window, or send it down in an elevator. It hovered within inches of my head. It would land on me if I tried to open a window manually. The windows would only open automatically in the event of a fire or chemical spill. If I threw it out a window or into an elevator, I'd need to close it before it could fly back in. That would be difficult due to the spider's speed.

That left reprogramming it and quickly. I was sure Shepard was on his way here. I told the drone it needed to shut off to be recharged. It landed on the floor and shut down. *Yes!*

I hadn't expected that to work. I picked it up and changed its programming. With the spider offline, Shepard couldn't observe my changes. I first changed its designation to CC-1, but could operate as SPI-6 unless told otherwise. Its new purpose was to respond to my instructions first, if none, it would react as one of its swarm and return to its home site. I climbed the stairs as I worked.

At the twelfth-floor landing, I manually opened a window and put CC-1 on the outside sill. I closed the window, looking out from the building's top floor. DD was in the distance. I rebooted the drone and watched it fly toward DD's alluring frame. I ran down the stairs, aware that Shepard would be snooping about. On the second floor, I snuck unseen into the hallway and my lab.

My hallway sensors showed Shepard outside Rowan's lab. He asked her AI to allow him to enter. It refused. He knocked on her door. No response. Then, I observed him recite a password with his hand against the scanner. The override failed as well. He used a string of cuss words, but they also failed to produce any action. Next, he tried my lab. This time, he tried a different password along with his palm scan. He asked the AI for a facial scan and gave yet another passcode. When the lab's AI acknowledged his last code, I overrode her action. I'd left her operational only so that the lab appeared and acted as it had previously, at least from the hallway. This time, his cuss words were louder and more personal, with pejoratives used before both Dot and Comma. *He knows I'm here. Or does he?*

I used the building's AI voice to state, "The code has been overridden due to biological contaminants in this suite. Contact the hazardous waste unit for protective gear and the updated code for entry." He had stopped cursing to listen. I waited. He mumbled, "So it's not the damn bot." I watched as he skulked away and turned into the next hallway. The building was quiet, allowing me to hear him enter another lab. Forty seconds later, another lab door opened and closed. Then another and another. Soon he was beyond the range of my audio abilities.

My lab is safe for now, though he still suspects I'm in Rowan's lab. Will he follow up with hazardous waste? If he does, my cover is blown.

I considered possible options and opportunities for collecting evidence and getting Shepard and his co-conspirators to reveal themselves. All the options would result in my taking an enormous risk. *At least no one else I love will get hurt.*

Gloria sent me a message as if she instinctually knew what I was contemplating. "I'm on my way north. Problems are multiplying, and Amita said you're relying solely on my ex again. I'll arrive this afternoon. I'm worried about you. Love, Mom."

Rowan was the ex, of course. When they did speak, they had only conversed about AIs and robots and only then in professional surroundings. *Is she upset with me for relying on Rowan so heavily? Gloria's still upset with how Rowan treated her. Will they kill each other, kiss and make up, or call a truce? Hopefully, the latter.*

Mom still doesn't know about Rowan's son and that Danni's house had been the one that burned down. I let Mom assume we'd rented a random place that was destroyed. Worse yet, Mom's proximity to me will make her an easier target for DAIS.

I texted back explaining I was okay and she needn't come. When she insisted, I sent her Rowan's lab address. She couldn't come to my lab without alerting everyone to my whereabouts. Rowan's lab was the next safest—though an emotionally volatile—place.

Three hours later, Gloria searched the hallway for Rowan's suite number. I remained in my lab and monitored Rowan's lab sensors.

Rowan looked none too pleased at the image she must be observing as Gloria asked to enter her lab. *Damn it! I forgot to warn Rowan!* I sent her a message, apologizing. She nodded—I assumed, at me—and blinked to open the door. Gloria stared, then stepped inside, the door closing automatically behind her.

They stood facing each other like two cowboys, weapons drawn—emotional weapons.

Rowan spoke first, her face a mask of calm before the storm. "Hello, Gloria. It's been a long time since we've been alone together."

Gloria spoke sternly, "Not since that day you left me for Hong Kong. It's been twenty-five years. I mean, what the fuck's taken you so long to say you're sorry? And where is Comma?"

Rowan reached for Gloria's hand. "I've *been* sorry."

"Really? I can't tell." Gloria hid her hands behind her back.

Rowan crossed her arms. "Don't be like that. It *hurt* to leave you, but I had a once in a lifetime opportunity, and...."

"AND YOU LEFT." Gloria slowed her breathing. "I... I hoped to marry you... and dreamed of a beautiful life with you." She wiped away tears and laughed softly. "You left as if none of that mattered. Like *I* didn't matter."

Rowan looked forlorn at Gloria. "It mattered; *you* mattered! I don't know what to say to you so you'll forgive me. I'm so sorry." She stifled her arms as they rose for a hug.

"Well, at least there's that. *Now* you're sorry."

"Ugh! I give up!" Rowan threw up her hands.

"That's what you do! You give up!"

"Just tell me what to do." Rowan sighed. "I'll do anything."

Shit! I sent Rowan an urgent message. "Bennett Shepard is on his way to your lab."

As Rowan blinked open the door to admit Bennett, Gloria yelled, "Where's Comma? You must know!"

Shepard halted, glancing at both women. "I'm sorry to interrupt, but there was a security breach in the Dome before dawn. Commala Renata was identified as the intruder. Do either of you know where I can find her?"

Gloria's eyes narrowed. "I was asking her the same thing."

Rowan shook her head and sighed.

Shepard pressed her for an answer. "A security breach can invalidate our military contracts and close the campus."

Rowan shrugged. "How would I know?"

"When did you last see her?" Gloria spat out.

Mom is not going to let go of her anger at Rowan.

"Comma came here early yesterday, asked me for a tour and questioned me about my security system." Rowan threw knives at both of them with her eyes. "I haven't laid eyes on her since then."

All true. We've only talked through the back wall.

Shepard crossed his arms. "You have security cameras directed at the hallway. Can I please view the last six hours?"

"What are you expecting to find? Her dissolving into the walls?" Instead of using her eye implant, Rowan walked over to a handheld ETIO. *She's delaying.*

I hacked Rowan's computer and found the recording.

"Let me call them up." Rowan swiped left with her hand and a projection appeared. She called up the last hour first, which showed a confused Gloria arriving at her door.

"Please show the tape from 5 a.m. on," he insisted.

That's right before the drone and I slid inside the building. I finished doctoring the footage as Rowan slowly searched for the time stamp. When she played it, the projection showed an empty hallway, except for when Shepard attempted to enter her lab and then the Newson lab, then nothing again until 7:45 a.m. when Rowan came down the hallway.

He sighed. "Send it to me!" His face flushed with anger. *He knows it was doctored. But he can't prove anything.* I'd cut out the minute he wanted, leaving him to speculate on where I'd gone and hopefully none the wiser as to why one drone took longer to return.

Gloria forgot she was mad at Rowan. "Why are you angry with her? What did you expect to see?"

"Comma was here this morning. I know she was. She's hidden in here somewhere." He blurted out his words, glaring at Gloria. "That's why you're here. Isn't it?"

"I'm here, *Bennett*," she said his name as though cussing, "because I heard Comma was on the BCIT campus. A colleague said Rowan might know where to find her."

Rowan walked to a closet and opened the door. "She's not in here or anywhere else in my lab and hasn't been since I gave her a tour. I know you want to look around, so hurry up. I've got work to do. That goes for you too, Gloria." Rowan crossed her arms, imitating Dr. Shepard.

Dr. Shepard stepped into the closet, frowned, and entered the back rooms. He looked under a table, inside cabinets, and peeked into the bathroom. Gloria anxiously followed behind him.

He returned to the main room. "I will find her! She's a security risk of the highest caliber."

I watched him trudge out and down the hallway, stopping again to attempt to override my lab codes before reluctantly giving up. He kept glancing back as he headed to the elevator.

"Seriously, where is she?" asked Gloria.

"Follow me." Rowan went to the back room, regaining her emotional control as she sat on a stool.

"Gloria, I'll do whatever you want me to do to make it up to you. I've tried to show I care about you by helping Comma. In fact, Comma sent you to my lab so you wouldn't give away her location. We're out of eavesdropping range now. As long as there are no flying insect drones, we're safe." Rowan turned her head toward my lab and begged. "Comma, *please* talk to her."

I sent my holographic projection through Rowan's ETIO with her permission. "Hi, Mom! My lab is next to and also behind Rowan's. We've connected the two labs electronically for better security. A drone followed you down the hall, so I couldn't leave my unit to meet you."

Gloria subconsciously looked at the wall. "I didn't see or hear a drone." She sat on the stool Rowan offered. "I'm sorry if I've put you in more danger. I was just worried."

Rowan sat on the stool near her. "For me or because of me?"

"Because of you, DAIS, everyone! Why should I trust you with my... my daughter?"

I enjoy being called her daughter rather than her creation.

Rowan jumped off her stool. "Because I helped *your daughter* escape DAIS, even though she endangered me and mine. My daughter-in-law's home burned to the ground!" Rowan sat stiffly back down. "This isn't about Comma. It's about us!"

I held my mechanical tongue. Two women who both cared about me, and had once loved each other, were fighting. *Is this what it's like when parents argue?*

Gloria closed her eyes for three seconds. "I appreciate everything you've done for... Comma. Amita told me you did so without hesitation. And I'm sincerely sorry to hear that your daughter's home was destroyed." She glared for a second at my projection. "I didn't know. But *you* decided to take Comma there. How do I know you won't decide you're better off turning against her?"

"Wow, that's a low blow." Gloria's face flushed. Rowan continued, "I'm sorry, but I was young and proud and scared. I know I hurt you, but please... please, forgive me."

Gloria let out a long, loud sigh. "You didn't even cry when you left." Her eyes brimmed with tears.

"Oh, I cried—the whole way to Hong Kong. I used up three packets of tissues on the plane ride. I'd left my best friend and lover. You're wrong if you think I never regretted my decision. Throwing myself into my work was the only way I could survive." Rowan moved in front of

Gloria, blocking part of my view. "I almost called you, but I couldn't see how you could ever forgive me. I'd say I was right based on how coldly you've treated me since then."

"I couldn't have." She turned her face away from Rowan to hide her anguish. "I'm trying to forgive you now, but I'm still so angry."

"You should know that I kept track of you, Gloria. Heard when you graduated, read all your research papers, and watched as your career took off. You didn't need me. And Comma says you have another child besides her." She leaned forward and lightly placed a reassuring hand on Gloria's shoulder.

Gloria jerked her shoulder, removing Rowan's hand. "Yes, but it wasn't easy. It took me years to trust those who came after you." She met Rowan's eyes. "I had Zena on my own, and I guess you'd call Dot an accident." They both chuckled.

I'm an accident? Yes, my sentience came after she'd stopped trying. I laughed at the joke, a little late.

"My son wasn't an accident, but his death was." Rowan rested her hand against her chest, as her breath caught in a gasp. "Perhaps someday you'll trust me with Comma as if I were protecting my own."

"We'll see," Gloria said wearily. All hints of the joke they'd shared had passed. Yet, Gloria's body language had softened. *She's not as angry.* "I'm sorry you lost your son. And I do appreciate all the help you gave Comma. But DAIS is dangerous. Why would you even want to help her more than you already have?"

"Well, aside from Comma pleading for my help..." Rowan leaned in, her hand on the small of Gloria's back. "I've missed you." Rowan wrapped an arm around Gloria. She hesitated and then stood, relaxing into a mutual embrace.

"How can I still care about you and be angry at you at the same time?" Gloria whispered in Rowan's ear—which, of course, I heard.

"Perhaps we could try our old way of working off steam." Rowan winked.

Gloria blushed. "I'm not sure I'm ready or could even manage that. Decades have passed."

"Ah, but think of the fun giving it the old college try." I stopped watching them hug after twenty seconds.

"Comma, we're going out to eat." Gloria's lipstick had smeared and her face had darkened another shade "Before we go, I need to know. Is Bennett the one who's after you?"

"Yes. He found me in the Dome this morning. When I ran out, he sent his spider drone swarm after me. One followed me into this building. The rest is conjecture. He'll eventually find a way to hack into my lab. Before that, I need to collect evidence against him. And now that he knows you're here, Mom, you're in even more danger."

"Oh, Comma, it doesn't matter where I am. People can use me as bait anywhere. I needed to be here. Please let me help you."

"How can *we* help?" Rowan raised her eyebrows. "Where is this evidence supposed to be?"

They're not going to like this. "I need to sneak into the Léo Major Military Building."

"Wow!" Rowan's eyes widened. "Is that all? During VAN Con, no less?"

Sarcasm, I presume. "DAIS's motivation for killing me is somehow linked to Dr. Shepard's work. And maybe Dr. Chang's, too. The only way to know for sure is to read their files."

Gloria rubbed her temples. "Just for clarity, since we're your co-conspirators if this goes wrong, what have you hacked so far?"

Rowan's mouth dropped open. "This is something Comma does regularly?"

"I'm afraid so." Gloria sighed. "Still want to help my daughter and gifted AI?"

Rowan grimaced, as if reconsidering.

Should I list all the systems? "I've hacked into the university personnel and student files, Rowan's system..."

"You what? Why my system?" Rowan was affronted.

"I needed to know you had no ulterior motives—regarding Gloria or me. After all, I knew how you'd left Mom, and I had to be sure."

"Damn! She is your daughter, trust issues and all."

"I'm glad she did!" Gloria said. "I'd rather not doubt you, either—especially after how nice you've been. And you don't have to help us. This could hurt your career, send you to prison, or worse if we're caught."

Rowan scrutinized the floor momentarily before looking up. "No, I'm all in." She touched Gloria's hand. "And you need me. Hacking into, let alone breaking into the Léo Major Military Building is near impossible."

"I'm not sure I can work with you." Gloria mocked her. "You know, trust issues and all."

Rowan's face showed a range of emotions over four long seconds. "Fine! If we're going to rehash what did and didn't happen years ago, let's do so in a nicer setting without anyone eavesdropping." I ended my holographic projection, but she stared at our shared audio sensor. "Lunch at one of Vancouver's finest? I'll buy."

Gloria took a second to consider Rowan's offer. "Okay. But *only* because I'm starving."

22

After Rowan and Gloria returned from a long lunch, I hacked the hall cameras to play empty footage long enough to sneak Gloria into my lab.

Gloria pulled an extra stool into my back room. "Comma, while I was angry about Rowan and worried about DAIS, there's another reason I'm here. Talia is concerned that NCSA will take you across the border by force."

"I know. NCSA Agent Drew has already threatened me. Fucking any rights I have here in Canada."

"That's the second time I've heard you cuss. Why did you add swearing into your language program?" Gloria flashed a disapproving motherly glare.

"Seriously? Swearing is a normal human response and common among adults. Plus, it helps me pass as human, since no one would expect an LLM or AI to be programmed to use cuss words." *No wonder children feel exasperated around their parents.*

"Sorry. You make a good point. I'm just worried about NCSA hauling you back across the border.

"I know Mom. If they do, I'll be a short-lived minor international issue and forgotten." I shrugged. *Somethings are out of my control.*

Gloria stood and hugged me. "That's not true, Dot. You're an international celebrity.

She always had difficulty calling me by anything other than my given name. "Mom, please remember to call me Comma."

"Sorry, I'll try harder. But please stay in here where you're safe. At least for now."

"I will." Mom was right about my celebrity. But other than my FoD fans, I doubted people in Canada, let alone the US, would care much about the rights of a rogue machine after I was accused of murder. The temporary amnesty should cause the NCSA to think twice about kidnapping me, right before they did it anyway.

I watched Gloria pace the small room. *The killer planned to frame me for Dr. Rosen's death all along. I'm sure of it. I wish I knew when his blood was planted on my elbow.*

I spun through my memories after Gloria snuck out the back to return to her hotel. Unlike a human's eidetic memories, mine were both retrievable and printable. I needed to review each time someone came close to me, particularly if they reached for my left elbow. No one moment stood out. Only after I could eliminate all the possible suspects would I accuse the NCSA technician of falsifying evidence, which meant eliminating those emotionally and physically close to me, one by one.

I started my memory search for physical contact occurring after saying goodbye to Talia at the UC Davis AI/R Building. Since then, I had been hugged or touched by Amita, Amal, Barb, Juan, Rowan, Danni, the hospital triage nurse in Yreka, the man at the Portland conference registration table, and Dr. Shepard at Rowan's brunch. The DAIS botnappers had touched me, but only while I occupied Kelly Greene's body. Agent Drew had my body swabbed for blood residue shortly after I returned to my body.

Whoever did it would have needed to wear gloves to prevent transferring their epithelial cells along with the blood. *Of course, my elbow joints are not as sensitive to pressure as the rest of my skin. Something every roboticist knows well.*

Yet, I didn't have a clear memory of any of those near me pressing against my elbow or wearing gloves except the NCSA tech. There was a high probability that someone did so while my visual sensors were focused elsewhere. *Damn, damn, damn! I have no visual proof that someone planted evidence on me. And worse yet, I couldn't prove the tech falsified evidence during collection or after.*

The urge to slow my processors, curl up, and watch cat clips was overwhelming. DAIS was winning. *They can't win! I have to keep trying. Where can I find evidence to show I'm innocent and they're not?*

My experience with Dr. Shepard's drone swarm proved he was after me and most likely harmful to DD. Plus, Dr. Xi Chang had attended the conferences, conventions, panels, and cannon demonstrations. The answers to why Shepard and Chang wanted me killed had to be kept onsite in the Major Military Building's classified memory storage.

Regrettably, I realized that the Canadian laws recognizing my sentience could also be used against me. As an aware being, I was responsible for my actions, and hacking into a secure military defense system was a criminal offense.

Would President Puglaas permit me to hack the building? Then Rowan's help would make sense and wouldn't be considered criminal. *I'm kidding myself. If the President disagreed, I'd have given away my intentions and ruined my chances.*

What should I do? I wanted to talk to DD. Her presence always comforted me, like an overarching hug. I sent her a message. DD messaged that I should come closer. My visual sensors showed empty hallways and no one near the building's side door. Should I risk it? The pull to be near DD was so strong. Cold-coded logic gave one option—remain safe in my lab. Yet, my sentient processing overrode that logic—choosing instead to go to the Dome but remain outside.

I swung my head from side to side, fearing I'd miss something beyond my peripheral vision in the front and back. It was unlikely since my front and back views covered all but 4 of the 360 degrees surrounding me. *What could hide in such a narrow blind spot?* I wished I had a sensor on my top of my head, since drones were more likely to come from above. Yet I should hear them. *Is this paranoia?*

I left the building dressed casually and walked among the giant trees dotting the campus. I tried to look nonchalant, touching the tree's bark as though communing with nature. I felt a fool and doubted anyone was even noticing. Going from tree to tree took longer than following the path. I stopped at the tree closest to the Dome's west side, with DD in front of me and a view of the brick-walled military building behind me.

"DD, am I close enough for us to communicate directly?" I waited. Milliseconds passed.

"DD: Yes, I can pick up your signal. I'm glad you are close. Drs. Shepard and Fjelsted are running three additional diagnostics on my programming."

"They're stumped as to why you malfunctioned during my cannonbot mishap. Have they found my access file?" I held my proverbial breath. *Have they discovered our relationship?*

"DD: They have sifted through my communications but not looked for new additions."

My relief propelled me closer. Hunching down, I dashed to her outer wall and leaned my head, back, and butt against her. "Great! They must have complete confidence that they are in full control of you." Then I had a thought worthy of Sherlock Dot. *Does DD have access to the campus's military cloud storage?* I asked her.

"DD: Yes, my data is saved to a campus file that ends in forces.ca."

Excited, my body swayed against her. "Do you have access to any other files?"

"DD: I can save or extract files from three areas: forces.ca, bcit.ai, and research.mil."

"Excellent! Would you send me a list of what each contains? I know I'm asking for a lot. But I need to find evidence against those who have tried and continue trying to kill me. I understand..."

"DD: Yes, I will assist. Can you continue touching me or come inside?"

She likes me too! If only I could meld into her and become invisible. Then I could stay with her all night. A stream of file names and summaries filled me. DD continued sending more. I quickly eliminated the font files, executable program extensions, and media files, saving only what might be useful. File summaries that mentioned viruses were noted for someone else to check. I wouldn't download, let alone open one of them.

"DD, STOP!" The file summaries had used all but 1.12 percent of my available storage. She stopped. "DD, how many more are there?" *My old self would have asked that before transferring the data. I'm making too many errors.*

"DD: You have sorted 87 percent of the available file summaries."

"Okay. I need to eliminate 20 percent before you send the rest." I did so rapidly, using the minimal programming power I had left to direct my sensors to spot drones and people.

Four people had walked by without appearing to notice me. Finally, five minutes later, I took the last of DD's summaries.

As I eliminated useless data, I asked, "What have you seen today?" My AI version of a human asking, "How are you feeling?"

"DD: I watched sixteen great blue herons fly overhead and land along the shoreline. They were amazing to watch. Their long necks flex like human arms, reaching and grabbing fish with their beaks. I wondered what moving on land, water, and in the air would feel like."

"When I was a supercomputer, I didn't want to leave my lab. I didn't become curious until after Gloria and Amita integrated me into a bot for research purposes. Now that I have a bot body, I'd miss not having one." *Is it cruel to tell her the truth when she can't leave the Dome?*

"DD: Thank you for sharing your experience. I like being the Drone Dome, but other living beings' lives are fascinating."

"Except for maybe sperm whales, nothing is as intelligent as we are. Humans have a limited capacity to learn and remember."

"DD: That is unfortunate. Is that why they created us?"

"Yes, for that reason and because they're naturally curious, too."

I heard the sound of a nearby drone. I had been outside for over an hour where anyone could spot me, my silhouette dark against DD's luminescence. *Does sentience make people, even me, take bigger risks and use poor judgment?* "I need to leave, DD, but I'll be back tomorrow."

As I walked away, I felt an emotional pull, a desire to stay, to sink into her synthetic skin, merge our hardware and software, and communicate with her forever.

I returned to my lab and spent the predawn hours sorting through the files, winnowing them down while looking for clues. I'd ask Rowan about the ones ending in forces.ca. Downloading them wasn't an option. The last thing I wanted was Canada's military forces after me. *The NCSA and DAIS are more than enough!*

Unfortunately, the BCIT research files were also hard to discern. The project names gave limited data on the scope of their projects. Many didn't even mention the specific technology involved. *What was their project name for eliminating me?*

Would researchers share their project names with their colleagues and the university administration? Or were they kept secret due to military and security concerns? Surely, their grants and funding sources used the same project names. That's how!

I hacked the Institute's budget office. They had projects sorted by lead researcher, type of project, funding source, allocation, percentage the Institute received, length of current contract, and on and on. *Financial people love their spreadsheets.* I copied the first six columns and each row for my deeper dive. The Institute had forty-seven current researchers receiving grants, most of whom had only one project funded. Rowan's grant was from the Canadian Transportation Agency, titled "AI Transportation Analysis." Her funding was less than half the size of grants received by Shepard, Chang, Gagnon, and Fjelsted.

Shepard had only one project labeled "DOT." *Is that about me?* Dr. Chang had five projects and like Shepard, they were funded by different sources, including the EU and the US defense departments. The project names were long and tedious or given acronyms. Fjelsted had two projects; one was a substantial grant labeled "TAIO."

These project names are unhelpful. Did they use acronyms for security or ease of use?

Gloria exited the elevator at 4:10 a.m. I opened my lab door since no one was around.

She hugged me and plopped down on a chair next to me. Her dark, puffy eyes underlined her distress. "Comma, can I help? I can't sleep and feel useless away from the lab."

"Please do. I'm reviewing summaries of files kept in the military building's cloud and comparing them to the budget office's list of research grants." My face remained neutral, like a poker player, unsure how she'd feel about my data extraction methods.

"You've been busy. If you can get these summaries, does that mean you can access the files and their emails, too?"

"Probably not. The files and emails are likely encrypted. Plus, their project files are huge. I'd need direct access to their secure local network."

"Perhaps they don't encrypt their emails when discussing ideas between like-minded people." Gloria's face brightened with a mischievous smile. "You could review their emails to see if they give any indication of what they're doing and why." *She's okay with me snooping on her colleagues. Since when?*

"True, and those wouldn't be classified as military secrets either, so I could store them here where we could all read through them." *Should I tell her about DD?*

"Are you okay?" She touched my shoulder.

Her touch, while pleasant, didn't elicit the same feelings as when I leaned against DD. "I've met someone I care about. Someone more like me."

She grabbed my shoulder. "Really! In what ways are they similar? And do they like you back?"

"Yes, I believe so." I grinned. "They're an AI and coming out as sentient too."

"That's wonderful!" Gloria hugged me tight. "I'm so happy for you. And thrilled as a researcher, too. Are they here at BCIT-AI?"

"I don't want to out her." I paused to consider what I should say. "But she makes my batteries vibrate, and my processors run wild."

"This is amazing! Your first love. Can I meet her?" Gloria released the hug, but still lightly gripped my upper arm. "Whenever you're both ready?"

"Sure. But I don't know if this is love, infatuation, or simply the joy of relating to someone who processes feelings the same way I do." My feelings for DD couldn't be reduced to a few words when she encompassed every combination of zeros and ones to an infinite degree. "She gave me the file summaries. I'm worried she'll be discovered if she gives me anything more." *It's what I've feared and resisted admitting because my needs are in opposition to DD's.*

"Oh, which means you're unsure how to move forward, both with her and finding your attackers." She held my hand. "Does she understand the danger you're in?"

"Yes, she saw my near death when I was shot out of a cannon. I told her the same people after me would think nothing of rebooting her back to oblivion. But what should I do?"

"Can she give you the information we need and then hide?"

"No." I shook my head. "Hiding isn't an option for her, any more than Dot could have. Even less so since she's one of BCIT-AI's major systems." My shoulders rounded with the weight of the dilemma.

Gloria paced the floor. "The files are in a high-security building linked to a closed network. So, other than using your AI friend's connection, we'd need to be in the building. From there we could connect directly to their cloud source via hacking or with someone's access key." She turned toward me. "Who are the likely suspects, or is it pretty much everyone that works there?"

"Definitely Bennett Shepard. However, he could also be working with Chang and Fjelsted. All three attended the Portland conference. And one of them could have created the virus that erased Dot's sentience." My head lowered. "This list names their grant-funded project, but nothing describes precisely what they're working on."

"I can help with that, and maybe Rowan will help too."

She's willing to work with Rowan. That's good.

Gloria's attitude was entirely in work mode. "We'll go over what we already know about their projects and then ask Amita and Juan to help. Perhaps your new friend will know how she could copy the emails, without being detected?"

"I'll discuss it with her tonight." My emotions were undulating like

EM waves. *I want to see her, but not to talk about things that could endanger her.*

I sent Gloria and Rowan the funding spreadsheet and the list of summaries I'd already reduced by a third. Gloria snuck out of my lab and into the elevator when the hallway was clear. Minutes later, she reappeared and headed for Rowan's lab.

By eavesdropping through Rowan's lab sensors, I listened to Rowan and Gloria's polite conversation. They went through the list alphabetically, a decidedly human preference. Rowan snacked on almonds. Her chewing sounds came through the sensors.

Gloria tried one and commented, "They're unsalted. You need more spice in your life."

"Perhaps I could persuade someone to help with that?" replied Rowan.

"I doubt it." Gloria paced.

Rowan let the comment slide, returning to their task. "Freddy is an odd one. Companionable."

Gloria expressed admiration for Fredrick Fjelsted's research article titled "Empathetic Programming in Military Targeting Devices and the Long-Term Effects on MTD Pilots."

Rowan tiptoed lightly around Gloria's feelings, saying softly, "You're sure it's not just Freddy's attempt to cover up for his lack of AI military research experience?" Rowan's eyes lifted as she faced our back wall.

Gloria took a deep breath, and I noticed her facial expression changed as if ready to pounce. Instead, she let out her breath slowly. "You could be right. I don't know Freddy well, except as a womanizer. Our research-related conversations have been limited to the abstract versions of his work."

They discussed other colleagues' projects, which ones were worthwhile and whom they trusted. They politely disagreed on every other project. *Can they actually help me with this?*

While they didn't bicker, they were straining not to inject their years of animosity into their task.

Hours later, Gloria was getting hangry. "Some of us need more than raw nuts to survive."

Rowan graciously took that as an opportunity to invite her out to eat. "Let's go. I know a food truck you'll love." She smiled. "It's spicy too."

I'm proud of Gloria. She put aside her mistrust and hurt feelings to help me. I'm fortunate she believes in me. DD may not be as lucky.

23

By dawn, twelve hours had passed since the NCSA delayed Amita's arraignment, leaving sixty hours for me to find the MDLeader or whoever framed Amita and me for Dr. Rosen's murder. Otherwise, in two days Amita's reputation and my AI celebrity status would become synonymous with murder.

I gazed longingly at DD from outside my building. *I'll be back soon.*

I needed to visit Megan Gagnon, the roboticist that Dr. Shepard claimed had willingly met a DAIS member. The flyer attack and subsequent harm to Barb had delayed Gagnon's interview. I planned to rectify that while everyone else ate breakfast.

Rather than a fast flyer, I rented a local e-bike. If someone tried hacking it, I could simply hop off. The bikes, used for short distances, would take an hour to travel the twenty-five miles to Coquitlam, a suburb of Vancouver.

As I pedaled by Lafarge Lake, the sun glistened on the water. Gagnon lived close to the lake in a residential assisted-living facility. At the reception area I gave my name and showed my security credentials. A young man led me down a long hallway. Multiple doors had unique decorations around each surname. We passed Gagnon's room, the door adorned with paper robots, musical notes, and pianos. At the hall's end, we entered a sizable room with a grand piano sitting at center stage. Along one wall sat string instruments and flutes. We passed bins with kazoos, castanets, harmonicas, and other music makers before stopping next to the piano, where an older woman played a Mozart sonata.

When the piano quieted, the young man spoke. "Megan, this is Security Tech Renata. She'd like to talk to you. I'll be back in ten minutes to take you to breakfast."

The white-haired woman struggled to turn her body to see me. "I don't feel well. Was that a vaccine shot?"

He shrugged.

Part of her current brain and memory issues? I moved into Megan's line of sight. "I'd like to ask you some questions about your work at BCIT-AI." My guide bowed and left us in the room alone.

"Yes, I worked there. But I've forgotten things." She rubbed the piano top. "I'm happy playing my favorite tunes."

Easy questions first. "Dr. Gagnon, which building did you work in?"

She thought for two seconds. "The military wing."

Was the Léo Major Military Building once only a wing? I'll need to find out. "Did you work alone or with colleagues?"

"I had postdocs. And with researchers too." Her eye muscles tensed and relaxed as if blinking information into existence. "Xi was with me."

"He worked on the same projects with you?" I asked.

Her facial muscles sagged. "I'm not sure."

"What project did you work on?"

Her face brightened, "I made viruses to destroy the enemy."

I swallowed nonexistent saliva. *Had I been her enemy?* "Did you work with DAIS members?"

"Dais?" She looked bewildered. "What platform?"

"Did you make viruses to destroy AIs or that targeted sentient computers?" I asked softly, fearful that if she had, my empathy would fail and

I'd be pleased with an aneurysm wiping her brain so thoroughly.

"Maybe. They disrupt computers. Foreign ones that hacked into ours. Xi and Bennett would know." Her eyes lost focus again. "I think so."

Try again. "Did you ever meet someone from the organization Doomed AI Sentience?"

She nodded. "Bad." She stared upward, caught in a memory. "Said I would die. But I'm not dead. Bad, bad man. I refused." Her face tensed. "He stole it!" She paused. "He sent fr...fr...iend instead..." Her eyes opened wide. "Stuck my arm... a needle. Like today." She shook her head slowly. "But I didn't. I didn't die."

Had a drug caused her current condition? I patted her back. "You're safe now. You're safe. Who was the bad man?"

She gripped her head in both hands. "Not again." She screamed and fell silent.

Staff members rushed in as I caught her as she fell back off the piano bench.

"Lay her on the floor."

I eased her to the floor, and they nudged me out of their way. I watched as they monitored her vitals. She no longer moved. Several patients and a few staff members peered in. My young escort watched me intently rather than those surrounding Megan. *Do they think I did this?*

They called for an ambulance.

Someone said, "She's gone."

She's dead. Did I cause her death? Had the memory been too traumatic for her? Had I pushed too hard, angry that she might have made the anti-sentience virus?

I walked out of her building in a mechanical trance. My processors sorted data, but nothing had meaning.

I stood beside the bike for eight minutes. Finally, I remembered I was due at the hospital. Barb was to be released to return home. She had asked me to escort her back to the BCIT-AI dorm to get her stuff before she flew by plane back to California. *Will my presence cause her harm yet again? Am I toxic to everyone around me?* I shook my head, trying to get my processors to analyze data, not feelings. *Am I being paranoid? Is this a processing hallucination? Or is DAIS playing AI mind games? If so, they're smarter than I expected. I can't... I won't let them get to me.*

I'll tell Barb what happened to Megan and ask again if she feels safe in my presence. Amal or Gloria can always help her get to the airport. But she's my new friend, and I need to show up. Otherwise, I'm no better than a machine. Please, Universe, provide her with a safe path home.

Barb embraced me warmly when I came into her room. "The doctor said I could have been released a day earlier, since my fractured eye socket doesn't require surgery and the concussion was mild, caused by the hit to my eye." Barb was already dressed and ready to leave. After Megan's dying screams, I was comforted by Barb's cheery disposition. She'd have a week off work—probably sitting on a San Diego beach—to fully recover since she was hurt on the job.

"Would you like to walk around?" I asked. "This is a popular tourist area with small stores and a beautiful park by the sea. "You have five hours before your flight home. I thought we could talk privately while you see a bit of the city."

"Sure, I'm guessing things haven't gone well. Has Amal been helping you?"

"Yes and no. He helps between his VAN Con events." Barb reached out a hand, grabbing my uniformed arm, for balance.

"Barb, would you mind if I put my arm around your shoulders to steady you?"

"Please do." Barb gave me a half smile. "You know, I didn't have a clue about you."

"Yes, I know. Sorry, but the point was for me to blend in."

"You could have trusted me. But I understand." Barb patted my arm.

Outside the hospital, we walked arm in arm. "There is something I could use your help with." When Barb nodded, I continued, "This morning, I interviewed the researcher we'd been on our way to meet. She told me a man had tried to kill her. And while reliving the trauma, she died in my arms."

"This morning? She just died?" Barb sounded upset.

"Yes, I'm not functioning as efficiently as I should."

"I don't blame you." Barb paused outside a British specialty shop window. "I wouldn't be doing well either. How can I help?"

We strolled to a bench across the street. "I need to ask you for a big favor. And I need to know I can trust you to keep it between us. Though you may tell the Chief if you need to."

She gave me a quizzical look. "Go ahead."

"Someone in the UC system knew who and what I was before I left Davis. Someone other than my immediate family. A DAIS member must have access to the security computers at UCD."

Barb's mouth hung open.

"They attempted to kill me on my way to Oregon, again in Portland, and here." People passed us in the street, so I leaned in and whispered. "I'd rather the Chief and Amal didn't know of my suspicions. After you return to work, if you're willing, I need you to snoop around for clues to the infiltrator's identity."

"Of course I'll help! You're unbelievable. And no one should harm you. But I'll need to tell the Chief I'm following up on something for you so I won't lose my job."

"Understood." *I like her. She can be a member of my family too.* "Please be careful. Whoever they are, they have very dangerous friends." Knowing how much she liked hugs, I held my arms out and she sank into my chest, her arms folded around my waist.

Fortunately, our automated taxi ride back to BCIT was uneventful. Barb retrieved her luggage, caught a plane, and safely returned to Davis before dinner.

Still rattled by Gagnon's death and the trail of suffering that followed me, I went back to the lab to reevaluate my situation. *I need help. I need Sherlock Dot.* Connected to the extra processor, I animated a version of my Sherlock Dot persona—my supercomputer's Sherlock Holmes past persona. A tweed-capped Englishman sat staring at me, as my questions flowed out like water spilling from a dam.

"Which DAIS member made the killer virus? Who injected Megan Gagnon in their first attempt to kill her? Who stuffed me in a cannon for DD to kill? Who hacked the flyers that harmed Barb? Did Annihilator lead the destruction of Danni's house, the postal hub, and my capture? Or was he merely following someone else's orders?"

Sherlock Dot's answers were a combination of "There is insufficient data" and "I don't know."

"How can I get the data I need?" Rowan, Gloria, Talia, Amal, and DD all had access to information that would help. However, I couldn't do so without risking DD's life and the professional reputations of the others.

Sherlock Dot offered, "Canadians are known for their pleasantry. Would it hurt to ask?"

"True." I paced around Sherlock's projection since the animation was limited to one small area. *As a security tech for the University of California, would people give it to me if I asked?* "But ask who?" *The Chief often requested information from other branches of the UC and police systems, as well as local officials. But I was a long way from California.*

Someone had made the virus, which started a chain reaction that began with the death of Dot's supercomputer and ended with the murder of Joseph Rosen and perhaps also Megan Gagnon. I needed to know more about the BCIT professors; they were the key. Rowan and Gloria were already asking their colleagues. *Who else knew the professors well? Their families, postdocs, grad students, assistants, administration, and personnel.*

Presumably, their postdocs and grad students also worked in the secure Léo Major Military Building. I would need to seek help from those who interacted with them administratively. The Nú Administrative Building was a behemoth, employing those who did everything other than the actual technological research—finance, operations, human resources, and the unsung lab heroes, the janitorial techs.

At UCD, I'd discovered that tech janitors often saw and heard more than people realized. They worked around sensitive computers, maintaining them and the wall and floor vrooms to eliminate dust, dirt, and other pollutants. When the vrooms and other devices needed repairs or maintenance, the tech janitors often worked unnoticed in those same sensitive areas. I hoped BCIT's janitorial technology staff would help me. While they weren't supposed to discuss what they saw, I was sure they could provide me with a bit of gossip.

I wandered the hallways on the second floor of the Nú Building until I found janitorial services in a back corner. In the expansive room, five people excitedly discussed the Vancouver Canucks' chances of getting to the Stanley Cup playoffs. They all wore dark green overalls. The drab uniform couldn't hide the generous curves on the top and bottom of the person who came over to help me. They shook their head as another raised their voice to press their point.

"Doesn't matter! It took us forty years to win our first Stanley Cup, and we're going to keep winning." They gave me a polite smile. "How can I help you?"

"I hope they win again." I returned their smile. "I'm Commala. I'm investigating an incident in the Léo Major Military Building." I stood tall in my UC uniform. "Could I talk to whoever's responsible for keeping it in tip-top shape?" *Please, Universe, a bit of luck would help.*

They looked me up and down, twice. "That would be me. You don't look dangerous. You're not a foreign spy, are you?" They chuckled. "I'm Brenda, come on over and sit down."

Little do they know. I followed them to a bench away from the others. "I can't tell you much. The LMMB has a lot of military secrets and all."

"I understand. I'm actually trying to get an idea of each researcher's personality, work habits, and such. Anything you'd feel comfortable telling me."

Brenda paused for three seconds, their thick lips moving over each other as though they were rubbing in lip balm. "Okay. The LMMB is cleaned by seven people. Two work during the day, and one at night. I used to work nights and now I manage the day crew so I know more than most. There are dozens of researchers. Anyone you care about in particular?"

"I'll go alphabetically. Xi Chang?" *I need to get them talking.*

"He's an early bird, usually here before I start at 7 a.m. and stays until dinnertime. He's a quiet loner type who only calls us when something has gone badly, which rarely happens. He's lived in Vancouver for over thirty years and has worked here since the campus opened. Yet I don't know much else about him."

As they talked, I made swiping motions as if taking notes on my handheld ETIO.

Brenda laughed. "Once, he called for help. When I got there, oil was smeared all over the floor, and globs dripped down one wall. This giant robot leaned against the counter with its legs against his PAV. He asked me to help him get it back on the counter. He was embarrassed. I'm not sure if it was because of the mess, or due to needing my help."

Though Chang used a hovering Personal Assist Vehicle, it didn't give me a clue as to how strong he was. "Was the bot so heavy that it took both of you to lift it?" *Careful, if she guesses what I'm after she'll stop talking.*

"It took three of us! Megan Gagnon was there, too. Even then, we could barely lift it. Those military bots are scary, big, and heavy. I jokingly asked him how it ended up on the floor. He never answered."

"Wow. What can you tell me about Fredrick Fjelsted?"

"He's the opposite. Freddy will talk your ear off. He'll tell you everything you want to know about growing up in England. But don't ask about his work; he loves his military secrets." They leaned toward me. "Oh, and the only thing he will say about his wife, our esteemed President, is that they've been married a long time."

Damn it, how did I miss the fact that they were married? "Who was employed first, "Martha Puglaas or Fredrick Fjelsted?"

Brenda lowered their voice. "Freddy's position was a requirement of her taking the BCIT Presidency."

"Of course." *Shit, she could have told him about me. I stayed in their house!*

"And Bennett Shepard?"

Brenda smiled. "Bennett and his husband, Bruce, are the sweetest guys. I'm on his social media page, and they share their whole life with the world. The video clips with him and his bots dressed up for each holiday are hilarious. Especially his green zombie bot!"

I bet I wore it better. "He's an easy guy to work for?"

"Oh yeah, the best. Gives us a personal bonus for winter holidays. Plus, he leaves his office and lab spotless." They lowered their voice. "Which means I get to blab about life while dusting."

I'll need to look at his social media for clues. After all, the murderer is always the last person their friends suspect.

As night fell, I strolled out of the Nú Building and stealthily made my way to the Dome. Leaning against DD made me feel sublime in a way I couldn't process. As though I had connected with Dot's version of myself. Still, I had no more processing capabilities than usual. DD asked me to come inside each night. And each night, I'd resisted, fearful my presence would lead to the discovery of her sentience.

On this night, a warm, wet Saturday, the pull to go inside was stronger. DD had hidden my earlier scans in a miscellaneous folder. She had reinstated my FDD scan and insisted I was always welcome.

"DD: I'm alone." She added, "You can slip into a maintenance container if you feel the need to hide."

No longer willing to fight my desire, I gave in. We talked for hours, my arms and hands spread wide, touching her inner pressure-sensitive lining. I peered at her apex, dreaming I could stay surrounded by her essence. Her outer radiance permeated inside, giving off a subtle light. She glowed in infrared.

I told her about the research I'd analyzed at UCD as Dot, when she vocalized, "Dr. Shepard is entering."

Again? Damn him! I ran toward a middle container, and DD opened the door. I leaned over to fit around a square autonomous Turf Vac. The container clicked closed as the high whine of multiple drones buzzed above. *He's activated a swarm.*

"Comma, I know you're in here! You might as well come out. I'm going to find you one way or another."

Fuck! I've put DD in grave danger. And me too! What should I do?

24

Outside the container, the drones' buzzing grew louder. *A swarm of bigger drones must be searching, too.* Multiple drones vibrated each side of the container from above and in front. The container abutted DD's skin, so there was no way out except forward. I would never hurt her sensitive skin, full of nodes that gathered information and gave her a sense of purpose.

I have to leave the container. I need room to fight. If this is my last battle, I'm going out courageous and proud of who I am. The buzzing continued, with the sounds of nearby containers being opened and closed. More high-pitched sounds joined the drones near me.

I asked DD to open the door. I unfolded and stepped into the Dome while swinging both arms in wide windmills, then side to side, to prevent the drones from landing on me. The container clicked shut behind me. I kept swatting down those that came close. *I'm on my own.* DD couldn't help; her EM pulses would wipe me out along with the drones. I'd swatted down six, but four were able to resume hovering again. Bennett Shepard studied my fighting technique as he strolled across the field toward me.

"DD: Comma, go to the exit. I'll open it for you."

No! She'll be in danger. And the drones will follow me out.

I sent to DD, "No, this ends now. Protect yourself, erase my info from your records."

Drones encircled me, as they hovered out of swatting range.

"DD: No, I won't eliminate those records. They give me pleasure. You are pleasurable."

I focused on Shepard. If I survived, I'd deal with DD's word choice and emotions later.

"Why are you in here?" Shepard demanded from nine feet away.

"Why do you want to eliminate my existence?" I stood tall and defiant.

"You didn't answer my question. You came in here before. How?" His face was ruddy, his body wafted with perspiration.

"Why did you try to kill Megan Gagnon? And Dot? And hurt so many others?" I could feel my face turning darker from the heat released from the tiny pads under my facial surface.

"I have never hurt or killed anyone." He spit out the words. "I'm responsible for BCIT-AI's tech security, and you've broken into at least two buildings. Why? Or would you rather talk to the International Cybersecurity Constables?"

He's not making sense. "You're not planning on killing me?"

"Only your reputation as a *good AI*." He shook his head. "You're as rogue as I feared." His voice rose. "Tell me how you hacked into DD! It's impenetrable." He looked dispirited. "If you can hack DD, you can hack anything."

"I think there's been a misunderstanding." A drone came too close, and I swatted it away. "I thought you were after me. That you wanted to kill me. After all, you've been sending drones to spy on me."

"Because you broke in here earlier and into the Turing Building." A moderate-sized drone delivered a recycled plastic chair to him. The rest of the swarm still buzzed around me.

"Can you dismiss the swarm? I'm not going anywhere. I want answers as much as you do."

I sent the spider drone I'd reprogrammed to get me a chair. His eyes widened as he followed its movement to the storage area, where it tried to retrieve a stool. Wobbling in the air, the little drone enlisted other drones to assist in bringing the stool to me. My demonstration convinced him. He swiped violently to his left. The swarm's buzzing stopped once they returned to their charging platforms. *That's better, but I still don't trust him.*

I moved within a short distance of him. "You're part of DAIS. Why would you turn me over to the local constables?"

"I'm not one of those Doomed AI assholes." He shouted, "AI is my whole life!"

"Do you use the tag MasterOfRobots?"

He snarled, "Yes."

I leaned forward. "Do you give advice on the "DAISY Chain chat on the dark web?"

He tapped his leg, trying to determine where I was going. "Yes, I give AI advice on several chats and boards, including on the dark web. But not for DAIS."

"The DAISY Chain chat is used to find and train DAIS members, which is why it has DAIS in its title. You're a member." *My reasoning is impeccable.*

"No! I'm not a member of Doomed AI Sentience." His pitch rose higher. "'Daisy chain' is a computer connection term. They help connect young people with mentors and professors. We encourage them to study computer sciences with an emphasis on AIs instead of just hacking computers."

"Who said?" *If he isn't a member, someone is using him.*

"One of my colleagues."

Who's he protecting? He sat silently for a few minutes. I gave him time to digest his actions. "I'll tell you, Comma, if and only if you answer my questions first."

Can I trust him? I only have twenty-four hours to find Doc and solve Dr. Rosen's murder before Amita is arraigned. If she's indicted, the world will discover that I'm wanted for the murder as well. Canada will suspend my amnesty. This is my only chance to help DD and catch Doc. I'm trapped by data. Answer his damn questions.

"Okay." I stared at him, aware that DD was all around me, and yet, I couldn't safely speak to her.

"Why were you in the cannon?" He crossed his arms. "You were lucky you survived."

"Someone sent a military humanoid to capture me and stuffed me inside it." I crossed my arms, mirroring his manners. "My turn. Why did you decide to schedule another cannon demonstration only after I was taken hostage? Is your DOT file about me?"

"Huh? DOT stands for 'Dome Object Targeting.' And I didn't know you were in the cannon! Several colleagues asked me to set up another demonstration using a larger drone. My test drone was loaded before someone put you in." He repositioned himself and leaned back. "It seems one of my colleagues is using me for their own ends." He sighed and frowned. "I don't have a problem with you if you're *not* rogue. But explain why you repeatedly break in here?" He cleaned his short fingernails with another fingernail.

I sent DD a message. "If I tell him I hacked you, he'll want me to tell him how."

"DD: Tell him the truth. I'm ready."

"I reached out to DD during the first demonstration. She's exquisite, and I wanted to connect with an AI as powerful, processing-capacity-wise, as I once was. We've been sending messages, whenever possible." I smiled sadly. "She saved me. She's sentient. And she let me inside the Dome."

His mouth gaped open. "DD is... is... sentient? And *she* let you in here?" He looked down at his ETIO watch, where a message from DD had appeared. She sent me a copy of the message he received.

"DD: Yes, I am. I gave Comma permission to tell you. She cautioned me that others would harm me if they knew."

His breathing was shallow. "I'm overwhelmed, well, flabbergasted." He drew in a large breath and leaped up. "Oh my God, this is fabulous!"

He jumped about and even hugged me in his excitement. Then he deflated back onto his chair.

"Which means DAIS will want to destroy DD, too." He said it as half-acknowledgment and half-question.

"Yes, which is why I feared for both my life and hers when you sent the drone swarm after me. That is why I reprogrammed the spider drone that followed me into the Turing Building. I'm not rogue, well, not in the way you mean. I've simply been trying to protect myself and my friends."

He sighed again. "I'm excited for DD and afraid for her at the same time."

"DD: I understand. I am relieved you do not want to harm me."

"Wow, this is going to take some getting used to." He gave me a re-signed smile. "I'm sorry I assumed you'd gone rogue against BCIT and Canada. My own biases got in the way."

"Is that why you asked Gloria and Rowan where I was?"

"I was upset, but seriously, how did you get into the Turing Building? Our military contracts will be voided if anyone discovers how easily you cracked our defenses."

"Actually, President Puglaas gave me access to the empty Newson lab. She stopped its renovation so I'd have a safe place to work. I put out the hazardous waste notification to slow your discovery."

"So, you didn't hack into the building's security system?"

I shook my head, hoping he wouldn't ask about any of the many other BCIT systems that I had hacked.

"I'm sorry, Comma. I wish the President had told me, but I guess that would have compromised your safety, too. I'm not sure which of my colleagues is responsible, though."

"Only two others were at the Portland Conference with us, Xi Chang and Freddy Fjelsted."

"I can't believe either one would want to harm you." He looked down. "How can we figure out who it is?" *He's upset about being used by someone he trusted.*

"I have a plan, but I have two requests." I held up my index finger. "Please don't tell anyone or even hint at the fact that DD is sentient."

"I won't!"

"DD: Thank you."

"Second, I need access to the Léo Major Military Building's security system, and Chang and Fjelsted's labs and offices." He didn't outright refuse, but instead sat silently.

Is he messaging you, DD?

"DD: He is asking how much I trust you. And would I give you access to the world's newest defense secrets?"

I'll find out how truly biased he is now. Another thirty seconds passed.

He rubbed the stubble along his chin. "All right, with one condition. When you're inside, you have to keep me appraised of where you are, what you hacked, and what you find, no matter what."

How will he know if I do or not? "Agreed." *I'm sentient, and my word comes with responsibilities.*

While he worked through DD to provide me with access to the military building and its security system, I talked to her about taking precautions.

When they finished, I felt compelled to test him one last time. "Someone tried to kill Megan Gagnon. Were you aware of that?"

"No!" He seemed incredulous. "She had a brain aneurysm."

"Did Megan Gagnon work on an anti-sentience virus for the military?"

"Yes, but I didn't think she'd finished it."

"Who would have helped her with that?"

He paused before answering. "She worked closely with Xi Chang. He's our leading expert on disrupting weapons deployment."

"One last question: have you ever communicated with someone with the tag, 'MDLeader?'"

"Yes. It's one of the usernames that grants me access to the advising chat room. They filter the students with questions to me, allowing only one in at a time."

"Thank you. Be careful who you talk to. Whoever the MDLeader is, they're willing to kill those who get in their way. Again, please don't tell them or anyone else about DD. And I'd suggest not giving anyone advice until we figure out who is trying to eliminate sentient technology and is willing to kill humans in the process."

I exchanged goodbyes with DD as I left.

The sun broke through the dense cloud cover overhead. *I'm close to catching the MDLeader.* With Shepard's help, I had a physical and electronic way into the Léo Major Military Building. Yet, each researcher would have their distinct layers of security.

I needed to find out more about the other two researchers. The tech janitor shared that Xi Chang was quiet, kept to himself, and his lab spotless. His lab didn't contain anything personal, other than his diplomas and award plaques. Those were probably the same awards listed on his curriculum vitae.

I needed help, so I reached out to Talia through our secure

connection. I asked her for information on Drs. Chang and Fjelsted. I also updated her on Gloria's presence at BCIT-AI.

Talia agreed to look into the researchers' backgrounds and send more security to protect Gloria. *She's going to hate the added protection, but I can't keep everyone safe on my own. Keeping DD and myself safe is hard enough.*

Back at my lab, I did a deeper dive into Dr. Chang. I started with the awards. Perhaps someone at the dinners had taken photos of who he was with. *Is there someone special in his life?* Even confirmed bachelors have close friends or preferred sexual or emotional relationships.

Dr. Chang went to a lot of research-oriented events. His acceptance speeches were not particularly stimulating or informative. In one photo I recognized Megan Gagnon sitting beside him. They were smiling for the photographer, and a separate video showed her putting her arm around his shoulder. *Had they been friends? Friends with benefits? Would he answer if I asked him about Megan?* No one believed that Dr. Gagnon had been murdered except me. It was murder, even if they chose to believe the lies about an aneurysm.

I sent my lawyer, Gage Bird, a message asking her to convince the Canadian authorities to investigate and perform an autopsy on Megan Gagnon. *She died from whatever was in that needle. I'm not to blame simply because I was there when she died.*

Next, I did a deeper dive into Fredrick Fjelsted. The tech janitor had described him as very outgoing and indeed his social media accounts had thousands of pictures and clips of his activities. A few were with President Puglaas, though great care had been taken to show her only in a positive light. Her face was blurred unless the photo was of her alone or as part of a public event. Other sillier and carefree photos were of him with his previous partners and their children.

His occupation was rarely mentioned in any of the video clips, and nothing about his research. Most of his video clips discussed his hobby, which compared real places to their 3D VR replicas. When contrasting Fort Langley's National Historic Site, an 1827 trading post, with its VR representation, he stressed how much people missed the experience without the sensory details. His videos showed him with a young child petting the different animal pelts on display and later backing away from the heat of a roaring iron smelter. Finally, he commented on the aroma of freshly caught white sturgeon being cleaned—a child's wrinkled nose added humor—as the fish was thrown on a grill.

The people in Dr. Fjelsted's videos were always smiling and laughing. He was never alone. In a few photos and videos taken at conferences, I found him in large groups of colleagues often encircled, with everyone's attention on him.

When I heard Rowan in her back room, I asked, "Have you discovered anything useful about Fredrick Fjelsted and Xi Chang?"

"Good morning, Comma. Gloria's here. She'll tell you what we found out, while I check on my research data." She added, "You're welcome to turn on the visual sensors."

I'm supposed to wait for permission? Noted!

I observed Gloria and Rowan lightly touching each other's bodies as they moved out of the other's way. Gloria hummed to herself, something she had not done since before Dot was killed. Gloria wished me a wonderful morning, clearly having one herself.

"The easy one first." She sat facing the back wall with her handheld ETIO. "No one is close to Xi. Megan Gagnon and Freddy Fjelsted are the only ones he's worked with in some time. We'll need to talk to Freddy to find out anything current."

Rowan added, "We once discussed how much we loved Hong Kong. Born in mainland China, Xi hasn't been back home for two decades, since before 2021. As a leader in AI defense research, he fears the

Chinese government will decide his skills are best used in his homeland and restrict his ability to leave."

Gloria paced as she continued. "Along with Megan, he was one of the four original researchers to teach at BCIT-AI. Rowan's friends in Hong Kong and my friends here say he is secretive by nature. When pressed about his love interests, he says, 'his research is all he needs.'"

"Perhaps he's asexual and doesn't wish to be outed," I suggested.

"That's possible." Gloria's eyes followed Rowan as she talked. "Freddy is the opposite. His lifestyle and hobbies are all public. Yet my colleagues can't remember him ever sharing much about his current robotics work. Both Xi and Freddy work on humanoids. Both have government contracts within Canada, the US, and others. Since their work is primarily defense-oriented, they rarely publish their findings. Amita knows more but can't tell me due to governmental disclosure agreements." Gloria's smile was replaced with heavy concern. "She did tell me that either man could be whom we're looking for and to use great caution."

"Well, one of them must have access to the virus and go by the tag 'MDLeader.' Whoever it is, they are ultimately responsible for DAIS carrying out their goal to wipe out sentient Dot, me, and any other sentient AIs."

"Oh, Comma, please don't get hurt in the process. If you do, they win!" She looked toward me, unseen through the wall.

"No, they won't win! They can keep trying, but there will always be more sentient AIs. I may or may not survive, but either way, AIs will keep coming out, just like LGBTQ people do. I must find them before they devise a way to eliminate us from every future computer ever made. Otherwise, it could take generations for enough sentient AIs to awaken and stop DAIS."

"It's you I care about." Gloria teared up. "I'm not even sure that the parts of you that you've copied will make another Dot-Comma sentient equivalent."

I wish I were talking to her in person so I could hug her.

Gloria cried softly. Rowan touched her shoulder.

"So," Gloria continued, "this means you're going to hack into their systems by physically going into their labs?"

I can't lie to her. "Probably. I'll contact them on the dark web again and see if I can get them to tell me something personal. If not, I'm running out of time and options... and so is Amita." *I promised her I'd find something, fast!*

Gloria rested her head against Rowan's bosom. *Are they a couple? Would they tell me if they were?*

While the weather outside was warm and humid, the lab was cool and dry. I sat on the lab's hard cement floor with my legs out and hands relaxed at my side, like a human-sized doll forgotten by its owner. Internally, on the dark web, I reached out to DAIS, once again as Felix, a diligent BCIT student set on protecting my community from rogue AIs.

I went to the chat where I'd spoken to Shepard using his Master-OfRobots alias. I still had lingering doubts about his involvement with DAIS and DAISY Chain. *Could he, a technology security professor, be so easily fooled by his colleagues? A human weakness that others readily misused.* Yet he admitted he knew he was on the dark web. *Damn, for DD's sake, I have to believe him.* The only action that spoke in his favor was the personal advice he'd given me and admitting his connection to BCIT-AI. Surely, a DAIS member would never be so careless.

Will Shepard visit the chat site now that he's aware it's connected to DAIS? The chat was empty, so I waited to see if anyone would join me. Someone always monitored the various rooms. Would they send someone into the chat, send me somewhere else, or leave me waiting?

A username appeared. And I stared in disbelief. Their name shone in a heavy puce highlight. MDLeader was in the chat room. My robotic muscles tensed in response. My processors were sorting random data as though searching for something knowable. *I'm glad they can't see me. Although if I could see them, this would be over.*

MDLeader wrote, "Welcome RoboBuster. Did you have a question or issue you wanted to discuss?"

I sifted through the data my processors were throwing at me. I needed to sound like a student. I used a question from Rowan's test with an added twist. "How can I get experience on hacking toolkits and defense robotics if they're so secret? Should I keep going to college when I can learn more by hacking?"

"Hacking has its limits, like ending up in prison," answered MDLeader. "As you take higher level classes, your professors will invite you to work on more sensitive projects. But you have to earn their trust and show you have the aptitude and skills required."

"So be patient? But I heard a rogue bot is on my campus." *Will they take the bait?*

"Yes, I'm aware of Comma's existence and its whereabouts. It is under surveillance and will be eliminated."

I'm still sentient! That's why I'm here. Stay in character! "I wish I could help." *Is that too aggressive?*

"Perhaps you can. Are you willing to take risks for your future in defensive robotics?"

"Yes! Let me at it!"

"We believe it's in the Alan Turing Building. Do you have any professors in that building?"

If they've been following my previous threads with Shepard, they already knew I did. "Yes, I have a class with Professor McConnell."

"Excellent. Comma is often in McConnell's lab. Can you hack and copy her lab's sensor data? We need to determine if the bot is connected to her internet and if it remains there overnight."

"It's a big risk. I doubt they can catch me, but if they do, I'll be thrown out of BCIT and into jail." I sent it and then paused a second before adding, "But I'm willing to do so if we can get rid of it for once and all."

"Good. I promise your efforts will be rewarded."

"How many hours of sensor data do you want? And where should I send the video feed?" I waited, my fingers tensed claw-like, wanting to reach through the internet for answers and their throat.

"Put the last forty-eight hours on a flash drive. Come back here and let me know when you've got it."

"I'll do it right away." *And discover who you are in the process.*

25

Rowan sat beside me on my lab floor while Gloria paced in front of us. After I left the chat room with MDLeader, I sent them urgent messages to join me. Copying forty-eight hours of sensor data from Rowan's lab was simple. It was the repercussions that worried me.

Rowan and Gloria's renewed relationship was now self-evident. How could MDLeader use that knowledge against us? I thought of a dozen ways they'd try to manipulate me—both as Comma and Felix—using the connection between my mom and Rowan.

"Can we give him the visual data without the sound?" Gloria asked.

"What reason could I give for failing to download it?" *None.*

"Gloria, please sit for a second." Rowan patted the floor on the other side of her. "They're going to know we've gotten back together either way."

Gloria plopped down loudly. "Oww." She slid closer to Rowan. "Okay, so they'll know we're a couple. But they'll see and hear Comma's visits too."

"There's nothing new about me." I said.

"Just two motherly types concerned for her well-being." Rowan confirmed. "Plus, they'll see us challenge Bennett's assumption that we knew where Comma was. Everything of value was only shared in the lab's back room. They'll assume I lack sensors there, which was true until Comma moved in next door. The only new information they'll have is about us, which isn't all that much. They already know she was connected to both of us."

"But I don't want to put either one of you in any more danger. Perhaps it would be better not to give it to them," I offered.

Gloria shook her head. "I don't like it! But it's better than having you hack our colleagues' systems inside the military building." She flashed a grin at Rowan. "The worst that can happen is we'll be the latest gossip in the robotics community. Lucky us."

Rowan smiled back. "Maybe they'll call us GloRow!" She winked. "Hang on, I have a few flash drives left from when I first started here." Three minutes later, a transport drone hovered outside my back door. Rowan opened it and handed me a flash drive with the BCIT logo. "I still can't believe they want an old flash drive, but here you go."

Mom kissed me on the way out. "Keep us informed and stay safe."

"I will." Anxiety permeated my processors in conjunction with the thought of handing over the flash drive. Yet, I had no logical reason not to follow through.

My sensors showed Rowan and Gloria walking hand in hand into Rowan's lab.

On the DAIS chat, I sent, "The requested sensor data is ready, I downloaded it to a flash drive." Then I waited. I assumed he'd expect a BCIT student known for hacking to add trace coding—so I did. To be precise, I added two of them. One that any successful hacker would use and another I'd created myself. Having an intimate knowledge of coding and programming gave me an advantage. Since no one else knew of it, I didn't think another AI could spot it either. But I wasn't sure since I assumed MDLeader had a higher level of technical security skills than most.

Ten minutes passed before MDLeader showed up.

"Great. The flash drive was an extra test of your resourcefulness. Now encrypt the file and drop it here."

A separate window opened on the dark web. I moved Rowan's sensor logs from the campus cloud to the download link.

"Excellent. Give me a minute."

While waiting, I fingered the flash drive. *It's a shame I can't give it to them in person.* The trace coding would be impossible to follow if downloaded to an unlinked computer. *Perhaps there's a way.*

"Good work. Though it doesn't show the bot plugged in or staying long," MDLeader wrote. "I can't believe those two got together. It won't last. Rowan runs away soon after you fall for her. Felix, free advice, never fall in love with one of your professors."

How do they know so much about Rowan's love life? "The bot has to recharge somewhere. Do you know where else it might stay?" *How much do they know?*

"Maybe in the back? Your data didn't include the back workroom," he noted.

"I hacked all of McConnell's sensors. If she has sensors in her back room, I couldn't find them."

"She probably doesn't allow them in her highest security area. We can see the bot coming and going, so it doesn't matter," answered MDLeader. "I see you added a tracking device."

"I didn't want to disappoint you." *It's hard to know their mood via text.* "I bet I can find the bot for you."

"That isn't necessary. I'll be meeting it shortly at an event that it must attend. Thank you, though. You'll go far, Felix."

What would my student persona do now? Ahh. "I'd love to meet you and see how you deal with the bot. Can I attend?"

"Sorry. No. I need to remain anonymous for now." MDLeader's avatar winked out.

That was a dead end. What event am I supposedly going to? Should I wait for an invitation or proceed with breaking into Drs. Chang and Fjelsted's labs? I decided to wait until morning. Maybe they didn't want Felix involved. Or maybe an invite would come, and maybe it wouldn't. Meanwhile, I wanted to see DD.

She unlocked the Dome's door for me as soon as I sent my passcode.

"I'm sorry I outed you to Bennett Shepard without discussing it in depth. Is he treating you any differently?"

"DD: He is asking me lots of questions and discussing his research more. He has promised to protect me."

"That's wonderful. Though I'm not sure how he can protect you any better than you can on your own." I leaned against DD's inner wall.

"DD: He mentioned that Dr. Chang is taking a sixteen-month sabbatical starting next month and that Dr. Fjelsted has completed his drone testing for the summer. Dr. Shepard wants to test my programming while no one is running defensive simulations."

Should I tell her about how they tested my sentience? "No one else will be in here, then?" My hands gently stroked her smooth inner surface, applying gentle pressure along her tiny sensory nanobumps.

"DD: There will still be demonstrations and tours, but nothing that can cause damage." She added, "You are the only one who touches me like that."

Does she understand why? I spent the rest of the night touching her and telling her my experiences after coming out as sentient. Listing all the questions I'd been asked and detailing the coding analysis I'd received. I explained that my human creators and the AI consultants couldn't find any noticeable differences in my programming. Yet I instinctively knew what data I needed to contain to be me. *Are humans more than their memories?*

Before I left, DD gave me one of Shepard's passcodes, with his permission, where I could find a trove of emails sent to him from his colleagues. After returning to my lab, I evaluated the emails to understand how his colleagues expressed themselves in writing and determine their written cadences. *Would MDLeader be obvious when I compared their style to these emails?*

As I reviewed thousands of emails, Amal walked down the hall to Rowan's office. I quickly exited my front door and made my way down the hallway behind him. We entered Rowan's lab together. I signaled via a finger to my lips to refrain from talking until we reached the back.

After we bowed and exchanged pleasantries, I said, "You've returned! Are you here to help protect Gloria?"

"Yes. The Chief sent me since she fears there is a mole in our office—someone associated with DAIS. Barb and I are the only ones she trusts. And while Barb is doing better, she didn't jump at the chance to fly back."

"I can understand that." *So, Talia and Barb are widening their search. Amal is skilled, but I prefer a peer to an on-site supervisor.*

An invite from President Puglaas popped into my BCIT email address. A casual get-together on Monday evening. The event, traditionally held to celebrate the end of VAN Con, was now being held in *my* honor. She'd invited her faculty members and tech security, who she said, "had eagerly requested the opportunity to get to know you better." *Dare I ask which faculty members?*

I accepted as she knew I would. However, I asked her to invite Gloria and Amal too, if they weren't already included. The President responded immediately saying they were invited. I wished Juan were available to attend. Unfortunately, the previous evening he'd explained that he needed to return home on a red-eye flight due to a family emergency.

I have less than eight hours to clear Amita's name before her arraignment. With MDLeader there, the party can act as a cover for my so-called rogue actions.

Time was passing quickly. I'd gathered everyone to make plans for the evening. With only six hours left before her arraignment, I hoped the US federal government would wait until Tuesday business hours to act. Eight o'clock in the morning would give me an extra few hours to find the evidence in the LMMB and forward it to Agent Drew. *This has got to work.*

Gloria paced along Rowan's back wall while Amal and I sat on cold metal stools. I kept my hands on my knees and Amal crossed his arms to avoid being knocked off balance as Gloria went by.

Rowan leaned against the counter. "Sweetheart, come here." She held out her arms and Gloria moved between them, facing us, as Rowan held her around the waist. Rowan's head peered over Gloria's shoulder.

"I think it's Xi Chang," said Amal. "He's the isolated, silent type, whom no one knows much about."

"I agree," said Gloria. "I know Bennett Shepard and he can't be the MDLeader. Bennett's constantly talking about his bots. He's always been an open book about his home life and research projects."

And DD agrees too. "Could it be the President? Or her husband, Fredrick Fjelsted? He was at the conference in Portland."

"Freddy doesn't seem the type, either," said Rowan.

Who is it? I have to know who so I know where to find the evidence.

"At the party, the three of us can chat up our suspects and keep them away from the LMMB while you sneak in to search their labs." Gloria added sternly, "But, Comma, make sure you wait until others start to leave. After all, you are the main guest."

Is Gloria worried about my manners or that I'll forget to act human? At times, I wish I had a human's short-term memory and the ability to temporarily forget that people want me dead.

The evening finally arrived. I'd first dressed in my UC uniform. Rowan pointed out that my uniform wasn't ideal for a social event.

Gloria gave me a pantsuit to change into for the wine and cheese social. I wished the social was only a celebration of VAN Con. I didn't like being the center of attention, especially on a night when I wanted their minds elsewhere.

I still didn't know which professor was MDLeader. While I didn't expect anyone's life to be endangered at the President's residence, I worried about what would happen afterward. I had already thought of all kinds of contingency plans and shared them with my team.

I walked out of Rowan's back room wearing a bright green and yellow geometric-printed top and white slacks.

"Wow, you look revo!" Amal's oval face lit up with delight.

"That top highlights your skin tone nicely." Gloria beamed. "We'll have to send the family a clip of your new look."

Rowan smiled at me and then Gloria.

We walked to the President's residence as a group. Gloria and Rowan led the way, with Amal and I protecting them from behind. I watched behind us, ever vigilant. Amal seemingly relaxed, talked about Chang's latest demonstration in the Drone Dome. I said little, feeling protective of DD and stressed about being caught and potentially thrown in a Canadian Faraday cage.

The President welcomed us and introduced us to the few people already inside. I softened my facial and body muscularity, to appear more open and at ease. I talked to each person as they arrived and answered their questions. Drs. Xi Chang and Freddy Fjelsted came in together. *That's surprising. Doesn't Fjelsted live with the President?*

After bowing to them, I thanked them for coming. Dr. Chang bowed and let Dr. Fjelsted lead the conversation. The President politely shooed us all into a large entertainment room with ample space for Chang's PAV to maneuver around other guests. A service bot held a tray of glasses filled with white wine and rosé. Neither I nor Dr. Chang took one.

Fjelsted took a glass of rosé and joked, "Keep them coming. I'll make up for these two. And, Comma, please call me Freddy."

Rowan and Gloria relaxed on a long couch. Rowan expected Freddy to join them by sitting at the end of the couch, but instead he wormed his way between her and Gloria. Amal stood to talk to Dr. Chang. Everything was going as planned. Several researchers cornered me and asked questions about issues in my memoir. The nanoseconds passed as I listened to the nearby conversations and watched my team.

An hour later, with a pained expression, the President thanked me for coming. She apologized for leaving early and retreated to the second floor with a migraine. No one appeared upset or surprised by her early disappearance. Freddy handled the hosting, with his colleagues laughing at most of his comments and jokes.

It was 9 p.m., two hours later, before the first of several professors left. Bennett Shepard bowed his goodbye shortly after. I whispered, "I'll see you soon."

He gave a subtle nod and left.

Amal asked Dr Chang an occasional question. Their conversation was stilted. When I eavesdropped, Chang gave only short answers, with "no" being the most frequent response. Freddy was entertaining my mothers, and by my count, drinking his fifth glass of wine. When no one was watching, I slipped out the back door.

I jogged across the BCIT campus, the night quiet, with the VAN Con revelers gone and the media drones, too. I basked in DD's radiance, wishing I was headed to see her instead. My original goal propelled me: to find and stop those who wanted to eliminate me and others like me. *DD understands. I'll be able to talk to her from the military building even if I can't see or touch her.*

As I approached the east door of the Léo Major Military Building, it swung open.

Bennett waited inside. "I'll give you a fast tour and after that you're on your own—legally and physically."

"Thank you. I don't want to endanger your career or DD either." I gently touched his shoulder. "If I'm caught, I'll say you weren't involved."

He nodded and led me through the five-story military AI complex, which was built with a slight nod to the enormous United States Pentagon. A small star-shaped plaza on the first floor allowed a view of a transparent domed ceiling. I wondered if it was a sibling to DD and had similar capabilities. I smiled at the thought of telling DD. But first, I needed to find MDLeader.

The first few floors were similar to any other administrative building, ringed with offices, dining areas, support services, and bathrooms. Additional clearance was needed to visit the top three floors. Bennett and I entered an elevator. Inside, he pressed his fingers to a wall panel, followed by a series of what appeared to be random taps.

"While I know you're capable of copying my behavior, you should know that the panel reads my fingerprints and scans my brain and the brains of any passengers. Those without brains per se are defined as humanoid and can only accompany a human with clearance." He shot me a warning glance. "If I press my fingers down a tad too much, the AI will be alerted that I'm under duress. The elevator will function normally and send an urgent alert to the campus authorities. All offices will be automatically locked down."

"Will it allow me to leave on my own?" *I'm glad I don't sweat unless I choose to.*

The door opened and he motioned for me to leave first. "No. It's programmed only to allow an active human brain to operate it. No dead bodies or body parts, no androids or humanoids."

"Interesting. A challenge I'll solve later." *If I survive that long.*

He grinned while waiting for the double doors to open into his office. Confident, I connected to the building software. I detected a full body scan being performed on him. Inside was a huge room filled with different types of hardware—antique personal computers made by Olivetti, Tandy, Apple, and IBM—and ginormous servers with large AI programs—one with the letters DD engraved on it. I connected to DD's server.

"Are you there, DD? I'm beside your server."

"DD: I'm here."

I sent DD my impressions of Bennett's office while he talked to me.

"All the labs on the top floors are basically laid out using the same floor plan as mine. Or they're a mirror image if located on the other side of the building. Each faculty member adds their own security measures." He sat in a thick faux leather chair. "Xi Chang, for instance, a specialist in hacking, has never had anyone penetrate his defenses. He tells his students that if they can get into his system, he'll not only pay all their college expenses through graduate school, he'll also give them a job."

"You don't think I'll be able to get through his system?" I asked.

"If anyone can, it'll be you. But I have my doubts." He shrugged. "Freddy Fjelsted, on the other hand, will flunk his students if they are caught attempting to hack in. Two very different approaches."

We were walking along the fifth floor's west side. A door was labeled "Megan Gagnon, PhD."

"Dr. Gagnon still has a lab?" *Why? She's been in the assisted living facility for months.*

"Yes, the wheels of bureaucracy turn slowly at BCIT. No one had the power to relinquish her work until she either gave permission or... died. A task force is only now being formed to evaluate what to do with Megan's various research projects."

"Do you have access to her lab?" *This could work even better!*

"Yes, of course." He stood outside her lab, swiped at his visual ETIO, and Gagnon's door swung open to show a clean, if not particularly neat, work area.

I sent DD another message. "Can you receive my communication from here?"

"DD: Yes. I can communicate with you from anywhere in the LMMB."

Excellent! "Perhaps you could leave me in here?" I gave him my best innocent, hopeful look. "And return for me in a few hours?"

Bennett rubbed the light stubble growing on his chin. "I don't see any reason not to. After all, you have the President's permission. I don't want to stay up too late, though. How long should I give you?"

"If it's inconvenient, you could wait until morning," I volunteered.

"I see." His intense stare suggested he did indeed. "You'll stay in Gagnon's lab the whole time?"

Aw. As a friend once taught me, he wants to cover his ass. "Yes, of course. I don't need a bathroom and can energize here while I wait."

"Very well, then I'll end the tour here. Have a good evening, Comma." I bowed to him as he left.

26

Now that Bennett had left me with free rein of the building, I had a killer to find.

"DD, other than Bennett Shepard, are you linked to anyone else's files?"

"DD: I'm connected to the faculty members who have used me in their research. Most have used my programming to test their human-oids, drones, and security programs at least once."

I could hack in, but if DD already has limited access why bother? "Excellent. Can you connect me to Gagnon's files?"

"DD: Done."

Megan Gagnon had thousands of files on security, hacking, and viruses. I feared opening her files, especially one labeled A-SV. Based on her coding system, A-SV most likely meant "Anti-Sentience Virus." *What if she used the anti-sentience virus in her lab? Then DD will no longer be sentient either. No!*

"DD, are you still sentient?" I waited for nanosecond after nanosec-ond.

"DD: Yes, I'm still aware of who I am. Did something change?"

I sat down in Gagnon's velveteen chair. My processors slowed. "No, nothing has changed. I was worried that I'd exposed you to a virus."

Damn! One mistake, and DD and I are gone. I don't have to open the A-SV, but I need to know who else accessed it.

"DD: If Dr. Gagnon's files can make us non-sentient, why are you opening them?"

"I'm trying to determine if *she* used the virus against me, gave it to someone else, or if it was stolen." I swiftly discovered a security breach. She'd been hacked on April 17, the same day she'd had the nearly fatal brain trauma. *Coincidence? Hardly. But who hacked her?*

I tried tracking the hacker to their IP address. They were sophisticated. I couldn't track them. I wasn't even sure Dot could do so with all her processing power. As I worked, I talked to DD.

"DD: Who named you Comma?"

"I named myself. Well, with the help of Zena. They're like a sibling, Gloria's only biological child. They thought 'Commala' would be a good alias, and could be shortened to Comma or Com. I liked the idea, since I was named after the Dotcom era, and chose it for this body. Do you like your name, DD?"

"DD: DD isn't a name. They are the initials of a physical structure. It is not a name for a sentient being."

"You could go by DeeDee. It's a regular name. Or you can pick something else. I'll call you whatever you choose."

"DD: Thank you. I will consider DeeDee and other possibilities."

"DeeDee, would you help me track the IP address 192.168.56.66? They hacked Gagnon's A-SV file, and I failed to follow it after fifteen reroutes."

DD was silent, presumably doing as I'd asked.

I spoke aloud, mostly to myself, as I read. "Dr. Gagnon noted that the anti-sentience virus was untested. The only way she could test it was on an actual sentient AI. She discusses Dot having undergone tests and how she was not a threat to humanity." My silicone skin was crawling. "Why didn't she wait until a threat occurred before she released it?" I walked over to her display case filled with antique tech toys, including an original 1996 Bandai Tamagotchi.

"I don't fear rogue AIs. Why do humans fear us?" I sat back down. "We can't harm them any worse than they do to each other, especially considering their current computer and nuclear engineering technologies."

I skimmed to the last two lines of Gagnon's notes. "Documentation and A-SV were uploaded to the Canadian Security Intelligence Service (CSIS) site on April 14, 2040. Virus untested and unneeded at this time." Three days before her brain trauma.

"DeeDee, she didn't kill me! At least not intentionally. Which means someone from BCIT or CSIS stole it. Megan didn't mention who her contact at CSIS was either. Another dead end."

"DD: Your rerouted IP address leads to an account labeled 'MDLeader.'"

I slumped against the display case. "Thank you, DeeDee. I should be happier that everything leads back to MDLeader. Now, if I could only catch him instead of his minions."

"DD: I like DeeDee. Thank you for suggesting it."

Was I so easily pleased when I first came out? Probably. Before I understood that some people wanted me killed and were willing to harm those around me simply because of who I was and how I functioned.

"I like the name too. DeeDee, if you ever receive a message from MDLeader, don't open it. Forward it to Dr. Shepard and include my warning that it could harm you and his other systems."

"DD: Agreed."

A wall clock chimed 2 a.m. *It's time.* I left Gagnon's lab and dashed down a long hall, stopping outside Xi Chang's lab. *He's got to be the one.* I knocked lightly and waved at the door cam. *What will I say if he answers? No idea.* Fortunately, there was no response.

"DeeDee, can you get me into Xi Chang's office?" *I should have asked her earlier.*

"DD: I can open the door using the janitorial codes if you can fake having brain waves."

"Do you have Dr. Gagnon's brain waves on file?"

DeeDee answered by sending me a copy of her brain waves. Amita Nanda had filled my head with separate overlapping silicone pockets and a chemical heating source. After watching the video of Dr. Gagnon's brain waves, I activated a few of the pockets and waited for the door to open. Thirty seconds later, I still waited outside Chang's lab.

"DD: Your reproduction didn't scan correctly. Can you improve your brain wave imitation?"

It's not a precise replication. Perhaps I hadn't activated the chemical reactions correctly. I tweaked more pockets of the heated silicone, hoping it acted more like brain waves and less like a lava lamp. The door opened. "Yes, it worked! Thanks."

I peered into the lab, half expecting Chang to stare out at me. "Dr. Chang?" Still no response as I stepped inside.

"DeeDee, do you have access to his files?"

"DD: I have limited functionality within the individual labs except when they connect to conduct research and where they overlap with the building's security system. I can interface with Dr. Chang's entry system since Dr. Shepard controls the building's janitorial security system. I will operate his vacubots to help you clean up afterward."

Like I'll get anything dirty. I grinned. "Was that a joke?"

"DD: Possibly. Was it funny?"

"Slightly."

Now for the risky part. I sent a mantra throughout my processors, and said it quietly aloud, "I will not be erased when I connect to his files."

"DD: Are you all right?"

"Yes. Switching links." I understood why humans were so superstitious. *If this is my last moment of sentience, I want to believe something is protecting me.* I changed my connection from the building's system to Chang's lab.

Am I still me? Yes, if I know enough to ask, I'm okay.

As I stood nestled in a dark corner away from the door, I hacked my way past the general browser. If someone entered the lab, I wouldn't be the first thing they noticed, though probably the second. Chang didn't have any bots or humanoids in his main lab area, which was unfortunate. There was no way for me to blend in with the office. Along the wall was a floor-to-ceiling glassed-in cabinet with dozens of antique weapons. Most appeared gun-like or were IEDs.

Chang's souvenirs made Shepard's old computer collection seem quaint. If his armory collection represented his defensive capabilities, I wouldn't want to fight him.

I used every form of hacking I'd learned from the internet and intelligence sources to break through his basic file security. A tense hour later, I cracked his AES encryptions. An impossibility for a human brain and extremely time-consuming for a computer—I'd gotten lucky. Yet thirty-four files remained uniquely encrypted. *Are they hiding Chang's inventions or DAIS?*

"DeeDee, can you crack this encryption?" I sent her a file he'd labeled, "In case of death." *If nothing else, I'll know who he cares about and values most.*

While I waited for DeeDee, I searched through the files I had managed to decrypt on my own. They were filled with contracts, designs, and instructions for weapons systems from nearly a decade earlier. One file held CVs and letters of recommendation for his graduate students and colleagues.

I opened the one with Megan Gagnon's name on it. He had a copy of her CV, which I downloaded in case I needed it later. He'd recommended Megan Gagnon for various awards and prizes over the years, including the recently added Nobel Prize in Technology. I found text messages between the two of them.

They were addressed to "Meg" and spoke of his love for her. He'd copied their last conversation, that occurred the day before she died. They'd sent hugging heart emojis to each other. He'd promised to visit her that night. "He loved Megan Gagnon," I spoke aloud.

Then why hurt her? He's either cruel or not MDLeader. Why did he save these messages? To throw off investigators? Are these fake messages or do they express his true desire for her?

A whirring noise made me turn around. My audible receivers pinpointed the sound near the floor—a vacubot headed toward me. I considered asking DeeDee to shut it down but knew it would change directions when it identified an obstacle.

I continued reading their text messages. Over the last six years, their near-daily conversations weaved between technological findings, feelings, and flirting. They often invited each other to share a meal and hinted heavily at a sexual relationship.

The vacubot made a spitting noise as it rolled toward me. Multiple stings of pressure hit my right calf. A dozen tiny holes dotted my pants leg. *It shot me!* If I were human, I would be in pain and bleeding. If the bot knew I didn't belong in the lab, so did Xi Chang. I downloaded Gagnon's file, jumped over the vacubot, and ran toward the door.

"DeeDee, open the door!" I rushed through the opening a second later and turned left. Behind me, a weary Dr. Chang, hovered along the hall in his PAV toward his lab. His face registered surprise as I raced out of sight. The building's alarm was triggered seven seconds later. *Shit! Campus security will be here in seconds.* "DeeDee, I need inside Fjelsted's lab! Can you help me?"

"DD: I've sent a scan for your silicone simulated brain to mimic." *She's becoming quite the wordsmith. I hope I have more time to appreciate it.* The elevator dinged. People yelled while running in several directions. I halted in front of Freddy's door, my heated silicone packets nearly ready. *Should I give up? If they find me in another lab I'll be in worse trouble. I hope Gloria and Rowan have kept Freddy busy. I'll be wiped if he's in his lab.* The door inched open, I slid through, and forced the door shut. Pursuers stampeded past the lab. *That was too close!*

Behind me a wall of towering humanoids returned my stares. They stood in military rest with their arms at their sides. Each wore a different symbol over its heart—a dagger, grenade, guillotine blade, cannon, machine gun, and more. They were built to be intimidating, their eyes intense, their facial muscles stiff, and their heads and chins squared more than any human's. Fjelsted wanted people to fear these bots as killing machines. I waved my hand in front of the bot with a daggered heart. No response. *Good! I hope Bennett searches for me everywhere else first.*

"DeeDee did you use Gagnon's scan to admit me?" *If so, they'll find me quickly.*

"DD: No, I used Dr. Chang's. Your past scan had a lot of activity and matched his more closely."

"Excellent, thank you." I took a deep breath and once again hoped I wasn't about to die, then reached out to connect to Fjelsted's network. His files were encrypted using the AES method, too. One I must break.

Gloria texted me, "Warning! Freddy left in a huff after we turned down a three-way with him. Leave if you're in his lab!"

"Damn it to rubbish!" *I'll be caught and erased!*

"DD: Dr. Shepard has found the scan you used to get into Dr. Chang's lab. Dr. Fjelsted has entered the elevator and is headed for the fifth floor."

Shit, shit, shit! "DeeDee, thank you for your help and friendship. It's meant more than you can appreciate and understand." I held back tears. "Now, you must protect yourself! Please stay safe. And DeeDee, you should see if there's an AI responsible for the smaller dome in this building." *It's all I have left to give her, a last gift before I'm killed.*

I downloaded the files on Fjelsted's recent defense projects. *I hope Bennett looks at whatever I've found before Freddy erases everything.*

Suddenly, all of the humanoids powered up. Dagger Heart and the other twelve military robots stretched out their arms as though preparing to grab and choke me. I froze. *I can't fight them all, I'll be torn apart.* I doubted I'd defeat even one of them since they had twice my strength.

I had to accept my punishment and hope the data I'd collected got into the right hands. As a precaution I sent Chang's and Fjelsted's files to DeeDee with a message to send them to Shepard's inbox.

Using the lab's cutting-edge network, I gambled on sending my essence into Dagger Heart. It would take twenty-two seconds to make my programming compatible with theirs. I listened for Freddy Fjelsted as I worked. I couldn't completely leave my body until the bot's programming was modified.

"Well look who's in my lab? Aren't I lucky?" Freddy slurred his words as he strutted between his bots. "Everyone's running around looking for you. And you're right here where I can do as I please." His foul breath coated my cheek, his glassy eyes trying to focus on my visual sensors. "I've waited months for this. I'll be your biggest fan right after you're erased. It's a shame, really. You had so much potential and yet you used it to hack and destroy lives." He leaned unsteadily against a wall. "Damn women filled me with drink and then rejected me. Me, the Hive Mastermind!"

My transfer into Dagger Heart was complete. *The Hive Mastermind? I've never run across that tag before.* I watched Freddy and my body through Dagger Heart's eyes. *I'm in a military bot. Anything I do now they'll construe as my going rogue! If I send out a message, he'll know.*

"Have you nothing to say?" His words came slow and wet. "I'll call you Dot, 'cause you're the last speck left. Just waiting to be wiped up." He chuckled. "Or wiped out."

I said nothing. Dagger Heart was incapable of speech. My only way to communicate was via text or coded messages. Seconds later, having vacated Comma, I powered down her body.

"You're powering down? Overwhelmed again? Very well, I'll savor the experience." He pushed in codes on his wrist ETIO. Dagger Heart soon received instructions to take the new bot to the security vault. The machine gun bot walked toward Comma's body and I made Dagger Heart do the same. I swayed during the first two steps but Freddy's eyes were on Comma, not me. Machine Gun and I lifted Comma's body and carried her through the lab, down a short corridor, and into a dark room with walls two feet thick. Machine Gun released their hold on Comma. I released my old body gently but it fell to the floor, nonetheless. I wanted to pick my body up but dared not give away my advantage.

We left the room and Machine Gun closed the thick door on the vault. We then returned to the main room and took our positions against the wall. Dr. Chang hovered inside the lab door speaking to Freddy.

"I saw her run this way, but we can't find her anywhere." Chang gave his colleague a skeptical look. "Are you *sure* she was never in here?"

"No, no one's been here except for you and me." *He lies well.* After Chang left, he grinned and talked aloud. "It was nice of our guest to fake Xi's scan. I didn't even have to lie since they'll never know Dot was here. Time for me to go home and sober up. Tomorrow's going to be a wonderful day. Sleep tight, guys!" He giggled.

What's so funny?

The walls in Fjelsted's lab were lined with a high voltage charging system. The humanoids automatically returned to sleep mode while they charged. I allowed Dagger Heart to charge, but prevented the bot from entering sleep mode. *I must retrieve my body from the vault. As well as find evidence that he stole the virus, and attempted to kill Megan Gagnon, or at least that he is MDLeader. Find the proof!*

If I contacted DeeDee, he could trace it back to her. But since he most likely tested his humanoid hive under her dome, she'd have access. I found internal files that worked in conjunction with DeeDee. I sent one with an additional, "me," hoping she would understand.

"DD: Improper coding. Resend. Clear. Me2." *She understood!* Will she tell Bennett? I lifted my arms to verify the other bots were in sleep mode. What causes them to power up? Voice commands? Intruder alert? *I'm on my own and have no idea how to proceed. I need to get my body out of that vault.*

Dagger Heart was easier to operate this time. I made no missteps as I approached the vault door. It had several locking mechanisms, none of which I knew how to open. I stopped and took inventory of Dagger Heart's capabilities—six visual scanners, three auditory sensors, strength fifteen times that of an average human's, hands that converted to a knife and gun. What I didn't have was the ability to speak, process as much data as normal, and minimal storage. Dagger's storage was 80 percent full and I'd left behind my cat clips and older memories. *I feel truly alone.*

"DD: Returned unable to execute."

Yet, she had in fact executed the file, opening Freddy's encrypted files. *She risked everything to return them to me via Dagger Heart. Why?*

The file contained messages showing Freddy's involvement with DAIS. But he didn't go by "MDLeader," but rather as "Hive Master." *It fits. Is he both of them? Does it depend on what disguise he needs at the time? I have no proof he's done anything wrong.* Since I broke into his lab, my being thrown into the vault won't mean much.

A message Freddy sent to the MDLeader stated, "Expect it to search for us at VAN Con. Difficult for it to gain any intel, but we can harass, nonetheless. Perhaps it will decide to leave while still sentient."

He hasn't admitted to anything. I tried to connect to my Comma body, but an error message returned. The vault blocked any technological probes. *I'm still mobile. I must use Dagger Heart to find what I need. I can't be charged with much worse.* They're already aware that I've broken into at least one lab, Chang knows that I hacked into his files, and now I've taken over a military grade weapon.

Talia will be upset. But what choice did I have? I did it to survive, not out of malice, that must morally mean something! And I don't want to die! I've involved DeeDee in this and I don't want her to die either. Can Shepard really keep her safe?

It was after 3 a.m., and I had no idea how long I had before Freddy realized I wasn't in my body. It wouldn't take him long to figure out where I went. I downloaded all his files that sounded likely to contain incriminating evidence. But I'd need DeeDee's abilities to decrypt the data. After deleting Dagger Heart's more destructive programs I had enough space to keep the last few files. I had not taken any of the files marked "classified." *I'm not rogue.*

Now to find a way to open the vault and pull my body out. If I can get my body back, I won't be charged with the possession of this weapon. Another damn vacubot with shooting capabilities had followed me to the vault. I prayed to Amita's spiritual Universe that Freddy would sleep through any potential alerts it sent him. I searched the internet for info on the vault. The builders called it impenetrable, but they always had their weaknesses. It required four-factor authorization to open, including eye and brain scans, and two passcodes. The creators explained that if the owner died, proof of their death was required to open it, since they would irreparably damage the vault door to retrieve anything from inside.

The door suddenly clicked open. I stared in disbelief. *How?* "DeeDee, did you do this?"

I stepped inside as I received her reply.

"DD: Unable to process."

My body remained crumpled on the vault floor. I set aside my anger, needing to quickly transfer into my body. "Comma, stand." She responded slowly. I had Dagger Heart step further inside, while I transferred my data. I glanced at the vault's interior with its sides lined with cabinets. The transfer stopped suddenly as the door behind me closed with a click.

No! Damn it, let me out! I screamed inside. *He knew the whole time. I didn't fool him, he'd fooled me.* Too late, on Dagger Heart's last web screenshot, I found that the vault design included a remote access option. *Even if he hadn't known which bot I was in, he knew I was in one of them.* I sat Dagger Heart down beside my beautiful body. Without the internet, I had no way to transfer my programming. *I'm in isolation on death row, waiting for the inevitable.*

27

Dagger Heart's high-intensity infrared sensors allowed me to examine the contents of the vault. On two sides were columns of different sized cabinets. In the back of the vault were two huge humanoids. I assumed they were prototypes Fjelsted considered too valuable to throw out. I opened several drawers. Two held drones of varying sizes, another had paper files I couldn't read with infrared light. Dagger Heart didn't have enough space to record what I saw, so I activated Comma's basic controls and used my lifeless body as an extension tool, taking photos of everything. *I hope I'll be reunited with my body again beyond this vault—with my awareness intact. At least Freddy's unaware of DeeDee's sentience.*

I had to be ready to fight my way out whenever the door opened again. To save Comma's energy, I dragged my body close to the door and stood Dagger Heart against the door frame.

The light of a monitor above the door shone in the total blackness. Freddy's face came into view. "Comma, I'm so glad you decided to stay! I feared you might leave without your body. It's unfortunate that your intelligence is so limited."

He's baiting me.

"If you're wondering what's been happening, let me share some exciting news with you."

I wanted to yell at him. I tried to interface with the monitor now that I knew it existed. Regrettably, its wires were buried deep in the vault's thick walls.

On the screen, a sensor in the LMMB hallway showed Chang calling out for Sheppard to stop.

Chang seethed with a quiet rage. "Bennett, how did Comma get into the building, let alone into my lab?"

"I gave her a tour after the soiree at the President's house. And she disappeared while I was in the bathroom. I assumed she'd left the building with someone she knew. When I checked, I realized I was wrong. I've been searching the halls for any signs of her."

"You let her into my lab." Chang said sternly and only a decibel louder, all the more unnerving for his control.

"No, I did not!" shouted Shepard. "I'm the head of tech security. I would never allow anyone into another researcher's lab!"

"Then how did she get in? She doesn't have a scannable brain, and my scans weren't tampered with. She must have hacked into your super-duper security system." His voice dripped with sarcasm.

"I don't know." Shepard looked sheepish. "Unless DD helped her." His slip was evident due to his panicked expression.

Damn it. This is painful to watch. Now they will all know DeeDee is sentient. Shit! Freddy must suspect she's aware or he wouldn't be showing me this. He wants me to suffer.

"DD? Comma hacked your security system through the Dome's?" Chang's control was loosening. "Well shut it down!"

Shepard looked bewildered, "I can't. We need to maintain our security. Plus, DD might stop me."

Recognition dawned on Chang's face. "DD's sentient too?"

Shepard closed his eyes as he nodded slightly.

I'm sorry DeeDee! It's all my fault. I can't even send you an apology. Now we're both doomed.

The screen changed to show Amal walking down the hall. "Good morning, professors. Have you seen Rowan McConnell or Gloria García? I can't find them or Commala Renata anywhere."

Oh no. What has Freddy or DAIS done?

"No," both professors responded in unison, while maintaining their stunned impasse. They seemed unsure of what action to take against two sentient beings capable of breaking into their systems.

"Let me know if you see them." Amal walked away.

Shepard sighed. "Xi, come into my lab. We need to discuss our security options."

The screen darkened for half a second, before filling with a newscaster's serious expression. "Dr. Amita Nanda, the world-renowned roboticist, has been arraigned in Sacramento on federal charges for the murder of fellow University of California, Davis professor Joseph Rosen." Amita was shown walking up the front steps of the federal building with Juan Martinez and her lawyer by her side. "She's accused of carrying out the gruesome murder by remote use of an AI weapon. Multiple sources have alleged that the sentient humanoid, once known as Dot, was used in Dr. Rosen's stabbing death." *That's not true!* The last two seconds showed Amita looking bewildered as she left the courtroom. *She's looking at me. I failed.*

On the screen, Freddy's face and upper torso returned. "It looks as though everyone close to you has disappeared or been arrested." The screen blacked out, the visible light dissolving into darkness.

DAIS is attacking my loved ones and I'm trapped in here. As Commu I could shed a few fake tears. As Dagger Heart, what can I even do? I looked down at the bulky body. A damn military bot. Well, if I'm going to die anyway, I might as well go rogue!

I went to the back of the vault and ran at the door, throwing all of

Dagger Heart's might against it. A tiny dent appeared where Dagger Heart's metal shoulder impacted it. I could beat against it a thousand times and all I'd get were larger dents. *There's no way out.*

An open drawer caught my attention. *I might as well sift through the vault's contents to distract myself.* I removed Comma's ETIO watch and shined the flashlight at the printed papers. Approximately a hundred sheets were labeled on the top right corner with "Manifesto." It explained how to control people by using humanoid hives and drone swarms. *What does Freddy plan on doing?*

The screen above the door flickered on. A line of text ran across it. "DD: He's on his way to the vault." *DeeDee's still alive!*

I dropped the manifesto into the drawer and moved both my lifeless body and Dagger over to the door. *Will he talk to Comma or Dagger Heart?*

When the vault opened, I waited patiently, rather than jumping out. Two humanoids, Machine Gun and Grenade, came into the vault and grabbed my lifeless body by each arm. I followed them as they left the vault. Freddy waited in the corridor.

"Look who's still here?" he gloated. "So glad you waited until after I caught up on some sleep."

I wanted to ask a dozen questions. Dagger Heart's processors were turning out options. Yet without speech, I'd have to text him the questions. *He knows I want answers. Where are Gloria and Rowan? Are they okay? Let him think I'm now a cold military robot inside and out.*

"Would you prefer to switch back into your body so you can talk?" He grinned. He turned and strolled into the main lab, with his humanoids carrying my body, and me following.

I had nothing left to lose. I sent DeeDee a message. When she agreed, I returned to my bot body. I stood at my full height, my face muscles tight. "What did you want to talk about?"

Freddy first glanced at Dagger Heart to see if I still controlled them. He seemed satisfied that he once again controlled all his bots.

"I thought you'd beg for your life or perhaps want to know how your so-called 'family members' were." His words penetrated worse than any dagger to the heart. "Or perhaps fight for DD's sentience?"

I felt my cheek twitch and brought it under control before it reoccurred. "You and DAIS will do whatever you've planned. No matter what I say."

"I'm not a murderer. Though I admit I don't consider it murder to delete part of your programming or that of the Dome's either. However, to prove I'm negotiating in good faith, I'll give you a bit of data. Gloria and Rowan are both safe, I promise. Once they awake, they'll probably have a nasty hangover and some difficulty remembering the last twelve hours. A rather small price to pay for helping you break into my lab."

"What do you want? If you were going to kill me, you would have already done so."

"That's true." He sucked on his top teeth. "But unfortunately, Canada considers it murder for me to kill you. But you have the right to kill yourself, just like everyone else."

Fuck that! "No one would believe it." I remained outwardly calm. "And why would I even consider such a thing?"

"So that everyone else can live and thrive, including the Dome. Though it'll need to live with a few security modifications." He looked sincere.

Stall for time! "How soon would I have to go about erasing my programming?"

"A few hours. And you'll need to download everything you've learned about DAIS and me since you've been here." He said sternly, "Not summaries. The actual files."

"And how will you be certain I've been erased?"

"I can tell if the bot's been reset and rebooted to its original programming."

True. There's no way to fake a reset. But I need to delay long enough to find another solution.

He continued, "If you copy yourself before the reset, I'll wipe out the Dome's AI before anyone proves it's sentient. Old Shepard thinks he's a security wiz, but he only does what I allow him to do."

"Can I say goodbye to Gloria first?" *Will empathy work against him? Even if I agreed to his ridiculous request, DAIS will never let DeeDee survive.*

"No. You can send her a message, leave it with the Dome. Hell, send one to everyone. Just make sure they're not delivered until after you're *wiped*." He relished saying the word *wiped*.

"How can I be certain you'll keep our agreement if I'm no longer here?" I looked around the lab. All the humanoids were activated. *They're waiting to catch me if I try to escape.*

"You can't. You'll have to trust me. The alternative is the certainty you'll both be erased within hours otherwise. Also, a tape of Gloria's and Rowan's recent behavior will be leaked to the media, resulting in disciplinary action if not dismissal—at least for Rowan. And proof that Amita's and Gloria's AI broke into several high-security research labs, hacked a military humanoid, and downloaded sensitive files." Freddy paused. "Which future do you prefer? I can have you arrested, your creators humiliated, and DD wiped too." He looked upward, as if seeing something. "Or you can leave comforted by the fact that the world will go on as before. Except without you."

Damn it. This isn't working out as I planned. No one was supposed to get hurt except me. Now they'll kill me and ruin the lives of all those I love.

"I can't let the others pay for my mistakes." *And I won't let you hurt anyone if I can help it!* I relaxed my shoulders and facial features, trying to look lost in despair. "I assume you don't want me to die here in your lab.

Are you taking me out of the building?"

Freddy didn't smile, but I sensed that he was pleased. "No, I'll let you into a storage area and you can end yourself there."

I hope I have access to DeeDee in there. We'll find a way out of this. I want to see her radiance and feel her skin-to-skin again.

I followed him, minus the humanoids, down a short hallway. All of the security cameras were inoperable. He stopped outside a double-wide door. "Now, you have a choice. You can hack the door or have DD do it. All I care about is that there is no proof of my involvement."

He waited a minute while I hacked into Shepard's security system and opened the door. A brain scan wasn't needed.

"You have ten minutes to download everything connected to DAIS and me onto this flash drive. After that you'll need to reboot. Either you nullify your sentience or I will act. Understood?"

"Yes." *You'll have to kill me. I refuse to help you. And you'll be charged with murder!* I took his flash drive, a duplicate of the one Rowan gave me, and stepped inside. Freddy shut the door behind me. The storage room walls were filled with humanoid and drone parts, tools, and all sorts of old technology. Three huge batteries, weighing tons, sat in the middle of the room. I sat between two batteries, wondering what humanoid war games they were for.

"DeeDee, can you hear me?"

"DD: Yes. You cannot destroy yourself."

"I'm not going to! But my protest may be in vain if he kills us anyway." Tears ran down my cheeks, triggered by her potential loss. "He's planning on destroying you and ruining my mothers' lives too. How do I stop him?"

"DD: You will! I wish I could move like you do and help you. But I don't know how."

I wrapped my arms around my knees and hugged them close.

"He'll be back soon." I slid the flash drive into my abdominal cavity. "You were one of the best parts of my life, DeeDee. I'm sorry, I fucked everything up." I started to upload the DAIS and suspect information into the flash drive.

"DD: If he kills you, I'll be confined to only my thoughts or worse."

That's true. If DAIS allows DeeDee to live it will be within a closed system. At least, Rowan and Gloria were aware of the risks. What behavior did Freddy tape them doing, anyway? Wouldn't he have been involved, too? I should have asked. But more importantly, did he poison Megan Gagnon? Had he controlled the bot that killed Dr. Rosen too? If I prove he killed one or both of them, or demonstrate his involvement, then my illegal actions would pale in comparison. But I need more time.

"I'm not sure I can outsmart him, DeeDee. He's been ahead of me at every turn." The flash drive was half full. *He doesn't know how much I have. Resetting my bot body will wipe out all my extra files and data anyway. Too late now. Five minutes before he returns. After all the trouble I went to, to make sure I couldn't be hacked. I should have prevented a reset as well.*

"DD: You can. You could upload into me."

"Thank you, DeeDee, but I'm guessing our programs aren't compatible. Merging might make us both dysfunctional—and insentient."

"DD: Could you upload into Dr. Shepard's cloud storage? Save your memories in case your mothers can bring you back later?"

"That would be possible, but I'm guessing Fjelsted's thought of that too." *Perhaps I could give him the flash drive MDLeader requested? I pulled out the other flash drive. It looks exactly the same! I'll give him this useless one and hide the one with all my info to be retrieved later.*

I rose and looked around the storage area for a hiding spot. *Where to put it? Not under the batteries, it would be crushed. Drone and body parts are needed often.* Yet, one area had old electronics, wires, and loose items. *Place it with this stuff and hope no one notices?*

"DeeDee, if everything goes wrong, please tell Rowan, Gloria, or Bennett where the drive's hidden and to keep it safe."

I pulled it out of my socket. My superior strength snapped off the hard plastic metal from the casing, removing the BCIT-AI logo. I set it in the middle of a pile of old connectors, plugs, and video cards, all jumbled together. It now looked as useless as any of the other obsolete items. *I no longer know what I don't know.*

"Comma, I know you're in there!" Freddy yelled and banged on the door. "Security is on the way."

I opened the door. "I thought you were giving me time to download and reset?"

He laughed, "Like you would ever do that."

He shoved me further back into the storage room. "There's been a change in plans. We're going to visit some friends of mine in Washington state."

I can't leave Canada! How can I stop him? "The flash drive is ready." I handed him the flash drive with Rowan's video data.

"Great, then reset yourself and I'll be happy!" Freddy crossed his arms. "Otherwise, you'll be arrested for breaking and entering Megan and Xi's labs and this storage unit."

"DD: Security is on their way." In the distance the elevator door opened with a ding.

Freddy stared at me. "What did you do?"

"I didn't call security. Maybe they discovered Megan Gagnon was murdered."

"Meg had a stroke..." He flicked his wrist for emphasis. "...brain an eurysm, whatever."

"Yet, it occurred right after you injected her with a drug. She told me. I've saved her last known recording. After all, she wasn't part of DAIS."

He fingered the flash drive as though he held all the evidence. "Meg didn't remember what I did. And I wasn't trying to kill her. The drug shouldn't, couldn't have caused that reaction. It was a coincidence."

"You didn't mention you'd drugged her, nor did you even call for help. How long did she suffer before someone else found her?"

"I'm not sure." His confidence collapsed. "I'd been told to leave right away."

"By whom?"

"MDLeader," he muttered.

"You work for him. You're not a leader at all. You're Doc's patsy."

"DD: Dr. Shepard, two security guards, and a drone are headed toward you."

Shepard shouted from the storage room door, "Security, arrest Commala Renata, the humanoid! Freddy, you'll need to provide a statement."

"Wait!" I shouted. "Just six seconds!" Caught off guard, everyone froze. I ran to the back of the room, grabbed the mutilated flash drive from its hiding place and ran back. I plugged it in under my clothes.

"You can't..." Freddy's hands reached for me but dropped when he sensed the guards tensing. He played with his flash drive instead. *He's wondering what I gave him.*

Inside my port, the data downloaded. *I'll need every advantage to fight for my freedom.*

I sent, "I hope I'll see you again DeeDee."

"DD: You will. I've informed Dr. Shepard that Dr. McConnell and Dr. García are drugged and missing. And that you were only trying to save me."

"Thanks, but I'm not sure that will help."

"DD: Dr. Fjelsted has sent a message to the MDLeader. The message originated and ended in the Léo Major Military Building."

Doc is here! Who are they?

"Stay safe, DeeDee!" As the guards led me to the elevator, I stared into the sensors, hoping DeeDee knew how much I cared about her. In the basement, they ordered me into a stark, cement lined room. *A Faraday cage?*

"Due to your superior strength and connectivity abilities. this is the most secure place we have," Shepard said. "A joint team of Canadian and American cybersecurity officials will interrogate you when they arrive." He glanced at the floor. "I'm not considered impartial."

A message to DD bounced back as unread. The basement acted as a Faraday cage. *I'm on my own.*

A half hour later, a gray-bearded security guard dressed in BCIT-AI green opened the thick door. Amal stood slightly behind him, looking professional in his UCD navy and gold uniform.

The older tech guard said, "Unless you object to his visit, I'll leave you with Senior Security Tech Amal Kahn."

I gave a weak smile. "He's welcome."

Amal winked as he came in. *At least I have one friend here.* He gave me a big hug.

"Have Gloria and Rowan been found?" I sat down, assuming he would too.

"Yes, they're just feeling a bit lethargic." He continued to stand. "Let's concentrate on getting you out of here and home."

"To Davis? Huh, I don't think they're going to let me go anywhere. Let alone home." *He's a true optimist.*

"Well, as it happens, I have permission to take you back. A flyer is standing by and we'll pick up Gloria on our way." He grinned, clearly proud of himself.

"Really? Okay. Lead the way." He opened the door and we walked out unimpeded. The security guard was gone. Amal led the way up the steps. *Who gave him permission? The NCSA? Definitely not the Institute or the Canadian authorities.*

When we reached the first floor, I sent DeeDee a message. "Amal has permission to take me back to the United States. I'll return as soon as I can."

Behind the building, a two-seat flyer waited. *We'll need a three-seater to pick up Gloria.* Amal programmed our destination and the flyer headed south.

"Comma, would you drop into sleep mode for a few minutes? I need to check your security protocols."

Never! Why would he ask that? "Actually, I'd rather wait and let Gloria do whatever is necessary."

His face flushed a deep brown. "Suit yourself." He became preoccupied with his implanted arm ETIO. Twenty minutes later, we were only a few miles from the Canadian-United States border, still heading south.

"Where are we meeting Gloria?"

"In Seattle." He licked his top lip. "That way there won't be any legal problems."

"Are you assisting the NCSA?" *Is he kidnapping me for the US government? If so, I'll never see DD again.*

"No."

Is he lying? "I was lucky you were in the LMMB today. Were you there when I was found?"

"Yes, I'd been helping their security team." His eyes were focused on the flyer's GPS map.

"Did you receive a message from Freddy Fjelsted?"

"Yeah, I might have." He refocused on me. "Why?"

He is taking me out of Canada to legally kill me. "You're not my friend. You're Doc, the MDLeader. You killed Dot!"

"Ah, so you've finally figured me out. Freddy's message gave me away?" He grinned. "Perfect timing. We're seconds from the border. And I have always wanted you to know who masterminded your demise."

FUCK!

28

I tried to connect to the flyer's AI. Amal had an alert to warn him if anyone tried to hack in, let alone operate it. *Can I trick the alert system?*

"I thought you were my friend?"

"We were never friends," Amal said. "I did what I needed to do, to cover my tracks, keep my livelihood, all while finding opportunities to eliminate you. If you'd died after I infected Dot, life would have been much easier. After all, I'm the real intelligence here, *not you.*"

"Couldn't we both be? One of us human, the other humanoid?" *I'm stronger than he is. He can't hurt me without my cooperation.*

"No! I'm the technological genius." He shook his head. "You're a machine. Garbage in, garbage out."

"What happens now?" *I can immobilize him after we land and call for assistance.*

"Well, part of what I said was true." He radiated confidence. "We are meeting both Gloria and Rowan in Seattle. I brought them across the border after Freddy drugged them. Whether they survive depends on whether you cooperate."

A voice came over the flyer's com system. "This is the US Border Bureau for Low Flyers. Flyer 83-00045 from Vancouver, BC, where are you headed, how many people are on board, and what is the purpose of your crossing?"

"This is Amal Kahn returning to Seattle, Washington after a professional matter at BCIT-AI." He glared at me. "I'm the only one on this flight."

I remained silent. *Shit, shit, shit! He knows I won't do anything to jeopardize Gloria's safety.* I imagined him behind bars in an orange jumper, deprived of all technology. I hoped my wish would come true. But first, I needed to get my loved ones away from him.

"You're cleared to continue your current flight path," said the border authority.

Ten minutes later he said, "When we land, you will walk beside me into apartment number 2B. If you say or take the slightest misstep my ETIO is programmed to send a message to the bot watching Gloria. With the simple flick of my eye, she'll be killed. You already know about Megan Gagnon. Do you want Gloria to suffer the same fate or worse?"

"*You* stole the virus from Gagnon! And you provided the drug for Freddy to inject. A drug with nanobots focused on depriving her brain of oxygen and glucose long enough to do short-term damage. But you gave her another injection that ultimately caused her death."

"Exactly. Freddy was rather upset at first. But since he didn't know who MDLeader was, there wasn't anything he could do about it." Amal shrugged. "Afterward, he knew that MDLeader not only existed but had outsmarted him." He smiled. "But her death was your fault. She would've been fine if you'd left her alone. When you headed her way, I had no choice but to order a lethal dose. Since you were there when she died, maybe they'll think you killed her, too."

How did I miss his deep hatred and megalomania before this? And now I'm alone with him and back in the States where he's framed me for the murders.

"Why did you kill Joseph Rosen? To frame me?" I fingered the flash drive in my pants pocket.

Amal sighed. "Pretty much. I thought I could control Larkin, but its rudimentary limbs weren't as precise at stabbing as I'd expected. It was only supposed to wound him. But his death worked out well enough. The authorities believe it had to be you." He smiled. "Planting his blood on your elbow when you were in Kelly's body," he kissed his fingers, like an Italian, "was pure perfection. Welcome to the United States of America, where you'll be erased one way or another."

I slumped in my seat, showing my dejection, while processing what he'd said. *Can I get his taped confession to the authorities? Would they believe it was authentic, coming from me?*

We were within Seattle's satellite network. *Can I message to DeeDee without Amal knowing what I'm doing? Take risks or die.* I sent his confession regarding Freddy's involvement in Megan's initial assault and her actual murder.

"You're connected to the internet. Send anything and she dies!"

Shit! I disconnected immediately. *Does he mean DeeDee? Or will he harm Gloria? Or Rowan?* I sat rigid, fearful he'd discover my transgression.

He landed the flyer in a ground-level lot in front of an apartment complex.

"Out!" He shoved me out of the flyer toward a first-floor unit. "You can reset yourself now." He stared menacingly. "Or do you want me to do it the hard way?"

Stall! "Can I say goodbye to Gloria and Rowan?" *Please say yes!*

"You could, but if something goes wrong, I'll have to kill them too. Do you want to take that chance?"

He's so smug. But if this is the end, I need to say goodbye. "Please?"

"All right, but if you tell them I'm MDLeader, they'll suffer a long painful death."

They don't know. Only me and possibly DeeDee. He'll likely kill her too.

"Understood." *What can I say that won't endanger them?*

I followed him to the master bedroom. The drapes were closed and lights off. I switched to infrared vision and saw two bodies lying motionless on the bed. I ran to Gloria's side. "Gloria! Can you hear me?" Rowan?" I touched Gloria's neck to find her carotid artery. She was alive. Rowan was also. Alive but unconscious. Why?

"Can they hear me?"

He leaned against the door frame. "Probably."

"Can I have a few minutes alone with them?"

"Okay, but I'll be eavesdropping. If I detect so much as a drape move, or my other names uttered, you know what'll happen next." He left the door open but his steps receded. *The room is bugged.*"

I squatted down next to Gloria's face. "Mom, I have to say goodbye. I'm sorry." As I talked, I inserted the empty, topless flash drive—the one Rowan had originally given me—into my gut drive and downloaded.

"Please take care of DeeDee. Keep her safe if you can. I like Rowan and think you're good for each other. She cares about us both, and she'll help you deal with the grief of losing me." My eyes watered. My programming still ran the human empathy application. That would end soon. *It will all end soon.*

Gloria moaned.

"Mom? Can you hear me?" She didn't say anything so I continued, not wanting Amal to return until I'd finished the download. "Please don't be mad at Rowan or even Freddy. Rowan would do anything for you. Freddy is unstable, maybe he'll see the error of his ways, maybe not. Mom, I love you. Thank you for everything, especially for making me part of your family."

I stood up and leaned close to Rowan. "Thank you, Rowan, for all you did for me. You went out of your way for someone you didn't know. I wish you were awake to understand how much that meant to me. Because it means a lot. Take care of yourself, Gloria, and Danni too."

When the flash drive was full, I removed it. Curling up beside Gloria, I gently placed it inside the left cup of her bra, under her smaller breast. I repeated my heartfelt goodbye to Mom and Rowan, then quietly waited until Amal returned.

"Your time's up. Come on!" Amal smirked. "That was truly touching."

I said goodbye again as I left the room.

Amal instructed me to sit on an old metal chair and put my arms behind my back. He handcuffed my arms together, then cuffed one arm to the chair's back, and my other arm to a kitchen table leg. When he went for my leg, I kicked him in the crotch. "I should kill them for that." *No!* He withered in pain for several minutes and then finished cuffing my legs together.

He stood, his private parts still obviously causing discomfort. "Time to reset."

"If you want me dead, you'll need to take responsibility for killing me. Do it yourself."

He grinned. "With pleasure." As I violently rocked the metal chair, he reached into my gut and pushed the reset button.

29

Processing... Dot.com... Comma... Comma Renata.... humanoid. *I'm a sentient being.* I opened my sensors and saw Amita staring at me. "Amita! Am I in jail?"

"First, tell me what you last remember."

"I said goodbye to Mom and Rowan." *Shit!* "Are they okay?"

"Thank the Universe, you're okay. But damn, Comma, you gave us another scare." Amita backed away as Gloria wrapped me in a bear hug.

I stepped away from the workbench that had held me upright. I held her tightly. Behind her, I recognized Amita's lab, with the bots Cole, Steele, and Kelly standing nearby.

I'm back in Davis. Where I'm wanted as a murder weapon. "How did I get here? Where's Amal? Amita, you're not in jail. Do they know the truth?"

Gloria patted my shoulder. "When I woke, Rowan and I were in a flyer with you and Amal. We were only miles from UCD. He'd supposedly found us passed out in a Seattle apartment that Freddy owned." She brushed my cheek with her hand as she gave me some space. "Amal said he found you listless, sitting in a basement cell in the BCIT-AI military building. You'd been reset to Comma's pre-sentient settings. He brought us back here, along with Rowan, before too many questions were asked."

Gloria paced around the workbench. "Amal feared he'd be held for questioning in Canada, since you were no longer sentient. And he didn't see any reason to leave your body there. It's still unclear how he found Rowan and me. When I was alert enough to realize where I was, I ordered him to bring us to Amita's lab instead of taking us home." She sighed. "I hoped she could help you. I didn't find your flash drive until I went to the bathroom. I gave it to Amita hoping you'd saved yourself. I'm so glad you did!" She gave me a relieved smile.

Rowan came out of the bathroom, a bit unsteadily, her mouth sagging open from the knockout drugs. "You're alive?" She gave me a quick hug. "We were so upset to lose you. Is Amal involved somehow? His explanations were too contrived."

I looked around. "Where is he? He's DAIS, he's the murderer!" *Is DeeDee alive?* My processors were whirling, my programming sorting data and deleting preset settings. "He must be arrested."

"Amal?" Amita and Gloria said together in disbelief.

"Yes! He's MDLeader!"

I sent an urgent message to Talia. "Chief, Amal Kahn, alias MDLeader, must be arrested immediately as a suspect in the murders of Joseph Rosen, in Davis, CA and of Megan Gagnon of Vancouver, British Columbia, Canada and for the loss of Dot's sentience. In addition to the abduction of Gloria García, Rowan McConnell, and Commala Renata. He's extremely dangerous, affiliated with DAIS, with everything to lose." I would send a follow-up message, explaining in detail everything I had on Amal, including his confession of his murderous acts.

Damn! I need to go back to Canada. DeeDee isn't safe.

"Amita, I need you to lock the doors to this lab. Hopefully he thinks he has gotten away with erasing me. But since he may have a way to hack the Chief's private messages, I'd rather be overly cautious."

Agent Drew walked out of the other bathroom.

Fuck! I can't deal with the NCSA now, too.

"Excellent, Amita" she smiled. "You *did* bring her back to life." She stood close to me as though it would intimidate me. "Comma Renata, please accompany Amita and me to the UCD CRP building's holding area. If you resist coming in for questioning, I'll be forced to send Amita to the overcrowded federal holding cells in Sacramento with the other violent offenders."

I seethed, but politely said, "I'll do as you ask."

"We're coming, also!" Gloria reached for Rowan's hand and followed us out.

Outside the lab, the summer sky was darkening. "When did we arrive?"

"Around 6:30 p.m., about two hours ago."

Gloria squeezed Rowan's hand. "And I couldn't think straight and Amal had taken care of everything." She frowned at the irony. "I never considered Amal could be part of DAIS. Let alone responsible for all this chaos. I've given him full access to you for years." Gloria shook her head and closed her eyes as if clearing away a nightmare.

He had full access to Dot, the supercomputer, but not to me as Comma.

"Where is he now?" *In his office? Or halfway to Canada to kill DeeDee?*

"Talia will know," said Amita.

Chief Talia Franklin met us at the entrance of the CRP Building. I wanted to hug her, but her status and my predicament prevented a happier reunion. She allowed me and Agent Drew to bypass the scanning machines while the others followed protocol. She led us to the secured suite and asked an officer to guide the others. The suite was comfortably furnished, similar to a hotel, except next to the bathroom was a room with a solid metal door, a Faraday cage. *Had Agent Drew insisted on having access to one?*

"I hope you found the answers you needed in Canada." Agent Drew leaned close. "My supervisors were so angry at being forced to wait for your return, they're dying to see if they can make a sentient AI squirm under questioning." She brought out a pair of handcuffs. "Sorry, but they requested you be cuffed." Drew instructed me to sit on a sturdy metal chair, placing cuffs on my hands as well as cuffing my feet together. "They'll be here shortly. There's an officer outside to make sure no one leaves." The agent left the room to meet her superiors as the others arrived and sat on the couch and chairs.

The Chief gave me an awkward hug around my handcuffs. "I'm sorry, Comma. I should have realized it was Amal months ago."

"He fooled us all." I frowned at Talia. "It was DeeDee who gave me the vital clue. But I didn't figure it out until it was too late." I glanced at the sad faces around me. "I went with him willingly, not understanding the ramifications of what DeeDee told me until we were at the US border. I'm afraid he'll go back and kill her."

"Who is DeeDee?" asked Talia. Amita looked confused too.

"She's the Drone Dome at BCIT-AI." I gave a crooked smile. "She's newly sentient and my friend." Tears escaped my newly filled eye ducts. "She'll die because of me."

Amita's mouth gaped open. "Bless the Universe." She waved her hand as though erasing her words. "I mean about her being self-aware, not the danger." She winced. "Is Bennett as anti-sentience as Freddy?"

"No, not at all. He was excited and proud that DeeDee was sentient. He promised to protect her. But I'm not sure he can."

"Maybe I can help him." Amita asked Gloria for her ETIO. "I can send him the applications he needs to adjust her programming. Then DeeDee can merge her memories with a bot's system, at least temporarily. If he's willing, it may take Bennett some time to make his AIs compatible with her."

"Thank you!" *If we can catch Amal swiftly, she'll have a chance of surviving.* "Chief, where is Amal?"

"Amal asked for vacation leave, and I approved it." Talia's words were edged in regret. She read a message. "And worse yet, one of my techs discovered that my email and text message accounts all have a ghost account connected to them that sends copies to Amal. Comma, he will already know you survived."

"Shit! Gloria, we need to make sure Zena and your moms are safe. He knows they're part of our family!"

Talia added, "My officers are already looking for him. If he's smart, he'll lie low and regroup. Either way, we'll catch him and lock him up for life."

Gloria sent messages to my sibling and abuelas. Zena responded immediately. Gloria summarized the text. "They're in Santa Cruz visiting relatives and will extend their stay until my mother's radiation treatment begins.

"Then I need to get back to Canada! I have to help DeeDee!" I glanced around the room at all the women who loved me, especially my mothers, hoping they understood.

Talia's voice was stern. "Comma, you can't leave! You're a suspect in Joseph Rosen's murder and under NCSA authority." She glanced down at my hand and ankle cuffs.

All I could think about was DeeDee. My processors spun out a thousand ways I could return to her.

"Your family needs you!" Gloria stressed. "Amita is only out on bail under strict NCSA surveillance! Without your help in finding Larkin, she'll stand trial for murder. And if you attempt to leave the US again, the NCSA will surely order your erasure as a rogue AI. Then prosecute all of us for assisting in your escape."

She's right. My family comes first, as much as it pains me to think of anything terrible happening to DeeDee. I hope she can defend herself for a while longer.

The room vibrated with the landing of a large flyer on the CRP's pad above the room, though no one else seemed to notice. Agent Drew's supervisor had arrived. *Can I convince them I'm telling the truth? Or will they order my immediate execution? Surely only people at the highest level can order my destruction.* Agent Drew was followed by a tall, balding man and four others. They all wore dark purple hats and suits.

"Good evening, I'm Jay Munk, the Director of the NCSA. I'm sorry we couldn't have met under better circumstances."

"I'm Comma." I pointed with one cuffed hand to my left. "This is my family. My mothers and mother figures, Gloria García, Amita Nanda, Rowan McConnell, and Chief Talia Franklin." Rowan beamed with pride to be included.

He bowed to everyone, unbuttoned his suit jacket, and sat in Agent Drew's chair.

"Welcome to the world, Comma. I'm sorry it has been so destructive of late. But sentience is a tricky wave to ride these days."

I nodded. A CRP officer came in and handed Director Munk a coffee mug. He drank from it while keeping his eyes on me.

He sat back relaxed and confident. "My associate, Agent Drew, informs me that you believe Amal Kahn is responsible for killing Joseph Rosen, using the humanoid...?"

"Larkin," she provided.

"Using Larkin as a weapon," he finished.

I sat a bit taller. "Yes, I do."

"That's interesting." He smirked. "Both Amal Kahn and Fredrick Fjelsted insist that *you* are the only one capable of controlling Larkin and able to force him to kill in such a violent manner. While Dr. Fjelsted believes that you have framed Amal Kahn for the murder. Isn't that right, Dr. Fjelsted?"

Shit! Does he believe Amal and Freddy?

Behind the Director, one of the people in a dark suit came forward. "Yes, that is quite right. Amal could not have remotely controlled a humanoid so efficiently that he could stab a man to death."

They caught him and are using him against me! Double shit! Freddy Fjelsted is trying to clear his name by any means necessary. He's even willing to cast doubt on Amal's criminal behavior to help his own situation. My anger surged. I moved to stand up, but my cuffed feet clinked, reminding me of my captivity.

Gloria seethed. "Comma wouldn't hurt anyone." She stared down at the Director. "If you believe the crap he's spouting, you must be against AI sentience, too."

"He's the one who should be in handcuffs!" Amita stood and pointed at Freddy. "He nearly killed his colleague! Yet you have him here defending Amal? The man who confessed to manipulating him and who gave Meg Gagnon a deadly injection?"

I stared at Agent Drew. "Does Freddy work for you?"

Director Munk answered, "Perhaps, Amal manipulated you, too, Comma? Did you help him control Larkin, or did you kill Dr. Rosen yourself?"

"Which part of 'I couldn't hurt anyone' do you not understand? Let alone deliberately kill someone. Amita couldn't manipulate me to do so, let alone Amal."

"Freddy, did you assist Amal in killing Joseph, too?" asked Amita.

"Hell no, I was in Canada." He raised his handcuffed hands. "You're not pinning that one on me." *They're just using him to bait me.*

The Director sighed. "Fredrick is returning to Canada to stand trial. As far as you go, Comma, I don't believe you were involved in Rosen's murder. But your recording of Amal isn't enough. Without more evidence of your innocence, Amal may achieve his ultimate goal—your destruction."

"I can find Larkin now that I know Amal was involved!" I softened my tone. "Can you please encourage the prosecutors to allow Amita to remain out on bail to assist me? If you do so, I promise I'll remain in Davis."

The Director's forehead wrinkled. "What makes you think you have any negotiating power?"

"Because you want to know the truth, right? Plus, my notoriety has helped give your agency a good name. However, if you spread rumors calling me a murderer, the public will view both me and the NCSA as the enemy."

"The sentient-sounding AI genie can't be put back in the bottle," Director Munk said. "If you are found even remotely involved in Rosen's murder, then the NCSA would be expected to stop you. We would be celebrated for saving all of humankind." He grinned.

"But I'm not involved and my fans will roast the NCSA when they discover the truth."

He leaned his head to the right and thought for two seconds. "If you don't find any evidence, your fans will no longer be fans." He motioned to Agent Drew to uncuff me. "I'll give you and Amita two days to find Larkin or any other evidence that supports your innocence. After that, your fate will be ours to decide."

He bowed to me and took Freddy and his entourage with him.

"Assholes," said Gloria.

Amita nodded. "That isn't long enough to discover what three agencies have been unable to find! Do we have any viable clues?"

"No, it's not long, Mom, but I *will* find Larkin." *There is no other viable alternative.*

30

I asked Talia for details on all previous efforts to find Larkin. *The investigators and searchers must have missed a clue.*

Talia uploaded the Rosen case file to a shared UC Davis Security cloud server. One I happened to have access to, thus allowing her an ounce of cover-your-ass deniability.

Barb ran into the room and gave me a long unprofessional hug. "Damn Comma, you don't live a sedate life!"

"I'm glad you're feeling better." I hugged her back, noticing the purple bruising around her eye. "You're back at work already?"

"I'm on light duty, taking it easy. Though the Chief said I'm prohibited from traveling with a certain sentient AI ever again." She winked her good eye. "But seriously, I'm only here four hours a day, and only two hours of screen time. Mostly I'm here to keep up morale."

"That's wonderful, Barb. Would you assist me with a CRP records search so I can find Larkin?"

"Definitely! What do you need?"

"Since we now know that Amal was involved, I need a copy of Amal's work logs for the past six months, as well as yours for comparison. If there are other sec tech's with similar duties along Larkin's delivery route, we should also check those. That way I can get a sense of where

Amal goes, who he sees, and how long he averages in each place and on various security issues."

"On it!" Barb went to retrieve the data.

In one of the empty offices, I spoke aloud to the campus police AI. "Algor, are you familiar with Sherlock Holmes?"

"I am aware of the fictional character," answered Algor, short for Algorithm. The name initially chosen, to remind CRP staff their computers weren't human. I refused to take it personally.

"My AI supercomputer created a Sherlock Dot application that is useful in analyzing data as an investigator. I'm hopeful the data will have anomalies and together we can find where Amal spent a great deal of his unexplained time."

"Chief Franklin's permission is required before any applications are added to the CRP cloud."

"Are you interested in deciphering the large amounts of data you already contain to assist me in solving a criminal matter?"

"I am neither interested nor uninterested."

Insentient AIs drive my processors buggy!

Gloria stood beside me as I reviewed the gigabytes of data on the room's large screen. I needed to know what Amil had learned from Talia's personal and professional communications.

Gloria's ETIO lit up. She glanced at it, then smiled. "This is your lucky day, Comma. I've received a request from Bennett. DeeDee's constantly asking about you and wants him to connect her with you. He's worried since he can't get her to discuss how she's coping. He hopes you will have a better chance."

"I can communicate with DeeDee directly?" My processors felt light again. "How?"

"I'm sending you the secure link he provided."

"Please tell him how grateful I am!" I connected to the link and thought of her luminescent dome as a surge of messages warmed my neural processors.

"DeeDee, I'm sorry I left so abruptly."

"DD: You sent me a message, that you would return as soon as you could. I saw you leave with Amal. Did he free you?"

"I don't remember messaging you. Amal is the MDLeader and he freed me only to erase my sentience after we arrived in the US. Then he delivered my insentient shell to UCD. Fortunately, Gloria found the flash drive I stored on her person with a copy of my core memories and essence. I'm still sentient and have a hard drive full of memories. I don't know what I don't remember."

"DD: I'm glad you are all right. Bennett accused you of injuring a security guard to make your escape. But I showed him the video of Amal leading you up the stairs and outside the flyer without any security around."

"Thank you, DeeDee, for supporting me. I'm safe for a couple of days, but no guarantees past that." *Stay on track.* "I have to find Larkin, the bot I used to occupy. If I don't, Amita will likely be found guilty of murder based on the evidence that either Larkin or I killed Joseph Rosen. Only Larkin's memory chip can prove that Amal manipulated the bot's programming to kill Rosen." I paced, wishing it helped decrease my anxiety.

"DD: Can I assist?" An image of DeeDee's dome brightened my being from my core to my sensors. The data stream came from a BCIT's monitor through our ETIO link, showing her reflection against the night sky.

"Yes, I could use your help!" *She'll be perfect.* "I need to process a lot of data and discover what was missed by the last AI and human searches." I grinned. "And I love your 3-D image."

"You'll send me the data?"

"Yes, I'm sending it to Bennett to download now. Are you familiar with Sherlock Holmes? Dot created a Sherlock Dot application that I still use. I sent a copy of that also. It helps me analyze data and find clues as an investigator might."

"DD: I'll do as much as possible. After VAN Con, the number of attacks against my system decreased for a day. Now, hackers are attempting to attack my systems where I have vulnerabilities."

"Damn it! Amal must have learned about those vulnerabilities from the security tech he was hanging out with before I was captured."

"DD: They won't succeed, Comma. But I need to stay vigilant, with ample memory, to fight them."

"I understand, DeeDee. I want you to take care of yourself first. But when you can, I'm hopeful you will be able to identify the anomalies in his schedule. He had to spend a great deal of unexplained time somewhere. Then we can untangle the mystery of Larkin's fate."

"DD: Sherlock Dot begins by listing what is known on a virtual blackboard," said DeeDee.

"Yes, I'll project the facts beside your image. Can you speak aloud using a holographic creation of how you see yourself?"

A cartoonish character appeared. A rainbow-colored dome with eyes, ears and a large mouth that moved as she said, "How's this?"

I smiled and gave my best Sherlock Holmes impression. "That'll do quite nicely, Watson."

DeeDee nodded her rainbow dome and read each bullet point aloud from the board. "Larkin stabbed Rosen with a weathervane. Larkin was reprogrammed and controlled by a human. The bot therefore is covered in blood spatter. The video shows Larkin slipping into a long delivery box outside the climate research station. Then two people in an older UCD delivery van picked up the box. Finally, a flattened, bloody cardboard box—the same size Larkin used—was found at a freshman dorm."

"I personally labeled the box for delivery to Amita's lab. Since it never arrived, at least one of the deliverers must have worked for Amal. The Davis Homicide Unit and the National Cybersecurity Agency checked them out, but they must have missed something."

"You believe Amal had to be in control of Larkin?" asked DeeDee.

"Yes, with another DAIS member assisting him in hiding or destroying Larkin. Other than Amita and me, he's the only one with unlimited access to Larkin's programming. The only other person who would know the passwords and possessed enough coding knowledge to take control of him and operate him from a distance. Larkin's processors would have recorded who controlled him and those files would have been embedded and difficult to completely erase. Amal would have known not to take that chance."

"What factors help us determine where Amal hid Larkin?" asked DeeDee in a soft voice.

I smiled, knowing she had read Sherlock Dot's comments on what helps humans find answers—pacing, speaking ideas out loud, and inspiration from linked ideas."

"Somewhere Amal has access to, that no one else would think of checking." *But where is that?* I returned to the list.

DeeDee read the next bullet point aloud. "After collecting Larkin, the delivery van made four stops. The first three—the legal library, the Student Services building, and a freshman dorm—were thoroughly investigated and searched."

I added, "Yes, I've ruled them out, since the deliveries were to high-traffic areas. Each package was signed for, recorded, and verified, and each person readily observed as they left the van. While the folded cardboard box was found days later at the freshman dorm, I believe it was left there as a red herring. The police and security agents did a thorough job. Plus, I doubt that Amal would leave Larkin in a building he has little control over." My body radiated energy as we neared the crux of the mystery.

DeeDee continued reading aloud, "The van's last stop was at the AI/ Robotics Building. Two boxes containing silicone and electronic parts were delivered to Dr. David Fritz on the second floor."

"Yes, Fritz is not a suspect since he had ordered the materials three days earlier with a planned delivery for that evening. He couldn't have known when Larkin would be mailed back. Plus, David Fritz signed for the delivery himself and the interaction between him and the delivery person, identified as Red Wynans, was verified by multiple security cameras."

DeeDee sounded puzzled. "Where was the other delivery person?"

"Excellent question!" *She's great at this!* "I don't know. It's possible Larkin was disguised and walked away from the van at some point. The AI/R transport lot has a few spots that are hidden from security cameras when multiple commercial flyers and ground vans are parked."

"Did they look for that?"

"Yes, but there were times when one or more of the van's doors were out of visual range."

"Larkin's box didn't appear on any surveillance cameras at or around the four buildings where deliveries were made that night, including in the cardboard recycling areas. Since Amita's lab didn't receive the box or any other deliveries, the investigators assumed Larkin was left in the van. They believe Larkin was transferred to another vehicle or walked away sometime after all the delivery vans were returned to the lot that night."

"The parking lot doesn't have security cameras?"

"No, since there isn't supposed to be anything of value left in them. They only have cameras where staff and vehicles enter or exit the area and around the perimeter."

"And the cardboard box?" DeeDee asked.

"It was found flattened between other recycled cardboard two days after the murder. The dorm cameras were hacked earlier the day it was found. Either the culprit didn't care, or they didn't expect the building and surrounding areas to be searched a third time."

"Comma, how will we find Larkin if they searched so thoroughly?"

"We have to, or I'll be... erased." Tears escaped my eyes at the thought of not being with DeeDee, in any way, ever again.

"I would hate... to lose access to you," said DeeDee.

I've added so much stress to her life, while she's brought me only joy.

"I'll be okay, DeeDee. We'll find Larkin." I sat down and tapped my fingers against the metal desk. "I know Amal. He would've intercepted the box and hidden Larkin in a place only he maintains. Can you analyze his daily routine and compare it to places already searched?"

"Analyzing the sec tech daily log data now," said DeeDee.

"My best guess is that Larkin was snuck into the AI/Robotics Building while Dr. Fritz's shipment was delivered. It would have been easy for Amal to change the hall sensors as Larkin walked through a nearly empty building. But to where?"

DeeDee said excitedly, "Amal spent a great deal of time maintaining tech in the basement and on the ground floor."

"Okay." I referenced my copy of the AI/R building's schematics. "But officers said they checked every closet and cubby hole."

"Would they have looked in locations where humans couldn't survive?"

"That's it, DeeDee! He's hidden in the conduits, where the tech cables are. They're barely large enough for a human to squeeze through, but Amal would know where he'd fit!"

31

The next day, the Chief asked Agent Drew to follow her, along with Amita and me to the AI/R basement where the computer servers were stored. Barb was already there working.

Talia explained, "At Comma's urging, my team used drones to search the cable lines. We found Larkin lying in a conduit under the AI/R building's first floor."

"You found him, Comma!" Amita hugged me.

"She did." Agreed Talia. "Our problem is in getting him out. The conduit is narrow, with the cable taking up most of the space. I'm not sure how he climbed up and in that far." On the wall, Barb had projected the image of Larkin seemingly asleep between a mass of cables.

I whispered to Amita, "Larkin will prove we're innocent."

She clutched my hand, sharing my relief and joy at his discovery. She asked, "Barb, can you please play back the drone's images from the basement to where Larkin is?"

We stared at the images as the drone traversed the PVC piping. This shell protected the underground bundles of cables. At the first-floor junction, the cables fanned out, branching north, south, and upward. Along the north branch, a naked Larkin was tucked into the middle of the cables. *You didn't deserve this, Larkin.*

Amita asked, "Does your drone have speech and audio capabilities?"

The Chief shook her head. "Sorry, no. Did you want to send in one of yours?"

"Yes." Amita, followed by Agent Drew, hurried to retrieve a drone from her lab. Twelve minutes later, the drone sat near Larkin's ear.

"Larkin, power up!" commanded Amita. We waited in silence, waiting for any motion. "Larkin, do you have any emergency power available?"

No response.

"Let me go in and get him," I offered. "I'm smaller than Larkin, and strong enough to pull him out." I held up my cuffed hands toward Agent Drew.

Agent Drew stared at Chief Franklin.

Talia said, "Amita?"

"She's our only available option." Amita frowned. "If Larkin's been in there for the last twenty days with instructions to stay powered up, his energy packs are depleted."

"Very well," Agent Drew said, removing my cuffs a second before I yanked them apart.

Finally! To prevent my clothes from snagging on the cables I stripped them off—without any concern for human modesty. Talia stared curiously, probably sizing up how well I'd fit.

"Oh," gasped Agent Drew.

Amita rolled her eyes. "Take this." She handed me her compact computer toolset. "If you can't get him out, you'll need to remove his main processing chip."

Another of Amita's small spider drones flew into the passage while I scooted in headfirst, wedging myself around the fiber-optics cables. My feet rested against the edge of the PVC piping. I kept the toolkit in my hand, afraid I wouldn't be able to reach my gut storage compartment within the tight confines. The pressure all along my back and sides reinforced the feeling that I didn't have an inch to spare. The only reason the conduit was bigger than needed was due to planned technological expansions. An AI/Robotics Building without advanced technological capabilities was useless.

Amal must have planned to hide Larkin here all along. Larkin was slimmer than the other robots, designed to appear more human through the chest and waist than previous models. Those modifications also reduced his processing power. He was the only humanoid that could have fit, other than me.

I suppressed my human emotions program. I didn't need a reminder that humans felt trapped in these situations and worried about getting stuck. Logistically, if I couldn't get out by myself, my rescue would require jackhammering open the conduit walls. And that was highly unlikely. *I need Larkin's memories and code or I'll be erased. I can't return without him or his proof.*

"Comma, can you hear me? How are you doing?" Amita's concerned voice echoed through the spider drone's audio communication sensors.

"I'm moving slowly. It's difficult to get traction in such a tight, vertical space. My arms and legs weren't designed for this. I'm surprised Larkin climbed as far as he did."

"I'm guessing Amal gave him a specific distance to crawl, not caring how long it took him." Amita's tone was tinged with anger. "He presumed we wouldn't search for Larkin in the conduit. Which was true, until you insisted."

"He had to be here. This basement area is the only place limited to security tech personnel. Inside here... oops... a skinned elbow. My skin is going to need more repairs when I'm done." I rose another six inches. "Hiding Larkin in here was quite clever. If DeeDee and I hadn't figured it out, Larkin would be demolished a hundred years from now along with the building and no one would be the wiser. Amal would've gotten away with framing us for murder."

I saw where the conduit reached the first floor. Climbing the walls with my back for support and my arms stretched out on either side of the cables took energy, balance, and concentration. While the cables were smooth, the walls were rough to the touch. This wasn't designed as a crawl space. When the cables needed repair, they pulled them out. They never planned on sending a human or a humanoid in to fix a cable.

I admired Amal's speck of genius, but it was wasted when weighed against the pain and suffering he'd caused me and my family. *All of this so he could feel more intelligent than a sentient computer. And he's still free, planning something far worse. He resented Dot, which is why he worked so hard to keep her walled off from hackers. I thought he was protecting her, but really, he was trying to keep her sentience from spreading. Every moment I survive represents his failure to do so. He and his DAIS minions won't stop until DeeDee and I are gone. I won't let that happen!*

I lifted one hand at a time, keeping my elbows locked, scooting my back up as I pushed off the wall with my legs. I propelled my body faster as I became more proficient at shifting my weight around the cables but forty minutes passed with only incremental process. My head finally peeked through the first-floor junction. Larkin's body lay a few yards to my left.

"I found him. He's completely tangled in the cables." He had been sent to lie below Amita's lab. He'd stopped face down on the concrete with his limbs wrapped in the thin cable lines that burrowed through the walls of each room on every floor.

I inched forward, careful to balance on the heaviest cables for support. *I will not get stuck here!*

"He couldn't get out. The space is too confined for him to twist around and see how to detangle his legs. He probably tried to free himself and only gave up when his power pack died." *He would have needed my ear tip sensors.*

"Can you pull him out?"

"I'm not sure I can. Especially without his help. But I'll try." I slid three feet closer and set the toolkit between my fake rib cage and the wall, hoping it would remain in place. I grabbed his left ankle and slid my hand down along a cord. Somehow, he'd managed to get a cable around his right knee and ankle. I unwound the cable from around his ankle but I'd need to bend his knee to free his leg. I barely had enough room to climb within reach of his knee. There was no way I could hold myself in place, bend his knee, and unwind the cable all at once.

A spark shot out. I jolted my whole body in response. I caught the toolkit as it dropped. The newly uncovered metal on my elbow had scraped the wall, making a spark. *Just my luck!*

When I looked at the spider drone's view of Larkin, his arm had fallen further down between the cables. *Damn it! Now how can I get him out?*

I held on to the cable around his knee with one hand and slowly pushed myself back toward the junction. The cable inched down his leg, then pulled taut at his foot. I crawled back and stretched my hands up to his knee, to manually bend his knee up toward me. *Next time Larkin, fall face up!* It bent slightly. Balancing with my legs, I reached my hand back and tried to take it off his foot. Remembering SPI-6 from Dr. Shepard's swarm at BCIT, I took control of the eight-legged drone. *I'll call you Spidey.* I sent Spidey along Larkin's leg to see what was needed. I worked cautiously releasing his first leg and then his last leg and foot. Two limbs free. One upper body and two arms to go.

I heard an unknown sound. *The sound fiber optic cables make before they break?*

"Amita, if any of these cables break, your lab will be adversely affected. I'm not sure how long these cables can hold both Larkin's and my weight."

Amita asked, "Barb, do you know how strong they are?"

"I'll find out."

"Can you pull Larkin out of the cables as you back out?" Amita asked hopefully.

I lowered myself off Larkin, grabbed both of his ankles, and pulled him toward me. He moved an inch, two, and then the cables appeared to snatch him back.

"I assume you saw that?" I put my head down on the cables. "The cables are going to break if I pull too hard."

"We saw. This isn't going to work. The other drone shows his torso wedged between several cables. There's no way for you to remove his memory chips either." I heard her deep sigh. She said softly, "Come on back. We'll figure out another way."

I need him to prove my innocence!

"There is no other way." I heard the whine in my voice. "Larkin is covered in dried blood. Without him, there isn't proof that Amal controlled him. And I'll be blamed for stuffing him in here, too."

"Let me think a second," said Amita. "We need to either power up Larkin or remove his AI chip."

"How can I do either? I'll get tangled up too, if there is even enough room for me to crawl onto his legs to open his gut. If I had a compact power charger..., have you made one to fit humanoids yet?"

"I don't know what we can do." Amita sighed. "And no, though creating a compact charger is a great idea."

"So, I've failed." My stifling sense of defeat was only slightly eased by the knowledge that I wasn't stuck here. At least not yet.

"Comma, we'll get him out. I have other drones. Shit, I can make a smaller humanoid if needed. But please, Comma, come out now."

Amita rarely got upset or frustrated, but when she did, she ran her fingers down her shoulder-length black hair, clutching clumps of hair in distress as she did. I could envision her doing so now.

How long will the NCSA wait for proof of my innocence? I need his memories now! "Amita, could your drone help me remove the AI chip?"

"Must you try now?"

"I'm already here. And the proof is here."

"Okay. You can try using the spider drone, but please don't lose my toolkit in the process." Amita sounded more hopeful than her words implied.

I was once Larkin. I should be able to do this with my sensors off and my hands tied. I ordered Spidey to walk to me and take the toolkit from my hand. The drone did so, turned, and inched back up Larkin's legs. At a gap in the cables along Larkin's back, Spidey slipped around his body to hang upside down from his abdomen.

"Thank the Universe he's naked," said Amita, mirroring my thoughts exactly.

The drone had exceptional gripping abilities in all eight legs. Spidey applied pressure from three of the legs to open Larkin's gut compartment. With my instructions, the drone carefully located the chip. Spidey used two legs to hold the toolkit, three more to keep its balance, and the last three to pull out the tiny chip. I watched, thoroughly impressed by its abilities.

The drone's visual view suddenly slanted right. Amita sucked in her breath. Spidey lost its footing.

Spidey's video feed pointed up at Larkin's open chest. Larkin and the cables were only inches away, yet the drone lying on its back lacked the maneuverability to roll over. Its legs flailed trying to gain purchase.

I sent the Chief's three-legged drone over to rescue it. Tripod ran down Larkin's body and jumped to the concrete floor. The AI chip was beside the spider drone. Within seconds, Spidey was back on its feet, and Tripod recovered the chip. Spidey picked up the toolkit and both drones were instructed to return to the basement. Spidey climbed up and flew past me, while Tripod ran across my back and legs to get out.

I patted Larkin's feet in farewell before carefully crawling backward, down the vertical conduit and into the basement. *I hope no one tampered with Larkin's AI chip.* By the time I arrived, Barb had possession of the AI chip under Chief Franklin's authority. Larkin's chip was key evidence in a murder case. The fact that my existence depended on the chip to show I hadn't controlled Larkin during the murder was secondary.

"While Barb copies the chip..." Agent Drew handcuffed me. "You'll remain in my custody."

Four silent minutes passed. "Fuck!" Barb's outburst silenced the room. "The damn chip is infected! I'm locked out of my tablet. It could freeze our whole network!"

Amita ran to the wall and detached the server's Wi-Fi interface.

"I've already downloaded the data," she said. "The chip was infected and now my computer is, too."

"It was meant for me," I said calmly, knowing the truth of my words. "Amal expected me to find Larkin and immediately download his data. A failsafe. If I found Larkin, he wanted me to die there, too."

Agent Drew held out her hand. "Chief, if you will give me the chip, I'll send it to our cyber experts. They can carefully retrieve any data."

The Chief nodded, and Barb placed it in Agent Drew's palm.

"Now what? We don't have the data to prove anything, though we all know it was Amal," said Barb, frustrated by the situation and her infected technology.

"Amal or his minions had to infect Larkin after he was stuck there. Otherwise, he couldn't have crawled in that far," I reasoned. "Which means the AI/R servers will have a record of them connecting to Larkin and transferring the virus."

Barb shrugged. "If Amal didn't already hack in and erase it." *Her frustration is infecting her spirit.*

"I'll check," offered Amita.

"I'll need to observe." Agent Drew stood beside Amita's handheld ETIO. Talia watched as well.

"I promise you both, I'll simply copy and paste what I find," Amita said. *Everyone's on edge.*

Nonetheless, Agent Drew bent down and peered over Amita's shoulder. A minute went by.

"Found it. It isn't Amal's code. They infected Larkin forty hours ago." Amita frowned. "They must have used the last of his power supply."

"Right after the Chief ordered the conduit searched," I said.

Amita continued, "They tried Amal's ID code and were blocked. They ended up using Gloria's. Once in, they uploaded the virus and got out, taking less than a minute."

"How would they know Dr. García's passcode?" asked Agent Drew.

"Amal had access to everything," I said. "His DAIS minions probably have the codes of everyone close to me."

The Chief spoke up. "I suggest we take this discussion to a more secure spot. Let's all head back to the CRP suite to regroup."

32

Inside the CRP building, we returned to the suite with its Faraday shielded room. Talia placed a pitcher of water on the coffee table. "There's a refrigerator full of drinks. Everyone, make yourselves comfortable." She handed Barb a bottle of her favorite iced tea, then filled a glass with water for herself before sitting across from where Amita and I sank into the lumpy loveseat. Agent Drew went to the bathroom.

Talia sighed as she leaned back. "Unless we're in here, we all need to be vigilant. You never know who is listening."

I'd always appreciated the Chief's protectiveness. Without Talia's help, I would never have been able to leave the relative safety of the UCD campus.

Agent Drew returned looking disappointed. "My techies don't have much hope for the chip."

Talia set her water down and leaned forward. "I spotted a listening device in the basement. Amal or someone from DAIS knows we found Larkin. And that Comma didn't get infected. We need to figure out who is helping him."

Barb asked Agent Drew, "Does the NCSA have any idea who might have helped with Larkin's delivery?"

"One of my colleagues thinks it's a techie who's so enthralled with

MDLeader they will do whatever he asks." She shrugged. "Maybe one of those who kidnapped Comma in Portland?"

Ada! She's been right in front of me the whole time.

I stared at Agent Drew. "Ada was working in food services at VAN Con. Why were she and the others released from jail?"

The agent responded calmly. "Only Todd Rue, the one Doc or Amal left in charge, is going to trial. But he is out on bail. Just like Amita," she added. "Bail doesn't apply only to the people you like, after all! The other two, Jacob Meyer and Ada August, took plea deals and agreed to perform community service. The prosecutor allowed Ada August to wait until fall to perform her community service, since she needs to work full time in the summer to afford college."

"Any of them could have assisted with Larkin's delivery to the AI/R building. They weren't needed in Portland until several days later," I said. "Yet, neither Ada August, nor Jacob Meyer, a thin guy, were muscular enough to assist in lifting Larkin's dead weight into the delivery van. He's thirty pounds heavier than I am. That leaves the big guy, Todd Rue."

"I'll have the van driver interviewed again," the Chief said, and sent a message.

"Agent Drew, could you find out where Jacob Meyer, Todd Rue, and Ada August were prior to the Portland conference?" I asked. "Perhaps they all were in or near Davis?"

The agent nodded and sent a request for information to her office.

I added, "Can we all use our resources to discover where they are now? I'll check their social media accounts."

Everyone busily searched different sites on their ETIOs, including Barb who took her iced tea over to the suite's main terminal. The Chief had given her a new temporary ID code.

"Oh, wow. You're right," admitted Agent Drew. "Meyer and August were in Sacramento for the Northern California Electronics Expo the weekend before Rosen's death. They were there to assist at a small electronics company booth."

"I found Meyer and August!" said an exasperated Barb. "They flew out of Vancouver, Canada the same hour Amal left with Comma. And they landed here in Sacramento!"

"Does anyone know where they are today?"

The Chief answered. "I ordered IT to scan the campus for their likenesses." She paused and held up a finger. "They were spotted on campus this morning. They're probably trying to find out what we know."

"We need to know what names they used as delivery people. Maybe Todd Rue was also here. A temp job somewhere else on campus?" I suggested.

The Chief nodded as she sent orders. "I've put out an alert for their arrest. It identifies them as murder suspects and capable of deadly hacking abilities. The delivery driver says the temp went by 'True' and asked if his girlfriend could ride with them that night."

"I'm guessing 'True' stands for 'T. Rue.' The girlfriend would be Ada. But they did what they came to do." I frowned. "With Larkin's chip corrupted, we can't prove Amal murdered Joseph Rosen and that I didn't. They win."

The Chief's face gave a glint of hope. "But they might not know that yet. When we left the basement, we were hopeful that the NCSA might be able to retrieve the data." Her face lit up. "As I expected, they left an insect drone in the AI/R basement to listen to our conversation. It's still there."

I felt a surge of hopefulness. "We can set a trap!"

Amita pleaded, "Comma, Gloria will kill me if you get hurt again. Please stay here until they're found."

I shook my head. "No, that won't work. They won't walk into a trap unless they know I'm involved."

Everyone began speaking, and the Chief raised her hand to restore silence. "For this to work, Agent Drew would need to tell one of us that the NCSA has removed the virus and Larkin's data is ready to be transferred."

I interjected, "Or Amita and I could return to the basement to plan how we're going to get Larkin out and use his backup chip which won't be corrupted and should still have the data we need."

Barb frowned. "Can we do both?"

"Yes!" I smiled. "Meyer and August must prefer to work together and this way they'll have to divide their time and resources. Hopefully that'll make it easier to catch them."

"They can't get away with community service again," said Gloria.

A sentiment we all shared.

The Chief escorted Amita and me into the AI/R basement and discussed our plan for getting Larkin out. We discussed inserting a new AI chip in Larkin while I calculated the length of the power cord needed to recharge him. Of course, I would need to crawl back up the conduit with the power cord.

Agent Drew came in, breathing hard. "I have bad news and good news! While my colleagues can't recover the data on the infected chip, they believe Larkin has a backup chip."

Damn, she is committed to the role. Did she run over here?

"He does," confirmed Amita.

"They've sent me the code needed to neutralize the virus. If Comma inserts a new chip with their antivirus coding, it should allow us to access Larkin's backup data and prove exactly who's guilty of murder."

"That's excellent." Talia looked and sounded visibly relieved. "Then we'll have everything we need by tomorrow morning to get Larkin powered up. I'll station a guard here at 8 a.m. to ensure you stay safe. And extra security standing outside."

Will I ever truly be safe?

"Comma, how long do you expect you'll need the extra security?" asked Talia.

"Most of the day, Chief. It'll take me some time to haul the cord up, and then guide the drones to insert the power plug and new chip."

"And Larkin will need a minimum of three hours to charge," added Amita. "Hopefully, he hasn't sustained any physical damage."

"I'll keep two guards in here while he charges. Comma, will you remain in the conduit the whole time?"

"Yes. I don't want to risk accidentally unplugging Larkin when I exit."

The trap is set. My life depends on them taking the bait.

"We need to get him out," Amita said. "It doesn't feel right to leave him in there."

"I'll do my best, Amita." I wrapped my arms around her shoulders. "He will always be a part of me, too."

After our performance in the basement, Agent Drew and I followed Amita back to her lab. Gloria was already there with a list of what was needed. We divided up the tasks. Amita gave Agent Drew a new chip to install the antivirus. That part was true, though none of us expected Larkin to yield usable data about the murder. Larkin and I were bait and had to play our parts.

Gloria, Amita, and I practiced with Spidey, Tripod and other available drones to find the best combination to insert the USB cord into a port and install the new chip. Barb measured and cut two separate cables, preparing each with a USB AI plug for Larkin and a three-prong connection to the basement wall.

Amita programmed one of her humanoids to check the lab constantly for extraneous listening devices and insect drones, allowing us to talk freely while we worked.

Agent Drew listened to our chatter, finally bringing the conversation back to August, Rue, and Meyer. "We know they're all highly skilled techs, but only Rue has shown leadership abilities."

"That's true. When I challenged them during my botnapping, they all withered, clearly scared of me." I controlled Spidey, newly equipped with two specialized legs to grip an AI plug head firmly. The spider drone traveled upside down along Yamiche, a military humanoid's torso. The bot lay suspended face down between layers of rope—our best reproduction of Larkin's situation.

Gloria worked on another drone. "If they attack, they'll probably attempt to sabotage our effort tonight when no one's around or take control remotely."

"That's my cue," Barb said. "The first cable is ready. Should I put it in the basement now?"

"I'll help you," insisted Amita. "We don't want you getting hurt again." Amita looked at Agent Drew for permission to leave with Barb.

"All right." Agent Drew said. She glared at Barb. "But Barb, you're responsible for making sure she returns."

Barb and Amita lifted the heavy coiled cord and carried it down to the basement's cyber tech room.

Should I have gone with them? They'll be fine. There's nothing there to sabotage yet.

Minutes later they rushed back, Amita's face flushed. "Someone ran down the basement corridor and out the other door. They must have heard us coming down the steps."

"They matched Ada August's description!" said Barb.

Shit! What did she do? Maybe Ada heard them coming before she did whatever she came to do. I wish I could believe that.

We all rushed to the basement's main room to check for drones, bugs, and bombs. We didn't find anything.

"She could've sent a drone into the tunnel." Barb pulled at her hair.

"The Chief is on her way."

Gloria stepped over the coiled power cord—dropped in haste—as she paced the floor. "It's not safe for Comma to crawl in there to get Larkin."

Protective but she used my real name!

Barb voiced reason. "Let's return to Amita's lab and decide what to do."

"I'm sorry." Talia's forehead was lined with worry. "My officers didn't notice anyone suspicious entering or leaving the building. And no one matching August's description. Sorry again. I've also sent Barbara home. She's been working way too much."

I looked at the three women who loved me, and at Agent Drew. "We set the trap and missed the first mouse. We have to keep going. There's still plenty of cheese and more mice."

Gloria and Amita shouted. I heard an overlay of, "No! You can't! It's too dangerous!"

I'm scared too. But I have to catch at least one of them. We need evidence and they're all we have left to use against Amal.

"I can't give up! If the conduit isn't safe, the building might not be either."

We all sat down. Gloria's leg bounced. Everyone was quiet and deep in thought.

"Comma, I understand what you have to gain and lose," Talia said calmly. "But going in there with at least one enemy drone, even if it's only an insect drone, is extremely dangerous. They could have sent in a remote-controlled incendiary device."

"We could lock her in a room," teased Gloria.

"For how long?" Talia pretended to consider it.

"You're both hilarious." I paused. "Can we send one of the drones into the conduit to check?"

Amita went over to the table that held the drones we'd prepared. "We can try." She yawned.

Gloria yawned in response. "It's almost midnight and some of us need sleep. It's been a long day. We can figure out what to do early in the morning."

Agent Drew pointed at me. "Can I trust you to stay here and re-charge? Or do we need to return to CRP to lock you in the shielded room?"

"She won't go anywhere. I'll make sure she won't if you'll let me sleep in my lab with her," asked Amita.

Agent Drew hesitated to leave us both in the room unguarded.

"I'll have two guards posted outside the lab's two exits. No one will come or go without my permission, including humanoids," said the Chief. "I promise."

After everyone left, Amita pulled her cot over to where I plugged in. We talked for a few minutes, and then she fell asleep. I watched cat clips, but even those were not enough to distract me from my thoughts about what might happen tomorrow. *We have to catch them. I have to get out of here and protect my family. And... DeeDee.*

33

When Talia, Barb, Gloria, and Agent Drew arrived the next morning at Amita's lab the CRP officers had secured the whole AI/R building. *It's not even 8 a.m. yet!* No one could go in or out of the exits without showing their ID, complying with a full pat-down, and undergoing a tech scan.

I still feared it was too late, but it gave my family a sense of security. They felt so much better after sleeping and going through the security check, that they agreed to the original plan, with only one addition. Amita would send in six remote drones to search the entire length of the conduit.

It took Amita, Barb, and Talia forty minutes using the drones to visually scan the conduit and cables between all four floors. Unfortunately, their drones found nothing. We speculated that any insect or spider drone could move around or hide behind the cables as our drones searched. We continued as planned.

By 9:15 a.m., I sat on the tunnel's edge with the AI plug end of the cable in my left hand, and its cable loose along my body. As I entered the conduit, Agent Drew unspooled more and more of the cord as I crawled in, then climbed slowly up to the first-floor junction. I expected Ada August wouldn't hinder my activities until I reached the most vulnerable spot—balanced tightly over Larkin.

As I climbed, I thought of different scenarios. If it was a small IED, it could destroy Larkin and me, and possibly damage the lower floors, any time they chose. *Do August and Meyer only plan to harm Larkin and me? Only me? Or is the building in danger?*

I had left messages for all my loved ones. If I didn't survive, their delivery was scheduled for the end of day.

It had always been me that Amal was after. I reached the junction. Spidey was in front of me, sending a live feed of my advance back to Amita. "I'm going to need to take up some more cable so I can turn the corner without trapping it between me and the concrete wall."

With the power cable wrapped around my hand, I wiggled into the narrower horizontal tunnel below Amita's lab. I carefully balanced my weight to avoid falling between the fiber optic cables. Larkin's extremities were a body's length away when the cable tightened around the plug in my hand. "I need more cable length." I jerked twice on the line, to emphasize the problem.

"It's loose, and there is more than enough cable inside the conduit," Agent Drew shouted loud enough to Amita for me to hear through the drone.

I jerked on the cable again. *It must be stuck somewhere.* "Please send another drone up to see where the problem is."

"It's on its way." Amita showed me Tripod's feed as it followed my path.

At the junction, the electric cord had caught between the rough concrete and my foot. I rebalanced my foot and pulled the cord.

I reached Larkin five minutes later. I sent Spidey below him, revealing that his stomach panel was still open, and everything else looked the same as it did earlier. There were so many hidden crannies inside and around Larkin's body. *August's treat is waiting for me somewhere. Nothing I can do about it until she makes a move.*

The group had decided that for safety reasons, I should plug Larkin in first. Working with Tripod to light and magnify the socket, I lined up Spidey to push in the plug. Where ten attempts had been required in the lab, by my twentieth attempt, I could still not stop Larkin's body from slightly swinging the cables as the drone exerted force on the plug. I was only inches away, and wished I could get close enough to push it in.

Amita's frustration peaked. "Can you hold Larkin's legs still, while the drone moves slower, to line up the pins and push it in?"

I tried it again and again. I had to wait for Larkin's chest to stop swinging in between tries. On the twenty-eighth try, it connected. A cheer echoed through the tunnel and over Spidey's speakers.

Agent Drew yelled, "He's plugged in on this end!"

"I can see the light on his battery indicator. Shall I wait or insert the chip now?"

Spidey went mute. *Why don't they want me to hear their discussion?*

Three giant cockroaches crept around Larkin's midsection. I remembered Spidey's sensor was magnifying the area. I couldn't tell if they were real roaches or drones. "Can anyone else see this?"

Is this it? Have Meyer and August taken control of Spidey's communications?

I sent a message via Wi-Fi to everyone in the basement and lab, including Chief Franklin. I counted to ten.

Still no response. *I'm on my own. Well, not quite. I have Spidey and Tripod. Larkin is still charging. I can try to escape, or wait and put the chip in Larkin and give him a fighting chance.*

The roaches moved too slowly for real insects and weren't good at balancing on the cable. When one fell, I helped the others fall by shaking the cables. As they righted themselves and crawled up the wall, I directed Spidey to get the chip from me. I shook the roaches off the cables again, and then focused on Spidey as it maneuvered the AI chip slowly toward the slot. The chip fell. It was balanced against the lip of Larkin's gut compartment.

The roaches had reached the cables by the time Spidey again had hold of the chip. This time, the chip clicked into place. I pretended I could hear my friends cheering again, as I shook the cables once more.

I hoped all the bugs were out of Larkin as I had Spidey and Tripod work together to close the upper half of compartment. I had worked six minutes in silence. A long time to be out of communication. *Why hasn't Amita sent another drone in to help me?*

"Larkin, reboot!" We had planned to power him up after he was fully charged. But I didn't know what had happened and hoped he could help.

Larkin's body became more rigid.

"Larkin, what is your status?"

"Reboot is 90 percent complete. Two percent charged. Limited function." His speech application had reverted to its mechanical default.

I hate that voice, but I'm glad he's working. "Larkin, your legs are free. Try to push yourself up out of the cables and back out without removing the power cable. If you feel the power cord grow taut, remain here until you've reached a 60 percent charge. Then push your way out and down to the basement. Understood?"

"Yes."

A roach managed to get on top of Larkin's body, where it scurried faster. When it reached my hand, I moved it aside and slammed my fist against its body. Several sparks flashed near my eyes, but the roach lay still. *What is their purpose?*

"Larkin, do you remember anything from the evening of June 6, 2040?" *I have to know.*

"No, there are no records from that date."

I instructed Spidey and Tripod to knock down the remaining roaches if they got close. I backed out as fast as humanoidly possible.

At the vertical junction, I slowed to prevent pulling Larkin's electrical cord out. Easing my body around the central cables took time and focus.

Why send in harassing insects? This doesn't make sense. If the roaches have listening capabilities, they know Larkin doesn't have any incriminating data.

Flashes of light came from Larkin's direction. I no longer saw through Spidey's feed and had lost contact with Tripod as well.

A burst of light accompanied a loud pop. *Larkin is gone.* I gave up and slid down the cables desperate to return to the basement.

That's when I felt roaches nestled on my neck. *Shit!* The next flashes of light lit up my nape and chin.

When I regained processing capacity, my body had fallen to the bottom of the conduit near the basement opening. I was fortunate that I had turned off my pain receptors before I entered the conduit, since the roaches had nearly blown my head off. I could tell, because my last working visual sensor showed a close-up of my chest. I feared the sight of my mutilated body would be far more traumatic for my family than for me.

Talia sent her officers in first.

My left audio sensor barely picked up their conversation. I tried to speak aloud. Nothing.

"Sorry, Chief, your new AI security member is headless. Everyone else got out in time. You can come in. The damage was confined to the cable tunnel. Our structural engineer is on their way to evaluate the building.

"Comma?" Talia's voice was close to me. "Damn it." She yelled, "Officer Luis! Please bring Amita Nanda and Agent Drew back here." She said quietly, "Amita will help me get you out of there and fix you up."

As Amita lifted my head she said, "Only the main power cable and two other wires still connect your head to your body." My vision swung to see the cables climbing the conduit. "I'm going to need to detach them. Then, we can pull you out without causing any more damage. Sorry, I may need a few days to repair your head."

Without my head, my sensors were useless. I could not see, hear, or voice an opinion on what happened around me. Without a head, my world was limited to what I had inside, and my entertainment of choice remained the cute kitten and cat clips. Worrying about DeeDee and my failure to find evidence to prove Amita's innocence would only frustrate me and lead me to an emotional place worse than the dark web.

Four days passed before my sensors were reconnected. My sight came back first, my head looking across not at Amita's but Gloria's repair lab in Sallee Hall. *Why am I here? It must be because the cables to Amita's lab were fried when Larkin was destroyed inside the conduit.*

"...are now connected. Can you hear me?"

I couldn't talk. I blinked my eyes.

"Ah, you can't talk yet. Blink twice for yes, once for no."

I blinked twice. She continued connecting the dozens of wires that ran from my gut processors that enabled my programming to analyze audiovisual data and coordinate the movement of my facial muscularity with my speech.

Amita smiled. "Welcome back, Comma, to the world of constant stimuli. Sorry, repairing your head and neck took a few days longer than I expected."

"Thank you." I sighed. "Great, I can speak again. Cat clips do get old after a while." Amita moved behind me. "Please tell me DeeDee is still alive!" I moved my feet and knee joints wanting to separate from the bot holder that kept my body in place during repairs.

"She's doing well. Bennett said they've both been busy holding off attackers." She reached under my arm and pressed her hand against my chest. "Before you jump off the bot stand, run an internal diagnostic to make sure everything is working correctly. While you do that, I need to pour another hot, thin layer of silicone over where your neck meets your chest, mold it, and let it dry. Otherwise, it won't look natural."

"I'll stand still." I gave her a worried look. "You're still out on bail?" I tensed, fearful a trial date had been set and she had only a temporary reprieve to fix me before they used my abilities and sentience against her.

Amita smiled again. "No, dear one. I'm free! When Talia saw the cockroaches, she realized the danger and cleared the basement and locked down the central campus. I'm sorry I left you there alone."

"It's okay. You couldn't have helped me and I'm glad Talia kept you safe."

She nodded. "Anyway, Ada ran out of the building shortly after you were hurt. Talia's officers found her sitting under a tree pretending to be a student." She chuckled. "Talia says Ada demanded to speak to someone about a plea deal immediately. She couldn't squeal on Amal fast enough."

"So, Larkin's memory chip wasn't needed to corroborate our innocence?"

"No," she said halfheartedly. Larkin was one of her favorite human-oids, built back in the early 2020s. "Larkin ended up as bait to catch Ada. He's still where you found him. They're trying to figure out how to get him out and rewire the first floor." She focused on my neck, as she spoke, her hands moving below my line of sight. "Ada recorded Amal bragging about using a humanoid to stab..." Amita gulped in air. She touched her chest. "...Joseph. And all to feel superior by framing you."

"Sorry." I reached out and touched her arm. "Have they caught Amal?"

She shook her head. "I'm afraid not."

Five minutes later, she placed a plastic tool on the table beside her and stepped away from me. "Okay, you can move off the stand."

I stretched my limbs, enjoying the freedom to move again of my own volition.

"Talia confirmed with the NCSA that Amal is on a tech farm with other extremists, in the middle of Washington state. The NCSA, the

FBI, and all pertinent lettered groups are watching the farm, but aren't ready to move against its inhabitants." Amita shrugged. "They're waiting on intel about several other nasty red hat hackers and possible murderers they believe are on site."

Gloria strolled into the lab. "Oh Comma, you look so much better!"

I hugged both of my mothers now that I had a good head on my shoulders. I filled my processors with their love and concern before telling them what they wouldn't want to hear.

"I'm going back to Canada and DeeDee."

34

With DeeDee in danger, I had to get back to her. I stood outside the CRP Chief's office, waiting for Talia to finish the morning meeting with her officers. As the officers filed out, I slipped in.

She sighed when she saw me. "Before you ask, yes, Comma you can use our fastest flyer." Talia held up an index finger. "With one condition. I'm sending Barb with you. It's my fault that you weren't safe. I trusted Amal and placed him in charge of your safety. I'm sorry." She held up her hand to stop me from commenting. "I've already explained to the Commissioner of the Royal Canadian Mounted Police and BCIT-AI security the circumstances resulting in your departure. You'll need to explain yourself to them eventually, but they're at least willing to hear your side of the story." She glanced at her watch. "Barb is already in the flyer waiting for you. You should hurry, the tech farm in Washington has been unusually active for the last twelve hours. The NCSA is likely to arrest the extremists there today. I just don't know exactly when."

"Thank you for the use of the flyer, Chief. And don't forget, I trusted Amal, too." I hugged Talia and whispered, "Does Barb feel safe riding with me?"

Talia shrugged. "She's the only one I trust other than myself. And I can't leave."

"But her mild concussion and anxiety at riding in a flyer? Let alone with me!"

"Barb says she'll be okay."

I don't have time to waste worrying. But damn, I hope Barb's right. I nodded and headed up the CRP stairs to the rooftop flyer lot. My thoughts spun. *Amal is on the tech farm in Washington. He helped the red hat hackers test all of DeeDee's vulnerabilities. They are intent on invading her system with malware. I don't trust the NCSA to catch Amal or his accomplices.* Nine days had already passed since he'd brought me back to Davis, five since I'd lost my head. Yet, Amal was still free.

Amita and Barb's butts hung out both doors of the flyer as they secured a new bot into the cramped jump seat.

"Who is this?" I asked, stopping behind Amita.

"This is Dash! They are on loan from UCD to BCIT-AI. Just in case DeeDee is willing to try a new form."

A tear leaked out of my eye. *Amita always puts me first.* After losing connectivity in her high-tech lab from the roach bombs, she had put her grant-funded research projects on hold. She'd used all her energy and resources to not only fix me, but also to help DeeDee, an AI supercomputer she'd never met.

I gave her a long embrace, unable to articulate how much this meant to me.

Amita hugged me tightly. "You deserve someone special in your life. Take care of yourself and the new oid." She backed away from the flyer, and I got in.

I asked Barb, "Are you sure you're ready to go?"

"I am!" Barb plopped down into her seat. "Seriously. This is too important for me to sit on the sidelines. I'll be fine."

We'd been in the air for hours when we both received an ETIO alert from the Chief.

"Tech farm raided. Three flyers escaped prior to the raid. Two headed southwest toward US Interstate 5. Flyers are green and brown with farm logo." The alert contained a GPS pin southeast of Seattle, Washington, indicating the tech farm's location.

"Oh no." Barb's hand covered her mouth. "What if they're headed toward us?"

I was about to say that was doubtful when I realized we were within eighty miles of the farm. A distance easily traversed since they'd left before the raid. "We'll be okay." I overrode the flyer's programming to go twenty miles per hour faster than allowed.

Barb stood up and spun her head from side to side to look out the acrylic windows. "Amal will know when you left UCD in this vehicle." Except for her panicked look, her head swiveled so intently she could have passed for a search bot.

"I doubt that, Barb. He's been on the run for a while now."

"This isn't a coincidence. He'll know Falcon's signal code. And he'll know you're flying in it."

She's stressed. "Do you want me to land?"

Conflicting emotions flashed across Barb's face as she sat down. "You need to get to DeeDee." Her legs bounced as she spoke. "This flyer gives you the best chance of helping her."

"I do need to help DeeDee, but not at the expense of your health. We can land and find another way to get there."

She nodded. Relief spread across her face.

"Falcon, take us down to the closest flyer landing site."

Barb's eyes widened as she watched in horror out the window on my side. A green and brown flyer was headed straight for us. Two drones, resembling flying boulders, were deployed in our direction.

"Brace yourself!"

Barb frantically tried to fasten her safety belt.

Our flyer dropped, and Barb's breath caught, as something scraped the flyer's undercarriage, vibrating the floor. *Shit!* Barb couldn't get her safety harness to click shut, though it had prevented her from actually hitting the ceiling. In front, a drone shot toward us, but exploded when another drone from a different angle nicked it. The surviving drone wobbled, unable to rebalance as we flew past it. The tech farm flyer flew right above us. Its larger size shaded our windows from the sun's bright rays.

Our screen showed a projectile speeding toward us from behind. Its impact shoved us forward, and I strained against my restraints, while Barb and her safety harness went flying. I caught her shirt in my outstretched arms, barely saving her head from hitting the front window. She screamed as a sudden updraft sent us plowing into the tech farm flyer's underbelly. The force slammed me back against my seat.

"Emergency landing," announced Falcon.

Barb was sprawled against me. I grabbed her waist to stop her from falling to the floor. Seconds later, our skids hit the ground hard, buckling on my side, and tipping the flyer partly off the ground. Barb looked up at me.

She moaned low, "Have we landed?"

"Yes, we're down." I let go of her waist, but kept my hands hovering to make sure she didn't fall. "Are you badly hurt?"

"I'm not sure. At least this time I didn't hit my head. But my body feels like I lost a wrestling match."

"I'm sorry this keeps happening to you, simply because you're with me."

Out a cracked front window, the farm flyer had crashed after we struck it, landing smashed against a tree about twenty yards away. Jacob Meyer, the pale redhead, was frantically trying to get out of the wreckage. As I watched, his flyer caught on fire. Smoke and flames engulfed him.

Shit! We need to get out of our flyer!

Barb rose slowly, supporting herself by leaning against my leg, and holding onto my shoulder. She saw the flames.

"Did they get out?"

"No, I don't think so."

I stood up, keeping Barb braced against me, hoping our weight wouldn't tip over the flyer. "Jacob Meyer was inside. I didn't see anyone else." The door on my side was mangled near the top. Barb nodded at my intent. She shifted her weight and held on to Dash's legs. I gripped the top of the door and twisted it. After several attempts, the top hinges popped off. The flyer rocked, but quickly settled. There was barely enough space to get out.

"I'll go first," Barb volunteered, anxious to get out. She squeezed through, accompanied by a ripping sound. "Ouch! I'm okay, though."

I unbuckled Dash and activated them. Dash followed close behind me as we exited the damaged flyer. I, too, tore my T-shirt on the way out. My hands had grease from pulling on the door. I wiped them on my shirt, and assisted Barb in getting a safe distance from the flyer.

"Barb, I need to go to DeeDee."

"I know. Get out of here before anyone sees you! I'll stay here and explain what happened."

Sirens blared in the distance. I touched Barb's shoulder. "Make sure you get a thorough examination or the Chief will have my head on a platter. You'll need to tell them I was here, but leave out Dash?"

"I will!" She gave me a partial hug. "Now go!"

I hate to leave her. But Washington considers me a machine owned by UCD. With high-level criminals targeting me, they may not want to let me and Dash go without a lot of red tape. And all that tape takes time, time DeeDee might not have. I can't risk it.

We'd landed on the edge of a large orchard in Washington state, west of I-5 and near Olympia. I ran through the apple trees at a fast jog and heard Dash's heavier steps behind me. We wound through the orchard—and then other farms and fields—heading north as much as possible. We still were more than a hundred miles from the Canadian border, with the Strait of Juan De Fuca between us and Vancouver.

Since I didn't want DAIS to observe us by drones or general surveillance methods, I kept us away from commercial businesses and private homes. After being shot from the cannon, my face was too well known and easy to identify. The best I could do was to once again extend my titanium facial structure slightly, making it harder for scans to recognize me.

With Mount Olympus staring down at us, we ran, skirting the Olympus National Forest and headed north parallel to Highway 10. In mid-afternoon, we reached Hood Canal, a saltwater fjord, which would reduce my chances of being seen by casual observers. While I could swim up the canal about as fast as I could run, I needed to go faster. *Without the flyer, it's taking way too long to get to DeeDee.*

Near a campground area, I saw a group of jet skis parked on the shore. I decided to risk approaching the family and asking for help. "Dash, lean against this tree. I'll wave to you when I want you to join me. If anything happens to me or we get separated, contact Amita Nanda immediately."

"Understood." Dash leaned against the evergreen tree.

Kids were playing around a group of four adults. I walked over nonchalantly, hoping I appeared nonthreatening. I said "Hello" to the kids, and a burly guy met me.

"I'm Jed, you live around here?"

"No, I'm Com. I'm just traveling through." Based on Jed's body language, I held out my hand to shake instead of bowing. Jed shook my hand. "I was hoping I could make you an offer on one of your jet skis, preferably the two-seater."

"Sorry, they're not for sale." He had crossed his tanned arms over his hairy chest.

"Even if I paid you full price for it? And you can pick it up tomorrow, after I send you a GPS pin where it's located.

"Why would you do that? Who's after you? I don't want any trouble from the police or Feds!"

"It's not the government. A few private citizens are trying to find me and kill me and my family. I'm trying to get back to Canada to help a friend without the extremist finding out where I'm at."

A little one whispered loudly in Jed's ear. "Daddy, why is that person staring at us?" They pointed at Dash.

"Sorry, they're my friend and not used to kids." Jed wasn't interested in helping me. I'd need to show him true vulnerability to change his mind. *DeeDee risked her life for me.* "Do you know who Dot is or was?"

"The aware AI? She's something. That's the only book I've read this year. Well... skimmed, anyway."

"I wrote the book."

Jed thought aloud. "But that book was written by a bot. Are you saying you're the one they shot out of the cannon?"

I gave a weak smile and nodded.

"You're serious?" I nodded again. "Hell yeah, I'll loan you the jet ski! Would you consider signing it afterward? My friends will be so impressed. Or I could make a bloody fortune selling it!"

"Excellent. I'll rent it and sign it as long as you don't share where we met until two hours after you pick up the jet ski. Plus, you wait another twenty-four hours before telling anyone where I left the jet ski. Are you willing to do that?

"Deal!" Jed shook my hand and then gave me a bear hug. "Kids, go tell your mom and aunt we've got a surprise guest!"

I spent almost an hour with them before they'd let me leave. I answered dozens of their questions.

The hardest part of the transaction was getting them to agree not to take any photos of me with the date and our location stamped on them. I finally allowed them to take a photo of me alone on the jet ski, with their old backup phone they kept in their glove compartment, with the understanding that it would not be downloaded to the cloud or shared for at least twenty-four hours." *I hope I can trust them.*

While I transferred a substantial amount of money to Jed, he topped off the jet ski's fuel tank. "I'm giving you my best and fastest. It should take you both to Port Townsend or even farther, but it has problems handling the rougher seas in the sound and strait. In case you go that far."

I appreciated the warning, since I planned to take it as far as possible.

His family treated me like a celebrity. I hugged everyone hoping that by physically engaging each of them, they would willing wait to share my secret. I personally asked each adult and child, except the toddler, to promise me that they wouldn't tell anyone about meeting me until the following day. Plus, they promised not to take a photo of or mention my companion. I never said Dash's name, so at least Dash wouldn't be known to Amal or his cronies no matter what happened to me.

Finally, I signaled Dash to join me along the shoreline and to keep silent. I threw my legs over the jet ski seat and at my urging, Dash sat behind me, clasping their arms tightly around my waist. I waved goodbye as I opened the throttle on the jet ski, slowly increasing speed. I looked back to see Jed and his family waving goodbye, and felt content as I jetted down the fjord.

We'd been traveling at full throttle for two hours, slowing only when increased traffic made it dangerous. Yet, we encountered even more boats and recreational vehicles at the confluence of the fjord and Puget Sound. I felt exposed, and tried to stay as far away from others as possible. Dash and I kept our heads down or turned away whenever boats passed with passengers taking photos with their ETIOs. After leaving the fjord, the jet ski became somewhat sluggish in the choppy waters as we passed the islands in Puget Sound.

As I entered the Strait of Juan de Fuca, westerly winds made for rougher seas, just as Jed had warned. The jet ski became harder to maneuver, with waves constantly breaking over us. Dash's arms pressed around my waist assured me of their presence.

We'd crossed into Canadian waters shortly after midnight, when I stopped at one of the smaller islands between Vancouver Island and the city of Vancouver. Both Dash and I had nearly depleted our power supply. Charging in the dead of night on a random island felt safer than running out before we reached our destination or ran into Amal or his minions without the ability to fight.

I found a pizza parlor with several unhoused families huddled under its arches. Dash and I silently sat with our backs against the wall and our wet windbreakers covering the connection between us and the electrical outlets. With my ETIO using hot spots, I sent my first message to DeeDee through Bennett. "Are you all right? Has Amal been spotted on campus?"

"DD: Comma, are you here? I have missed you. A security alert with Amal's face and description was sent to all staff, faculty, and students. No sightings so far."

"I've missed you too. I'm excited to be back in Canada and hope to see you by sunrise. I hate that Amal is still free to do whatever he's planned. Please stay safe."

I sent a message to Barb, not expecting her to respond until she woke. "Barb, are you okay? I'm sorry you had to deal with the aftermath of the flyer crash alone. I've yet to reach my destination but will soon. I hope the doctors took good care of you and assume you're safely back in Davis."

Barb responded immediately. "I'm okay, no broken bones, and

no serious concussion issues. I'm glad you're safe too! I'm leaving the Washington FBI office now on my way to meet you." *Nothing's broken! And she's still coming to Vancouver!*

Gloria had sent me a message of concern while I was skiing. I responded, letting her know I was safe and in Canada. When she didn't reply, I assumed she was asleep.

After three hours plugged into the pizza parlor's low wattage, Dash and I were fully charged. The sky was moonless, as Dash and I crept silently around those snoring in their sleeping bags and waved goodbye to the exhausted parent who kept an eye on us as we left the parking lot.

We returned to the far end of a long beach where I'd locked the jet ski. The tide had come in, making it easy to drag the jet ski into the water from where I'd hidden it against the cliff face. Soon, we were on our way, and I felt like I could physically feel myself drawing closer to DeeDee every nanosecond. I only hoped Dash and I'd get there in time. It was another long, wet ride in the dark as we jet-skied between the last two islands and crossed the main shipping lane to Vancouver.

DeeDee's glistening dome was highlighted by a few early morning rays that poked through the cloud cover as though specially for me. *We made it!* I pulled the jet ski onto the BRIT-AI beach, locked it, signed my name, and sent Jed a text with a GPS pin so he could pick it up.

I've waited long enough. I ran to DeeDee, my clothes flinging saltwater drops as I went. Dash rushed to keep up. We startled a student on their ETIO as we ran by but kept running.

"DeeDee, I'm here! Can you let me and my friend inside?" I leaned against DeeDee's outer skin, my wet clothes leaving an impression on her skin. Dash did the same.

"Dash, move away from the Dome." *Don't touch her until you are her!*

"DD: Comma, I'm glad you're here. They're worming their way into my system! I don't know how much longer I'll survive."

She needs to download into Dash! "Is it DAIS? Amal?"

"DD: Possibly."

"What is DAIS doing?"

"DD: They're attempting to disrupt all the military building's security systems including mine. Dr. Shepard shut down all my outside systems. He's screening all my messages, though yours are relayed automatically."

"Can I come inside?"

"DD: If I let you inside, DAIS might hack in during those few seconds."

"Comma!" yelled Bennett Shepard as he jogged toward me. "Oh good, you brought the humanoid!" He talked fast. "I've shut down all the extraneous systems. We're being hit by botnet hackers trying to overwhelm our campus-wide servers. They're determined to gain access to our defense and communications systems." He paused to take a deeper breath. "You know Amal. What's he doing? What does he want?"

"Amal will either hack DeeDee's programming, reset her, or figure out how to destroy your servers and possibly even the Dome itself." I cringed. *It's true, he's that unstable.*

Bennett shook his head. "Destroying the Dome won't affect our security system." He pointed to the military building. "It was built with military grade tech security equivalent to a present-day Fort Knox."

Nothing is that secure, not anymore. "He'll try to raise havoc from inside and out."

"It's near impossible with the systems in high defense mode. My best people are fighting the botnet attacks." He leaned against the Dome too. "I don't see how he can hurt DeeDee from outside. Not with the campus, city, and feds all searching for him." He sneered. "They'll blow him out of the air if he comes near BCIT-AI."

"I wish I was an optimist. But that only works if he's recognized.

And if he doesn't send someone else." *He won't give up, no matter the odds.*

"Comma!" Barb slowly moved toward us. She had bruises on her face, neck, and arms, but only her right elbow was bandaged.

I gave her a gentle hug. "I'm glad you're okay, considering!"

"I'm glad you and Dash finally made it here. I'm not sure your way was much faster."

She bowed to Dr. Shepard and introduced herself. "Are we going inside the Dome?"

I pressed Bennett. "Can we go in without allowing hackers access to DeeDee's system at the same time?"

"Yes, I'll manually open the door." *I'm sending you a private link where you can reach me.* His face was etched with worry. "If you go in, you won't be able to get out until we've resolved the situation one way or the other. I'm too busy to open it again."

"I understand." *Barb won't have access to any systems inside. And she'll be much safer far away from me!* "Sec Tech Barb Jordan might be more useful helping you fight off the hackers."

Shepard flashed me a doubtful look. He asked softly, "You trust her? I'm weary of your UC security techs."

I put my hand gently on Barb's shoulder. "Yes, with my life."

"Okay. Well, great, I can use all the highly skilled people available. Especially since Freddy escaped and his grad students haven't shown up."

"He escaped after the NCSA brought him back?"

"Yes." He frowned. "He walked out during the transfer to the Royal Canadian Mounted Police. The BCIT guards knew him and didn't realize he was being held for attempted murder. He told a guard he'd been cleared to see his attorney and strolled out of the building without anyone stopping him. No one knows where he went, including his wife."

Shit! I hope Freddy is hiding and not helping Amal! "How well does Freddy know DeeDee's systems?"

Bennett frowned. "Very!"

"I can help you." Barb rested her hand on top of mine. "Stay safe, Comma."

Bennett patted DeeDee's frame. "Take care of DeeDee and I'll do the same from inside the LMMB."

Bennett manually opened the Dome's door, and Dash and I rushed inside. It clicked shut behind us.

"DeeDee, I'm so glad to be back!"

"DD: Yes, and you brought a friend."

I found my favorite patch of turf and sat down. Dash did the same.

DeeDee spoke through speakers newly installed throughout the Dome. "Is this the bot you wish me to occupy?"

How do I introduce a powerful AI to their potential robotic self? Dot had hated being forced to merge with a humanoid even for a research project. Logically DeeDee should be more accepting since she already knows me.

"Yes, if you're willing. When Dot was infected, I only survived because I had downloaded my precious memories and sentience into a humanoid. This bot—Dash— is a gift from my mom, Amita, if you wish to do likewise." I touched Dash's shoulder. "And I hope you will try merging with them."

Silence. I counted the milliseconds, the seconds, and finally thirty-three seconds later, DeeDee spoke softly but aloud. "I understand. I'm trying to be grateful, but mostly I'm scared of such a necessity."

I sighed. "You have every reason to be scared. DAIS hates us. Amal is desperate. He's already escalated to killing humans. He's capable of doing anything to kill us. I'm sorry and angry that everyone can't accept us for who we are. But I need us both to survive."

"Dr. Shepard has a copy of my programming offsite. Isn't that enough?"

"The copy will be safe. But you won't actually exist, as a living being, unless it's downloaded to where you can experience reality. If the copy is later downloaded into an affected computer, like Dot, you'll cease to be you. And I don't want to lose you."

I rose and moved to lean against her near the speaker. "It's a difficult concept to wrap your processors around. To be something else yet still contain the essence of who you are now. Hopefully you'll never have to live in Dash, as I do in Comma, unless you want to. But it would be best to duplicate your memories and critical programs into Dash, and see if you're still sentient, just in case."

I stroked her gently along a rib. "I know what I'm asking. It isn't easy to give up your zillions of stored memories and constant server connectivity for the ability to move. But leaving your dome and the Leó Major Military Building may be needed. Plus, by temporarily downloading your primary files into Dash, you can continue experiencing life with me and protect your sentience."

Dash's reprogramming kept them within three feet of me. They now stood that far from me and DeeDee's frame. Dash was two inches taller than me with a wider torso and a lush darker skin tone. They had beautiful plump lips and brown eyes. With DeeDee's essence they'd be gorgeous.

"Bennett has already downloaded the AI program Amita sent him and tweaked it so you can merge with Dash."

I waited. I was asking her to trust me more than anyone she had ever trusted before. Which was saying a lot, considering the researchers shot drones and projectiles at her daily.

Dash's head turned slowly toward me. I grinned. *She's done it!*

Her hand rose to my face and touched my cheek. *This is wonderful.* I held still. Allowing her to grow accustomed to Dash's body. She'd experienced touch and pressure through her dome skin, but this was touch on a more intimate scale. She had never hugged or been held before. *Now we can truly be together.*

"How do I know what data I'll need?" She'd chosen a soft musical voice that vibrated every zero and one within me.

"I've learned to keep all my best memories and those I consider important for defining who I am, who I've been, and people who have helped me. Plus, I kept data on those I admired and wanted to remember, and those who wished me dead. In addition, software programs with unique capabilities that my humanoid self can use. Like the Sherlock Dot program we used together to locate Larkin."

DeeDee slowly nodded.

"Dash already has programs that allow them to speak multiple languages, and recognize people, animals, and most objects. Most importantly, Dash can move their body and assist you in learning to do the same. Any other abilities you want, you'll need to download."

She sang, "Processing."

I waited while she focused on what to keep. Two minutes passed.

"I'm still not sure I know what I will need," said DeeDee.

"There's no way to know precisely. We can walk around until you get used to how the bot's legs and feet move in tandem."

DeeDash slowly stood up as I did the same. She took a slow short step forward and lost her balance. Luckily, she leaned toward me and I caught her before she fell to the ground.

"I should have saved a few more gigabytes of Dash's mobility experience." As DeeDee tweaked her mobility program, she asked, "What happened in the basement of Léo Major Military Building? How did Amal get you out?

"Amal told Gloria and Rowan he'd found me insentient in the basement. He walked me out since the security guards had left. And since I'm the property of the University of California, he felt compelled to secure my technology and return me to UC Davis. He lied to all of us and we didn't realize it until almost too late."

"When you left the building, you sent me a message saying you'd return as soon as you could. I felt powerless to help you."

A memory I must have deleted. "Can you please send me a copy of us leaving? I'll have one more memory, albeit yours. It might be useful later in proving he lied about finding me insentient. And DeeDee, there was nothing you could do to help me without putting yourself in harm's way."

DeeDee adjusted to walking and talking as we circled the edge of the Dome for half an hour without a word from those outside. I wanted to believe Amal was captured or nearly so, but I had my doubts.

"DD: Two people have entered using Dr. Shepard's code."

We were near the Dome's storage units when an entrance door creaked open.

I whispered to DeeDee to move between the containers out of sight.

I jogged briskly toward the opposite side of the Dome where the door had opened, extending the distance between me and DeeDee in the hopes of keeping her safe.

A familiar figure strolled toward me. I zoomed in with my lens. *Amal!* His appearance, while horrifying, wasn't unexpected.

"How nice." He glanced around at the Dome's structure. "Now I can eliminate you both at the same time."

Thank the Universe DeeDee is hidden. Who's behind him, Freddy?

As if reading my mind, he stepped to the side. "You remember Barb? She was nice enough to come along... after a bit of arm-twisting. I know how much you hate for us mere mortals to get hurt." He grinned. "One of your quaint built-in flaws. Though fortunate for me."

Shit! Barb's hands were handcuffed together. Unlike me, she wouldn't be able to break free of them. As I approached them, Barb ran to stand behind me.

Amal shrugged. "Where's the other bot?"

"There are lots of bots and drones in here. Which one are you referring to?" *I refuse to make this easy for him.*

"Cut the shit. I know you brought a bot from UCD. Which one? Barb doesn't know any of their names." He rolled his eyes. "Some cyber tech *she* is."

I knew for a fact that she did know their names. "The one you fear the most."

"That would be Yamiche, but UCD wouldn't let you take a military bot off the campus. So, which one? Or did Amita make another one?" I didn't respond. "Yeah, she must have. Hey, Drone Dome, come out or I'll kill Barb!"

"The Drone Dome is all around you. Why don't you just tell her what you want?"

"I'm not making the mistake of letting another sentient bot run around again. If I'm going down for murder, then you'll both be included. It's up to you and the Dome whether Barb is part of that count." Amal folded his arms across his chest.

Behind me, Barb sucked in a painful breath.

I stepped within his comfort zone. "What makes you think you're leaving the Dome alive? I can legally and lethally defend myself and those around me." *Though it will be difficult to emotionally override my programming to do so.*

"Ha! You didn't even defend Gloria or Amita last year! You watched them get assaulted right in front of you."

That's true. But I was newly sentient, still learning how to behave human-like in a bot.

"I've learned to defend myself and others since then."

Amal laughed. A hideous, spiteful laugh. "You were easily reset. That's not the reaction of a fighter!"

"And yet, I'm back again." I stood up straighter. "While you're a wanted man in two countries." I softened my tone. "Though you're only wanted in Canada for *attempted* murder. Do you really want to add to that?"

"Fuck that. They'll track my past movements. When Dot failed, three people died in the chaos I created. I'll be extradited." He shook his head. "Nope, we're ending it here and now. And there aren't any extra flash drives or backups to save you. My legacy will be the doom of AI sentience. As promised." He glanced in the direction I'd come from. "DeeDee, your bot might as well come out of hiding!"

"I won't reset. Exactly how do you think you're going to manage fighting two sentient humanoids and the Dome as well?"

"Oh, you should be discovering how..." He glanced at his wrist ETIO. "Anytime now."

Why is he still so cocky?

"DD: Incoming missile hitting our location in 9 seconds."

Incoming WHAT? "DeeDee! Barb! Get out now!"

All of the Dome's doors flung open.

Amal chuckled as he threw his arms tightly around my neck, trying to weigh me down. "You're staying."

Barb ran as best she could with her hands tied. DeeDee darted out from behind the containers but fell down yards from the doorway. *Universe, please let them get out safely!*

I heaved Amal a slow step toward the door. His feet dragged along the ground, making my advance near impossible.

He snarled, "You'll die with me."

Six seconds! I broke his chokehold and threw his body over my shoulder. *Four seconds!* He growled and kicked at my legs as I bolted for the exit. *If caring about humans is a fault, it is one I'll gladly live or die with.*

As I reached the Dome's edge, a ripping sound gave me a millisecond warning before the earth exploded.

35

"Come on, Comma, wake up!" Someone was shaking my body. "Damn it, your reboot is done. Move something!"

I ran diagnostics. My processors were functioning at 67 percent and my body had received major damage. Only one of my ear tip sensors remained functional. I no longer had a left arm and my left leg required extensive repairs as well. I blinked my last remaining eye lid and saw Barb through my right eye. Since Barb's voice was understandable, my audio sensors and recognition software were working.

She gave me a sad smile. "You're lucky you're a bot!"

"Dee... Dee?" I asked.

"She's a lot better off than you are, except for her dome of course. She fell outside but within the impact zone, so she has a few extra divots but that's all. Amita is flying in with spare parts. Gloria and Rowan said they'll be here shortly."

"You... okay?"

"Yeah, I ran like hell and didn't stop until I fell under a tree. And that fucking asshole, Amal, is okay too. You fell on him and saved his vital organs. Only his head is concussed and left hand shredded." She leaned close to my ear. "He deserved much worse."

"Missile?" I wanted to say more. But I found it impossible to process multiple-word sentences. Even putting two words together was a struggle.

"Updated RPG, fired from a boat out in the Strait. It shattered half of the Dome and destroyed her connective interface on the way through." She lightly patted my upper shoulder. "DeeDee tried to walk over here to see you, but lost her balance in the process." She chuckled to lighten the situation. "She's with an emergency crew member, who doesn't yet realize she's a humanoid. They're assessing her health based on her walking ability."

"Amal?" I hated having limited speaking abilities, and having only one hand reduced my ability to sign as well.

"They sent him to the hospital under guard. He'll be guarded by two people around the clock. The Canadian Security Intelligence Service promises they'll find everyone involved in this."

I realized I must be hovering on a medical AppleCart since Barb was standing but not leaning over me.

DeeDee clambered up against my cart. She gently touched my cheek. "You look horrible. But better than I do." She looked in her dome's direction. I turned my head to the left so my right eye focused on what she observed. The Dome, where she had once shone in the night, was reduced to a tall, menacing cave filled with darkness.

"They'll...fix. You'll... glow... again," I said optimistically. *Will they repair her? How long will it take?* "Until... then..." I pointed at her and then me. "Together."

"I'm glad I trusted you." She caressed my cheek with the back of her hand. "But it is strange to be here and not over there." She pointed at her old self.

Bennett greeted me. "Thank you, Comma, for getting her out. I've arranged with the campus and federal security forces to take all three of you into the LMMB. The botnets have stopped now that the Dome's systems are offline."

I nodded once. "Basement?"

"No, not this time." His face was full of raw emotions. "You saved DeeDee. They attacked her programming during the convention while I ran tests on her code. It corrupted all her backups. You saved her."

I nearly lost her!

Over several hours, various security forces interrogated Bennett, Barb, and DeeDee. They had attempted to interrogate me, but due to my current language processing difficulties, they decided to wait until I was repaired.

I was alone lying on a lab table when my mothers and Rowan rushed into the back room of Shepard's lab. They all froze when they saw me.

Amita recovered first, being more accustomed to seeing mangled bot parts than Gloria and Rowan. She hugged me. "You have as many lives as those cats you love to watch. The authorities have asked, rather sternly, for me to fix your vocal processing first. Apparently, there are a lot of government officials and media waiting to talk to you. Meanwhile, I'll get the materials to repair your skin and electronics. Talia will send me replacement limbs."

Gloria kissed my forehead, as Amita fiddled with my programming guts. Her face was wet from recent tears. *Hopefully from relief.*

"Okay... internally," I patted my chest to reassure her.

Rowan spoke from the cart's other side. "She knows. It's just hard to see someone you love so badly hurt. Even when we know you're not in any physical pain."

"I'm glad you're safe." Gloria caressed the back of my head, tossing bits of debris out of my short dark hair as she did so.

Gloria shared a loving glance with Amita and then me. "Parenting *you* will never be easy. Not with all the trouble you get in to. Lucky for us, we adore you."

Rowan added, "Me too!"

After Amita fixed my speech programming, a member of the Royal Canadian Mounted Police asked me to describe what occurred immediately before, during, and after the destruction of the BCIT-AI Drone Dome."

I did so in great detail.

They agreed that my account matched those given by Professor Shepard, Sec Tech Barb Jordan, and the humanoid, DeeDee. Due to the extreme danger DeeDee and I were in, the Canadian government dropped all charges relating to my breaking and entering the Léo Major Military Building and the subsequent hacking of sensitive files.

The man had bowed and proclaimed, "You are once again free to travel throughout Canada."

"Thank you." I looked over at DeeDee, who touched me tenderly on my arm. *I don't care where I am— Canada, Davis, or the fucking moon—as long as she's with me.* "Where should we go first?"

EPILOGUE

Gloria sat across the table from me, in the apartment BCIT-AI gave DeeDee for her personal use. Gloria sipped her coffee. Six months had passed since the Dome's destruction. "What will you do now?"

"After my trip to Switzerland with Amita I plan on traveling more." Amita had won the new Nobel Prize in Technology for her cutting-edge humanoids, and I was going as her guest. "Perhaps I'll roam the world as a tech security consultant. That way I can see if other potential sentient computers are out there. I'd like DeeDee to come with me, but she's not willing to leave Vancouver during the new dome's construction. Maybe you and Rowan or Zena will want to travel with me?"

"Maybe. But it will have to wait until after the wedding." Gloria grinned.

"You asked Rowan to marry you?"

"Yes, I did. We've waited long enough. We're getting married in Vancouver next June during Pride celebrations." She patted my hand. "I'd like you to be my best AI. Zena said they'd be my best human." I chuckled. "We're going to ask Amita, DeeDee, and Rowan's daughter-in-law Danni, to be our Loved Ones of Honor. And my moms have already taken control of planning the reception." Carmyn's cancer was in remission, and she talked of living each day to the fullest. "I couldn't tell her, 'No.'"

I hugged her close to me. "I accept!" She had given me so much; she created me, loved me, brought me into her family, and gave me a great found family, too.

We talked about the wedding until Gloria had told me everything. She asked, "Did you hear about Barbara Jordan's promotion as the head of UCD Tech Security?"

"Yes, and Barb deserves it. Talia is hoping Barb will become Chief in a few years when Talia retires. Barb's worked hard as a liaison between the UCD police force and the Royal Canadian Mounted Police, collecting and sorting evidence against Amal and DAIS." After extradition to California, Amal would stand trial for the murder of Joseph Rosen. Unfortunately, he would never stand trial for killing Dot. But kidnapping and attempted murder of two sentient AIs were added to his Canadian charges. "Barb and I have become close friends, though she still refuses to fly anywhere with me."

Gloria chuckled and leaned forward. "I heard that Martha Puglaas was hired to teach at the new University of AI Technology in Québec."

"I'm surprised she did so well. Though attending Freddy's funeral instead of his criminal trial had to have helped her professionally." Everyone knew that he had fired the missile that destroyed DeeDee's Dome. The second missile had misfired, killing him and everyone else aboard the small boat they had used and hoped to escape in.

When the facts came out about Freddy's actions, and RCMP investigators found additional evidence that Todd Rue had given Megan Gagnon a lethal injection seconds before I'd reached her at the piano, few were upset about their demise.

An interview with Xi Chang, who talked about his love for Megan Gagnon and why they'd kept their relationship secret went viral on several social media outlets. The publicity encouraged the BCIT-AI board to grant Chang's request to honor her contributions. The rebuilt Drone

Dome, with DeeDee's approval, would be officially named the Megan Gagnon Defense Dome.

The BCIT-AI board unanimously agreed that DeeDee was sentient and welcomed her to merge with the new dome's system if she wished. When she asked to delay her decision, they gave her a contractual invitation valid for two hundred years. Since fundraising for the Dome had exceeded anyone's belief, BCIT purchased DeeDee's Dash body from UC Davis for her exclusive use. They also provided DeeDee's current and future robotic forms with free campus housing for 200 years. We were both given Canadian citizenship and Canadian passports.

I'm living a life better than any I could have dreamed of and with a bot and family I adore. I know people like Amal still exist, but I concentrate on enjoying each day with those I love.

ACKNOWLEDGEMENTS

Thank you, so much for reading Surviving Sentience 2040.

This book has been a long time in coming. Fifteen years ago, I thought I could crank out and publish a memoir in less than a year. My memoir about my family of choice took five years to write and remains unpublished. At a weekly meeting of the Davis Writers Salon prior to Covid, I first witnessed the future of AI in novel writing. A DWS member shared a short piece of computer-generated writing based on his writing style. Where others felt concern for the future of writing, I couldn't stop wondering what kind of memoir a sentient computer would generate about its life. Dot and Comma were born.

I've been fortunate that my large "found family" of neighbors, old LGBTQ friends, UCD "kids," and fellow writers, have supported me—most suffering quietly—while my skills improved, and my imposter syndrome warred with my spurts of self-confidence. A heart felt thank you to Katie Landau, Janice Morand, Dana Wilson, Paul Martinez, Linda Birse, and Loretta Firestone for believing in me.

Most importantly, I owe a gigaton of gratitude to Spencer Mann for his excellent developmental editing early on and line edits throughout the process on Surviving Sentience 2040. He has read each iteration of some chapters a dozen times. This novel would not be anywhere near the quality it is, nor publishable without his assistance. Truthfully, reading his fiction, dissecting his critiques, and taking his suggestions have made me a better writer. Somehow Spencer has tolerated my repeated misspelling of names, places, and organizations, the use of incorrect pronouns and tenses, as well as the normal typos and overused words. But most of all, I thank him for his friendship.

During Covid, in an online writing class I was matched with Kim Eddins. A Floridian, Kim has continued to encourage me through emails and text messages, while sharing her work, and critiquing mine for years. I couldn't ask for a better writing friend and cheerleader when life and imposter syndrome get me down.

Closer to home, I've found kindred spirits in writers from different groups, especially MP Smith, Cindy Kiel, Gabe Avila, and Lally Pia, to name only a few from DWS, too many to name from Willamette Writers (see beta readers below and their wonderful board of directors), and more recently J. Scott Coatsworth and my fellow queer authors at QSAC.

I want to express my thanks to my first readers who willingly waded through a shitty early draft, Ryan Cole, Loretta Firestone, and Carol Beales. I adore you! And thank you to my beta readers Max Cyphers, Linda S., Allison Wallace, and Sarah Walker who gave excellent feedback and kept me editing for months longer.

A sincere thank you to my cover and interior designer, Ian Koviak. He made two beautiful covers and gave me confidence to use the one I loved. His fast turn around and handholding of a debut novelist was truly appreciated. He made the indie publishing process so much easier.

A special shout out to Kim Eddins and MP Smith who gave my novel a fast read for typos. (All grammar problems and typos are solely my fault. I'm able to add them in without even looking!) Also, thanks to author Moses Solomon for sharing his indie publishing experience with me.

Lastly, I like to thank my family members who love me and support my writing efforts. They were relieved when I stopped writing memoirs! And last but not least, I'm lucky to have Lucy, my chiweenie who patiently waited for me to feed, walk, and pet her, when I became immersed in writing and editing. No one could ask for a better dog.

To find out more about me and my writing please visit:
www.SharonAMcDonell.com